Dead Tones grabs you on the first page and doesn't let go. I ate up R. Z. Crompton's first two books, and this is the best yet. Each book is that much better than the last. Look for Crompton on the Booklist in the not too distant future.
Karen Cohen,
Book Manager
Community Relations Coordinator
Hastings Entertainment SuperStore

The backdrop for Dead Tones makes this a really unique reading experience. Loved it!
L. Dale Barnett, Director
Union High School,
Renigade Regiment

R.Z. Crompton's desire to have authentic Cherokee history should be applauded. Dead Tones is a must read for anyone wanting a great mystery or a peek into Cherokee lore.
Sequoyah Guess,
Author and Culturalist

DEAD TONES

To Helen
I hope you enjoy
Rita
2-15-98

R. Z. Crompton

Zoller Publishing, Inc.
P. O. Box 461661
Aurora, CO 80046

Dead Tones

_____

Book cover design by:

R. Z. Crompton

This book is a work of fiction. Names, characters, and incidents are either products of the author's imagination, are used fictitiously, or are used with permission. Any resemblance to actual events or persons, living or dead, is entirely coincidental.

Copyright © 1997 by R. Z. Crompton

All rights reserved. Written permission must be secured from the publisher to use or reproduce any part of this book.

Library of Congress Cataloging-in-Publication Data

CIP 97-090968

ISBN 0-9649438-2-4

R. Z. Crompton

This book is dedicated to:
All of the students, mine included, and teachers who have participated either as the basis for characters or as readers who helped me bring this story to life.

The Union High School Renegade Regiment Marching band. The students provided me with endless inspiration and entertainment. I'm happy to tell you that no one really died on the trip to Texas.

Nichols Junior High School in Arlington, Texas. Two of the Nichols students participated in the writing of the zoo scenes.

"Hard work and persistence turn our God given talent into a work of art."

by R. Z. Crompton

R. Z. Crompton

Acknowledgements:
Weber's Superior Root Beer Drive-in Restaurant, Tulsa, Oklahoma.
Bourbon Street Cafe, Tulsa Oklahoma.
Dallas Zoo, Dallas, Texas.
Medieval Times, Dallas, Texas.
Sequoyah Guess, author and culturalist.
Tulsa Band, Tulsa Oklahoma
Alice Blue-Mclendon, D.V.M.
Graham Design Associantes, Inc.
Ray Davis: thank you for the technical advice.

Dead Tones

R. Z. Crompton

Introduction

Orange and blue flames danced in the cool darkness as teacher and student quietly listened to the night's chorus. Crickets answered the frogs' deep crescendo with their own high pitched whine while the breeze rustled the last of the autumn leaves in an irregular rhythm. The chill in the air was a nice contrast to the heat of the campfire, but tomorrow would be cold as the wind gradually shifted to the north.

"Grandmother, I don't understand why someone wants to hurt me."

"The crystals tell me your body will not be harmed. It is your spirit which will be tested," answered the old woman as she stared into the glowing embers. "Your friends will also be tested."

"Why?" asked the younger woman.

"Some will die."

"Die! Who? Why?"

"I don't know who or why, only that it will happen soon." The old woman watched her granddaughter. The first girl of her oldest son, Sarah was the chosen one, the natural successor to the old woman's Cherokee power and magic. But Sarah lived in a different society than her predecessor, and it was old woman's responsibility to teach Sarah how to live the Cherokee traditions in this new age. The old woman felt heavy with anticipation. The test facing her granddaughter might destroy both of them. Sarah needed strength and encouragement, and that was one thing the old woman had plenty to offer. " I have been preparing you for this. We've always known the old ways of our people would collide with your new world. Only you can decide if you are strong enough to make the old teachings work in this strange place where you live."

Dead Tones

"I'm frightened. You've never tested me like this before."

"This is not my test, Granddaughter. You will be faced with an evil from your world, a world I do not know."

"But you always know the evil you have to fight."

"Not this time. This danger is not Cherokee made."

"Then why am I involved?"

"You will be blamed for this evil," said the old woman.

"Me? Why should I be blamed for something I didn't do?"

"Really, Granddaughter," smiled the old woman. "Lots of innocent people have asked the same question. The answer is very logical. You will be the easy target."

"Will you help me?"

"Now what do you think?" smiled the old woman.

"I know. I'm sorry I asked. Can you make a spell to protect me?"

"A spell will not stop this person from blaming you, but look for who is yelling the loudest and you will be close to the one who is hiding. Now go home. Come back tomorrow night. Your friends will need all the help we have to give."

"How many people are involved?" asked Sarah still not fully comprehending what she had to face.

"There will be many people in this. You will know soon, dear, very soon. Tomorrow. You will be able to feel the discord among your friends here." The old woman moved her hand over her heart. "I always feel the evil here first. You will too."

Sarah stood up, brushed the seat of her pants and walked over to the old woman. "Thank you Grandmother. I will meet you at the campfire after sunset."

"Yes, dear, but make sure your homework is done. Your mother still gets angry with me for taking you away from her."

R. Z. Crompton

Sarah smiled as she bent down to help her mentor to her feet. "She knows I love her, but she knows I love you differently. That's what makes her jealous." Sarah pressed a soft kiss on the sun wrinkled face. "Let me walk you back to the house tonight."

"Yes, dear. Tonight I will take your help. I'm a very tired teacher. Be careful going home. You have a long drive."

"It's my time to think about what I've learned."

"Good girl," responded the old woman as she slowly limped her way back to the dimly lit house.

R. Z. Crompton

CHAPTER ONE

    ShyAnne Rennae Mayfield maneuvered her purple Geo through the heavy Friday afternoon traffic on Peoria Avenue eventually turning into the parking lot in front of Weber's Superior Root Beer Stand. Traffic in the Brookside area of Tulsa, Oklahoma, always seemed congested as it hustled through the narrow streets in a busy part of town. Shy pulled up next to the red jeep where her five best friends were already waiting for her to join them. After turning off the key, she laid her sunglasses on the dash then ran long fingers through her cascading waves of curls. When she glanced in the rear view mirror, she noticed the dark blue eyeliner smeared around the corners of her aqua eyes. She quickly tried to wipe away the misplaced make-up before getting out of the car.
    Monica was the first to notice the anxiety on her friend's face. "Shy, what's wrong?"
    "Everything. I really need something to drink." ShyAnne moved through the parked cars toward the small orange building with Monica scurrying to catch her.
    "Shy, what's wrong?" Monica asked again as she stepped up beside ShyAnne.
    "Allison was admitted to the hospital this afternoon."
    The announcement caught the attention of the others trailing behind them and started a barrage of questions. "Why?" "When?" "Will she be okay?"
    ShyAnne tried to answer all the questions in a logical order as they walked toward the door of the restaurant. "Mr. B. called me into his office during last hour. Ali's mom was with him. Mrs. Hayes wanted to know who Allison had eaten lunch with, and who she'd hung

Dead Tones

around with in the morning. The doctors think Ali might have been poisoned. It was awful. Mrs. Hayes was so scared."

"Poisoned?" Mike jumped in. "How?"

"They have no idea. That's why all the questions. I do know after lunch Ali said she wasn't feeling well. So Mrs. Hayes figures whatever's making her sick, she got into before noon. I didn't know she'd gone home until I was called into Mr. B's office this afternoon. Ali drove herself home, but she was so sick Mrs. Hayes took her to the hospital."

"How bad is she?" Monica asked.

"Really bad," Shy answered softly.

"Oh, My God. You mean like she could die, that bad?" Krissy was nearly in tears when they got to the door.

The six teenagers silently crowded into the small entrance. Mike was left holding the door as the others squeezed to form a line in front of him. Mike looked at the small lunch counter and realized that as last in line, he was probably going to be the one left standing. "I don't know why we have to come here," he growled. "There's plenty of restaurants where we can go in and sit down."

"Oh, stop complaining," Monica hissed. His complaining irritated her. Mike was the cynic of the group. He could find the flaw in every situation. However, he added a crisp reality to the group's over optimistic view of life. The girls enjoyed teasing him; and since he was not only intelligent and talented but incredibly buff, they enjoyed matching wits with him, pitting their optimism against his pessimism. "When you get to pick the meeting place, you always pick that slimy burger place."

"Yeah, but it's close and we can sit down."

"Oh, suck it up, Mike. What, you on the 'padded pony'?" Krissy demanded. All the girls snickered. "You've been PMSing on us all day."

"Bite me," was Mike's only defensive remark. "I like greasy burgers and..."

"We know. We KNOW. You like to sit down. So here. Sit down." Krissy and Monica squeezed closer to ShyAnne, so Mike could move in and sit on one of the stools by the window. "I suppose you want us to order for you too," she added.

"Well, now that you've offered."

"Krissy, why do you encourage him? Did you miss the chapter on women's lib in history?" Monica snipped at the blond standing beside her.

"Of course not, but I'm broke. If I order and deliver, he pays for both of us," she whispered back. "Don't worry. I'm on the leading edge of this relationship. I just don't let him know it."

"Sometimes I wonder if you know it," Monica added sarcastically. "So what are you going to get?"

Krissy answered Monica with some of her own sarcasm, "Duh, what do I usually get? A root beer float. How 'bout you, Shy."

"The usual," she answered flatly as she stared out the plate glass window at nothing. Turning back to get a place in the short line, she added, "no, I don't feel like eating. Just root beer tonight."

"You sit," Monica directed. "I'll get it for you."

"Thanks," Shy replied, letting a puff of air escape when she hit the seat.

Now Mike became concerned about Shy's mood. She was normally the "smiley face" of the group. Her transparent sunglasses covered with little black and yellow faces were considered the trademark of her personality, so the frown was grossly out of place. Besides, this was one girl who never passed up a chance to eat. Mike stared at her. She was long, lean, gorgeous, and terribly upset. While the others ordered, Mike moved closer to ShyAnne. "Shy, there's more to this than Allison's being in the hospital. Isn't there?"

Dead Tones

Taking a deep breath, she admitted, "Yeah, lots more. Mrs. Hayes talked about poison. She wants to believe Allison got a hold of something that caused an allergic reaction, something easy to fix. She's assuming it was an accident."

"Yeah, that's what we're assuming too. Right?"

"Maybe. What if it's not an accident? What if ...?"

"Don't even think about it, Shy. You're suggesting... I can't believe anybody would hurt Ali on purpose, and I'm the negative thinker in this group," said Mike proudly defending his position. "The role doesn't fit you. You'll feel better if you have one of those awesome chicken sandwiches with the rest of us."

"What? I thought you didn't like coming here." Shy was finally pulled back into the group's more traditional conversation.

"Yeah, but I never said I didn't like the food. I just like giving you a little crap from time to time. It's good for you." Mike's devilish grin brought a smile to her face. "What I'd like to know is how you can come to the most famous hamburger joint in the city and order chicken? Don't you feel like a traitor?"

"What are you talking about?" Monica asked; she'd been paying close attention to Shy's comments. The four girls had been friends since they'd started playing in the high school band four years ago. Mike and Sean were added to the group later more by default than anything else. Before the teenage hormones really kicked in, the two boys slowly became indispensable, loyal friends. The girls hadn't paid much attention to the fact that two of their best buddies were guys. In fact, sometimes they felt sorry for Mike and Sean. After all, it was really a dirty trick for fate to put such great people into male bodies. But then puberty arrived, and the girls realized the guys deserved the bodies Mother Nature had handed out because their brains were certainly hooked up to the rest of their male anatomy. Now the girls saw not only steadfast friends, but good looking, deep-voiced masculinity. Putting up with the traditionally stupid boy behavior was easier since they'd established their loyalty first.

"Don't you ever read Mrs. Mayfield's articles? She wrote about this place last year," Mike informed her.

"Really?" Monica's question was full of surprise. "I didn't know we were coming to a famous place."

"Famous? Who's famous?" Krissy was always a little slow on the up take which provided the others with endless amusement.

"This place, Krissy. It's the place that's famous not a person," Mike answered her.

"Oh." She sounded disappointed, but then added cheerfully, "Why?"

Sarah, being slightly annoyed with the flippant way the conversation had changed, offered the explanation. "This place is famous for its hamburgers and root beer, and because it's old."

Most of the kids visiting the bright orange building at 38th Street had no idea that Weber's Superior Root Beer Drive-in Restaurant was the oldest restaurant in Tulsa. In 1891 on a farm in Bowden, Oklahoma, Oscar Weber Bilby put a grilled hunk of ground beef on a homemade sourdough bun. Lots of places claim the title of original hamburger king, but all the other early makers of America's favorite sandwich used slices of bread. Not only do the Webers still use the original piece of pigiron as a grill, they are considered the only master root beer brewers in the world.

Krissy ignored the sound of irritation from Sarah and Mike. If Mike was the cynic of the group then Sarah was the silent brooding type. "Well, I agree with Shy about this root beer," Krissy added. "This is absolutely the best stuff in town. And the food is a lot better than that place of yours, Mike."

"Yeah, yeah. But I like to sit down."

Dead Tones

"In case you can't tell, you ARE sitting down," Sean said over his shoulder as he waited for his burger. Sean was the only true burger lover of the bunch. "Shy, I hope your mother remembers I'm the one who told her about this place, about the best sizzling hamburgers in town. Man it's a good thing your mom enjoys her history as well as a good burger. The rest of you never did appreciate the fact that the grill back there made the very first hamburger in 1891."

Shy corrected his claim, "I beg your pardon," she tried to sound offended, "I do pay attention and for your information, it wasn't the grill that made the first burger; it was placing the burger on the homemade bun which made history, and that was done by a woman."

"That's just the way life should be: the man does the grilling while the woman holds the bun," Sean declared proudly.

Monica shoved her fist into the guy standing in front of her. "That's the most disgusting, sexist thing you've ever said. Unless, of course, you mean that it's normal for the women to make history while men take the credit."

Gasping for air, Sean whispered, "Whatever you say, my Dear." Then he picked his order up and moved toward the counter where Mike and Shy were waiting.

ShyAnne laughed as Monica turned away from her still recovering boyfriend to hand her a frosty mug of homemade root beer. Shy tipped the ice cold mug up savoring the taste of the frothy, brown liquid. Then she served the rest of her problem to the group. "Hey guys, ya know Mrs. Hayes was supposed to be one of our sponsors."

"Yeah, so what?" Mike asked as Krissy handed him a frozen mug and grilled chicken sandwich.

"Well, she can't go."

"Of course, she can't go," Krissy stated matter-of-factly. "Her daughter is dying."

"Krissy," ShyAnne snapped. "Allison's not going to die. She's our friend. She can't die."

"Sorry, Shy. I didn't mean to upset you. I know you two have been friends like forever." Krissy was certainly slow with the wit sometimes, but Shy knew it was more of an act than anything else. Besides Krissy would never intentionally hurt anyone, especially Shy. ShyAnne was her best friend. The only friend who understood and respected her mind and goals. To everyone else, Krissy was the stereotypical blond. She knew she was the butt of a lot of jokes and usually lived up to the stereotype with great pleasure. One day she'd have the last laugh, and she'd be laughing all the way to Wall Street.

Krissy loved dabbling in the stock market with the money her grandfather gave her every year for Christmas. The two of them challenged each other to put together a profitable portfolio during the next twelve months. Then both brought their financial report to the family gathering on Christmas Eve. With the winner declared and congratulated, the next year's contest started on Christmas Day. Originally, Krissy's mom hated their money talk on Christmas. In her opinion, it added more stress to the money factor on a holiday which was supposed to be focused on God. After years of complaining, Krissy's mother realized just how fantastic her father and his gift really were. Gramps was giving Krissy self-confidence and independence; important things that couldn't be bought and placed under the tree. Gifts every parent wanted to instill in a child, but most rarely found the magic formula between the discipline that helps and the discipline that hurts.

In the early years Gramps always won the financial game, so Krissy had to buy the double scooped ice cream cone, which symbolized the winner's trophy. Eventually, Krissy realized buying shares of stock like Matel and Toys R Us just because she liked the toys was not the smartest decision. However, buying Disney had been

Dead Tones

a good choice, but more by accident than intellect. The last couple of years, however, she'd out invested him and was proud of her portfolio and its profits. Now she read the Wall Street Journal.....rather than the Sunday toy advertisements. Krissy learned to pick her stock based on corporate earnings and annual dividends rather than the brand name embroidered on the butt of the jeans. Eventually the family began looking forward to the intense discussions regarding assets and liabilities. The Aunts and Uncles listened eagerly as Krissy and Gramps talked about their strategy and returns on various blue chip stocks. Krissy had gone from a listening, sometimes bored student, to a competent opponent. Investing was a hobby now, but eventually it would be her livelihood and Wall Street her home. ShyAnne was the only person who knew about Krissy's little hobby.

Shy continued her explanation of the problem she was facing, "The point is the band is short a chaperon. Mr. B. told me this afternoon that we need to find a replacement for Mrs. Hayes. You know how he is." ShyAnne hung her head in defeat.

"Yeah, we know. 'A parent in every room'", Sean sighed.

"So find another parent. What's the big deal?" Mike asked.

"By five o'clock tomorrow morning?" asked Shy.

"There's got to be an extra mother going along just for the fun of it. There always is," Monica offered.

"My God, we've always got parents up the butt," Mike added.

"Why can't we just add one more girl to four rooms? We've slept on the floor before," Sarah suggested in her stoic voice.

"I already suggested that."

"And?" Mike let the word hang in the air.

"For some reason, Mr. Krammer thinks my mother should fill the empty spot."

"Your Mom? For sure!" Krissy snipped sarcastically. "She'd rather have her nails ripped out than chaperon a band trip."

"I know. The last time I asked her, she said maybe after the Second Coming of Christ." The girls laughed.

"Why?" Asked Sean. "We aren't that bad."

"It's a long story. And it's not the kids she hates." Shy nearly choked on her root beer when she looked through the huge plate glass window. "Hey, look at the kid out there." She tilted her head toward the window as she lifted her mug to tip the last drop into her mouth.

"What kid?" Mike asked. All eyes looked up searching the parking lot filled with cars and people. The November afternoon sun was low in the sky making it difficult to look through the westward window.

"The little blond boy sitting on the back of the white pick-up. See, the one picking his nose."

"I see 'im. He's sitting on the top of the cab. There!" Krissy pointed at the small figure in a dirty yellow T-shirt and blue jeans sitting cross-legged and running a forefinger up his nose.

"Yuck!"

"Ewww!!!. He's eating it." Monica's mouth made a loathsome twist, and she put her onion ring back on the tray.

"Oh, gross!! Gross!!" Krissy turned away from the window.

"At least it's fresh picked," Mike snickered.

Laughter filled the small front room of the Root Beer joint. The six people, crammed onto the five chairs, didn't realize their body motion was causing a shift until Sarah suddenly slipped through the wooden seats.

"Ahhhhh!" She yelled grabbing for the counter but found only the small container of french fries. She continued to fall, landing on the floor with her fries flying through the air. Even the reserved Sarah couldn't keep from roaring with the others until tears ran down her cheeks. It'd been too long since she'd had a good laugh. Life had become too serious since her grandmother started teaching her the old

Dead Tones

medicine philosophy. The medicine of her Cherokee ancestors was not just a bunch of home remedies, it was an intricate part of the Cherokee religion and heritage Sarah was proud of.

Sarah was still laughing as she pulled the fries out of her long silky strands of brilliant black hair. One leg, having slipped through the middle of the four legged bar stool, was now precariously hanging through the gold stabilizing bar; so she had trouble getting any leverage necessary to stand up.

Monica was the first one to jump off a stool and lend a hand. "Sarah, you hurt?" She expected to see a long brooding face, but was pleased with the beautiful grin looking up at her.

"Fine, I'm fine," Sarah answered still giggling. "But I think I'll use this graceful move as my exit since my french fries are no longer edible."

"Yeah, I gotta get goin' too. I'll give you a ride," ShyAnne offered. "The sooner I get home, the more time I'll have to work on my mom."

"Do you want us to come along? You know, strength in numbers," Mike stated.

"Thanks, but no thanks. My mother hates feeling set up; and if we all pounce on her, that's exactly how she'll see it. She'd say no fer sure."

"But what are you going to say?" Sean asked.

"I'm not sure yet."

"You've gotta have a plan," Monica announced. "This is our last Regional Final; and I, for one, don't want to miss it."

"Me either, but my mom is a master of the 'frame or be framed' technique. I've watched her verbally trap an interviewee more times than I can count. My dad hated arguing with her because he could see the web she was weaving, but he couldn't keep from getting stuck. I'm better at the game than he was, but I'm no match for her."

R. Z. Crompton

"If you don't want us to come along, we'll stay and finish eating; but I think you need us," Krissy said, taking another bite of her sandwich.

"I'll help her come up with some kind of strategy on the way home," Sarah replied as she brushed the french fry remnants out of her waist long hair. "C'mon, Shy. I gotta get home." She headed for the door.

As ShyAnne walked toward the door, Monica yelled after her, "I'll call you."

"No don't. If we're in the middle of a heated debate, I don't want her to have time to refuel her argument. I'll call you when I have her answer." Shy pulled her keys out of her purse as she walked out the door.

"Good Luck!" Sean yelled before the door closed.

ShyAnne, taking four large graceful steps, was next to Sarah before she reached the car. The smile which had illuminated Sarah's face was gone. Shy wasn't really surprised. Her friend had been especially gloomy the last week or so. In fact, even carrying on a conversation with her had become difficult. The mysterious coal black eyes rarely focused on anything concrete. They seemed to be looking for a distant place, a place of the spirits, that only Sarah could relate to. Sarah's brief lapse into the realm of reality when she'd fallen off the stool was the first time Shy had seen her act like an eighteen year old since she'd started learning the old Indian ways. Shy worried about the pressure Sarah seemed to be under to carry on the traditions. Was she just complying with her Grandmother's wishes, or was she so totally dedicated to the ancient medicine that she was willing to give up her youth?

"I'm glad you're giving me a ride home, Shy. I wanted to talk to you about Allison."

Dead Tones

"Why, Sarah? Do you know something about where she was today, or what she might have eaten?" Shy asked as she pressed the button on her key chain to unlock the car door.

"No, but I heard you mention to Mike about the possibility of her being poisoned."

"I never said that," said Shy as she opened the car door and reached for her smiley-face sun glasses.

Sarah slid into the passenger side of the car, pulling her seat belt across the front of her chest. "You didn't say it, only because Mike stopped you. I understood your meaning even without the words."

"You're right," she sighed, "the thought did cross my mind, but I can't really believe someone would want to hurt Allison. My God, she was voted Band Queen last year even though she was only a junior. That's never happened before. Traditionally, only seniors have been voted Band Queen; but the kids put up such a stink, Mr. B. had to let the election stand."

"I know, but I've been wondering about the..." Sarah's voice trailed off.

"Wondering about what, Sarah?" asked Shy.

Sarah hesitated for a moment trying to frame her words so as not to sound ridiculous, "I know it seems silly to you, but my grandmother told me last night that something bad is going to happen to me and my friends. Something evil that she doesn't understand."

"An 'evil'? Oooouuuuu," Shy let the sound linger as she pulled out into traffic. "You better not let Mike hear you talk this way. He already thinks you're on the loony side of reality. Could you be a little more specific?"

"No," she answered emphatically. "I can't be more specific! I just know Grandmother is always right."

"So you have nothing you can show me, nothing you've heard?"

"Only a feeling, a very bad feeling, Shy. Trust me."

"Maybe you're just feeling this way because your grandmother is teaching you all that negative crap."

"Gran is teaching me how to ward off evil, but whatever is going to happen she said it would start soon. I can feel it, just like she said."

"Yeah, well maybe you're imagination is working overtime. No disrespect intended, Sarah. I've just never believed in the presence of spirits; good or evil."

"You believe in God, don't you?"

"Of course I do," Shy sounded offended that Sarah would even ask the question.

"Then you have to believe in the Devil too?" Sarah's remark was more of a question, and she turned her head to watch Shy's reaction.

"I guess so, but I don't like to think about it."

"You have to. That's the classic example of good and evil. If your religion can have good and evil, why can't mine?"

"I don't know. I never think about my religion being based on good and evil. I think about the power of God, not the Devil."

"How can you separate the two?"

"The only thing I know fer sure is that you're almost home, and this conversation is not helping me prepare for the argument with my mother." ShyAnne turned the car into Sarah's subdivision just east of Sheridan at 73rd St. "Do you have any words of advice, Oh mighty Medicine Woman?"

"Shy, don't joke about the magic. I'm not a medicine man."

"Sorry, but if you're not a medicine man...woman, then what are you?"

"There is not an exact translation. Di-da-hv-whi-sgi is my Cherokee title."

"Di-da....da." Shy stumbled over the sounds. "Say it again."

Dead Tones

"Try 'Healer'. That's the closest translation I know. What you don't seem to understand is that I can't be a good Healer unless I know all the magic: good and bad. As far as the Cherokee are concerned, good and evil aren't two separate things. They're part of one circle. I can't fight the evil unless I know what it is."

"Sarah, you talk as if the evil is alive."

"It is alive. I can feel it." Sarah opened the car door and looked back at Shy. "And yes, I do have a suggestion for you. Be honest and straight with your mom. You'll do fine; and, by the way, she'll say 'yes'." There was a calm reassuring sound to her voice. It was the sound of confidence, absolute assurance. Sarah's prediction gave Shy a sense of peace as she put the car into reverse. "Thanks for the ride."

"Yeah, sure thing. Thanks for the advice." ShyAnne gently stepped on the gas and backed out of the driveway.

****

Sylvia Hayes stopped her pacing as the silver haired man walked into the hospital waiting room. Anticipating his words by the sour look on his face, she came to the conclusion that the diagnosis wasn't going to be good. Her husband had escaped the stress of waiting by hiding in a six-month old copy of People Magazine. Sylvia hated his ability to detach himself from reality, but then he'd perfected the habit over the last eighteen years.

Philip Hayes, who couldn't seem to control his receding hairline any more than he could his expanding waistline, tried to concentrate on the words in front of him. Hiding behind the dog-eared pages, he'd been gazing at words telling a trivial story about some new Baywatch Beach Queen making a big splash in the movies. He had no interest in the superficial woman or her story. His desire was to keep from speculating about the fate of his daughter; he was hiding from his fear. His baby girl, eighteen now and graduating in the spring, was dying; and there wasn't a damn thing he could do to stop it. There was nothing he could do about the years he'd wasted not spending time with her. In his silence, the regret was as ominous as the fear. He wanted to scream, he wanted to cry, he wanted to hold Allison while she still knew he was her daddy, but he held his emotions at bay using the old magazine as a shield.

Philip nearly ripped the magazine in half when the doctor entered the room. He didn't need to hear the grim edict. The news was in the older man's dark eyes.

"Mr. and Mrs. Hayes," Dr. Rayborn paused while he rubbed his open hand across the stubble on his chin. His eyes closed for a brief second hinting at his fatigue, and then he continued. "Allison is as comfortable as we can make her. Unfortunately, she's continuing to get weaker."

"What can you do for her? What's wrong?" Mrs. Hayes questioned, barely able to keep her tears in check.

"I'm pretty sure she doesn't have a bad case of the flu as you suspected. We've completed the early tests and started a more extensive viral and bacterial culture. So far all the results are normal."

"Isn't that good?" asked Sylvia.

"Not really. It means it's going to be harder to find out what's wrong. The symptoms she has and the results we aren't finding in the test just don't support your theory of the flu. We tested for the more common flu bugs going around the school and the results were negative. However, not all of the bacterial or viral infections would show up in our preliminary tests. Some of the cultures take a couple of days. But I don't think we'll find much."

"So what's wrong?" Philip Hayes growled as he rose out of the overstuffed green chair.

Dead Tones

"Well, my gut feeling is that she's been poisoned."

"Poisoned?" Philip Hayes snapped. "How in the hell was she poisoned?"

"That's the million dollar question. I need you to think back over the last twenty-four hours. Track her steps, where she's been, who she was with, what she ate and where. Any little thing might be a clue that can help us."

"Can't you treat her?" pleaded Mrs. Hayes.

"We're running a series of tests trying to identify any foreign substance in her blood, but we could run a thousand tests before finding the exact poison. It could take days, even weeks, for us to identify the right substance. We can't even do all of the tests here. We have to send blood samples to a reference lab. Frankly, she doesn't have that much time."

"Are you saying Allison could die while you're still running your damn tests?" yelled Mr. Hayes.

"I'm afraid so," Dr. Rayborn answered meeting the other man's stare.

Sylvia reached for the pale mint green wall to steady herself. "Oh, my God. Phil, what are we going to do?" She tried to hold back the tears threatening to spill onto her cheeks.

"Think about what she did today, Syl."

"Mrs. Hayes, can you think of anything she ate that might have gone bad, any lunch meat, or leftovers? Did she eat anything for dinner last night that you two didn't?"

Mrs. Hayes shook her head negatively as she played the day's events over in her head.

"Please understand my next question. I don't mean to cause you more pain, but I have to ask if she could've taken anything herself?"

Philip Hayes took the insinuation of suicide as a personal affront. His fingers rolled into tight fists with the knuckles turning white as he formed his response. "My daughter didn't try to kill herself!"

"Mr. Hayes, no parent wants to think his child would want to die, but it happens. It's tragic, but it does happen."

"Not my daughter. She was happy, loved. Not Allison, not my baby." As the reality sunk in, he fell into the chair. "It's possible," he sighed, "I guess. I really don't know." His voice seethed with pain. Philip Hayes didn't know his daughter any better than he knew the man standing in front of him.

Sylvia squared her shoulders and stiffened her resolve to address the two men. "Dr. Rayborn, I can assure you that Allison didn't take anything on purpose."

Phil moaned as he added, "But I pushed her. I always pushed her for better grades, to work harder without ever listening to her. I never told her I loved her."

"Well, that part's true. You never said much of anything positive to either of us. But I did. I took care of her. When you left the room, I gave her the reassuring strokes she needed. Allison was...is a good girl. She always wanted to please you. To make you proud, but you were never satisfied. I covered for you. For eighteen years, I covered for you, made the excuses for your absence, eased her disappointment when you said stupid, angry words."

Philip Hayes was dumbfounded as his wife made her accusations. "I don't understand, Syl."

"Of course, you don't. You never did. I've been your servant and errand girl for years. Pick up this. Don't forget to call so-and-so. Did you get my shirts? The steak is too done. The coffee is bitter. You criticized me long before Allison was old enough to understand what was going on. I was ready to counter any comment, any order

Dead Tones

you gave her. I wasn't going to let you destroy her confidence. Whether you know it or not, she IS a good girl."

"Are you suggesting I don't love my daughter?"

"I'm stating a fact, my Dear Darling Husband. You may love her. You might even think you love me. The sad fact is you have absolutely no idea how to show your love or any other positive emotion. You're a negative man."

Phil looked out the door of the small waiting room and then back at the doctor standing behind his wife. "Sylvia!" He said barely above a whisper. "I can't believe you're saying all this..."

"Afraid somebody might hear the truth? You were more passionate about the leather seats in your car than you were about us. The way you rubbed that damn oil into them every weekend. If only you'd caressed me the same way." Her chin quivered at the final accusation.

"Sylvia, that's ridiculous. I never...caressed my car."

"You spend more time cleaning your car than you do with us. Can you even remember the last time you did anything with Allison?" She paused for a moment, but there was no response to the question.

"The only time you talk to her is when you're both at the dinner table. That's what's so sad. She wanted a daddy. A loving, time giving daddy. Ya know something funny? Every time I hear some wishy-washy do-gooder telling me how wonderful it is for a family to sit around the dinner table together, I just want to smack her," snapped Mrs. Hayes as she whipped her hand through the air to hit an imaginary person. "Who decided that eating around one table could make everything in a family hunky-dory? What an idiot! Dinner time was a chance for you to do your military drill. You always found something to yell about. Your daily menu didn't consist of your favorite food items; it was made up of the issues you enjoyed throwing at each of us."

R. Z. Crompton

"You're exaggerating," Philip insisted, shaking his head back and forth. He was trying to think about dinner last night. They had argued; or more accurately, he'd yelled and they had listened.

The crackle of the hospital intercom stopped Sylvia for a second. She didn't want Philip to miss a single word. "In fact," she continued, "the last six months or so, your nightly tirades were like a game for us. We compared notes before dinner and made bets with each other about your choice of topic. Sometimes we even made things up just to add spice to the game."

The man was stunned by his wife's declaration. She'd never acted like this before. "You and Allison have everything it's possible for me to provide. Syl, I've tried to work hard to give you a home."

"No, what you gave us is what you wanted us to have. It was easier to give us stuff than it was to give us yourself."

"Why didn't you ever tell me how you felt?"

Now it was Sylvia's turn to be silent. It was true. She'd never complained. All these years, and she'd never confronted him.

Dr. Rayborn stood silently behind the short petite woman who'd certainly been a beauty a few years ago. The slightly graying, dark brown hair curled softly around the naturally pretty oval face. As a single man, he could see himself dancing on the balcony at the Country Club with this woman wrapped in his arms. Maybe she was ready to get out of the kitchen, he mused to himself.

"Sylvia?" Philip wasn't going to let her off without an explanation. "As long as you opened the door of this conversation, tell me why you never complained before."

She straightened her stance as if getting ready for battle. "I didn't have a right to complain." The statement was given matter of factly.

Dead Tones

"What are you talking about? I may not have been the most attentive man in the world, but I never stopped you from speaking your mind."

"Don't be an idiot. You know why I never complained. In spite of the fact you were rarely around, you did provide a home for us and for that I'm grateful."

"Sylvia, what are you talking about? Why wouldn't I give you a home? You're my wife. Allison's my little girl."

For the first time in years, there was emotion in his voice. Closing the gap between them, Philip looked down into her eyes. "What are you insinuating? "

"Jesus, Phil, do I have to spell it out for you?" They hadn't mentioned, even hinted at the past, and now she was about to dump it at his feet.

Philip didn't deserve to be humiliated; but then, on the other hand, their silence all these years hadn't served them well either. Maybe a little shock treatment would help. Sylvia was due. Her frustration had been boiling for years, but she'd always kept the lid on tight. Well, he wasn't going to sulk his way out of this like he did everything else.

"Sylvia! What on earth are you talking about?" He asked again.

"I've always been grateful that you married me. You didn't have to."

"For God's sake! You were pregnant with my child. Of course I had to marry you. That's what we did back then. Men didn't abandon their responsibilities as easily as they do now. Abortion and birth control weren't as handy. Passion had a price, and we paid."

"Yes, we paid. But I had Allison to fill my happiness. I poured everything into her. I always felt like I'd trapped you. And you stayed. I was your self-imposed prison sentence. Your punishment for passion."

"That's not true."

"Yes it is, Phil," she sighed. "The passion we shared in the back seat of your Chevy was gone after I told you I was pregnant. You married me, but the light disappeared from your eyes. I had no right to complain. All I could do was make sure Allison didn't make the same mistake."

"Does she know about...about the pregnancy?"

"She's not stupid. Some basic science and math was all she needed to come up with the questions. I told her the truth. In the beginning, I think she found the whole story wildly romantic; but when she was older and realized we had serious gaps in our relationship, she began to realize safe sex protects more than just health."

"You mean she's...Our little girl is...?"

Sylvia smiled at his naivete. "She's eighteen and has had a serious boyfriend for two years. I thought it was better to be straight with her than to watch her follow in my foot steps."

"If you were so damn unhappy, then why'd you stay with me all these years?" he growled at her. "You could've made it on your own. Why did you waste all those years on me?"

Well, she'd finally pushed a button. He was showing a little anger. "Silly me," said Sylvia sarcastically, "I never gave up hope that you'd come home from work one day and sweep me off my feet like you did that night out by Keystone Dam."

"I work hard for you and Allison. I'm tired when I get home." He sounded apologetic.

"You're a vegetable when you get home, a non-communicating, non-functioning vegetable. Shit, there were times when I thought I'd have to give you oxygen."

Phil looked across the room at Dr. Rayborn listening intently to their conversation. "Sylvia, this is not the place for such a discussion."

Dead Tones

"Oh, I think it's a great place. Our daughter, our only connection to each other is lying in a bed down this wretched hallway while you're feeling sorry for yourself. I'm not going to let you think for one second Allison tried to kill herself. So stop with the self pity and help fight for her. If you've got any feelings for us at all, get your ass into that room and convince her you love her."

Philip watched speechlessly as his wife picked up her purse and headed for the door. "Where are you going?"

Sylvia didn't turn around; her hands were shaking and the lump in her throat was growing. She was afraid she'd lose her nerve; cower to him as usual. If she apologized now, everything she'd managed to say would be wasted. *Be strong. For Allison, be strong,* Sylvia said to herself before answering her husband. "I'm going back to the house to see what I can find. I already talked with her friends and teachers, but I didn't go through her room."

"Sylvia, you should stay with Allison. I'll go."

The absurdity of Philip's going through Allison's room brought a chuckle from Sylvia as she turned to face him; and with a new flare of irritation she answered, "You go through her room? You've got to be joking. What would you look for? You have no idea what belongs in her room and what doesn't." Sylvia paused as another possibility came to mind. "Wait a minute. Are you afraid to stay? Afraid you might get too close?"

Philip wanted to answer. He needed a quick come back, but he wasn't good at banter, especially when it came to his wife. Their conversation was usually limited to the general happenings of the day, never anything as taxing as a heated, two-sided debate. That's what their marriage was missing: the heat. He watched with new respect as his "used to be" docile wife turned and walked away from him.

Dr. Rayborn hadn't said a word. He'd thought about excusing himself from their discussion, but listening to Mrs. Hayes was the best entertainment he'd had all day. However, now that she was gone, he felt awkward and had to say something to cut the tension in the room when Philip looked back at him. "She's just upset about Allison. Ya never know how people will react to the bad news."

"Maybe. But I think my wife won't be the quiet homemaker anymore. What should I do?"

"About your daughter or your wife?"

"My daughter," Philip answered sarcastically. He knew Rayborn had been amused at their conversation.

"Right now, I think you should take your wife's advice and talk to Allison. She might be able to hear you. If she becomes conscious, try to find out where she's been and with whom. In the meantime, you might try a prayer."

A prayer? Philip's conversations with God hadn't been any better than his family discussions at the dinner table. Sylvia was right. Even though he'd never thought of her as his prison, he'd never let her get close to him again either. She and Allison had been his duty, and he'd served his time. *So, maybe I served without a smile on my face. She never complained. Was she serving her own sentence? Sorry, Syl, I never stopped to consider what you were going through or how you perceived my actions.* Maybe it was time to change a few things in his life. Trying to formulate some words of love, Philip trudged slowly through the sterile white hallway toward his daughter's room.

Dr. Rayborn watched the dazed Mr. Hayes walk away with heavy drooping shoulders. The man's life was unraveling, and the only thing he could do was hope for a guardian angel to give him strength. Not much consolation for a man who's spent all of his adult years hiding behind thick walls of emotional isolation. And Mrs. Hayes? Well, if Mr. Hayes didn't take care of his lovely wife, the doctor might just step in. This woman had some latent passion prime for tapping. He smiled at the prospect of dancing to soft music while he caressed

Dead Tones

the delicate skin. Then a devilish mental image sent a chill down his spine. *Oh yes, this man needs more than a guardian angel. He needs a God Damn Saint.*

R. Z. Crompton

CHAPTER TWO

With a deep breath feigning courage, Shy opened the back door and walked into the large white kitchen. Mr. Hairy Monster, or more affectionately known as just plain Hairy, was waiting for her with his big brown eyes, licking tongue, and happy dog shuffle that made her glad to be home.

The room was dark and silent, which wasn't unusual. Shy walked around the corner of the island in the center of the kitchen and placed her purse and backpack on the counter before bending down to give the big yellow dog the loving caress he wanted. Hairy was a devoted friend, and he listened well without offering stupid advice. As long as Shy talked to him, he'd sit tilting his head from one side to the other. Deep brown eyes looked tenderly at the girl sitting cross legged on the floor in front of him.

"Hairy, has Mom had a good day? Hmmm?" She scratched behind one floppy yellow ear. Hairy answered by cocking his head to the other side, so she would get the other ear as long as she was down at his level. "I sure hope she's in a congenial mood." The dog gave a low moan of comfort as he rolled over hoping for a brief tummy rub. "Sorry, boy. I have to talk with Mom. Come with me. C'mon." Standing up, ShyAnne patted her leg in command for the dog to follow her. Hairy obediently jumped to his feet, following close enough for Shy to keep her hand on his head.

Shy's mother worked in her office at the front of the large brick house until Shy came home from school. Then they made dinner together and discussed the day's events. Normally, this was a very relaxing time for ShyAnne. She enjoyed chatting with her mom about

Dead Tones

classes and friends, and she liked hearing about the new assignments Claire had received from her editor.

Claire and ShyAnne had been on their own since the divorce three years ago. Shy was happier with just the two of them living together. The split between her mother and father had been long in coming and painful for all of them, and it had left her mother very bitter about marriage and men in general. Then, within weeks of signing the final legal papers, she had the chaperoning incident with Mr. Krammer, the assistant band director at the high school.

Mr. Krammer accused her of letting the girls under her supervision out after curfew. By the time he realized the girls had slipped Claire a couple of dramamine in her coke, putting her soundly to sleep, the damage was done. Claire lumped Krammer into the same category as her ex-husband and refused to ever chaperon again. Mr. Krammer had apologized profusely, but Claire wouldn't back down. He'd made a fool of her; and as far as she was concerned, he ranked right up there with all the other three legged jerks she'd encountered over the years.

Claire had been a writer with the local paper for several years; but after the divorce, she was on her own for a living. She wanted no ties to the rotten son-of-a-bitch, so she didn't ask for any child support for Shy. Besides, she didn't want the guy to have any reason to stay in contact with them. ShyAnne, who agreed with her mother, heard from her father on Christmas and her birthday, and that was fine with her. She didn't miss anything about him, especially his yelling. There had been no kindness in him let alone love. Claire had protected her from the verbal abuse as much as possible, and Shy was grateful. She had been old enough to understand the three of them were failing miserably at family life. Shy and her mother portrayed the loving family life much more successfully without the miserable man around.

Writing full time became very lucrative when Claire was out

from under the stress of a rotten marriage. Within two years, she had a syndicated column and several free lance offers from national magazines. In spite of Claire's professional success, Shy worried that her mother's one intimate relationship was with her computer. All of her human interaction was via the Internet, not exactly a wholesome relationship. Maybe it was time for Shy to push her mother back into the world of warm human bodies rather than little square boxes.

Claire Mayfield, clicking away at the computer in front of her, looked up when her daughter strolled into the room. "What's up, dear? You ready for some dinner?" Light brown silky curls draped gracefully across her forehead and then past the collar of her bright blue sweater. Light hazel eyes decorated the beautiful ivory complexion.

"Yeah, I'm starved. A bunch of us stopped at Weber's, but I didn't have anything to eat. How was your day?" Shy asked, plopping herself down on the green leather sofa setting opposite the large walnut desk. She took a brief look around the room. Large windows with only a side-swag for decoration allowed light to fill the room all day long. Claire was determined to get as much of the outdoors crammed inside as possible, so she'd had colorful flowers planted and several hummingbird feeders hung where she could see them while sitting at her desk. Ceiling to floor bookshelves filled the wall behind her. Admiring the professional flavor of her mother's office, Shy vowed to have one just like it. However, Shy wasn't aspiring to a writing profession; she was going into the field of medicine, specifically surgery. She had the grades and test scores. All she was waiting for was the acceptance letter from Texas A & M along with a scholarship. With no scholarship offer, Shy was stuck with her second choice and a full ride. Her friends had encouraged her to take the full ride, but Shy was determined to pack her bags and move to College Station.

Dead Tones

Claire's enthusiasm was evident. "My day was great. I've been asked to do a special feature on the Bourbon Street Cafe for next Sunday's paper. I love writing about good restaurants, and this is one of my favorites. How come you didn't eat? You always grab a snack when you're at Weber's. And you usually bring me one of my favorite burgers. What's wrong?"

ShyAnne smiled at her mother. "You know me too well, Mom. I had a really bad afternoon."

Claire turned away from her computer in order to give her full attention to the daughter lounging in front of her. The last couple of years she'd blossomed into this beautiful, confident woman. Claire was immensely relieved considering the first fifteen years of her daughter's life had been spent in the same house with a rotten man. Shy rarely complained; so if she had a problem tonight, it was worth listening to. "Okay, tell me what's up. I'll help if I can."

Shy had to watch herself now. She didn't want her mother to think she was being set up. *Be honest and straight. That's the best. Just like Sarah said.* "Allison is really sick. She's in the hospital, and they don't know what's wrong."

"I'm sorry, Shy. When did she get sick?"

"This afternoon. Her mother told me after school when I was in the bandroom. They think it was some kind of poison."

"My God. Her parents must be frantic with worry."

"Her mom was also a chaperon for the band trip. Mom, we are supposed to leave at five o'clock in the morning. If we don't have another chaperon by midnight, the trip is going to be called off. What are we going to do? This is my last Regional. I don't want to miss it."

"I'm sure you don't, along with every other senior, Shy. Mr. Barnett will find someone."

"Mom, he called me."

R. Z. Crompton

"You know how I......," her answer was interrupted by the sound of the doorbell. Before Claire could finish her answer, the front door, which was visible from Claire's office, popped open.

"Hey, you guys home?" called a sweet perky voice.

"Aunt Nae, how are you?" ShyAnne met her aunt in the middle of the room and placed a loving kiss on her cheek. The shorter version of Claire didn't realize she'd just stopped her sister from giving Shy a negative answer to a question that hadn't even been asked. ShyAnne was grateful. She needed time to reframe her request. "Where's William?"

"He's home doing some serious bonding with his dad," Rennae answered as she gave a loving stroke to Hairy. "Hey, boy, how ya doin'?"

"Yeah?" Shy's comment was more of a question. She wasn't sure how much bonding a four year old could do.

"They bought several new pieces to William's Thomas the Train set today. When I left, the two of them were on the floor putting the new track together. Thought I'd get out of the house while Daddy was playing trains. I don't know who was having more fun: the man or the child."

"Aren't they one-in-the-same?" Claire asked with a cynical tone.

"Ah, come to think of it, most of the time they are; but ya know, it works for me. When I think about wanting another child, I just pretend the father is the second son, and that's the end of my longing." Rennae laughed as she waltzed across the room and slipped onto the sofa.

"I think I'll get some packing done while you two talk," said Shy.

"I didn't know you were leaving town. So you've finally decided to run away from this strange creature who lives with a box?"

"Close, Aunt Nae. The band is supposed to be leaving for Denton, Texas, tomorrow. We have Regional Finals on Saturday," Shy answered with little enthusiasm in her voice.

"Good Luck."

"Thanks, Nae."

Dead Tones

"You don't sound very excited for a teenager who's escaping for the weekend. I thought you enjoyed these trips.

"There's a major problem this time. One of the girls is in the hospital, so her mom can't chaperon. No chaperon - no trip."

"Why can't your mother go?" Rennae asked raising an eyebrow as she looked at her sister, who was considering various ways of killing the only blood relative she had left in the world besides ShyAnne.

"Oh no, you don't. You know very well why I won't go."

"I understand why you won't go, but you **could** go if you were inclined to do it for Shy. After all she is a senior, and there aren't many trips left."

"Rennae, I don't want to go."

"Claire, you spend all of your time behind your computer. It's not healthy."

Shy didn't want to be a silent observer of this conversation, especially since she had an ally. "Mom, I agree with Aunt Nae. You spend too much time alone."

"Stop! Both of you, just stop. Shy, did you call her before you got home? I'm sure this is a conspiracy, and you, young lady, will be shot for treason." There was no touch of humor in Claire's voice as she looked from sister to daughter.

"No, but I wish I had been so devious. And don't change the topic, Mother. It would be good for you to get away for the weekend."

"In case you haven't noticed, I like being by myself," snapped Claire.

"Well, it's a damn good thing because in a couple of months Shy leaves for college, and you won't have anyone," said Rennae.

"I'll still have Hairy." At the sound of his name, the old dog sauntered over to sit at Claire's feet.

"That's not exactly the companionship I had in mind," offered Rennae.

"So, oh wise sister, tell me what I should do."

"Well, now that you've asked, I think you should find a man and get married."

ShyAnne cringed at the boldness of the suggestion. Her mother hated men, absolutely hated the opposite sex. She sighed, believing the argument lost as she listened to her mother laugh.

"Married? Why in the hell would I want another husband? That's like wanting a perpetual hemorrhoid."

"I'm serious," Rennae snapped. "You can't have a meaningful relationship with a little gray box that says 'hello' or 'good-bye' depending on which button you push."

"I prefer a man I can turn off. Besides I have plenty of meaning in my life. And I certainly don't need a real live man to screw it up."

"Actually, a good screw is exactly what you need," said Rennae.

"Rennae!" Claire snapped.

"She's right, Mom. You can't count on Hairy for all of your needs."

Claire reached down caressing Hairy's large blonde ears. Hairy cocked his head slightly to get the full pleasure of the massaging fingers. "Hairy is plenty of companionship, and he doesn't spit toothpaste all over the bathroom mirror."

"Yeah, but when he has a gas attack, he ranks right up there with the best of them," Shy acknowledged.

"He does have his toxic moments. On the other hand, he never ridicules or gives unsolicited advice. In my opinion, he's the perfect male partner. When he becomes annoying, I can't turn him off, but I can put him outside. I could never do that with your father. Man, what a royal pain in the ass he was."

"Dad might not have been the prime father figure, but I really don't think all men are like him. Most of my friends have great dads. You

Dead Tones

could at least get out and socialize. Do you even know a single man?" she challenged.

"Yes, I know some single men. Lots of them, in fact," said Claire defensively. "And who died and made you mother?" Claire asked staring at Shy. "And why do I have to socialize with men. I know your friends' mothers. We talk frequently."

Shy ignored the last part of the comment and continued. "You only know them via the telephone, and that goes for most of the male friends too. And I think you're using the term friend very loosely here. If you subtract the interviews you do, then you've taken away most of the people you're putting into the category of friendship. Now, I agree that a lot of those rescue workers you've gotten to know are pretty buff, but they all live in the mountains. When was the last time you went out to lunch with a man or a woman for that matter. And Nae doesn't count."

"Well, Derrick and I had lunch last week, and I'll see Tom next Thursday."

"Mother, Derrick is your banker and he's at least fifteen years younger than you."

"Ten, maybe ten years younger. Who cares?" announced Claire.

"I agree, age isn't important if the desire is there; but, like I said, he's your banker," said Shy.

"He's a man and single. Maybe there is desire on his part," added Claire.

Nae jumped into the conversation, "Get real, Claire. What would he want with an older woman? And who's Tom?"

"He's her accountant, and that doesn't count either," offered Shy.

"I bet you can't get a date with either of them," Rennae challenged.

"Who said I wanted a date. I don't need a date if I'm not looking for a husband."

Claire's sister was ready for the final push. "Okay, you're not ready to get married. I really don't think any of those band students are looking for an old woman 'to have and to hold 'til death' and all that crap, so go on the damn trip."

"And what about Krammer? I don't want to even see the guy."

"Get over it, Claire. That was two years ago. You've got to learn men aren't necessarily rotten; they're just different. Besides, I'm sure the guy isn't going to want to marry you anymore than any of the other boys."

Shy was dumbfounded. Her aunt had reeled her mother into the net like a master fisherman, and her mother hadn't even seen it coming. Aunt Nae was a genius. However, her mother hadn't answered yet. "Please, Mom. I'd really like you to go. After all, you were planning on going anyway."

"What are you talking about? I wasn't going."

"I've seen you before, standing in the back or at the opposite end of the bleachers. I've seen you at almost every competition the last two years."

"Is that right, Claire? You were going anyway?"

"Okay! You've made your point. Call Barnett; tell him I'll go. But he'd better put Krammer on a different bus." Shy ran for the phone. When she was out of hearing range, Claire continued, "Damn you, Rennae. You tricked me."

"You mean you can't believe I beat you at your own game. May I remind you that you didn't invent the 'frame or be framed' game all by yourself. I was always your greatest challenge," said Rennae proudly.

"You're a rat. I assume you're going to take care of Hairy?"

"Yeah, otherwise you'll use the poor dog as an excuse not to go."

"I certainly can't get him in for boarding this late. You want to take him home with you?"

"Guess I'd better. Stupid dog won't let me into the house when you're gone."

"That's what he gets paid for. He doesn't let anyone in the house, especially rats like you."

Dead Tones

"You just hate losing. Now, how 'bout the bet? What's at stake?"

"What bet?"

"The date bet. I bet you can't get a real date, lunch or dinner, before next weekend."

"I really don't care what you think."

"Oh c'mon, Claire. Play the game. It'll be fun. Like being in high school again. Now who's it going to be."

"We aren't in school, and I don't play tricks on my friends."

"So you do have male friends. Tell me about Derrick."

"There's nothing to tell. He's my banker and my friend."

"Has he asked you out?"

"Maybe," Claire smiled. Rennae was manipulating her again, and doing it very well. "Nae, stop. I don't date."

"Claire," she whispered, "Don't you every get.....you know.....horny?"

"Rennae! That's none of your business."

"Ah, so you do. Maybe you don't need a husband, just a 'boy toy' for a few months of female pleasure."

"I think you've screwed up my life enough for one night. I'll call you at four thirty tomorrow morning just so you know how much I appreciate you."

"Give me a glass of wine, and I'll help you pack. By the way, don't take dramamine from band members."

"Oh, thanks a lot." Claire's voice oozed with sarcasm. "I really don't need anymore help or advice from you."

"I'll get my own glass." Rennae walked out of the office toward the kitchen. Before Claire could shut down the computer, her sister was back in the room. "What does Derrick look like anyway?" She asked handing a glass of Merlot to Claire.

"He's tall, blond and has a cute, tight ass," Claire offered.

"Really?" Rennae sounded astonished at her sister's description. "I don't believe you. You're making him up."

"Believe what you like. I really don't care," Claire glared haughtily at her sister.

Rennae, sipping on the deep red wine, considered Claire's answer. "I think you're bluffing. Derrick's your banker. How do you know if he's got a cute butt?"

With a sly smile, Claire stated matter of factly, "I told you he's more than just my banker."

"I won't believe it 'til I see it." A frown washed onto her face. "Why didn't you ever tell me about him. You're not good at keeping secrets from me." Again doubt presented itself. "Didn't you even tell Shy about him?"

"Of course not. I knew you'd both jump to conclusions. Neither of you seem to understand that I'm happy being single. I'm not so lonely with my computer box."

"We worry about you. It's just not healthy to live with a box."

"Give it a rest already! I'm comfortable with myself. You have to feel lonely to be lonely, and I don't feel lonely. When I need human contact, I go to your house." Claire tipped the long stemmed wine glass to her lips.

"So you were lying about having a relationship with Derrick?" Rennae was sure she'd caught her sister in a fib.

Claire's eyes danced with mischief as a sly smile spread across her face. "I wasn't lying. However, I don't kiss and tell either. I don't need to." She picked up her glass of wine as she pushed back her chair and stood up. This conversation was over. She walked out of the room with Hairy at her heels and left her sister sitting on the sofa.

Rennae was stunned by her sister's confession. *So the recluse isn't so reclusive after all. Maybe there's still hope for her.* "Claire, wait." She followed her sister down the long hallway into the kitchen. Claire was

Dead Tones

pulling a pan out of the cupboard. "Do you want to eat with us? We're having spaghetti."

"No thanks. I've got to cook for the boys later. So tell me."

"Tell you what?"

"Do you still get horny?" Rennae whispered looking over her shoulder as if someone might be listening to a National Secret.

"I'm not dead, Nae."

"So you do!" She declared softly as she leaned over the edge of the snack bar.

"Why are you whispering?"

"I didn't think you wanted Shy to hear us."

"You think she'll be disappointed to find out her mother isn't the perfect stoic? She's a big girl, Rennae. She can handle it." Claire pulled a couple plates out of the cupboard while she waited for the water to boil.

"I'm sure she'll be relieved. Your daughter seems to think your life is plugged into your computer."

"I don't need a man, and I wish you two would stop trying to push me into something I don't want. Now if you'll change the topic, I'll pour you more wine. Otherwise take your matchmaker ideas home."

"More wine please." Claire poured more of the red liquid into Rennae's glass. "Is he any good?"

"Who?" Claire asked as she poured the chunky garden spaghetti style sauce into another pan.

"Derrick, is he any good?"

"At banking or loving?" Claire waited for clarification and tried not to laugh at her sister's reeling imagination.

"I really don't care if he can add or not."

"Well, I keep going back." Claire smiled at her sister. Claire could imagine the wheels of her sister's mind turning. She was beginning to feel just a little guilty about weaving this story. Oh well, her sister deserved to be strung along after luring her into that damn band trip.

Rennae finished her glass of wine in one gulp. "I think I'll head home. It must be time for William to eat and go to bed."

"Why? It's only half past six."

"I have something important to ahhh....to discuss with his dad." She headed for the kitchen door.

"What's wrong, Nae?" Claire smiled at her sister. "You lookin' for a little lovin' yourself? Maybe you're the only one here who gets horny."

Rennae turned only for a moment, "Bite me!", was her quick response and the door closed.

"Hey, you forgot Hairy." The dog's ears perked up at the mention of his name.

Rennae was opening the door in a split second and looking down at the dog. "Let's go, Hairy." Hairy looked at Claire for permission to follow another's instructions.

Claire bent down on one knee in order to see eye to eye with her devoted companion. "Be a good dog for me. Go." She gave the command and pointed to her sister. Hairy hurried for the door. "Take good care of my dog."

"Get a date, or I'll hold him for ransom." The door slammed behind her.

Nag. Nag. Nag. Hopefully, Derrick will help get her off my back for awhile. Sorry Derrick, hope you don't mind being my lover for a while. Claire smiled at herself with great satisfaction. Having Derrick as a lover wasn't such a bad thought. *After all, he does have a cute little ass.*

"Mom?" ShyAnne interrupted her mother's fantasy. "Mom? What are you grinning about? You've got that sneaky look. Where's Aunt Nae?"

"I'm thinking about....about your manipulating aunt," Claire didn't feel like bringing up the subject of Derrick again, so she jumped into a

Dead Tones

more volatile topic, "... and how I owe her a big one for tricking me into that band trip of yours."

"You're still going aren't you?" Shy asked as she leaned up against the long white counter edged in dark green to match the color scheme of the white wallpaper covered with delicate long stemmed tulips.

"Didn't you call Barnett already?"

"Yup. I didn't want to give you time to change your mind."

"I'll go because I love you."

"And because Aunt Nae talked you into it. You were going to say 'no' before she got here. Weren't you?"

"I was hedging."

"Hedging? Really, Mom. I was under the impression you couldn't get the word 'no' out of your mouth fast enough.

"I hadn't made up my mind yet."

"Man, am I glad Aunt Nae showed up."

"I'd sure like to know how she ended up coming over at that specific moment. I'd swear she had an inside track to our conversation. Here, take your plate and sit down." Claire handed Shy the filled plate and then picked up her own. "Did you tell Barnett to make sure I'm not on the same bus as Krammer?"

"I did. You're safe. And, he said 'thanks'." She walked into the dining room just a couple of steps in front of her mother. The two of them always ate in the dining room at the formal table. It would have been so easy to eat at the kitchen counter. Easy to lessen the importance of the little time they had together. After the divorce, Claire had been determined to make dinner time a pleasant experience for them. After years of absolutely no sense of family, dinner for Claire and Shy had become a symbolic celebration of times lost.

Claire responded to the words of thanks with the resignation that she was doomed to spend the weekend with too many people in a space too small for her comfort zone. "He's welcome. You're welcome. And my sister is having a good time tonight thanks to me." Claire stated flatly as she sat down at the round walnut table.

"What? How do you know she's having fun?"

"Nothing. Please pass the Parmesan cheese. Did you call the hospital about Allison?" Claire asked reaching for the dish in Shy's hand.

"Yeah. There's no change. At least that's what the cranky old nurse said. She wasn't going to give me any information at all. I should've told her I was Mrs. Hayes. She wouldn't know if I was telling the truth or not."

"What if Sylvia was standing there?"

"Then she would've taken the call and answered my questions. She knows how worried I am. This is depressing for all of us. Maybe we shouldn't even go to Texas."

"You're not usually so pessimistic. What else is bothering you?"

"What if Ali was poisoned on purpose?"

"Are you serious?" Claire looked at Shy with new interest.

"Mom, when was the last time you heard someone was poisoned by accident? Food poisoning maybe, but that should be pretty easy to track. Allison's the only one who's sick. If it was contaminated food, don't you think someone else would be sick by now?"

"Not necessarily. Maybe Allison ate a bigger portion."

"Sarah's suspicious too."

"About what?"

"Evil spirits," answered Shy showing a slight irritation.

Claire almost choked on her wine, but she didn't say anything.

"Ya know, Sarah's all wrapped up in this Cherokee medicine stuff. I'm not sure if she's just superstitious or if she really feels the evil."

"So you think learning the ways of her people has warped her ability to think logically?"

"I don't know. She's so serious all the time. She relates everything to her grandmother's medicine, to good and evil."

Dead Tones

"That doesn't mean she can't think clearly. Sarah just analyzes her thoughts according to her new standard."

"But I can't help feeling she's looking for the evil in everything. It's like she wants to find the bad side even if there isn't one."

"Sarah's a smart girl, practicing her new art. She's entitled to a mistake in judgement here and there."

"I don't necessarily think she's made a mistake this time. I just think all this evil stuff is eerie."

"If you deny there's evil in the world, then you're the one not thinking rationally."

"I don't deny evil; I just didn't think it could be so close."

CHAPTER THREE

  Five luxury charter buses hummed their toxic diesel tune as the students, looking for the perfect seat, plowed through the aisle. Shivering uncontrollably, Claire huddled in the seat by the window. Shy had warned her to dress warmly, but Claire had ignored the advice. After all, it was early November, and they were going to Texas. How cold could it get? Claire rationalized that she'd be better off dressing for the longest part of the day since they would be spending most of their time outside. She really didn't want a bunch of heavy clothes to drag around all afternoon. Shy had walked out of the house with a pillow, blanket and winter coat. Claire insisted her daughter was over compensating for the chilly morning. In a couple of hours the sun would be up and shining through those big windows. The bus's occupants would slowly roast. Well, it was still pitch black outside as Claire watched girl after girl, including her own daughter, board the bus with pillow and blanket possessively in tow. Either the boys were dumber, or their macho egos wouldn't let them admit they needed anything more than the red and white band jacket. Hopefully, the hot air of conversation and body heat would raise the temperature of the bus to a comfortable level, or the five hour trip to Dallas was going to be miserable for Claire.

  Turning to stare out into the darkness, which would become the parking lot in another hour, Claire's thoughts drifted back to her evening conversation with Shy about Allison and the possibility of intentional poisoning. The idea hadn't really sunk in until Sylvia showed up at the front door around ten. She appeared exhausted and disheveled as she stepped slowly over the threshold when Claire invited her in for a cup of tea.

  "Actually, Claire, if you have something a little stronger, I'd sure appreciate it. I can't even think straight anymore."

  "Sure, Sylvia. C'mon in." Claire lead the way into the family room where she had a poorly stocked bar. "Is there anything else I can do for you?"

Dead Tones

"Thanks for taking my place on the band trip. Mr. Barnett told me Shy was going to ask you. Ya know, I haven't missed a trip in three years," Sylvia admitted softly. "And I always pack a care package for the kids and these energy bars." Sylvia handed a shoulder bag to Claire and then wilted onto the deep burgundy love seat. "The kids like the bars before they compete cause they give them more stamina. My job on the trip is kinda like being 'Joe the fix-it man'. Anybody who has a problem with his uniform comes to me. I've got this bag full of fix-it supplies. Everything from duct tape, safety pins and shoe polish to extra socks, gloves and shoes. Over the years, I've tried to log every uniform problem we've had and plan a 'fix-it' strategy. You can't begin to imagine what can go wrong with those goofy uniforms. I also carry a few extra things for the girls. Somebody always forgets the time of the month."

"Thanks. But you didn't need to bring all this over," answered Claire feeling guilty about her lack of forethought to consider she might have a job to do. She'd been so focused on her own upcoming discomfort, the fact that the kids were going to a major competition had slipped her mind.

"When I got back to the house tonight, I found the bags sitting on the counter. They were already packed, and I knew you'd need them. Actually, I don't want to see the stuff sitting around. It reminds me of the fact that Allison isn't going." Then the tears rolled uncontrollably down the pale, exhausted face.

"Oh, Sylvia, I'm so sorry," said Claire trying to comfort her. She sat for several minutes with her arms around the sobbing woman and allowed her the time to cry out her grief. As the tears began to subside, Claire reached for the small snifter of deep amber liquid. "Here, sip on this, Sylvia."

"Thanks," was the soft reply. "I'm sorry for breaking down on you, but I couldn't at the hospital. The pain has been building up all afternoon and I just couldn't hold it in any more."

"It's okay. I understand."

"Claire," tears brimmed the sad eyes, "What am I going to do? I'm so scared."

"Does the doctor have any idea what's wrong?"

"When I went back late this afternoon, he had no news. Allison was slipping deeper into a coma, and he had no idea of what was causing it. I've back tracked every step. There was nothing different in her day, nothing unusual. I talked to all of her friends. I've been able to account for every minute, and there's nothing to help the doctor. Nothing!" Sylvia gulped down the last of the brown liquid. "It's good, Claire. What is it?" she asked handing the glass back.

"*No Cello*, a black walnut liquor. Can I get you another?"

"Please," said Sylvia handing the delicate glass back to Claire. "I've never heard of *No No...No* what?"

Claire, happy to talk about something else, smiled. "It's *No Cello*." She pronounced with the best Italian accent she could. "I got hooked on it when I went to New Orleans a few years ago. I can't find the stuff in Tulsa, so I have a friend in Chicago send me a couple bottles for Christmas every year." She poured a glass for herself this time and returned to sit beside Sylvia. "How's Philip doing?"

"Not too well. I think this is the first time in eighteen years he's felt any emotion at all."

"I didn't realize you and he were ....." her voice trailed off. Claire didn't know how to word the question without sticking her foot in her mouth, and humble pie was not her favorite dessert.

"Nobody does. In fact not many people have even met him. Philip was never much into the family scene."

Dead Tones

"Yeah, I know what you mean," said Claire with plenty of sarcasm. "Steve wasn't much of a family man either. I just got to the point where I couldn't take the hostility anymore."

"Everyone's noticed you and Shy have been much happier since the divorce. Even though I didn't know Steve, I know you're better off without him."

"Did you ever think of leaving Philip?"

"No. Our situation's complicated. I felt obligated to stay, and I guess he did too. Although I'm surprised he stuck with us all these years."

"Why?"

"It really doesn't seem important now. But if Allison....if Ali," tears dripped off her lashes again, and Sylvia took a sip of the *No Cello*. "Well, we may not have a reason to stay together."

"Do you have any idea what you'd do?"

"Financially, you mean?"

"I don't mean to pry, Sylvia."

"Like I said, I'm surprised Philip stayed all these years. I've been prepared to be on my own with Ali for a long time. Of course, I never told him this."

Claire had a new and deep respect for the woman sitting next to her. Sylvia was much stronger than Claire had ever given her credit for. She'd always considered women who stayed in a loveless marriage as weak, but Sylvia, for some reason, had swallowed her pride and stayed with Philip. She had given up living in order to give Allison a father. *That's one hell of a commitment to your daughter, my friend.*

"Sylvia, I don't want to pry, so please don't tell me if you'd rather not, but why did you feel so obligated to stay with a man you don't love?"

"I never said I didn't love him. I love the memory of the man who's Ali's father. I know that man is somewhere deep inside the person I've been living with. For the memory, I was willing to hope and pray for the memory to be a reality again. Maybe God's punishing us for our...our stupidity now and back then."

"I don't really understand."

"Philip was and I suppose...hope...still is a very loving, passionate man. When we were in high school, our senior year, he gave up the cheerleader for me. I was a nobody. I lived in the wrong part of town, dirt poor. I don't know what he ever saw in me. I've tossed all the details over in my mind for years, but I still wonder why Philip gave up his life for me. He was the school hero, played football and basketball. Every girl in the school drooled over him. Philip dated me. My dad always said he was looking for an easy target...you know what I mean."

"Yeah, I know."

"He literally swept me off my feet. I was head over heels in love; and by graduation, I was pregnant. Well, his parents had always accused me of being a gold digger; so in their eyes, I'd proved them right. My father accused me of being a poor slut just before he threw me out of the house."

"You don't have to tell me this."

"I know, Claire. However, you're here, or I'm here at your place, and I guess I need to tell someone the story. No one else has ever heard all the details. In spite of his father's anger, Philip never wavered in his commitment to me. Unfortunately, he couldn't escape his father's accusations either. Philip's passion was left in the back seat of his Chevy, but he never left my side. Now you know why I couldn't leave him. He gave us a home, and went to school at night. When he got his degree, he found a great job, but he never left me. As far as I've been able to tell, he's never strayed either. I owe the man, Claire. He could've walked away eighteen years ago."

"You're right. I think I'd have stayed too. My relationship with Steve was never so passionate or so unselfish. We both made the

Dead Tones

mistake and hated each other for it. I made the mistake of thinking a baby would help an already terminal marriage. When I asked Steve to leave, he couldn't get out the door fast enough. At least you have the image of a hero in your past."

"The house and job didn't seem like much to live on this afternoon. I really let him have it, right in front of the doctor."

"How was he when you got back to the hospital?"

"He was sitting by Allison holding her hand. I was surprised. The tears were still flooding his eyes. It was all I could do to keep from throwing my arms around him."

"Why didn't you?"

"I've made the first move several times without a response. It's his turn."

"Sylvia, this is not the time to be stubborn. Maybe he needs forgiveness for these past years."

"I don't know that I'm ready to let things wash away just yet," answered Sylvia, handing the small glass back to Claire.

"Another?"

"No, I've got to get back to the hospital. Claire, I know you don't want to do this band trip, but try to have fun. For ShyAnne and yourself, forget your last trip. Just go with the flow, ya know what I mean?"

"I think I'm going to find out about five o'clock in the morning."

"Do me another favor, please?"

"Sure." How could Claire refuse her? She'd probably have jumped off a cliff for the woman after the conversation she'd just shared.

"Listen. Listen to the kids talking."

"What am I listening for?" Claire's curiosity was piqued.

"Kids talk amongst themselves. They say things they won't say to an adult; brag, ya know."

"Yeah, I'll listen, but for what?"

"I don't really know. All I do know is that every person Allison was with is going on this band trip. One of them knows more than he's saying."

"Sylvia, do you think someone poisoned Allison?"

"My gut tells me there's more to this story than what I know." Sylvia got up and headed for the front door.

"Shy and I will find out as much as we can. I'll call you Sunday night when we get back."

"Thanks, but if you find out anything, please call me from Denton. The doctors don't have a thing to go on. One little tidbit of information could save my baby's life."

Claire's heart went out to the woman standing in front of her. She surprised herself when she reached out to hug Sylvia. "I'll do whatever I can. You take care. Call me if you need to talk."

"I will," said Sylvia and she closed the door behind her.

Claire was jolted back to the reality of the freezing bus when a body plopped down beside her. She was shocked to turn and find herself staring into the face of Scott Krammer. Stunning blue eyes danced in front of her while the fragrance of his body filled the space between them.

"Hey, Claire, thanks for coming along," said Scott with a jovial twang to his voice.

One of the boys bumped Scott's arm. "Hey, Mr. Jazz. How ya doin' this mornin'?"

"Fine, Josh," answered Scott with a warm smile on his face. The gangly Josh continued to stumble his way down the aisle. Scott turned back to Claire, "Poor Josh, his feet grew faster than his ability to control them. We're always amazed when he gets through a whole performance without tripping over himself, but his heart and effort are in the right place."

Dead Tones

Scott's dark sandy hair was slightly disheveled as Krissy brushed past him with her blanket. "I'm really sorry Mr. Krammer. You okay?"

"No sweat, Krissy. Are you and your deadly companion there going to pick a fight further back?"

Krissy laughed. "No." She gave the man a brilliant smile.

"Hey, just make sure you and Mike behave back there."

Krissy blushed, "Mr. Krammer, I can't believe you'd say such a thing in front of Shy's mom."

"Hey!" The shout came from outside the bus. "Who's holding up the traffic? Get movin'."

"Yeah, yeah. Hold your horses," yelled Krissy over her shoulder, but she started to move on with Mike right behind her. Like Krissy, he didn't make any comment about seeing Claire sitting beside Mr. Krammer. He figured the less said about the previous encounter between the two of them the better.

Claire watched the easy exchange between student and teacher. According to Shy, the kids idolized the man sitting next to her. *Remember, you don't like this guy. I don't care if he is good looking and nice to the kids. He's an inconsiderate ass!! I don't like him!! Besides, he's never been married.* Claire caught herself analyzing the man. *There must be something wrong with him. Shut-up, Claire, you're making excuses for yourself.*

"Yo, Mr. Jazz." A tall young man loomed over the seat in front of Claire.

"Good morning, Jason. I hope you're planning to take a seat in the back."

"Why? You want to keep this good-lookin' woman all to yourself?" Before either of them could frame a response to the outlandish comment, the boy went on. "It's great to have you along, Mrs. Mayfield."

"Thanks," answered Claire.

Jason returned to the flow of traffic headed for the back of the bus. Just before he was out of Claire's hearing distance, he added, "By the way, be careful of girls handing out dramamine."

Claire actually felt sorry for the man next to her. The apology was written on his face. She took only a second to analyze that she could go through the next forty-eight hours with the reputation of being a bitch or a mom with a good sense of humor. For Shy, as well as herself, the second option seemed the better of the two. *It's time to get rid of the anger. If Sylvia can have fun, then so can I.*

"Thanks for the advice. I'll keep my eyes open this time." Claire caught the glint of approval in Jason's eyes.

Scott smiled. He was impressed with the play on words. "'Keep your eyes open'. Good come back, Claire."

"Thanks," said Claire feeling uncomfortable with the conversation. *Change the topic. Quick!* "I thought you....you"

"Were going to be on a different bus?"

"Yeah."

"Well, there was a problem with the directions. Dale has to ride on the lead bus, so we don't miss our exit. Sorry, but you're stuck with me."

Claire had no audible response for the man. She simply turned her head away from him and continued to shiver in silence. She wasn't sure how to proceed with the man she'd declared hatred for. Her only comment came in silence. *Okay, Krammer, maybe you're not an ass.* Claire found herself caught between the promise to Shy and Sylvia to have fun and her supposed dislike for the man sitting next to her. Admitting she'd been wrong was not easy. And the man sitting next to her made it difficult for her to remember the man she'd hated two years ago.

"Here, you're freezing. This'll help."

Dead Tones

As she turned her head, the aroma of fresh ground coffee aroused her senses. *Hot coffee? Anything hot would do, but good hot coffee was more than she had hoped for. Scott Krammer, you certainly know how to surprise me.* "Thanks." Claire took great pleasure in letting the warmth of the cup flow through her hands. "Where did this come from?"

"I had a thermos with me, but I know better than trying to open anything while the kids are getting settled. Be careful. It's really strong."

"Just the way I like it, strong and black," Claire responded finally letting a smile of gratitude linger on her face. A slight lurch of the bus told her they were moving. The caravan pulled out of the parking circle past the large astro-turfed football stadium and onto Mingo Road.

Krammer continued the conversation, "Really? I've never met anyone who'll drink my coffee."

"Are they afraid you might poison them?" Claire, remembering her conversation with Shy the night before, nearly choked on her words.

"I guess so. Hope you don't agree."

"Actually, it's about like my own. No wonder ShyAnne never developed a taste for my coffee. I guess I didn't realize I made it so strong. Did you hear anymore about Allison this morning?" Claire couldn't help thinking about her promise to Sylvia. Did someone know more about what had happened to Allison?

"When Dale called the hospital this morning, she was the same. We are all upset, but if we don't keep the kids focused on this competition, the whole season is down the drain."

"I know. Shy wondered if you shouldn't call the whole trip off. But when Sylvia came over last night, I got the feeling she didn't want that."

R. Z. Crompton

"I can't believe how sick Allison is. I talked to her yesterday morning before class started. She'd come in early to make up a test she'd missed, but we almost ran out of time because she was sure someone had rummaged through her locker. We visited about some students' lack of respect for other people's possessions. Then she broke her reed and had to get a new one. By the time I had her calmed down and convinced no harm had been done, other kids were starting to filter into the office. I didn't want her testing while she was so upset, but Allison's a talented young lady. Once she set her mind to playing, she did very well.

"Did you tell her mother?" Claire asked as she barely avoided making physical contact with Scott's shoulder when the bus made the tight curve onto Interstate Forty-four toward Oklahoma City.

"Tell her what? About the test? Why?"

"About someone being in Allison's locker."

"No. When I saw Sylvia yesterday, I never thought about it. Kids leave lockers open accidentally all the time. Allison wasn't missing anything. Why?"

Claire wasn't sure how much to say. If she confided in this man, this man she was trying not to like, she might be showing too much of her hand. *I think a poker face is best. He'll really think I'm nuts if I start suggesting murder.* That was the first time she'd actually put a word to the action Sylvia had suggested. The evil? Could it be this close to them? "No reason, I guess. Sylvia's trying to put all the details of the day together. Maybe it's important."

"Maybe. Do you want some more coffee? I'll refill your cup before I go check on the kids in the back. I like to do at least one walk through early in the trip just to remind them I'm watching."

"No thanks. You better save some for yourself."

"I've got plenty of coffee, but you'll have to share the cup with me."

Dead Tones

Claire was wondering how desperate she was to stay warm, and then heard herself answering him before she knew herself what her answer was going to be. "I don't mind sharing." *My God! I can't believe I just said that. My body is selling out for a little comfort. I'm weak.* "Don't you have a parent sitting in the back?"

"No. Dale figures the kids have earned the right to sit back there without an adult looking over their shoulder. I agree, even though some of the parents have expressed other ideas."

"I guess I can see their point."

"These kids work several hours every day for weeks. Their only reward is the competition, to perform, and to win. Marching isn't an extracurricular activity for them; it's an attitude, a life style. You'll see. Besides, keeping the parents up front is more for the parents protection than the kids."

"What do you mean?"

"Let's just say the kids don't really appreciate having a babysitter, and you weren't the first victim of the 'dramamine surprise'. However, I'm glad to say that you were the last, as far as we know."

"Gee thanks. I don't know whether I should feel glad or just stupid."

"The kids work hard, but they aren't saints. We always keep an eye out for liquor, cigarettes, or drugs."

"I guess there's not too much they can do on a bus."

"I wouldn't go that far. Just because we don't catch everything doesn't mean they don't do it, or keep trying. They're teenagers; its in their blood."

"You mean physical contact too?"

"For starters. If a couple of kids are inclined to partake of the pleasures, then having a parent two or three seats away isn't going to stop them."

"How do you know they don't have alcohol back there?"

"We don't know absolutely. However, any of the kids dumb enough to think we believe it's really ice tea in those bottles should come up with a new idea."

"Really? They do that? What about drugs?"

"If they get caught with any of that stuff, they're out of the band. When we catch somebody, the example of suspension usually deters others for a while. Then all we have to deal with is the stupid antics."

"I suppose dramamine isn't considered a drug?"

"Sorry," Scott answered shaking his head, "too many of the kids get motion sickness. By the time we get to Oklahoma City, at least one will be complaining." Scott reached up into the space above his seat. "Here's the thermos. Help yourself. I'll be back in a few minutes."

"Thanks," said Claire looking up into the dancing blue eyes.

******

"ShyAnne! Shy, did you see your mom?" Krissy nearly jumped over the seat trying to get Shy's attention.

"What's wrong? Did she get off the bus?" Shy was worried something would happen causing her mother to renege on her promise. Maybe Mr. B. wouldn't cancel the trip if all the kids were on the bus already.

"No. She's on the bus, but guess who's sitting beside her?" Krissy fell into the seat across from Shy and made Mike crawl over her to get to the seat by the window.

"Really, Krissy, you could've let me in first," hissed Mike. "I wasn't going to fight you for the outside seat."

"Yeah, yeah," was the simple response. Krissy, the bearer of bad news, had more on her mind than Mike's inconvenience. She'd

Dead Tones

missed the chance for the aisle seat enough times to know "first come - first serve" was the rule of the land. And she didn't want Mike to block her view of Shy's face when she told her the news.

"Is B. sitting with her?" asked Shy, wondering about Krissy excited state.

"You wish. It's Krammer!"

"Mr. Krammer's on this bus? Oh my God. She'll kill him!"

"That's not the impression I got. Really, Shy, they seemed fine. But man, was I ever surprised." Krissy added as she shoved a bag under the seat in front of her.

"Me too!" She admitted still wondering why her mother hadn't just gotten up and walked out.

"I'm surprised you even talked her into coming, let alone sit beside Krammer," said Mike, trying to get comfortable in the small space by the window.

"I didn't convince her to sit beside Krammer," snapped Shy. "Maybe she's just waiting for the kids to move out of the way before she tries to get off the bus."

Mike put in his two cents worth of advice. "Relax, Shy. She looked okay."

ShyAnne turned to Sarah, who was sitting next to her. "I can't believe Barnett let this happen. He knows how she feels about Mr. Krammer.

Sarah, covered with a soft red and white blanket and trying to sleep, didn't seem concerned. "Don't argue with the spirits, Shy. Now be quiet."

"Sarah." Shy nudged her friend's arm. "Sarah, what are you talking about?"

"I'm trying not to talk at all."

"Sarah," Shy snipped softly, "What are you talking about?"

"Really, Shy. It's nothing," offered Sarah.

"My mother agreed to come on a band trip which she absolutely hates doing, and now she's sitting with a man she's been cursing the last two years. Don't you think this is just a little unusual?"

"Did you get help convincing her to come on this trip?"

"Yeah, how do you know?"

"Don't argue with the spirits," said Sarah pulling her blanket up around her neck.

"Damn it, Sarah. What are you talking about?"

Sarah sat up looking at her friend. Shy rarely used a foul word, and now she had Sarah's attention. "I was up most of the night with Grandmother. She helped me with the spirits. We asked for help convincing your mom to come on the trip. If they see fit to help her overcome her anger, then don't fight it."

Krissy was all ears. "Really, Sarah? You cast a spell on ShyAnne's mom?"

"Shhh. Krissy, be quiet. I don't want people to know I practice my medicine on my friends. They wouldn't understand. And I didn't cast a spell. I simply talked to the spirits."

Krissy was consumed with excitement. "Can you ask the spirits to help me?"

"Me too! Me too!" Sean, who was seated beside Monica in the seats behind Shy and Sarah, jumped into the conversation. "I've got a huge test in chemistry next week, and I just don't get it."

"None of you get it," snipped Sarah. "I can't use my magic carelessly."

"Why not? Don't you like us as much as you do Shy? You'll cast a spell on her, but you won't use your magic to help your other friends?"

"Shhhh!" Sarah snapped. "Krissy, you're being silly. You don't need my help."

Dead Tones

"No. I suppose I don't," admitted Krissy softly. "But I can think of someone who does. Did you ask your spirits to help Allison?"

"Yes, but it's hard to fight a spell that has already started; and it's especially hard to fight what we don't understand. All I could do was to ask the spirits to protect Allison from the evil in her body."

"What's so hard to understand? Isn't a bad guy a bad guy?" asked Sean.

"Grandmother has been teaching me about the Night Walker and the Raven Mocker. I can understand this evil. It is the other side of the medicine circle for me. I cannot understand the evil I feel around us now."

"What about your grandmother? Can she help?" Shy asked giving the Cherokee medicine more respect than she had yesterday.

"She is helping. As much as she can. Don't forget there's a big difference between Tahlequah and Tulsa.

Tahlequah, Oklahoma, seat of the Cherokee Nation's government, was established in 1840 after a quarter of the Cherokee people died while making the hike from northern Georgia and Alabama through Tennessee to eventually settle in Oklahoma, a waste land not considered valuable to any white man. The deadly walk became known in the history books as the Trail of Tears. In spite of the devastation caused by white man, the Cherokee returned to their system of three part government. They set up a system of elementary school and seminaries for men and women and published the first news paper in Oklahoma in both English and Cherokee. Cherokee Nation Bingo is a major form of entertainment for all Oklahoma residents and a great source of income for the Cherokee. Sarah made the hour long drive from Tulsa to Tahlequah and back again with great pride.

"No one in Tahlequah is going to question Grandmother's right to practice her medicine," continued Sarah. "It's a little different, however, in the High School parking lot."

"I guess," Shy acknowledged. "Up until this episode with my mother, I had my own doubts about your spirits."

"The band needed help and you needed convincing. The spirits wouldn't have stepped in if they didn't agree."

"Sarah, was Allison poisoned?" asked Monica leaning around the seat in front of her.

"Grandmother and I think so."

"Why? Who?"

"We don't know. It's only our suspicions. We might be wrong."

"I doubt it," whispered Shy.

"Will it happen again?" Krissy asked.

"I don't know. But the evil isn't gone. It's still here."

"Hey, guys, what are you so intently discussing?" Krammer had managed to get down the aisle of the bus without ShyAnne and the others noticing. Of the graduating seniors over the years, he was going to miss this group of six the most. It was hard to lose his favorites every spring, but these kids had become his family over the last four years. Maybe that's why he had wanted to make amends with Shy's mom before she graduated. Scott knew Claire hadn't stopped sponsoring band trips because of the dramamine those three girls had slipped into her coke. She'd stopped coming because he'd accused her of being lax. He felt the greatest guilt when he saw Claire watching their competition from a distance. That was the last time he'd lost his temper with a parent. He'd accused the wrong person, and the accusation had stripped ShyAnne of her mother's participation in an activity that consumed most of Shy's time.

"Nothing special, Mr. Krammer," responded Shy. "How's my mom doing up there?"

"She's fine. Thanks for convincing her to come along."

"I had lots of help," she answered nudging Sarah's leg. "But did you have to sit right beside her?"

Dead Tones

"When I got on, the only choice I had was between your mom and Charlie."

"Ewwwww," was the combined response.

"I don't care how much your mom hates me; she smells so much better than poor Charlie."

"Everybody, in fact, everything smells better than poor Charlie," responded Sarah.

"True, but he's got great rhythm and can beat the daylights out of the bass drum."

"Yeah, on the other hand, he's a danger to our air quality," offered Krissy holding her nose.

"I bet my Mom's freezing," said Shy not able to imagine peaceful co-existence between Krammer and her mother.

"As a matter of fact, she is. We're sharing my coffee, but I'm afraid that's not helping much."

"Are you serious? My mom's sharing your coffee?"

"Yeah, are you really that surprised? We're even having a pleasant conversation," continued Scott with a big smile on his face.

Shy turned her head toward Sarah and winked. "Wow, Sarah. You've got some powerful friends. Here," Shy offered her blanket up to the man standing over her. "Give her this. I'll share with Sarah if she doesn't mind."

"Not at all." Sarah moved to offer some of her red and white blanket to ShyAnne. The cover was more than just a blanket woven in the school colors. The colors symbolized good medicine and turned the blanket it into a protective cloak, but Sarah offered the cover without an explanation of its significance.

"Thanks, I'm sure she'll appreciate it." Krammer took a few more steps toward the back of the bus.

ShyAnne couldn't help but hear the crude comment vibrating from behind them. "Hey, Mr. Jazz, you gonna cuddle up with the pretty lady?"

"I think I'll pass, Jason. I don't need to trap my women on a bus. My dates actually agree to go out with me."

"Touché, Mr. Jazz," Jason slurred.

ShyAnne smiled. Jason was a great baritone, but heavily endowed with book smarts he was not. In fact, he was rather short on intelligence all together. In spite of his genius with music, Jason was constantly struggling to keep his grades up. His music gave him a chance at a life and a future only because his fellow band members teetered, coaxed and encouraged him. A student who didn't make the grade check didn't go on the band trip, so the kids often worked together studying for tests and finishing projects.

Scott returned to the front of the bus and handed the blanket down to Claire. "Shy thought you might need this."

"Thanks. I can't believe it's gotten so quiet. After all that noise when they were getting on, I thought I'd need ear plugs."

Scott slipped back into his seat. "It quiets down quickly in the morning. Most of the kids want to sleep. They're teenagers. They stay up all night and then sleep as long as possible. Some of the others will put on a headset. Eventually, they'll be yelling for a movie."

Claire looked around noticing the television monitors mounted throughout the bus. The bus had a beautiful gray and orange interior; and Hal, the driver and keeper of the bus, was determined to keep his luxury liner looking fine. There was even that hint of newness in the air. He'd given strict instructions about not sitting on the arms of the seats or laying in the aisle. "This vehicle doesn't move until everyone is in a seat," Hal had moaned. The kids sprawled out in the middle of the bus had grudgingly picked up their pillows and folded themselves into a designated space.

Dead Tones

Claire wrapped the blanket around her legs and pulled it up over her arms. The coffee had been good, but the blanket did more to warm her body. Scott's long legs didn't fit easily into the small space, so Claire moved hers as far over as she could. However, in order to move her legs out of his way, her upper torso angled toward him. There was no way around it. If Scott was going to abide by Hal's rule to stay out of the aisle, he wouldn't be able to avoid touching Claire. She knew this and enjoyed watching him struggle to keep space between them. The masculine size of his body had escaped her attention until he tried to cram it into the small area. Claire cuddled down taking as little space as possible and tried to relax. The warmth provided by the blanket and Scott's body soothed her shivering body. Claire fell asleep.

****

A bright flash of light sent Claire flying straight up crashing her head into Scott's chin. It took a second for her to get her bearings. "What happened?" The sun was up now bearing down through the over-sized windows. Several of the shades had been pulled down to ease the glare on the television monitors. Claire's blanket was no longer wrapped tightly around her upper torso but lay loosely in her lap.

"Wow! Great picture." Agreement came from several girls standing around Scott's seat.

Scott, nursing the pain in his jaw, was trying to untangle his legs from Claire's. In spite of his effort, he hit the gray seat in front of them several times. This was one of the rare times when Scott Krammer became annoyed with some crazy stunt. After more than a dozen years of being part of the Renegade Regiment teaching staff, he was pretty numb to the silly teenage antics. He'd run the gamut from surprise to shock and even disappointment until he'd developed a technique of teaching that managed and inspired the kids without taxing himself to the breaking point every year. Once he'd learned how to relax and enjoy the kids, their respect and devotion to him had grown. Once in a while, however, one of them got under his skin. The picture was no big deal, but he certainly didn't want to push this tenuous friendship he was sharing with Claire. There was no telling just how far her good nature would go, and images of her temper flashed through his mind.

"Jennifer, what are you doing?"

"Pictures for the banquet. We don't get good candid shots of you very often."

"Hey! Quiet up there. We can't hear the movie," shouted a male voice from the rear of the bus.

"Drop dead, Sean!" Jennifer yelled back. Then looking down at Scott, she oozed in a soft, sing-songy voice, "You and Mrs. Mayfield make such a cute couple."

Claire blushed and looked up at the monitor just in time to see a black and white cow flying through the air. A large twister chased after a red truck. She rubbed the corner of her eyes trying to get her contacts to focus. There was no denying that she'd fallen asleep and ended up cuddled into Scott Krammer's body. Obviously, Scott had befallen the same fate. Now dear, sweet Jennifer had a record of their slight indiscretion for everyone to see.

"Sorry, Claire. You okay?"

"Yeah, fine." Claire was more interested in the redhead standing in the aisle. There was nothing sweet about the glare in her deep green eyes.

"C'mon, Jen. Let's see who else we can get in a compromising position." Abby pulled Jennifer away from the front of the bus.

Dead Tones

"Wouldn't it be great if Mr. Krammer and Mrs. Mayfield got together?"

Claire and Scott didn't miss the comment, and no one in the front rows missed Jennifer's response.

"No way, man. She's old enough to be his mother."

The words, full of malice, intrigued Claire more than hurt her feelings. *A full blown bitch already. I wonder who lit the fuse on her tampon on fire?*

"Sorry, Claire. Jennifer's a little high strung." Scott tried to make excuses for Jennifer's bad behavior. "She does have a mouth on her."

"Good manners are learned at home, Mr. Krammer. She's not your fault."

"Please call me Scott?"

"Why? Because I'm so much older than you are?" asked Claire with a cynical touch.

"You aren't older..."

Claire cocked her head and raised an eyebrow. "Don't patronize me, Mr. Krammer. Of course I am."

"The point I was trying to make is that we are the adults on this trip. Therefore, we are equals. Age has no bearing."

"Okay, we're equals."

"So call me Scott. And a couple of years doesn't make much difference anyway." He threw in quickly.

Claire couldn't help smiling and wondering how many years really were between them. *At least ten, maybe more. He's right though. In this case, it really doesn't matter.* All the sponsors and teachers on the trip were considered equals. The teachers took care of the performance; but without the parents to organize the lodging, meals, and a dozen other details including the money, there would be no trip.

"Just for your information, Jennifer isn't high strung. She has a mountain size crush on you."

"No way. How can you tell in just a couple of minutes."

"It's a woman thing, I guess. And Shy's told me the majority of the girls, at one time or another, have a thing for you before they graduate."

"Oh yeah, give me a break."

Claire was surprised by his innocent reaction. She couldn't believe he'd never notice, but he seemed sincere. "Why is it so hard to believe? You're an extremely attractive, single man. They become young women while under your leadership. Is it so ridiculous to believe you're probably the first man, besides their fathers, who impresses them? Think about your influence on these innocent minds, and bodies."

"Don't kid yourself, Claire. They aren't as innocent as you'd like to think."

"Then why is it so hard for you to admit you might be the focus of their..."

"Lust?" He jumped into her thoughts. Beginning to feel uncomfortable with the direction of this conversation, Scott felt the need to defend himself. "These kids are my family. My own sons and daughters. I've never considered..." he stumbled over his words.

"Scott, now you're the one being naive. Even though you see sons and daughters, they don't see a father. I wasn't accusing you. I was only trying to help you understand Jennifer's reaction to me."

"I just never thought of them...feeling that way. Man, do I feel like an idiot."

"Most men are from time to time. Some more than others."

"Am I in the more or less category?"

"Well, it depends on when you ask me. Two years ago you were definitely in the 'more' category."

Dead Tones

"And now?"

"Up until this last discussion, you were in the less category. On the other hand, if you have any more coffee to share, I won't move you back."

"Coffee coming up."

****

"Sarah, are you still sleeping?" asked ShyAnne softly. She hadn't been able to rest at all. Every time she closed her eyes images of medicine men dancing around Allison's bed raced through her mind. Maybe that's why Allison was still alive. Maybe the spirits were keeping her alive until the doctors could find out what's wrong with her. *I've got to find out who did this to Ali. That would be the most help. Then the doctors would be able find an antidote.*

"What's on your mind? I can't sleep either."

"I want to figure out who did this," whispered Shy.

"Did what?"

"You know, who tried to kill Allison."

"Wait a minute, Shy." Sarah, with a serious gleam in her coal black eyes, sat up in her chair. "'Kill' is a really strong word. And she isn't dead."

"Only because your spirits are protecting her. If you think she was poisoned on purpose, then someone is trying to kill her. And it was your grandmother, not mine, who said someone was going to die. If we can figure out why, we might find out who."

"ShyAnne, you're trying to play a dangerous game. My best advice to you is protect yourself and leave the games to those better prepared to play."

"Are you chicken?"

"No. Just more intelligent. I respect the powers I don't understand. You don't."

"So you won't help."

"No. I'll be too busy trying to keep you out of trouble. And please don't tell Krissy," begged Sarah.

"Oh that'd be like telling the wind. The four corners of the earth would hear about our plan before we got to Dallas. Thanks, Sarah, I knew I could count on you. Now where do we start, Oh intelligent one?"

"Hey, the buses are pulling off. I wonder why," questioned Sarah.

"I don't care why. I just want to walk around for a few minutes." Shy reached across the aisle and poked a finger at Krissy. "Wake up. The buses are stopping."

"Why?" Krissy asked lifting her head off Mike's shoulder.

"I bet somebody needs a smoke," answered Shy.

Yawning first, Krissy looked at her, "Kids can't smoke on a band trip."

"Not one of us, Silly. One of the parents."

"Oh, yeah. I forgot about them."

The buses pulled side by side in a small lot. A throng of anxious bodies headed for the bathroom in the small restaurant. Claire waited for the students to file past. She wasn't in any hurry to get out. It was still too cold outside for her liking, so waiting in the bus while the others stood in line seemed the wiser choice. After all, they wouldn't leave her in the bathroom. The kids certainly managed to get off faster than they boarded, and no sooner had the last one stepped off the bus and Scott was back looking for her.

"Did you look through that bag Sylvia gave to you?"

"Not yet. Why?"

Dead Tones

"One of the girls is car sick. Sylvia usually packed some dramamine."

"I'll check." Claire reached under the seat for the large shoulder bag. Pulling it up onto her lap, she unzipped the side pocket and systematically started the search for a tiny tube of white pills. After several minutes, Claire pulled a white container out of the middle compartment. "Found it. Illusive little thing. I'll take it to her, so I can get her a glass of water from the restaurant. I don't think it's a good idea to have her drinking out of a community bottle. She might have the flu."

"Yeah, the last thing we need is a bunch of kids puking their guts out on the field."

Claire stood up and followed Scott to the door. Feeling the gust of chilly air, she turned around to get the blanket. Scott stopped and waited for her. As she stepped out, he reached up to offer her a steadying hand. Claire was surprised at the gentlemanly gesture. She wrapped the blanket around her shoulders and took his hand. "Thanks. By the way, who's sick?"

"Sue. She's sitting at the first table by the door."

Claire followed Scott into the old building. The line for the bathroom weaved through the kitchen and then in and out of the old tables. *Great, must be a one holer. We'll be here all day waiting for the girls to get done.* Claire assumed the girl sitting with her head on the table was Sue. As she slid into the booth, Sue lifted her head. The petite elegant features were pasty white.

"How ya doin'?" Claire asked slipping into the booth.

"I feel so crummy. Mr. Krammer said you might have some dramamine."

"Yeah, here." Claire opened the container and dumped one pill into the open hand. "I'll get you some water and soda crackers."

Claire had returned, handing the glass to Sue before she could put her head back on the table.

"Thanks."

"Do you always get sick on these trips?"

"Not for a long time," answered Sue, hoping desperately that the tiny white pill would make her feel better.

"Did you eat anything for breakfast?"

"No. Last night I realized I was short of reeds for my clarinet; so while everybody else ate at the breakfast buffet this morning, I got one of Allison's extra reeds and started breaking it in. I grabbed a coke as we left." Sue dipped a couple of napkins into the leftover water and wiped her face and neck.

"How did you get a reed from Allison?"

"We have each other's locker combination. We look out for each other...share and all that stuff. Ya know? Most of the clarinet players keep extra reeds cause they break so easy during marching season."

"Maybe the coke on an empty stomach triggered your nausea."

"I guess it's possible." Sue paused as she wiped the back of her neck and then her forehead. "In fact, come to think of it, the only time I got sick as a freshman was when I stopped with Jack at the Quik Trip for a coke on our way to the school. Jack graduated that spring, and my mom would never stop for me. Will this work by this afternoon?"

"It should kick in shortly. Sit up front in the bus and look straight out the window. No reading or side windows. Okay?"

"Yeah, okay."

Before Claire could get out of her seat, another pale face was looking down at her. "Sick?" The poor girl nodded her head. Claire stood up and motioned for the young lady to take her spot. "I'll get you some water."

Dead Tones

"Thanks, Mrs. Mayfield," moaned Kate.

Scott was headed for the table with a glass in each hand. "We've got another one. She's in the bathroom. Jane will need a dramamine too. Kate, won't you ever learn to sit up front?"

"Eww. With the parents? I'd rather be sick," she moaned again.

"Why don't you take something before you get sick?"

"Sometimes I do, sometimes I don't get sick at all. Every time I get on the bus, I hope I've out grown my motion sickness; my brother did."

"Guess what?" said Krammer, frowning at the miserable girl sitting in front of him.

"Not yet, huh?"

"You got it, sister. I hope you'll be ready to march."

"Have I ever let you down?"

"No, Kate, you haven't. I just think it's silly to be so miserable when you don't have to be. You're a senior, you're supposed to be smarter by now."

"You sound like my dad," snipped the tall, lanky brunette.

"Point made, but no sympathy."

"I don't need sympathy, only a little white pill."

Sue wasn't completely without humor. "Maybe you forgot your little white pill a few weeks ago and its morning sickness rather than motion sickness."

"Maybe. But I bet I'm out on the field and you're in the hospital." Kate swallowed the pill with a water chaser and got out of the seat just in time for Jane to take her place.

"Is she always so pleasant?" asked Claire watching the young lady saunter away.

"Not always. Sometimes, she's worse," said Sue.

Scott came to Kate's defense. "Meow, Sue. You and Kate bicker about everything. And I do believe you usually start the catty conversations. Here's your water, Jane. Get your dramamine and head for the bus. You too, Sue."

The girls did as they were told while Claire tried to get her chance at the bathroom. By this time the women had overtaken both the men's and the women's restrooms, so the line was moving along. Any of the adults who couldn't live without a cigarette had discreetly nursed their habit outside.

Claire didn't see Shy walk up behind her, but she recognized the greeting. "Yo, Mom. How's it going?"

"Hi, honey. I'm worried about the three sick girls. Have you heard about any others?" asked Claire as she turned around to see her daughter, Krissy and Sarah in line behind her.

"No. But a couple girls always get sick."

"Why do only the girls get sick?" asked Claire.

"Oh, that's easy to answer," reported Krissy. "The guys are already so rotten inside, they don't know if they're sick or not."

Giggles floated through the restaurant catching Scott's attention from the other side of the room. His gaze stopped with Claire. He appreciated the view and the returned smile. She was tall for a woman, but still several inches shorter than his six foot two inch frame. He liked the rich brown hair curling around her face and then hanging barely to her shoulders. Scott didn't care if she was older or not, he'd had a school boy crush on the feisty Claire Mayfield ever since their first argument two years ago. No matter how hard he tried to convince ShyAnne to drag her mother to the band events, Claire always managed to stay at arms length. When Dale had asked if he could put up with riding on the same bus with the irritable lady, Scott had jumped at the chance. He hadn't even looked to see if any other seats were open. The seat next to Charlie didn't count. Claire could

Dead Tones

snarl at him the whole trip and it wouldn't make a lick of difference. He wasn't going to give up that seat beside her.

ShyAnne didn't miss the eye connection between her mother and Mr. Krammer. "Mom, I'm so sorry."

Claire brought her attention back to the girls around her. "About what, dear?"

"About Mr. Krammer. Mr. B. promised he'd be on another bus."

"It's a....well, it's working out okay. Maybe he's.....matured in the last couple of years."

"Mom, don't fall for his charm like all the rest of us." Shy warned.

"What on earth are you talking about? I'm not falling for him. My God, one of the girls reminded me I was old enough to be his mother."

For the first time Sarah joined the conversation. "I think that's a bit of an exaggeration, Mrs. Mayfield."

"Thanks, Sarah. And you can all relax. I certainly wouldn't want to fight most of the girls in the band for this guy's attention."

"Mom, from the look of the smile he gave you, I don't think you have to fight at all."

"Shy, don't play matchmaker. It makes me angry." Claire slipped into the vacated washroom and locked the door.

"Good grief, Sarah, what kind of spell did you put on my mother? You're the one playing matchmaker."

Sarah wasn't good at hiding her inner thoughts from Shy, but then a smile slipped out and gave her away. "I didn't actually put a spell on her. I only asked the spirits to help your mom see the benefits of being on this trip. How was I supposed to know that Mr. Krammer was going to be one of the benefits?"

Krissy sighed, "I think it's cute. Mr. Krammer has been hounded for years by teenagers. No wonder he wants an older woman."

"Krissy, be quiet," muttered Shy. "I don't want her to hear us. Besides, just because my mother hasn't bit his head off, doesn't mean she's ready to marry him."

Krissy, the eternal romantic, wasn't ready to give up. "Your mom might just surprise you."

"Oh come on, Krissy. You remember the explosion between them the last time. What else would you expect from them? Mr. Krammer is going to suck up, and my mother is going to control her temper. Forty-eight hours later the two shall part company and never meet again."

Sarah was more optimistic. "Don't argue with the spirits, Shy."

"Really, Sarah. It's going to take more than Cherokee medicine, magic or not, to get my mother, the president of the 'I Hate Men Club' to give some guy the time of day. I don't care how good looking, intelligent, or wealthy he might be. If he has three legs, he's at the bottom of the food chain."

"You're starting to be as cynical as Mike," pouted Krissy.

"Ladies, head 'em up and move 'em out." Mr. Krammer came up behind them. "You're gonna have to use the john on the bus."

"No way!" Shy snapped. "You wouldn't make us do that. Nobody uses the 'relieving facilities' on the bus."

Relieving facilities? Yeah, whatever you say. "Sorry, girls, we gotta get goin'."

"We can't," stated Sarah flatly.

"Why not?"

"The boys used all the toilet paper."

"Now why would they use all the paper if they never use the john?"

Dead Tones

"Well...." All three girls started laughing, but Sarah continued the explanation. "Well, they didn't use it for the normal reasons."

"Can you be a little more specific?"

ShyAnne was the one to drop the details of the boys' earlier escapades. "They stuffed the toilet paper in their pants."

"They did what?" Krammer was astonished.

"They were making bets about whose, you know..." the girls giggled again. "You know...whose a..."

Krissy came to her rescue. "Whose 'thing' was the biggest. They used the toilet paper to, shall we say, enhance what Mother Nature bestowed on them."

"Jesus, what a bunch of morons." Krammer shook his head. "Please hurry up."

"Yeah, sure thing, Mr. Jazz," oozed Krissy.

Claire exited what was normally the men's room and met Scott's gaze. "Anymore sick kids?"

"No everything is pretty normal. Guys acting stupid and girls getting sick. A little dramamine and they'll be ready to march. I wish I could say as much for the guys."

"What'd they do now?"

"Trust me, you don't want to know. Ya know, it amazes me how these kids can be so grown up one minute and nearly regress to diapers the next."

"Are you speaking of men in general, or did you have specific ones in mind?" Claire asked with a touch of humor.

Krammer didn't miss the jovial hint in her question. "I don't remember specifically eliminating the girls from my comment. I can personally testify that most of the females on this trip are not destined to become rocket scientists no matter how spacey they might seem."

"You're right. We all have our moments: good and bad."

Now Scott faltered, afraid he'd insinuated more than he'd wanted to. "I didn't mean...."

"Relax, my feeling is if you can't act like a child once-in-a-while, you're probably dead."

"In that case, I should have a long life. I'm going to get everybody in here moving. Will you push the herd along in the parking lot? We've got to get going.."

"Sure. How much longer 'til we get to the University?"

"It's still a couple hours to Denton. We'll eat lunch first then head for the campus." Scott noticed the thin denim jacket hidden by the blanket still held in place around Claire's shoulders. "You have anything warmer to wear?"

"Not really. I just threw a few things in a bag last night. We're going to Dallas; how cold can it be?"

"You're going to freeze your buns off. Didn't ShyAnne tell you there's a cold front moving through? This is as warm as it's going to get. By this afternoon, the north wind is going to rip right through that blanket."

"I'll figure something out." Claire said sounding more confident than she really was. "Right now I'm more concerned about making sure those girls are able to march. I'll stay in the bus if I have to."

"That's no fun."

"That's life.

CHAPTER FOUR

    A sea of buses met the Renegade Regiment as they pulled into the University of North Texas parking lot. Competition had started early that morning; but because the better bands were usually scheduled for a later performance time, the Regiment didn't have to be ready to take the field until three o'clock. The semi-truck bearing the Renegade Regiment logo was already in position for unloading. As soon as the last bus stopped, the transformation was complete. Unruly teenagers had become efficient competitors anxious to match their skill against some of the best in the country. The doors of the buses opened allowing a wave of people to wash toward the semi which had been carefully packed the night before. The loading team, consisting of approximately a dozen students, climbed into the truck.
    Large racks of uniforms were carefully handed out of the back door, where waiting sponsors were ready to match uniform to student. Another door was opened allowing the pit equipment to be passed assembly line fashion out of the truck. Once these large items were removed, the hat boxes and smaller instruments were unloaded. As the truck was being systematically emptied, the kids were undressing in the parking lot. Claire watched in amazement as girls stripped down to strange combinations of boxer shorts, long underwear and sports bras. She was more concerned about the cold temperatures than the lack of modesty.
    "Shy, aren't you freezing?"
    "I just don't think about it anymore. We've got to change and that's all there is to it."
    "What do you need me to do? What does Sylvia do?"

Dead Tones

"Just stay in one spot. She usually stayed near Allison," answered Shy as she pulled her black trousers up over her hips. "Anybody who needs help will find you, but it's easier if you stand still. Hey, Mom, I'm really glad you're here. Thanks."

"I'm really glad I came. Sorry it took me so long to figure out I was wrong."

"Does that mean you'll go to Nationals with us?" ShyAnne smiled hopefully.

"Possibly. As soon as you guys are dressed, I'm going to run and get something warmer to wear."

"Told you it was going to be cold. Here, put my cuffs on me," ordered Shy.

Claire obligingly wrapped the silver cuffs around the red sleeves hooking the Velcro securely. "How's Sue? Have you seen her?"

"She's getting dressed, but she looks terrible. I don't know how she's going to get through the solo," wondered Shy.

"Sue's playing for Allison?"

"Yeah. Ali was first chair. With her sick, Sue's got to take over."

Claire stepped in closer to her daughter and whispered, "Do you think Sue wanted the solo bad enough to make Allison sick?"

"Mom, you sound like a 'Jessica Fletcher' wanna be."

"Honey, you know these kids better than I do. Sylvia's sure there's more to Allison's condition than she's been told, and she asked me to find out. So what's your opinion about Sue? She had access to Allison's locker."

"I didn't think you and Sylvia knew each other that well," said Shy.

"We don't, or at least we didn't until last night. Let's just say there's an understanding between us now. So?"

"Sue and Allison weren't good friends, but they weren't enemies either. Sue's been trying to get first chair away from Ali for two years, but Allison's the better player. Ali respects Sue's ability; and after Ali graduates, Sue will get all the solos."

"What's the likelihood the solo next year will be for a clarinet? Allison is getting lots of exposure with this solo."

"I hadn't looked at it that way. But Sue's sick now too. She wouldn't poison herself before the solo. Ya think? No. Frankly, I don't think she'd have the guts to poison herself after the solo either, even to cover herself. And she's not that kind. She's an honest competitor. Ya know what I mean?"

"Yeah, I..." Claire didn't have the chance to finish her thought.

"Mrs. Mayfield, I need some shoe polish." Kate came rushing through the throng of moving red and black soldiers.

"Wow! You sure look better."

"The power of the little white pill is wonderful. Shoe polish? And an energy bar too, if you have them."

"Oh, sure. Right here." Claire reached down into the back for one of the bottles of black polish. The energy bars were in the other bag. Claire pulled up a handful which were quickly claimed by the students within grabbing distance.

"Mrs. Mayfield?"

"Yes?" Claire turned around to see Jane standing in front of her. "What do you need?"

"I was wondering if you have any more of those energy bars?" asked Jane.

"Yeah, here you go." Claire handed another bar over. "How you feeling?"

"Better, a little tired," She held up the bar in her right hand as if to show why she needed the energy. "Better, though."

"Good. I was worried about you."

Dead Tones

"Thanks, gotta go." Jane headed for the designated warm-up area.

The kids lined up now for safety pins, hair pins, self adhesive Velcro to replace pieces which had fallen off the cuffs or to hold something else together. Claire was impressed with the kids' ability to fix, make do or improvise. Nothing stopped the preparations for competition.

Once the kids had their uniforms securely put together, they collected their horns and started the process of warming up. Uniform racks, cases and anything else laying on the ground was loaded back onto the semi, and the doors were locked. Claire almost put her bag of tricks in with the uniforms, but she had the last minute vision of someone losing a glove. She flung both bags over her shoulder and headed for the stadium with the other sponsors.

"Claire, it's really good to see you. I loved your last article." Jessica, Monica's mother, came up beside Claire. "I knew you were on the same bus as the girls, but I didn't get a chance to talk to you. Ya know, Sue was on our bus, and she's having a bad time. I'm worried about her."

"Yeah, Shy said she was still looking pretty sick. I hope she makes it," said Claire pulling the blanket tightly around her. She hadn't noticed the chilly temperature while she was helping the kids get ready, but now the wind seemed to go right through the blanket. "Jess, I'm going to check our show time and then run off to the nearest mall to grab a warm coat. Do you want to come along?"

"Love to. How we going to get there?"

"I'm going to call a cab. I don't think we'll have much time, but I can't sit out in this weather all day, and I'm sure it'll be colder tonight. I'll end up sick too."

"Can I make a suggestion?"

"Sure, anything to save time and my health."

R. Z. Crompton

"There's a Caché store at North Park. After you call the taxi, call the store and tell them what you need. One of the associates'll pull what you need. We'll be in and out within thirty minutes," said Jessica.

"Sounds like a good idea to me."

"So, Claire, I hope you don't think I'm being too forward, but I'm over forty, so I don't have time to beat around the bush."

Claire burst out laughing. "Jess, being over forty has nothing to do with your boldness. I remember you at those PTO meetings when the girls were little. You always said exactly what was on your mind. Probably shortened the meetings by a couple of hours."

"What can I say? I didn't have time to waste then cause the kids were a handful, now I'm too old."

"So what's on your mind?" Claire asked as she walked toward the pay phone.

"You and Scott Krammer are the newest couple being talked about. Frankly, I was shocked to hear the news." Jessica never paused for a breath let alone give Claire a chance to defend herself. "I thought you hated him. Boy was I surprised to hear you two were cuddled up in his seat. I..."

"Wait a minute," said Claire when someone answered the phone. She asked for a cab to pick them up at the northeast corner of the campus and hung up the receiver before turning her interest back to Jessica. "Who are you listening to? Are you sitting in the back of the bus with the other space cadets?" Claire flipped through the phone book looking for the number to Caché.

"No, I'm not." Jessica sounded almost hurt that Claire would question her source of information. "Actually, I always take the seat between the last sponsors and the first students. You wouldn't believe the information I can gather listening to both sides. Usually the truth

Dead Tones

is somewhere in the middle of the two sides of any given story. In your case, man, both sides are singin' the same song. So tell."

"Why? Are you going to go back to set the record straight?"

"Oh," Jessica sounded disappointed. "Don't tell me it's not true. We were really hoping you two would work out."

"Why?" Claire dialed the other number and waited for an answer. She told the lady on the other end what she needed and then asked her question again. "Why?"

"We all like Scott. He's wonderful with our kids, but he's still single."

"Jessie, that's his choice. C'mon, let's go wait for the cab." Claire, weaving in and out of the noisy crowd, headed for the entrance with Jessica at her heels. Music, filtering through the stadium, continued to rise in volume until the resounding crescendo vibrated the stands. Claire could feel the music pulsating in her veins. She'd rather stay and watch the competition, but freezing didn't sound like much fun. She noticed a few other shivering adults with blankets wrapped tightly around their shoulders. A few were buying sweat shirts with the Regional competition logo printed on the front. It was comforting to know other dummies had assumed it'd be warm in Dallas. Claire turned her thoughts back to Scott. *I can't believe I'm defending the man I was so busy hating last night. I can't believe Jessica's doubting the man's devotion to his job just because he's not married.* "Why can't Scott be single?"

"It's not natural."

"Who decides what's natural? You? The other parents? A committee? Your afternoon Soap Opera?"

"Of course not, but he's thirty-three and never been married. What does that tell you?"

"He's happy being alone," said Claire matter-of-factly. "Maybe, being a teacher is enough satisfaction. Let's face it, after spending all day with a bunch of screamin' kids, would you want to go home to some more?" Claire had a scary thought. *Would Scott ever take advantage of a teenager's crush? How does he know they aren't so innocent?* "Doesn't he have family here?"

"Scott's not from around here. I think he's from South Carolina, the Charleston area."

"Why did he come here?" Claire saw the cab coming toward them.

"To teach, of course. But that's not the point. People who spend a lot of time alone always turn out to be kind of weird." Jessica strung the sound of the vowels out making the word much longer and sleazier than it should've been. "Ya know what I mean?"

Claire stepped up to the cab when it stopped. "I think you've been watching too many Soap Operas. I spend lots of time alone, and I don't think I'm so weird. If the parents have a different idea, please let me know." Then she directed her attention to the driver. "The Caché store at North Park, please." Without uttering a word, the cabby hit the gas.

"You don't count, Claire. You were married once."

"Being in a rotten marriage is better than no marriage at all?"

"Yeah, it proves you're not...you know," said Jessica stalling.

"Wiiieeerrrd." Claire tried to imitate Jessica's pronunciation. "You guys don't really think Scott Krammer is gay?"

"We'd rather have him gay than messing with our daughters."

"So you're not worried about the boys?" asked Claire.

"Well, I suppose when Justin gets into high school I'll worry about him."

"What do you want from me? I don't know anything about Scott," offered Claire.

"We...I was wondering if you like him?"

Dead Tones

"I don't know. Up until a couple of hours ago, I hated the man. Now it's a maybe."

"So you two aren't exactly seeing each other?"

"No. Like I said, up until a couple hours ago, I hadn't talked to him in two years. And 'NO' I absolutely will not try to find out if he's straight or not. I don't care."

"What about Shy. Aren't you worried about her?" asked Jessica.

"Scott Krammer is her teacher, a very good teacher; and that's all he is."

"What about Allison? Monica told me she's had a serious boyfriend for a long time, but none of them have ever met the guy. Maybe it's Krammer. Maybe he's the father of her baby."

Claire jerked her head to look directly at Jessica. She was shocked by the accusation. "Baby! What baby?"

"I thought you knew. Ya know, he did give her private lessons," added Jessica.

"So what. Lots of teachers give private lessons."

"Yeah, but Krammer plays the trumpet. Allison's a woodwind."

Claire had no rebuttal for the comment. However, she did think it was unusual for a brass teacher to give woodwind lessons. *I'll have to ask Shy about this. She'd know if Allison was pregnant.* "I'm sorry Allison had to get sick in order for me to find out how much I've been missing the last few years."

"Yeah. Some of the kids think she took some pills on purpose," said Jess.

Claire could barely contain her frustration. "Jessica," she snapped, "You've got to stop listening to the rumors. Allison didn't try to kill herself."

"Then somebody tried to kill her. Krammer?"

"Jess, you're being ridiculous."

"Why? If she is pregnant with his baby, he certainly has a good reason to get rid of her," snapped Jess.

"How can you make these allegations so easily? You've known Scott for years. Do you really think he could do this terrible thing?"

"It happens in the movies. Why not here?"

"Your mind is running amuck. Get control, girl." The car pulled into the mall parking lot. Claire hated to admit Jessica's idea made sense.

"Okay, if you don't like that possibility, how 'bout this one? Ya know Sarah's been learning the old Indian medicine. It's possible..."

"Don't even think it, Jess."

"Why not? She could be practicing her magic on the kids."

"Stop! My God, you've been overdosing on fantasy. If you don't stop, I'm going to pay the driver to take you back to Tulsa. You don't get all this gossip by listening between the seats."

"When we volunteer at the Print Shop, we talk about stuff."

"You gossip," accused Claire.

"I like to think we speculate about the various possibilities."

"Speculation quickly becomes gossip when you start passing it around."

"Claire, you're trying to deny reality. Allison's been poisoned. Right?"

"Possibly. Sylvia's not sure."

"Denial," said Jess accusingly. "She was all over the school yesterday trying to retrace Allison's steps. If Ali was just sick, Sylvia would've stayed at the hospital. That leaves two choices: suicide or murder. What do you think?"

"I think your cup of imagination 'runneth over' and all that crap."

"Do you have a better theory?"

"Yeah, I do. It's somebody we don't expect," snapped Claire.

Dead Tones

"You've been reading too many novels where the bad guy is the last one you'd think about. In real life the bad guy is usually the most obvious."

"Well, forgive me if I'm not ready to turn Sarah or Scott over to the police just yet. You're just guessing. Proof would be nice," said Claire.

"Let the cops get the proof."

"Jessie, don't ruin somebody's life on speculation alone. Allison may come out of this coma and tell her folks exactly what happened. You'll feel really stupid if she's having an allergic reaction to something she ate."

"Maybe. But I think you're dreamin'."

"What did you think of the lady trying on evening gowns?"

"Didn't the manager call her Peggy? The long black dress with the white color draping around her neck and down the back was absolutely gorgeous. I've never seen a dress like it. The way the color turned into white accordion pleats and hung all the way to the floor." said Claire.

"It made Peggy look so tall and slender. I'd kill for a body like that. Ya know, you could wear a dress like that."

"Where? To my computer?" asked Claire, not really expecting an answer.

"Oh, I don't know. Peggy was going to some black tie fundraiser in Dallas. Buy a couple of tickets to the Waltz on the Wildside at the Tulsa Zoo in June and ask someone to go with you. You're old enough to ask a guy.

"Jessie, if I wanted the dress that bad, I'd just buy it and wear it to my desk," said Claire.

The cab came to a stop at the front entrance. Claire paid the man and hurried for the door. She had to get back to the stadium. Only now the urge was less to see the competition and more to protect

R. Z. Crompton

Sarah and Scott from the wild rumors that were flying around. She wanted to protect them from her own doubts too. Jessica's ideas weren't as far out in left field as Claire wanted them to be. *I knew I shouldn't have come on this trip. Something bad always happens when I'm a chaperon. But I've got a promise to keep. Unfortunately, I don't like the options so far.*

******

Dale Barnett stood in front of his band. His pride sparkled in his eyes and the kids could see it. "Great warm-up. You're ready for an outstanding competition," yelled the director. The kids cheered his vote of confidence. "The only show we have to beat is our last performance. We can do that. You've all worked hard. Let's make it sizzle, gang. This is our field!" yelled Barnett. "We're right here. In Denton, Texas! The United States of America. Planet Earth! Milky Way Galaxy! Period! Dot!!! Exclamation Point!!!!!!!"

The traditional words of inspiration were met with a loud, "Exclamation Point!" from the band members. Then cheers of excitement rose above the other bands warming up. Mr. B. could verbally stroke his band members until their adrenaline raced through their veins. Rows of soldiers dressed in the red and black uniforms waited to prove their worth on the marching field. "We've got a few minutes 'til we have to head for the field. Everybody take ten."

Sarah, standing next to Shy on the saxophone line, moved closer for an intimate conversation. "Sue wasn't in the line up. Have you seen her?"

"She's with Mr. Krammer. I don't think she's going to march."

"Who'll do the solo? That's one of the high spots of the performance," added Sarah.

"Don't know. Who else knows it. She and Allison were the only ones who'd practiced it. Ya know, Sarah, I listened to lots of little conversations while we were getting dressed. Nobody's talking

Dead Tones

about Ali. It's too bad she's not here, but I'm beginning to wonder if we're not just yelling 'wolf'," said Shy.

"What do you mean?" Sarah asked.

"The little kid who kept yelling wolf when there was nothing wrong. Maybe we're trying to make more out of this than there really is. I've been thinking about who'd want to hurt Ali, and nada, nothing, nobody," explained Shy.

"That's not exactly true," said Sarah, taking off the silver helmet. "Allison's a sweetheart. There's no doubt about it. Unfortunately, not everybody likes sweet, popular kids who get more than their fair share of the attention. Shy, you want everybody to be nice and get along; so it's hard for you to see the anger or jealousy lingering after a practice."

Shy removed her helmet also taking care not to damage the large black plume of feathers which turned the simple silver hat into an elegant completion of the conservative uniform. "You're exaggerating."

"About you seeing all white and goodness or about the kids of darkness?"

"Both, and stop being so symbolic. It sounds goofy when you talk like that."

"Sorry, it's the Cherokee in me."

ShyAnne didn't want to believe what Sarah was telling her, but she knew it was true. She'd heard comments, rotten things, about Sarah. Sarah wasn't an 'injun' or a 'squaw'; unfortunately, when she talked like an Indian medicine man, some of the kids realized that she was different. The only way they could deal with 'different' was with meanness. Sarah was an intelligent, moral person; and it made Shy angry when she heard others make derogatory remarks about what they didn't understand. Shy remembered how furious she was when Jennifer called Sarah a witch in front of several parents. Now Jennifer, she was one who could hate anybody for any reason. That girl would carry a grudge to hell and back.

"I suppose Jennifer could be a candidate for rottenness."

"Watch the kids interact. It's not so much what they say; it's the look in their eyes, the body language. We've all got to stay focused on this competition, so nobody's really talking about anything but the show. Wait 'til the pressure's off. Then we'll get a better idea of what people are thinking about Allison."

"I bet Mom calls the hospital tonight to let Mrs. Hayes know the results of the competition. We can make an announcement about Ali's condition. That'll get kids talking about her again."

"Good idea," said Sarah as she put the helmet back on her head. "Hey, let's march this one for Allison."

"For Allison." Shy held our her hand for a handshake to seal the promise.

CHAPTER FIVE

Claire climbed the steps of the bleachers carrying only Shy's blanket draped over her arm. Not wanting to hold her clothes through the long hours of evening competition, she'd instructed the taxi driver to stop at the Radisson, so she could leave her shopping bags with the concierge. With Jessica's help, Claire had managed to spend nearly a thousand dollars in less than thirty minutes. She tried on only one outfit, not to see if it fit, but to wear it out of the store. The red down-filled jacket with the fur lined hood was perfect for sitting in the bleachers. Black stirrup pants with a red and black angora sweater would keep her warmer than the thin denim she'd been wearing. On her way out of the mall, she'd made a quick stop at Dillard's for boots, long underwear and a winter scarf with matching gloves. The evening part of the competition would last several hours, and now she was ready to enjoy herself.

Scanning the long rows of the stadium for a familiar face, Claire finally spotted some of the other parents. There wasn't much room left anywhere, so Claire squeezed in by Trish while Jessica sat one row up by a couple of dads.

"Claire, it's good to see you again."

"Thanks, Trish. How are things at the print shop?" Claire's attention jumped to the field. A large band had just finished their performance and was leaving with a tremendous roar from the crowd.

"We're swamped with the Sonic coupons. Last year we did seventy-five thousand, but this year Sonic ordered over one hundred thousand. I'm gonna have coupons chasing me in my dreams."

"Are those the coupons that go out during the Holiday Season?" asked Claire.

Dead Tones

"Yeah, why?"

"The only time of the year Shy seems to bring home a ton of Sonic burgers is during the Christmas season. Now I know why she's so generous." Claire looked at the program she had on her lap. "How much longer 'til we're on?"

"There's one more band before us. Ya know, we could sure use your help at the shop next week."

"Trish, how much a...." Claire wasn't sure how to ask Trish about Scott. "How much 'speculating' do you guys do down there?"

Trish wasn't sure where Claire was going with such a strange question. "Speculating about what? The price of tea in China or the future decline of the oil prices in Tulsa?"

Claire smiled. "I was thinking a little closer to home. What do you hear about the teachers and the students?"

"I hear lots. What I believe is a different story. Can you be more specific?"

Claire chastised herself for being so ambiguous. She should've remembered Trish was pretty level-headed. Gossip was gossip. Straight to the point would get a better answer. "What do you know about Scott Krammer?" Claire kept her eyes on the field. Another band was taking position. The girls in the color guard scurried around the field placing their colorful flags in strategic positions.

"Probably more than most of the folks around here. Don't forget, we've already had two kids graduate from college. We've been around almost as long as he has. He's talented, handsome, and most of the kids think he can walk on water." Trish opened a thermos and poured herself a cup of hot chocolate. "Would you like a cup?"

"Love one. Where'd you get this?" asked Claire.

"My son lives down here. He delivered it just after I called him and begged for mercy," replied Trish.

"Thanks. What do you think about Krammer? As a parent, I mean?" Claire asked.

"He has a right to a private life. I think all of the teachers do."

"I agree. That was one of my arguments when I heard the accusations. Unfortunately, I don't really know enough about him to defend him. I did fine as long as the topic was general; but when the comments became more specific, I had nothing to go on. Why did he come here to teach?"

"Scott left Charleston for his own reasons. Reasons he didn't want to share with the folks around here. He has the right to leave his past behind. We all do," said Trish.

"I guess it depends on what the past is, Trish. Do you know why he left?"

"Yes, I do. It's personal but not illegal. As far as his reputation here, I pretty much agree with the kids. Is that enough?"

"Do you think it's weird that he's never been married?"

"What are you getting at, Claire?" Trish asked sipping her hot chocolate.

"Rumor suggests he might be gay."

Trish nearly spit her hot chocolate on the head in front of her. Choking as she tried to swallow the mouthful in order to speak her mind. "Claire, my God, where did you get an idea like that?" Trish didn't give Claire a chance to answer. "No, he's not."

"How can you be so sure?"

"Carl, my oldest, was one of the first graduates to have Scott all four years. With band, concert band and jazz band, Carl got to know him fairly well and so did we. After Carl graduated, the two of them became even closer."

Claire didn't understand where Trish was going. Everything she'd said so far leaned toward the two men being lovers. "How close were they?"

Dead Tones

Trish became indignant. "Not like that. They used to drive from Tulsa to Dallas to party for a weekend. Scott was afraid to be seen partying with a woman in Tulsa. He knew being single could lead to lots of rumors. He did, has done, everything to lead a straight, clean life. Who in the hell is passing this....this stuff anyway?"

"Does he still leave town to party?" asked Claire.

"He's had a girlfriend in Dallas from time to time, nothing serious. He stays with Carl when he comes down," explained Trish.

"I think it'd be good for him to party and be seen in Tulsa," suggested Claire.

"Why?"

"I'm afraid the kindling is being laid for a big fire, and I don't want Scott to get burnt. The best thing he could do is find a local woman for a few weeks."

"Why are you so concerned about Scott? I know there's a bad history between you."

"One incident does not make a history," responded Claire.

"With you two it did."

"We had one argument. He was defending the kids and the school; I was defending my ego. So maybe I over reacted."

"Ya think? Just a little, maybe? The rumors make the 'incident' sound so much more interesting than you do," said Trish.

"Yeah, I bet." Claire found herself wondering for a second time that day what the gossip was about her lifestyle. She didn't really care. Her livelihood didn't really depend on what this group of people thought of her. However, Scott's reputation could be destroyed by one false story taking root.

"Claire, I knew you were just coming out of a rotten marriage. Your fight with Scott was more about your hatred for Steve than any real dislike for Scott. You didn't even know him. Unfortunately, Scott was the target of your anger. Nobody else understood that. Did you?"

"Guess not, but I really don't care. I don't want to see Scott become a victim of something so silly. That's why I asked you the questions. Shy has never had anything but compliments for the man, even though she's kept her comments to a minimum around me. Trish, there's more to the rumor," stated Claire, as if making a confession. "I didn't realize you were so close to him. Maybe you can help."

"What can be worse?"

"Allison's pregnant and Scott's the father."

"Holy Mother of God!" Trish shook her head. "Somebody has way too much time on her hands to be thinking up all this junk."

"It gets worse. Speculation is he tried to kill her so no one would find out," said Claire.

"Do you believe this crap?"

Claire was silent for a moment. She didn't really know enough about the man to pass judgement one way or another. "I don't want to, but I honestly don't know. There's no proof against him."

"Exactly."

"What can we do?"

"Really, Claire, I think you can do more for him than I can," said Trish winking at the woman sitting next to her.

"No way, Trish. It'd never work."

"Why not?"

"Really, Trish. It takes two to play. Why would he want to tango with an older woman, especially if he likes to go dancing in Dallas?"

"I heard about you sleeping on his shoulder this morning."

"So what? One innocent encounter doesn't mean anything. We both fell asleep."

"Claire, as far as I know, Scott has never sat next to anyone on a bus trip. He always sits alone so he can spread those long legs out.

Dead Tones

If the driver insists on the aisle being clear, Scott has no where to put his legs but in the space next to him. That doesn't leave much room for another person."

Claire remembered how difficult it had been for Scott to fold his legs into the tiny space directly in front of him. "There weren't too many other seats available when he got on."

"He's the teacher. He can have any seat he demands. The kids don't argue with him. He sat with you because he wanted to."

"Yeah, right. Give me a break. He's at least ten years younger than I am. He won't have any trouble finding a young woman who will put all these ugly rumors to bed."

"Are you talking literally or figuratively? Claire, I know for a fact because he told me, he doesn't want just any woman."

"Trish, I can't lead him on. It's not right for me or him."

"Then talk to him. Tell him what you suspect. The two of you can put the rumors to bed without your ever pulling back the sheets." She smiled and nudged Claire in the shoulder.

"Trish you're terrible. First of all, we're just barely on speaking terms. Second, if Scott has as much integrity as you seem to think, he'll presume I'm a horrible person for even making the suggestion. Since you're such a good friend, you should talk to him."

"I plan on it."

"Wait a minute. Trish, please don't suggest anything that will make us both uncomfortable." Claire looked at the woman sitting next to her, but Trish wasn't paying any attention to her request.

"Quiet, now. There's the kids getting ready to take the field."

Claire's eyes jumped back to the field searching for Shy. The pit crew efficiently moved the percussion instruments into place as the students took their opening positions. Five white and gold, Egyptian looking tents designed to add flavor to the show, were carried onto the field by the marchers. This performance is what they'd worked toward for nearly four months. The prelims. The kids had to do well in prelims or there'd be no finals. Only the top twelve bands would be showing off tonight.

A loud voice boomed through the stadium, "The Bands of America is proud to present the Renegade Regiment from South Side High School in Tulsa, Oklahoma. The Renegade Regiment will be performing Ottorino Respighi's Belkis' 'Queen of Sheba'." The announcer introduced the directing staff and acknowledged the bands' many accomplishments over the years. Claire watched members of the colorguard, dressed in white with elaborate feather head dresses to represent the Queen of Sheba, take their places scattered tactfully throughout the marchers.

Immense pride filled everyone connected to the Renegade Regiment. The collection of trophies and pictures over the last fifteen years not only lined every nook and cranny of the bandroom, but Mr. B. had dozens of them at home. Oklahoma Bandmasters' Association had awarded the state championship to the Regiment several times. Each new class of marchers had an incredible legacy to uphold, and they took the challenge seriously. The band had won trophies at the Fiesta Bowl in Phoenix twice, performed at both Disneyland and Disney World, and marched at the Indianapolis Five Hundred last year. The shows, costumes and trips were incredibly expensive; so when the kids weren't practicing, they were out earning money. Fortunately, the parents controlled the fund raising and never missed a chance to add a penny to the pot.

Stephen, Kevin and Joy, the three drum majors, took their positions and declared the Renegade Regiment ready to perform. The bold sounds of the first piece echoed through the stadium as the marchers went into motion. Claire could feel her own adrenaline pulsating through her veins. Then she saw Sue standing near the pit. Why wasn't she marching? Claire watched, waiting for Sue to move.

Dead Tones

Within minutes, the girl stepped up to the microphone. Her melodic sounds floated elegantly through the air, and Claire let out a sigh of relief.

When the solo was over, Sue stepped back from the microphone and off the field. Scott Krammer was watching her. The girl was really sick and he'd felt guilty letting her play; but like most of the kids, she played for the good of the others. Without this solo, the opening number would've lost its punch.

"I have to play," she'd told him when the rest of the band was warming up. "For Allison, for you and for everybody out there. I have to play."

Scott had agreed to let her play as long as she used the microphone and didn't try to march. "Promise me you'll go back to the hotel as soon as you're done."

Sue had agreed. "I promise. But I'm sure I just have the flu. Mom and Julie have been in bed all week with some kind of bug. I tried to stay away from them. Guess it got me anyway."

"I guess it did. Rhonda will be waiting to drive you back." Scott left Sue standing at the sidelines ready to take her position. Then he'd given strict instructions to Rhonda. "I can't watch out for her once the show starts. As soon as she's done playing, take her to the hotel. Don't let her talk you out of it."

"I'll watch her." Rhonda had agreed sharing Scott's concern for the girl.

"If you think she needs to go to the hospital, take her. Don't wait for me. Here's my credit card, charge it if you have to."

"Don't worry." Rhonda had assured him. "Alex will have the car waiting for us at the front gate."

Sue finished her solo and barely heard the round of applause for her sensuous portrayal of the Queen of Sheba, when Rhonda whisked her off the field. Scott never saw her again.

R. Z. Crompton

The show was brilliant and the kids knew it. The whole band moved like a beautifully sculpted body waltzing over the field, every organ, every muscle in tune with the other, not just knowing the beat of the music, but living it. The color guard hit their last toss at exactly the same second the band played it's last note. The perfection echoed through the stadium when the movement ended. Vigorous applause met the students as they paired off and exited the field to the snare drum cadence.

The kids were proud of their performance, but there was no reason to celebrate yet. Their job wasn't finished. In spite of the superb effort, they took nothing for granted. It was bad luck to speculate about winning prelims, especially when several excellent Texas bands were still waiting to perform. Texas had a longstanding reputation of producing fantastic marching bands, and they were in Texas. The interim would seem endless.

The band was back at the semi before Claire and the other sponsors arrived. The truck had been opened, and most of the kids had already changed into street clothes. After the uniforms and instruments were packed out of the way, there was time to relax and, of course, wait. Dinner would be eaten in the parking lot when several hundred Subway sandwiches were delivered. No one was going to leave until the final scores were tabulated and announced.

ShyAnne finally found Claire standing by her bag of tricks and replacing some over-used velcro. "Hey, Mom, great coat. Where did you find it?"

"Hi. Wonderful performance! I'm so proud of you."

"Thanks. Did it really look okay when Sue just stepped up to the mike?"

"I doubt if the judges knew anything was wrong. The only reason I noticed was because I knew she was supposed to play under one of the tents. Actually, I think it was better with the mike. The music had a more profound effect on the audience because it was easier to hear."

"Good. Now, what about that coat? Do I get to borrow it?"

"Nice, isn't it. Looks better than the blanket."

"Yeah, just a little." Shy shook her head to give added approval. "It looks more like you."

"And how am I supposed to look?"

"Not too 'momish'."

"I'm sorry," said Claire with a questioning lift of her eyebrow. "What's 'momish'."

"Old. I don't like you dressing old."

"I don't either, and I'm sure you'll tell me when I do."

"Count on it. Have you seen Monica or Krissy?"

"Yeah, they checked their uniforms and headed for the bathroom. What are you going to eat? You hate Subways."

"I'll eat the chips."

"That's all? How can you march tonight if you only have chips."

"Easy. I had a good breakfast and lunch. So what if I miss dinner. Ya do what ya gotta do."

"I suppose you do. I'd forgotten how serious you guys get about marching. You're all pretty good about taking whatever comes along."

"After you've brushed your teeth a couple times spitting into the street gutter, ya kind of loose that prissy, prime and proper attitude. If you don't, you're gonna spend lots of time being miserable."

"Does that go for the sponsors too?" asked Claire.

"Pretty much. But you cheated by going shopping this afternoon," said Shy.

"I thought you liked my new coat."

"I do, but you still cheated." Shy teased. "Would you call about Allison if you get a chance?"

"I already did. She's about the same. If they can keep her stabilized for the next couple of days, the doctor thinks her body might be able to fight off whatever made her sick."

"Does he still think its poison?"

"I'm afraid so." Claire finished the mending job and hung the uniform with the others. "Are you hearing anything suspicious from the kids?"

"Not really," answered Shy, leaning up against the truck. "Sarah suggested we get the competition over before we try to analyze anybody's motives."

"Have you ever met Allison's boyfriend?" Claire looked around to see if anyone was close enough to eavesdrop. The last thing she wanted was to spread more gossip.

"Why?"

"I've heard a ton of rumors this afternoon. I was hoping you'd be able to give me some insight."

"So?" Shy waited for her mother to answer, but there was no response. "Mom, you gotta tell me what you've heard if I'm going to help."

Claire recognized the young lady approaching. "Sarah's coming. I'll talk to you tonight."

"She's okay. But Krissy might be with us tonight. I love her; unfortunately, she's a compulsive talker. On the other hand, she probably knows more than the rest of us put together."

"Who does?" Sarah only heard the last part of their conversation.

"The gossip queen," answered Shy.

"Krissy is our connoisseur in the art of gossip," announced Sarah with a sense of pride.

"You make her sound respectable. I think of her more as the 'energizer bunny'. She just keeps going and going."

Dead Tones

"Her talent will serve her well in the future," declared Sarah.

Shy wondered if Sarah knew about Krissy's plan to be a stockbroker. Krissy had sworn her to secrecy, but she could've done the same thing with Sarah. "Mom was wondering if I'd ever met Allison's boyfriend. Have you?"

"No. She talks about him all the time, but I've never even seen a picture of him."

"That's kind of strange, isn't it?" asked Shy.

"She says he's not from around here," said Sarah.

"Then why does she carry birth control pills in her purse?"

"I have no idea. Maybe they're just for show. Ya know, like she's bragging."

Claire had been listening to the exchange without interrupting. She didn't like the possibility that Scott could be Allison's boyfriend. If the girl carried birth control pills instead of pictures, then she probably didn't want anybody to know who the guy was. It made sense. Scott certainly couldn't take her to the prom without losing his job. "Shy, why was Allison taking private lessons from Mr. Krammer?"

"Because she had the solo and he wrote the music. Is that important?" Shy dodged the football flying at her head. "Hey, watch out."

"Yeah, yeah," yelled Justin in his sarcastic whine.

"I just thought it was odd since he's a brass player, and she's a woodwind."

"He only teaches a woodwind when he's written the music."

"Shy, is that..." Claire wasn't sure how to word the question without sounding spiteful. She was afraid Shy would blame her suspicions on their last band trip.

"What?"

Claire decided to take a different path. "Has Mr. Krammer ever talked about a girlfriend?"

"No. And I can see where you're going with this, Mom. Mr. Krammer would never abuse his position."

"You don't know that for sure. Have any of the kids talked about the possibility?"

"Yeah, some of the girls dream and drool over him, but he's never given any of them the time of day. He's our teacher and friend; that's all," stated Shy emphatically.

Claire's suspicions waned a little when Sarah also defended the man. "I have to agree with Shy about this one. I've heard a couple of the girls hope for a little indiscretion; and frankly, I'm sure they'd brag about conquering the man if there was any reality to the fantasy."

Claire was taken back by Sarah's comment. She'd assumed it'd be Scott taking advantage of the girl. "Sarah, you're implying that one of the girls might try to seduce Mr. Krammer."

"Might?" was the sarcastic reply. "'Have tried' is a more accurate way of describing the situation."

"Really?"

"Mom, you gotta get out of the seventies. You know, equality and all that crap. Mr. Krammer would be a big trophy for some hot blooded girl to hang from her headboard."

"And hang is the operative word here. His career would be hung out to dry," said Claire still not wanting to believe what she was hearing. "Could Allison have threatened to 'hang' him over her headboard?"

"Is that the rumor you heard today?" ShyAnne asked almost accusing her mother of playing in the dirty game. "Who'd say such an ugly thing?"

"It's not important who said it, only that someone said it at all."

"What else did you hear today?"

"A bunch of disgusting stuff."

Dead Tones

"You might as well tell us. We'll tell you what we know. And hurry before Krissy finds us."

"Could Allison be pregnant?"

ShyAnne didn't answer right away. Allison had hinted to her about a sexual relationship with some mysterious guy. Shy had thought Allison was fibbing until she found the pills in Ali's purse. Allison had no reason to lie. If she was having intercourse, she could be pregnant in spite of the pills. "I suppose she could be, but I don't think she'd have been able to hide something like that from all of us."

"It could be a motive."

"For what?" Shy was afraid of the answer. "Don't say it. I know," she answered with a deep sense of melancholy.

Sarah understood the implication in a broader scope. "Ya know, Shy, it could be the motive for suicide too."

"No way," responded Shy. "Allison wouldn't kill herself because of a baby. She and her mother had talked about it. Her mom didn't like the fact that Allison was sleeping with her boyfriend, but she didn't get nuts about it either."

Claire agreed with her daughter because of what Sylvia had told her the night before. Sylvia had lived through the family arguments, the shame, and the soiled reputation. She'd never treat her daughter the same way. Claire would have bet a cold night in the bleachers that Sylvia had had a good heart-to-heart with her daughter. "The next time I talk to Sylvia, I'll ask her."

"Do you think Allison would've told her mother?" Sarah asked.

"Yup, I sure do," admitted Claire. "However, I don't think Ali would've told her if Scott Krammer's the father."

"Mom, do you think Mr. Krammer would do such a thing?"

"I want to say 'no', but I have no idea," said Claire sounding almost ashamed of her doubt.

"Maybe it's another man who has as much to lose as Mr. Krammer does," offered Sarah.

"Any suggestions?" Shy would've entertained anything that would exonerate her favorite teacher.

"Girls, when we get back to the school tomorrow night, let's go through Ali's Band locker. We need a name or a picture, even a letter to prove there's a boyfriend."

"Someone besides Mr. Krammer, right?"

"I hope so. I really hope so," said Claire. "On the other hand, it'd prove he's not gay."

"I was wondering how long it'd take you to hear that one," sighed Shy.

"Is he? Is that how you know he's not having an affair with Allison?"

"He's straight, Mom. We've spent enough time talking over the years for me to be pretty sure. He enjoys a good looking woman when he has the opportunity."

"And just how do you know that?"

"I like getting to the band room early, especially on Monday morning. The teachers always talk and laugh," she paused and winked at Sarah. "They ahhh.... like to discuss their weekend escapades, sometimes in rather graphic detail. Mr. Krammer's no saint. He just has the good sense to play out of town."

"In this case, less sense would've been better."

"Mom, it's just gossip."

"Not if this turns into a murder case."

Shy and Sarah finally realized how dangerous this gossip could become. Their eyes met and the message was sent and received. They had a lot of work to do. Claire missed the exchange between the girls mainly because her gaze fell on the man coming up behind them. She almost felt relieved to see him.

Dead Tones

"Hello, ladies. The sandwiches are here. You guys going to eat?"

"Hey, Mr. Krammer. How's Sue?"

"I'm not sure. When I called the Radisson, they hadn't registered as far as I could tell. Rhonda might've taken her to the emergency room."

"What about tonight? Who's going to play for us?"

"Andrea's going to do it."

"Andrea!" Shy was surprised. "Why not Kate? She's next in line."

"Andrea works better under pressure. Believe me, it'll be a miracle if we can pull this off. Kate get's too emotional."

"Does she have the music?" asked Shy. "She's got to have the music." The tone of panic was in her voice.

"Excuse me, but you seem to forget who wrote the score for this competition. I may not be able to put the exact notes down on paper; but as long as the timing and sound are the same, nobody will know the difference. She'll give it her best shot.

"How much longer 'til we hear the scores?" asked Claire.

"Dale's waiting at the judges' booth now, but we'll hear the announcement over the loud speaker before he gets back. Shouldn't be much longer, so go eat." Scott motioned his head toward the big boxes sitting on the ground. He wanted them to leave, but Shy wasn't getting the message. Finally, Krissy gave him the help he needed.

"Hey, Shy. I've been looking all over for you guys. Let's grab a coke and go watch the boys play football."

"Watch? No way. I want to play." Shy took off for the field of green spread out on the other side of the semi.

Sarah reluctantly followed the two of them. "I don't do football," explained Sarah to man beside her. "I guess I could cheer them on."

"Don't strain yourself," instructed Scott.

"Trust me, I won't."

"It's good for them to have some fun. Makes the waiting easier." Scott offered taking Shy's position against the truck.

"Why didn't we just go to the hotel. It's nearly across the street."

"By the time we got them loaded and unloaded, we'd have to get them back on the buses to return. Besides, some of the girls would hurry to their room with the idea of taking a quick nap. Naps are bad news. Sleep destroys the drive to win."

"Really?" Claire felt better about the man standing in front of her. Shy and Trish, two people with no connection to each other, had given her the same story about Scott. Mesmerized by the blue eyes and warm smile, Claire looked past the man standing in front of her. No wonder the girls were crazy about him. He could easily seduce one of them. Claire looked back into the dancing eyes, wondering what kind of man was there. *Shit, he could likely seduce all of them if he wanted to. Some women will do anything for a smile like that. Who are you Scott Krammer and why did you leave South Carolina?*

"Did you enjoy the show?"

"Absolutely fantastic," answered Claire. "I sat with a friend of yours."

"I heard. Although, I know Carl better than I do Trish. She was concerned about some of the gossip floating around."

"Jesus, word travels fast around here."

"Gossip is like an Oklahoma grass fire; you can't out run it."

"I wasn't trying to. When Trish told me you were a good friend of the family, I wanted her to tell me the rumors weren't true. Then I'd hoped she would warn you about the danger you might be in."

"Well, she warned me. Now I'd like the chance to prove to you they aren't true."

Dead Tones

"Right now?"

"I didn't mean like right this minute. I've got to help Andrea get ready for tonight. On the way back to Tulsa, you can ask me anything you want." Scott turned to walk away.

"Sure. Good luck tonight."

"Thanks, we're going to need it."

Claire didn't like the feelings of confusion creeping though her mind and body. She was still cautious and doubtful about his integrity, and yet hoping he was the saint the kids believed him to be. Unfortunately, white knights have a tendency of falling off the horse into a big mud puddle. Was he a teacher or a weirdo? He was most definitely a man, and she promised herself that the warm fuzzy feelings she felt when he smiled at her were simply indigestion.

The crackle of a microphone caught everyone's attention. The kids were disappointed when a deep voice stated a staff member from the Renegade Regiment needed to return an important phone call. Claire was instantly worried about Allison. *Sylvia would wait until we got back to town to give us the bad news? She'd never put such a dark cloud over the band. It's Sue.* Claire was sure the call was about Sue. She wondered if the news was good or bad as she walked toward the sandwich line. Subways weren't her favorite either; however, going without supper ranked right up there with freezing. *Been there, done that, didn't like it at all.*

"Hey, Claire, did you get a sandwich?" yelled Trish.

"Not yet. I was busy talking with the girls and Scott."

"I noticed," said Trish trying to hide the big grin.

"I'd really hoped you wouldn't say anything until we got back to Tulsa."

"Why?"

"Cause here he's got to deal with sick kids, rewriting music, and keeping the rest of the band focused. He shouldn't have to worry about some stupid gossip."

"Well, I told him because I was afraid he wouldn't see you after the trip, and I didn't want you to go away thinking badly about him."

"I don't believe in rumors. There's no proof. Remember: innocent until proven guilty?"

"We all believe the principle; most of us just forget to apply it to daily life."

Claire, staring out across the lawn, simply nodded in agreement. She didn't see the flying object heading straight for her.

"Yo! Hey!" screamed Mike. "Heads up! Mrs. Mayfield!"

Claire finally shot a glance upward just in time to see the flash of red sail before her eyes. "Ahhhhhh!" Claire jumped back into Trish nearly knocking both of them over as she tripped over the edge of the curb.

"Mrs. Mayfield, you okay. I'm really sorry."

"I'm fine, Mike." Claire reclaimed her balance with the help of Mike's stabilizing grasp on her arm.

"I'm so sorry. Are you sure you aren't hurt?" Mike was more afraid of offending her than hurting her. "It's my fault. I should've been more careful." He was still holding onto her arm.

"Mike, stop. I won't break."

"I know, but I don't want you to be angry with me."

"Did you do it on purpose?"

"No, of course not."

"Then I'm not angry. Go. Play." Claire commanded the young man in front of her.

Scott approached Claire, Trish and Mike from behind and heard most of the conversation. "Mike, you beatin' up on the sponsors again?"

Dead Tones

"Hey, Mr. Jazz." Mike tried to sound nonchalant and innocent. "Not at all. I was just..."

"Go on. Get out of here," said Scott in a sorrowful tone. There was a heaviness to his words that caught their attention. Mike didn't walk away. He wanted to find out what was going on.

"Mr. Krammer, did you get the scores back? We didn't make finals, did we?"

"I don't know yet. Now go join the others."

"I know something's wrong. What's up?"

"Mike," there was more of a plea to the name than an order. "You'll know soon enough. Now go."

Mike walked away slowly with the red frisbee folded under his arm. He'd hoped to pick up some idea of what was wrong. Then he suddenly picked up his speed. Within minutes he'd have the whole drumline back to find out what was going on. Krammer would eventually say what was on his mind.

Scott waited for Mike to get out of ear shot before he started talking to Claire and Trish. "I answered the phone call. It was about Sue. She's...she's..." He didn't need to put the rest into words. The shock and disbelief on his face finished the explanation. Scott struggled to keep the tears from filling his eyes. *Don't cry! Don't cry. A man doesn't cry.* He reminded himself of the words his father had thrown at him when his sister died several years ago. *That damned old goat was too mean to cry.* Scott let his anger for his father overtake the grief.

Claire reached out to touch his arm. "What happened?" she asked softly.

Scott just shook his head trying to get control before Mike and the rest of the drummers came back to hound him for the news. He took a couple of deep cleansing breaths, but couldn't get the heavy weight of grief off his chest in spite of his rotten memories. The pain reminded him vividly of his sister and his mother. "Sue died in Rhonda's arms on the way to the hospital."

"Oh, no," gasped Trish. "How awful."

Scott was still trying to digest the severity of the situation. "My God, have I become so obsessed with competition that I'm willing to let a child die for me? Trish, tell me I'm not the monster that was standing at the sidelines letting a dying girl play."

"Scott, don't do this to yourself," said Trish softly. "You love these kids. I know you do."

Claire was aching for the man. His grief was pale compared to his gut wrenching guilt. "Scott," she reached out touching his arm, "Sue would've played no matter what you said to her. We all saw how sick she was, but no one else said anything to stop her. My God, we're mothers. If anybody should've noticed how sick she was, it should've been one of us. She said she had the same bug her mom had been suffering from all week. We just assumed that's all it was. The flu. That's what we wanted to believe."

"I'm...I was," he corrected himself, "I was her teacher. It was my responsibility to stop her."

"You aren't the only teacher here. Any one of them or us could've stopped her. It's not your fault," insisted Claire.

"That's right, Scott," added Trish, trying to make him feel better. "Did Rhonda tell you if the doctors have any idea why she died?

Scott gave a deep sigh before answering, "They're guessing. It might be a combination of the flu and the stress of competition and waiting so long to get help. It might even have been some kind of complication with her heart."

"Sounds like a logical guess to me," followed Trish.

"The key word here is 'guess'. A logical guess could be anything lethal," offered Claire with a touch of contempt, "and there's nothing we can do about it. How's Dale taking this?"

Dead Tones

"He's ready to pack everybody up and go home. He probably knew Sue better than any of us; consequently, he's taking it pretty hard."

Claire's mind was calculating the possibilities. "Why did he know her better than you? I thought you were giving her the private lessons."

"There's almost two hundred kids in the band with another twenty girls in the color guard and only a dozen or so staff members and technicians. We all have certain kids we get to know better than others. For the most part, my core of kids are jazz players; since I teach all the jazz bands when marching is over. I just happened to be working with Allison and Sue on this solo part because I wrote the music. Both of them were in the Wind Symphony last year, so they spent more time with Dale. Chris, on the other hand, knows all the drummers."

"So what was the relationship like between Allison and Sue?"

"They weren't real good friends. They were competitive to the point where it got in the way of any tight friendship. Why?"

"Just wondering. Sue told me she'd gotten into Allison's locker before we left. Exactly how competitive were they?" continued Claire.

"The normal," answered Scott. "They respected each other's ability, but neither spent much time wishing the other good luck. As for getting into the locker, Sue probably needed something. They weren't enemies either if that's what you're getting at," said Scott defending the two girls.

"As far as you know, they weren't enemies just rivals. One can lead to the other."

"They certainly wouldn't hurt each other over a solo."

"You're right. I guess I could see Sue hurting Allison for the chance at the solo, but Sue's the one who died." Claire had no idea where she was going with her suspicions, but she couldn't deny the gut feeling that the two sick girls had more in common. "Scott, don't you think its kinda weird that your first and second soloists are out of commission?"

"I never thought of it like that. One, two, three," Scott's voice trailed off.

"What are you thinking?" asked Trish.

"I'm agreeing with Claire. It could be more than a coincidence that my two top players have been replaced. I'm worried about Andrea."

"Is it possible Andrea might hurt somebody for the opportunity to play?" Claire was at a disadvantage because she didn't know the kids very well.

"No. Besides, she wasn't next in line for the part. I've watched her work under pressure, and her location on the field made her the best choice. She had no way of knowing I'd pick her if the other two weren't available."

"Then I'd worry about her safety too," said Claire.

"You two are crazy. You make it sound like we've got a serial killer with us. You don't even know how Sue died. Maybe she did have the flu." Trish replied.

"Sorry, Trish. But don't you think it's strange for Allison to be in a coma and Sue to be dead?"

"Weird, strange, spooky and any other adjective you can add. However, Allison's still alive and in Tulsa. Sue died here. We don't even know if they had the same symptoms."

"Well, as a matter of fact, they both assumed it was some kind of flu. I find that extremely suspicious. Last I heard, when you get the flu, a fever and some vomiting are run of the mill symptoms. Coma and death are not."

"It doesn't mean murder either," added Trish flatly. "We could be dealing with some exotic, new virus."

Dead Tones

"That sounds just as bad. And a virus would strike at random not the first and second chair in order."

"Well, I'm not ready to call the cops yet. There's absolutely no proof of either."

"I know, Trish," admitted Scott. "However, I think I'd better keep an eye on Andrea. I don't want her coming down with any strange disease."

Claire knew it'd be next week before Sue's body was transferred back to Tulsa. An autopsy would certainly be done in order to establish cause of death; unfortunately, that left plenty of time for another disaster. Claire wanted to get away for a few minutes to call Sylvia. She had several questions now which might help tie the two girls together. If there was no connection, at least she would feel better. However, Scott would feel more guilty than he did already.

"Are we going to march tonight?" asked Trish.

"I don't know. Some of the kids will want to pack up and go home. The others will think about what Sue gave up to play that solo, and they'll want to compete. Once Dale's had the chance to talk to the staff and sponsors, he'll make a decision about how to handle the kids. My guess is that he'll let them vote about staying or not." Scott needed to check on Andrea, so he excused himself with a request, "When the drummers come back, and believe me, they will, please don't tell them what's going on until Dale decides how he wants to handle this."

"What exactly would you like us to say? Mike tuned in to your anxiety in less than sixty seconds. He knows something's going on. How are we going to lie to a bunch of them?"

"Frankly, My Dear, I don't give a damn," Scott couldn't resist the comment in spite of the situation. Playing the word game with Claire was a natural. He'd have enjoyed himself more under better circumstances.

"Hah, hah," said Claire. "You're cute."

"I know," said Scott looking over his shoulder.

"Man, I'd hate to see you two interact without this stress. You're perfect for each other, and you don't even know it," offered Trish.

"You're nuts. We play word games, that's it."

"No, that's first. The rest is yet to come."

"What rest? Trish, there is no 'rest'."

"You're in a state of denial, Claire. When are you going to wake up and realize there is male flesh to have and enjoy?"

"I hope never. My life is fine just the way it is. Please tell me why...why in the world you and my daughter and my sister and everyone else in the world think I cannot be happy without a man in my life?"

"It's really quite simple. Man was not meant to live alone."

"Man maybe, but a woman can live very happily alone."

"Claire, I meant 'man' in a generic way. We are all social animals and the earth is like a big ark: the animals match up two by two. It's the norm of our society."

"Well, I don't live within the norm, and I'm very happy as a 'one' animal household."

"Existing is not the same as happy."

"Trish, I don't know you well enough to have you telling me how lonely I am. My daughter and sister spend most of their free time giving me the speech. I have to take it from them simply because I can't throw them out."

"Okay, okay. I get the message. It's your affair." Trish added extra emphasis to *affair* and dropped the subject. "What are we going to tell the drummers?"

Dead Tones

"Nothing. If we aren't standing here, they can't ask us any questions. Come on. Let's get out of here." Claire led the way into the crowd of students and sponsors waiting for the marching results.

CHAPTER SIX

Director Dale Barnett, trying to control his own grief, stood in front of his band. The staff and sponsors had spent the last couple of hours nursing themselves and the students through the devastating news about Sue. Rhonda had returned only long enough to tell Scott and Dale the details of Sue dying in her arms. She broke down crying as she told them of Sue's request for the band to perform without her. "She knew, Scott," sobbed Rhonda. "She...she knew she was dying, and there wasn't a damn thing I could do but cradle her in my arms." Rhonda's husband held her until the tears subsided. "I promised her the band would march."

Dale wiped the water from his eyes. "I don't know if they'll be able to perform, Rhonda. I don't even know if we should. Why don't you go back to the hotel and try to rest. I'm sorry you had to go through this."

Rhonda didn't leave until she put in one last comment, "It's what she wanted, Dale."

"Yeah, I know." The reservation in his voice was clear.

"Let's tell the rest of the kids," suggested Scott. "Most of them already know what's happened. If they vote to go home; we'll pack up."

Dale shook his head. "You know they'll want to march."

"Probably. I think we should give them the option."

"Maybe, but what about the solo part? That's going to be a big empty spot. I suppose we could use it as a moment of silence?"

"I don't think so," answered Scott, thinking about the impact of the silence. "Too many of the girls might break down and end up running off the field. Andrea's ready to play. She'll be all right."

Dead Tones

"Okay," said Dale with a sigh, "we vote."

Dale admired the tenacity of his students who wanted to march. Only a few of the sponsors had agreed with his first inclination to pack everybody up and head for Tulsa. The kids had been adamant about finishing what Sue had started for them. Her solo had put the polish on the second place finish which was the best prelims standing ever for the Regiment. When Stephen pointed out that leaving before finals would be an affront to Sue's memory, the rest of the band members were quick to agree. The vote to march the show in memory of their friend and classmate was nearly unanimous.

Looking at the crowd of faces waiting for his words of inspiration, Dale took a deep breath before saying, "This is hard for all of us, but I honestly believe you're doing the right thing. Sue was totally dedicated to her music, and somewhere she's watching and thanking all of you."

Several of the girls were openly sobbing now. He'd have to do better than this if they were going to take the field in a few minutes. "Would anybody like to say a few words?" He needed some help and hoped desperately someone would come forward.

"A prayer, Mr. B. Maybe some divine inspiration will help," offered ShyAnne. She had known Sue well enough to respect her talent, but that was it. According to Allison, the girl had been fiercely competitive musically. Shy remembered watching Sue with a group of clarinet players during the summer band clinic; she was an exacting section leader not allowing for any excuses. "I want results, do you hear me. No excuses, just results. Now do it again," she'd yelled. The memory brought a smile to Shy's face. Sue was tough on the girls, but then she'd taken each one aside and shown her what to do. Sue's line was the first to master its marching set every time. The girls respected the tiny brunette who barely came eye to eye with any of them. Sue was a great leader, and now Shy felt guilty she'd never taken the time to get to know her better. They hadn't shared any classes or other interests for that matter. Sue was more of a classical music lover, while Shy preferred jazz. Their paths crossed occasionally on the marching field; but after the season was over, they'd rarely spoken to each other. Now Mr. B. was waiting for Shy to say something wonderful about a girl she hardly knew.

"Dear Heavenly Father, please give us the strength to march our show tonight. Sue played for us this afternoon. Help us..." her voice faltered. Shy inhaled slowly before finishing, "Help us play for her now. Sue, wherever you are, this one's for you, Babe. Amen." Shy, not wanting anyone to see the tears running down her face, stepped away from the center of the circle. She could still hear the open sobs.

Claire was standing with several of the other sponsors behind the kids. "Trish," she whispered, "they can't march like this."

"I know," answered Trish. "It's hard to play a horn while you're sobbing. Even Dale is having a hard time."

"Do you see Scott anywhere? I'm worried about him," said Claire.

"Me too. He feels so guilty. I think he's sticking close to Andrea. He's getting paranoid about his soloists."

"Do you blame him?" asked Claire. "I'm sure glad Shy's not on his list of soloists."

"Man I sure hope he was right about Andrea's ability to work under pressure. I know I couldn't go out there and play," offered Trish.

"If all these tears don't stop, there won't be a show," added Claire, looking at the kids standing in front of her. Heads and shoulders were shaking from the grief. The black gloves wiped away the wetness because no one had enough tissues for the job. Claire had never met Sue, but this group's display of grief was saddest thing she'd ever witnessed. She found herself trying to control her own tears as

Dead Tones

she was pulled into the emotions of the group. Claire hurt for the kids standing in front of her.

Dale's hope for divine help was waning, and then he heard the muffled sound. At first the words were barely audible, then slightly louder. One of the boys from the back repeated his shaky chant, "Hey Sue, for you."

A deeper voice joined in, "Hey Sue, for you."

The soft click of a drummer added to the rhythm, "Hey Sue, for you." Click click, click click. The new cadence was quickly picked up by the others until a louder, stronger chant rose from the group. Dale, thanking God for His intervention, finally believed his band had a chance of marching the show. He didn't know if he'd have been able to muster the same determination and was glad he wouldn't be put to the test.

The chant washed through the band members cleansing them of their grief. As the words grew louder, strength and determination replaced the tears. "Hey Sue, for you." Click click, click click. Everyone shared the new resolve to offer a memorial to a dedicated friend. They had a job to do, and they were going to do it for Sue. The cadence grew louder, more defined; and the marchers paired off to make their entrance into the stadium.

The trek to the entrance was only a couple of blocks, but it seemed like miles to the sponsors who helped the ground crew set up the pit instruments. They didn't clear their minds for the performance like the students did. The parents had time to think about the significance of what was happening. The adults marveled at the students' ability to go out onto the field after what had happened, and a new respect developed for those goofy kids, who only a few short hours ago were throwing frisbees and stuffing toilet paper down their pants. Claire finally understood that marching wasn't just an activity; it was an attitude. Something that gave the kids confidence and discipline: a direction in life. The soft rhythmic beat of the drumline vibrated through Claire gradually replacing doubt with pride. She was sorry she'd missed the last two years.

The students knew the drill. Each marcher focused on a mental image of the show, the music, the color. The chant "Hey Sue, for you" reminded them of why they were going back onto the field. Tears were on the brink but held in check by their determination to live up to the memory of the friend who'd died only a few hours ago. There was only one set of dry eyes as the band stepped onto the field. One person was not marching a memorial but rather a victory.

Finals competition began with twelve bands having an equal opportunity to win. Darkness had been replaced with stadium lights hours ago when the first band had taken the field. The Renegade Regiment had drawn the eleventh spot. ShyAnne and Sarah were standing next to each other waiting for the announcer to ask if their band was ready to march.

"Sarah," whispered Shy, "you okay?"

"I just want to get it over with. There's no thrill this time."

"I know. I usually have to pee just as we hit the first note, then the urge goes away."

"Me too," acknowledged Sarah. "This time I only have a heavy feeling on my heart."

"What are your spirits telling you?"

"To be careful," was all she could say before Joy lifted her arms to lead the band.

When the kids took their ready positions, they weren't thinking of beating a Texas band; they only wanted to play. Every note played sang out to the lost soul, the lost friend. Every step was in perfect unison. Andrea's solo was as difficult for each person on the field as it was for Andrea herself. It was the consummate symbol of why they were there, and Andrea played each note from the depths of her soul.

Dead Tones

The effect wasn't lost on the audience. It was mesmerized by the ethereal motion on the field. With the burden of competition replaced with the desire to create a memorial, every marcher stepped with his heart instead of his brain.

The kids were emotionally drained when they left the field in the two man formation to the soft drum cadence, "Hey Sue, for you." Click, click; click, click. Everyone was filled with a great satisfaction of knowing he'd not only managed to march the show but had created a wonderful memorial. Only one person on the field felt no remorse, no grief, no loss.

The audience and other bands showed their appreciation for the remarkable performance with a standing ovation which went nearly unnoticed by the Regiment as it marched out of the stadium. The cadence didn't take the band far. There was only one band left to march, so staying just outside the entrance made more sense than trying to get into the stands. Finding an out of the way spot where two hundred kids can casually wait isn't easy; but finally, the kids were led around to the back of the bleachers where they could relax for a few minutes. Tears rolled down the cheeks. There was no celebrating after this show.

Monica stood with her head resting on Sean's shoulder. "This has certainly turned into a rotten trip."

"Yeah," he agreed softly.

"Ya know, I was the one who taught Sue her freshman year. She was great. Practiced her music every night, always on time for practice. I'm glad we're graduating this spring. I'd sure hate to have to come back next year."

"What about Nationals?"

"I forgot. We do have Nationals in two weeks," moaned Monica. "What are we going to do? We know Andrea can play the solo if Allison is still sick."

"It's more than that," responded Sean. "I doubt if the band will be able to muster up the desire to compete after Sue's death. I bet we don't make it," said Sean.

"Make what?" asked Mike as he came up behind Sean with Krissy on his arm. Her eyes were still wet: and on this rare occasion, she had nothing to say.

"I was just telling Monica that I doubt if we'll be able to recover for nationals in St. Louis. It's only two weeks away," replied Sean.

"Well, my guess is it's going to depend on what really happened to Sue," offered Mike.

"Why? Sue's dead. Isn't that bad enough?" asked Monica wiping her eyes.

Mike was uncomfortable with all this emotional crap. "People die, Monica. It happens everyday. I'm sorry, but that's just the way it is. What's important is why she died."

"I can't believe you're so damned apathetic," hissed Monica.

"Oooow, 'apathetic', big word for you," said Mike with the strong implication that Monica was a little short of change when it came to matters of the mind.

"Eat shit, Mike. It was on our vocab list last week. You can be such an ass."

"Yeah, yeah. But see what I mean? Life goes on. Are you willing to forego your senior year's national competition because a classmate died? I'm sorry it happened. She was a good kid, cute too. But I don't want to give up nationals."

Krissy jabbed him in the stomach before adding her thoughts. "I want to know what happened. It's bad enough Sue died, but if she was...if..." her voice faltered, "if somebody helped her along, I want to know."

Mike was astonished at her accusation. "I was thinking more of some nasty virus or flu bug infecting a bunch of us, not murder."

Dead Tones

"Well," announced Krissy with new control, "I think it's just too weird that Allison and Sue got sick with the flu and are out of commission. Sarah agrees."

"Sarah and her Indian voodoo? Don't tell me you believe her and her stupid spirits," snapped Mike.

Krissy stiffened her back and her resolve. "Ya know what? I'm tired of your attitude that everything you disagree with is stupid. I'm tired of your insinuations that I'm stupid. Obviously, you slept through our conversation on the bus this morning. Too bad. Your limited ability to accept anything new or different makes you the stupid one." Krissy walked away before Mike had a chance to recover.

"Wow, life does go on," said Monica feigning deep concern for the possible broken heart.

"Bite me," was Mike's quick response.

Sean couldn't control his snicker any more than Monica. "Life sucks, doesn't it?"

"You can bite me, too."

"Mike, I'm sooooooo impressed with your extensive use of vocabulary. I guess you did make your point though," continued Monica. "I would like to know why Sue died; however, I really doubt it will have any bearing as whether or not we march at nationals."

"Maybe we should summon up Sarah's spirits for advice," said Mike with ample sarcasm to annoy Monica.

"Krissy's right, Mike. You really can be a moron. C'mon, Sean," directed Monica. The command demanded he make a choice: his girlfriend or his best friend. He was damned if he did and damned if he didn't. Man, fate was dishing out a load of shit on this band trip. He'd never seen things go from bad to worse so fast in his life. Now instead of drawing strength and support from each other, they were fighting.

"Monica, you're over reacting just a little." Sean tried not to sound patronizing. He didn't want to alienate either of them.

"You're choosing him over me. Fine!" she snapped. "Just fine."

Sean grabbed her by the arm as she tried to walk away. "I don't want to choose at all," he said apologetically. "We are all friends in a difficult situation. We shouldn't fight."

"Well, I guess it takes the bad times to separate the real friends from the friends of convenience." Monica jerked her arm out of his grasp and pushed through the crowd. She didn't need to go far. ShyAnne and Sarah were on the outer edge of the group consoling Krissy.

"It was just a matter of time," cried Krissy. "I knew we wouldn't last much longer."

"Why?" asked Sarah.

"I'm going back East to college. Mike's staying here. He's been offered a full scholarship to TU. I know he doesn't want a long distance relationship."

Shy knew more about Krissy than anyone, and she doubted it was Mike who didn't want the long distance relationship. "How do you know? Did he tell you?"

"Not exactly," answered Krissy.

"What exactly," extra emphasis was placed on 'exactly,' "do you mean?"

"He tried to convince me to stay in state. I don't want to."

"So it's your impression that since he wants you around, he won't tolerate long distance?" queried Sarah.

"I guess so."

"Maybe you're the one who doesn't want to deal with the distance."

"I guess so," admitted Krissy softly. "I don't know what I want," and she cried again.

Dead Tones

"It's okay. We can deal with this tomorrow. Right now you've got to pull yourself together. We'll be going back onto the field in a few minutes. C'mon, Krissy, dry your eyes," begged Shy.

Neither Shy nor Sarah saw Monica approach, but they heard the string of adjectives spewing from her mouth, "shithead, moron, asshole, dog breath, turd face."

"Let me guess," said Sarah, "uhh, is it possible you and Sean had a fight? What do ya think, Shy?"

"Wow, that's a tough one. Shithead? Moron? Turd face? Sounds like a pretty typical description of the male anatomy."

Monica laughed and even Krissy had to smile. "He was being a jerk. Took sides with Mike after Krissy accused Mike of being a moron. What was I supposed to do?"

"I'm sorry," said Krissy.

"Don't worry. It's good for him. I don't want the guy to think I'll roll over and play dead for him. Keeps him on his toes. Know what I mean? We'll be fine...I hope."

"Ya know, it was really rotten of Sue to die on us this way. Everybody's a wreck," observed Krissy.

"Oh yeah, like it was her choice or something," snapped Monica.

The whistle sounded and everybody, putting their individual concerns aside, came to attention. All of the finalists had to march back onto the field for the judges to announce the results of the competition. The students expected to march in a block formation into the stadium; however, this time the line up was single file. Rows of various colored uniforms flowed over the green turf, offering a rainbow affect to the audience. The kids felt uncomfortable being strung out. It was difficult to draw strength from each other in a single file line, but within minutes they'd arrived at the designated spot and lined up in the traditional block formation.

The announcer started with the bands from the smaller school districts. The Regiment stood at attention. As far as the kids were concerned tonight's mass band formation was only a formality. They'd done their job: marched their memorial. They wanted this night to be over.

Cheers rolled through the stadium when the announcer called, "Drum line, first place: Renegade Regiment."

The kids were stunned as Joy, Kevin and Stephen went forward to receive the trophy.

Again the announcer, "Third place...Second place....First place for Color Guard: Tulsa Southside Renegade Regiment."

Roars from the crowd echoed across the stadium.

"Third place...Second place...First place for music: Renegade Regiment.

"Bands of America is proud to announce the over all first place winner of the Texas Regional competition: Tulsa, Oklahoma's Southside High School Renegade Regiment."

Joy, Kevin and Stephen approached the judges for the fourth time accepting the large BOA trophy on behalf of their band. Cheers erupted from the crowd as the parents and students jumped to their feet showing their approval of the judges decisions. This was the first time the Regiment had ever placed first in a regional competition. Slowly the reality of their accomplishment set in. What a wonderful gift for a friend.

"Shy," whispered Sarah.

"Yeah?"

"I wonder if she's watching."

"You tell me. You're the one with spiritual connections."

Again the crackle of the microphone was the prelude to the announcer's first words. "The judges and I have just been informed that the Renegade Regiment would like to dedicate their performance

Dead Tones

and trophy to a classmate. We are very sorry to inform you that Miss Susan Walsch, the young lady who played the solo during the preliminary performance, died this afternoon.

Cheers became an awkward silence which hung over the stadium. Then the first clicks of the drum cadence filtered up to the fans. Click click, click click

"Hey Sue, for you," answered the drummer's song. What should have been the victory lap became a final tribute to a friend as the Regiment marched one more time around the stadium. Within minutes the other bands and the audience joined the chant, "Hey Sue, for you." Click click, click click.

"Hey Sue, for you." The sound pulsated through the air. For this one minute there were no rivals in the stadium, only people paying respect to a fellow musician.

The emotions were raw when the band finally exited the field. None of the trophies would ease the pain. First place had been an empty victory, leaving everyone anxious to be gone from the stadium. The kids and sponsors headed straight for the truck. Changing into street clothes and packing the uniforms and instruments was a silent drill.

Scott escorted Andrea to Claire. "Andrea tells me she's staying in your room?"

"Yeah. Why?"

"Please don't let her out of your sight. I have to make sure some of the other kids are okay."

Claire instantly had a mental replay of two years ago when she'd let a couple of girls slip her enough dramamine to knock her out. She'd been extremely embarrassed and angry when Scott had accused her of letting the girls party all night. Now he was trusting her to protect Andrea from some unknown danger. "I'll watch out for her," answered Claire.

"Oh yeah, Andrea, don't let her," he nodded his head toward Claire, "drink anything from anybody," ordered Scott with a quick smile.

"Hah, hah. Why do you joke around when everybody is feeling miserable?" asked Claire.

"Because...I don't know. I guess because we need it."

Claire returned the smile and directed her attention to the girl beside her. "Let's find Shy and Sarah. I don't know what's taking them so long to get back here. This is where we were supposed to meet."

"I saw them go into the bathroom right after we came off the field. Krissy and Monica were with them."

"I suppose it takes a little time to get out of that uniform."

"Yeah, but at least they don't have to put it all back on. See here they come." Andrea pointed in the direction of the restrooms, and sure enough the four girls were trudging along carrying a red jacket in one hand and a horn in the other. They weren't in a hurry.

"C'mon, girls," yelled Claire. "We're waiting to pack up those uniforms."

Shy added a spring to her step, but she didn't exactly hurry. "Sorry, Mom. We're pooped. It's been a really awful day."

"Doesn't it help at all that you won?"

All the girls shook their head negatively. "We could've come in last and I wouldn't feel any worse," explained Shy.

"Yeah, she's right," added Krissy. "Maybe it'll mean more to the freshmen next year after the tragedy of Sue's death has faded."

"I doubt it," offered Sarah. "This will always be remembered as the year Sue died not the year we finally won first place. Ya know, it's kind of ironic that we work and work, year after year to win a Texas regional; and when we finally do, it doesn't matter."

Dead Tones

"Yeah, there's no glory in a memorial trophy," said Monica. "Ya know what's really sad?"

"What?" the others asked in unison.

"The fact that Andrea hasn't gotten the credit she deserves for her solo."

"You're right," said Sarah. "Sorry, Andrea. You really were incredible."

"It's okay," stated Andrea. "I understand. I don't feel any better than the rest of you."

"I'm surprised you aren't like in hiding or something," suggested Krissy.

"Why does she need to be in hiding?" asked Monica.

"Really, Mon. You are like really slow in putting this together."

Shy and Sarah smiled at Krissy's lapse into her ditzy blond conversation. "It's in her blood," smiled Shy.

"What? What'd I say?" asked Krissy.

"Like really, you don't know," teased Sarah.

Krissy blushed slightly, "Ooops. Sometimes it just slips out."

"Like it's really okay, Krissy. We love you just like you are. However, you better leave all that 'like really' stuff here at home when you leave for Princeton," suggested Shy.

"Princeton?" questioned Sarah with a new respect for her friend. "Are you going to Princeton?"

"Shy!" admonished Krissy, "you promised you wouldn't tell."

"Sorry, it just slipped out," she apologized.

"Yeah, like I'm really sure," accused Krissy. "Oh well, it was bound to come out eventually. I got my acceptance letter last week. No scholarship, but I didn't really expect one."

"Congratulations," offered Claire. "I'm really impressed. Didn't know you had it in you."

"I owe it all to my grandpa. He gave me unlimited inspiration."

"Have you told Mike?" Monica asked the question Krissy didn't want to hear.

"No, I haven't. All he knows is that I'm considering going out of state."

"I see," sighed Shy.

"What? What do you see, smarty?"

"I see why it's easier to argue with him rather than tell him the truth."

"I'll tell him when I'm ready."

"You won't have to if you aren't dating anymore, right?" asked Sarah.

Krissy wasn't in the mood to be pushed against the wall, and she wasn't going to answer anymore questions about college or Mike. "I'm going to the bus." She handed her uniform to Claire and walked away.

"Well, I guess she told us to shut up," said Monica.

"I guess she did," agreed Claire. "Now hurry up and give me those uniforms. Andrea and I are ready to get on the bus too."

"What did Krissy mean about my being slow putting things together?" asked Monica.

"Neither Allison, the first soloist, or Sue, the second, could play. Mr. Krammer had to pick number three. What do you think? Do you see a pattern forming?"

"Sure do. Andrea, you naughty girl. How could you do such a terrible thing?" joked Monica.

"Me! I didn't do anything."

"Exactly, and I doubt anybody else did either," said Monica.

"Monica," Shy was astonished. "You're a traitor. You agree with Mike. Neither of you are willing to consider murder."

"I don't actually agree with him. Maybe there's a virus or some other awful disease going around. I'm afraid we might all get sick.

Dead Tones

But you're right, I don't think one of us tried to hurt Ali or Sue. Hopefully, next week we'll find out why they got sick. Hopefully, before somebody else ends up in a coma or...or dead. We've got to find out what's going on if we're going to get to Nationals."

"Nationals? Mr. B. won't give up Nats," said Sarah.

"He won't have a choice if a bunch of us are sick," added Monica.

Sarah didn't say a word, but the roll of her eyes told Shy that Sarah's spirits disagreed with Monica.

Claire was the one to move the conversation along. "I think you need to get on that bus over there before you're all left standing out here in the cold. We can worry about everything else tomorrow. Now move it." Claire, grateful she'd bought the winter coat and gloves, was still chilled to the bone and quickly followed the four girls to the heated bus.

The scheduled celebration at the Radisson was canceled. Kids immediately claimed their bags and headed for their rooms. Those who weren't exhausted, didn't feel like a party. Claire had to wait in line with the other sponsors for the room keys.

"Ya know, Mrs. Mayfield, I think I could wait with Shy and Sarah. No one can hurt me if I'm with them."

"No way, Andrea. I promised Scott...Mr. Krammer I wouldn't let you out of my sight."

"I think he was exaggerating his request. I'm not little enough for somebody to drag me off."

"Doesn't matter. Until we get to our room, you stay right beside me."

Andrea just shrugged her shoulders. She obviously felt out of place standing with all the sponsors especially when they started drooling over how wonderful her solo had been.

"How'd you learn the music so fast?"

"It was only a few notes. No big deal."

"Really? You sounded wonderful."

"Gee, thanks. But I just did what any player would've done," answered Andrea feeling guilty about the attention. She would've loved the credit for a great performance but not at the cost of a friend's life. Sue had helped her on several pieces of music over the last two years, so Andrea had felt obligated to do her best.

"No, you were wonderful," oozed Mrs. Baxter, "and under such tragic circumstances too. I hope Scott Krammer appreciates what you've done."

"Yes, he does," responded Scott coming up behind Andrea and Claire.

"Mr. Krammer, please let me go with Shy and Sarah. I'll be careful, really."

"Sorry. I absolutely refuse to let anything happen to you. If I can't be with you, Mrs. Mayfield will be standing next to you. Claire, this is my room number. If anything unusual happens, call me. And don't let her out of your sight no matter how much she begs."

"Okay."

"Mr. Krammmmer, please," begged Andrea.

"Nope," he answered before leaving again.

"No offense, Mrs. Mayfield, but I grew out of a babysitter several years ago."

"I understand. Please call me Claire and then think of me as your bodyguard. Lots of great people need a bodyguard."

"Thanks."

Claire was handed two keys and she suggested to Andrea, "let's find the girls and get some sleep."

The lobby emptied as quickly as the keys could be passed out. Dale and the other staff members went to check the hallways, while Scott was left in the lobby to make sure everybody had gone up to a

Dead Tones

room. He was surprised to find Abby slumped over on a couch in one of the dining areas.

Scott reached down to shake her gently. "Abby, Abby?" His first thought was that she was ill or worse. This time he spoke loudly, "Abby!"

"Oh, Mr. Krammer. I'm sorry. I must have fallen asleep."

Scott couldn't miss the swollen eyes and the hick-up sound left after a terrible bout of crying. "Abby, are you okay?"

That was definitely the wrong question because the tears started all over again. "Ohhhh, Mr. Krammer, it's my fault...it's my fault Sue is...is dead. I'm soooo sorry."

Scott was confused. "What are you talking about? What's your fault?"

"Awwww," she bawled again throwing herself into Scott's arms.

There was nothing he could do but put his arms around her and try to offer some comfort. "Abby, Abby, it's okay. Tell me what happened."

Abby, still sobbing, laid in his arms for several minutes. This certainly wouldn't look good to anyone who came around the corner. Scott already knew the rumors floating around about him, and this would only confirm the suspicions. He had to get her to calm down and talk to him. At least it was late, and most of the staff was gone. Thank God the parents and students had made a quick exit. All he needed now was for Monica's mother to walk into the room. *Water, maybe a glass of water would help. C'mon, kid, give me a break. Tell me what the hell you're talking about.* Scott was desperate to get out of her arms, but she wasn't cooperating. "Abby." She didn't respond. "Abby! Stop crying." She tried to get some control of her emotions. "I'm going to find you a glass of water, then we're going to talk about what happened."

R. Z. Crompton

"Just call the police, Mr. Krammer. I might as well turn myself in," sniffed the hysterical girl.

Get a grip, Abby. You always over react. "Why don't you tell me what happened before we call the cops. Now sit here until I get back." Scott hurried across the empty dining room and through a swinging door he hoped would lead to a kitchen.

Abby, hoping to gain mercy from her teacher, broke into another fit of tears. She was sobbing effectively into her hands when he walked back through the door with a pitcher and two glasses.

Scott poured half a glass of water and offered it to Abby. First he needed to get her attention. "Abby. Abby!" He sat back down on the sofa. "Abby, please get a hold of yourself." She finally lifted her head and took the glass. "Now tell me what happened."

Abby shook her head affirmatively. "I killed her. I wanted Sue dead and I killed her."

"Can you be a little more specific?"

"I wished her dead and...and...and she died," sniffled Abby.

My God, she is just slightly nuts. Scott was pretty sure Abby had nothing to do with Sue's death, but he wasn't ready to send her off to her room yet. "Why'd you wish her dead?"

"Because...because she stole Bobby from me. He was mine. Then she smiled at him and he dumped me for her. I called her really nasty names and I wished her dead. And now...and now she's dead. I'm soooo sorry." Again she threw herself in his lap and sobbed.

Damn, I shouldn't have sat back down. "Abby. Abby! C'mon, girl. Get some control. You cannot wish someone to die. Can't be done."

"Of course you can, Mr. Krammer. Indians do it all the time."

"What are you talking about?"

"Indian magic. The spirits can kill somebody if you know the right spell. Just ask Sarah. Her grandmother taught her all about it."

Dead Tones

"But, Abby, you aren't a medicine man."

"Oh, I know that. But if they can wish somebody dead, then I can too. And I did, cause she's...she's dead," and again the sobs of guilt.

Scott didn't doubt her feelings were genuine. However, he did doubt her power to wish Sue's death. He wished he'd called Claire when he'd gone into the kitchen. She could've come down and given him a hand with Abby's over active imagination. It was odd that the one person who'd probably pass the harshest and quickest judgement on him was the person he would've asked for help. Oh well, she wasn't coming to rescue him; and he had to get Abby out of his lap. "C'mon, Abby, you've got to get to your room."

"But, Mr. Krammer, aren't you going to call the police?"

"No. They'd throw you in the loony bin before they'd put you in jail. You didn't kill Sue."

"How do you know?"

"I just know," said Scott as he stood up hoping she'd follow suit.

"This wouldn't have happened if she hadn't stole Bobby from me. He was mine," whined Abby still sitting on the sofa.

"You can't make a boy or anybody else love you no matter how hard you try or how much you wish. It just doesn't happen that way," answered Scott thinking about his father. *You just can't wish for love, Abby. I know, believe me I know.* Scott felt sorry for her. "Abby, try to understand what I'm going to tell you. I know it's hard but when a relationship is over, one person is always the 'dumper' and one is the 'dumpee'. Now the 'dumpee' never likes getting dumped on. It's no fun, but those are the facts of life. It doesn't matter how old you are, it never changes."

"You mean there's no 'happily ever after'?"

This girl had overdosed on fairy tales. "No, there's no 'happily ever after' and you can't kill somebody by wishing for it."

"Really?" she asked sadly.

"Really. Now are you ready to get some sleep?"

"I guess so." Abby finally stood up.

Scott bent down to retrieve her coat, wrapped it around her shoulders and led her to the elevators. He was grateful reality had finally touched her and she was out of his lap. He needed a clean escape. Over the last twelve years he'd had a few close calls. He assumed all of the teachers did from time to time. Some student suffered a tragedy, and a teacher was left to pick up the pieces. Thankfully, he'd never been caught in a compromising situation. No matter how innocent he was, people loved to gossip; and he'd seen gossip destroy a career over night. Scott thought about what Trish had told him earlier. *Shit, some people just make the rumors up as they go. Just because I'm not married, I'm either gay or abusing my students. Life can really suck. Why is a different lifestyle a threat for so many people? Why?* Scott shook his head trying to rationalize about the dark side of human nature. He'd never understand why so many people wanted everyone to be carbon copies of themselves.

The elevator door closed and a student stepped out from the shadows. Scott and Abby had not gone unnoticed, and Abby would not go unpunished.

CHAPTER SEVEN

Andrea, sitting cross legged on the green and red flowered bedspread, listened intently as Shy and Sarah filled her in on their suspicions. Andrea had been sure Mr. Krammer was just being over protective, now she was glad he'd assigned her a babysitter. "Mr. Krammer wouldn't try to hurt me, ya think?"

"Na, if he was the bad guy here, I don't think he'd a been so urgent about you staying under Mrs. Mayfield's protection," answered Sarah.

"I agree. He was wonderful all afternoon. I almost died when he asked me to play the solo. I can't imagine anybody saying 'no' to him. Those big blue eyes are so awesome," sighed Andrea.

"Grab a piece of reality, Andrea. And please don't let my mother hear you talk that way. The last thing we need is for her to have more doubts about his motives or possible desires."

"She's in the shower," responded Andrea. "How much can she hear?"

"You'd be amazed. I think she's got sonar built right into her brain. Sometimes she knows what I'm thinking before I do."

"Na, it's just one of those 'mother' things we'll develop too when we have kids," said Sarah.

"I'd like to have a little bit of that sonar now, so I could figure out why somebody's trying to kill our clarinet players. Anybody want a snack? I think there's some chips or cookies in Mom's bag," said Shy, getting off the bed.

"Yeah, I'm starving," answered Andrea. "I didn't get a chance to eat much before finals. I was too nervous before I played, afraid I'd puke on my feet while I was playing that damn solo."

Dead Tones

Sarah and Shy shared a quick glance. Andrea never swears. "You okay?" Shy asked Andrea. For the first time Shy and Sarah noticed the stress on her pretty face. "Do you feel sick now?" Shy almost sounded paranoid.

"I'm tired and hungry. And scared. You can't do anything about the scared, but you can feed me."

"Come to think of it, I'm starving too. There was no way I was going to eat one of those yucky subways. Let's order a pizza."

"Great! Have 'em bring some coke too. That way we won't have to leave our room to get a drink," suggested Andrea.

"I better tell mom," said Shy walking toward the bathroom door. Then she stopped, "Na, let's tell her after we order. That way she can't say 'no'. It's easier to beg for forgiveness than to ask for permission."

"Neat philosophy. Who do we call?" asked Sarah, pulling a phone book out of the night stand.

"Anybody listed in Denton and still open," answered Andrea. "I'm not real picky when I'm starving."

"I hear ya." Sarah called three places before finding somebody who'd still deliver. Shy and Andrea changed into their version of pajamas: boxer shorts and a grossly baggy sweatshirt.

Andrea was the first to plop back onto the bed. "Can you even imagine Mr. Krammer being gay? What a waste of beautiful, male flesh."

"No kidding. Do you know how stupid all the girls would feel?" asked Shy. "I mean, we've all had a crush on him at one time or another."

"Oh, fer sure," agreed Andrea.

"I'm sure a few of the guys, too," added Sarah.

"What do you mean? Why would a guy have a crush on Mr. Krammer?" asked Andrea innocently.

R. Z. Crompton

Shy and Sarah looked at each other and then smiled back at the rather naive girl sitting across from them. "Think about it for a second, Andrea. It'll come to you."

Andrea cocked her head like an obedient puppy trying to understand a master's request. Then her face, turning bright red, twisted into comprehension. "Ewwww! Gross! You mean some of our guys are...are...like wow, weird, happy campers, funny? You mean like that?"

"Cute choice of adjectives, but yeah," answered Sarah.

"Who?" asked Andrea.

"Wait a minute," injected Shy. "This has gone far enough. Sarah, you don't know for sure, and right now if my mother hears anything that sounds slightly like gossip, I'll be grounded until retirement: mine not hers. There's enough rumors flying around without us adding fuel to the fire."

Just then the bathroom door opened, and Claire asked, "Who's adding fuel to the fire?"

Shy smiled at the other two girls before answering, "Nobody, Mom."

"Who left these in the bathroom?" asked Claire. In her hand were three green marbles.

All three girls bellowed with laughter until Andrea finally claimed them.

"I don't understand what's so funny."

"Andrea, are you going to enlighten her or should we?" asked Shy.

"They're my green marbles," again snickers from the other two. "All the clarinets put marbles in their sports bras. It's sort of symbolic."

"I'm sure it is. So?"

Dead Tones

"Well, we'd hate to lose our marbles while we were marching, so we carry them in a safe place," continued Andrea.

"Should I even ask if the color has any significance?"

"Only if you want to know," said Sarah.

"Our clarinet mascot is Mr. Horny and..."

Claire interrupted, "Mr. Horny is green. So what's with Gummy Bears?"

"Oh, that's tradition. Mr. B. gives everyone a Gummy Bear before we march. We lick it and stick it to our horn. It's supposed to bring us good luck. After the show, if we marched perfectly, we get to eat the whole thing. But if somebody missed a step, he only gets to eat the feet. Somebody else might have to eat the head."

"I get it. How long 'til the pizza gets here?"

"See," said Shy. "Sonar."

"What?" asked Claire over the sound of the blow dryer.

"About fifteen minutes," yelled Shy. Then she grabbed a pillow, sprawled out on the bed and directed her attention back to their mission. "Sarah, grab some paper. Let's write down our suspects and their motives. Maybe that'll help."

"Good idea," said Sarah jumping off the bed to get her notebook. "Where do you want to start?"

"I suppose with the obvious. The first and second clarinets are the ones who were hurt. All we have to do is figure out why," suggested Shy. She looked at Andrea.

"So, now am I your best suspect?" accused Andrea.

"Welllllll, no. Not exactly," stammered Shy.

"Thanks for that vote of confidence." Andrea was hurt. "You're right though. If you're gonna look at all the possibilities, I suppose you have to look at me. I'm soloist number three."

Sarah thought for a moment before saying, "Shy, if your theory is plausible, then I'd look for somebody who'd already learned the music. Mr. Krammer had to rewrite the solo this afternoon for Andrea to learn. If she had planned to be his third choice, my guess is that she'd have learned the original music, or at the very least brought it with her."

"Good point," added Shy smiling at Andrea. "Looks like you're off the hook. Feel better?"

"Much," answered Andrea, with a big sigh.

"Andrea," said Sarah giving her a knowing look, "there's no way you could be guilty. Shy was pulling your leg."

"ShyAnne! How can you joke about something so serious?"

"Because there's absolutely no way *you* could hurt somebody. You're too...too soft," admitted Shy. "Besides, Sarah would know if the evil spirits were in you. Wouldn't you?" asked Shy hoping Sarah would back her up.

"Maybe, probably. I don't know. I can't detect evil in any specific person. Otherwise I'd know right away who was doing this. It's just a general feeling I get. Anyway, back to our task. Andrea, have you heard anyone besides Allison and Sue practicing?"

"Nope."

"You were surprised when Mr. Krammer picked you, right?" asked Shy.

"Yeah."

"Maybe somebody else was surprised too. Who would have been his most obvious choice?"

"I would've picked Megan or maybe Kate. They're both good players and have marched longer than me," answered Andrea while she ran her brush through her thick hair.

Sarah thought about the two girls. "I don't think Kate would care. She has nothing to gain from all the attention."

Dead Tones

Claire had been listening intently to the conversation and wanted to know more about Megan and Kate. "Isn't Kate the other girl who was sick?"

"Yeah. Why?"

"Just wondering," said Claire. "She and Sue don't get along very well, or was their animosity only in my imagination?"

"Dislike isn't really a strong enough word for their feelings," responded Andrea. "Hate." She thought for a second and then confirmed her own opinion, "yeah, mutual hate sounds about right. They've hated each other since grade school."

"Why?" asked Claire.

"I don't really know," answered Andrea. "It's just always been that way."

"Hmmm." The conversation between the two girls was coming back to her. "Kate almost threatened Sue this morning."

"Really? What'd she say?" asked Shy.

"Kate said she'd be on the field while Sue was in the hospital."

"Is that all?" responded Shy.

"Yeah, isn't that enough. I didn't think much of it this morning, but now it seems rather significant."

"Not really, Mom. You're just not used to hearing how cruel kids can be to each other. Actually, what Kate said was pretty minor compared to some of the stuff we hear."

"Okay, so tell me why isn't Kate interested in the attention?"

"There's no advantage for her," answered Sarah.

"Why? Isn't she a serious player?" inquired Claire.

"She's a great player. But her interest isn't in music," said Shy.

"Yeah, remember that awesome demonstration she and her dad gave least year in bio? All those beautiful tropical fish," explained Andrea.

"Yeah, her dad was absolutely the best speaker we had all year. Mom, his work is fascinating."

"What do they do with tropical fish?" asked Claire.

"Kate's helping her dad with medical research using tropical fish. They dissected some while we watched. We got to see the parts of the fish that are important to the research. I'd never seen Kate so intense. She's a natural scientist," added Andrea.

"Okay, so Kate's off our list cause she has nothing to gain from being the soloist."

"That's my opinion, Mom. I doubt if she'd even want to play. Like Andrea said, her passion is science, not music. She's out here for the fun."

"So what about Megan?"

"Well, she's a good player and really works hard," said Andrea. "I don't know if music is that important to her either. At least I never get the feeling it is."

"Mom, did you have time to call Mrs. Hayes?"

"No, why?"

"Well, I feel kind of guilty dissecting my friends without any concrete reason to believe Allison's illness and Sue's death are connected. Know what I mean?"

Before Claire could answer there was a knock at the door. "Yeah, the pizza's here. I'm hungry too." Claire grabbed her wallet and headed for the door. Surprised to open the door and find Scott standing behind a young man in a blue jacket with two flat boxes resting on his right arm and a two liter bottle of coke in the other, Claire handed a twenty to the pizza man and then moved aside inviting Scott into the room without saying a single word to him. Claire felt guilty, she'd been caught letting the girls do something unsanctioned just like last time.

"Hey, girls what's up? Did ya get any pepperoni?"

Dead Tones

"Yeah, how'd you know we were getting a pizza?" asked Shy.

"I knew somebody would. After all these years of band trips, there's just some things that always happen and ordering pizza is one of those absolutes. All I have to do is wait for a delivery man to come through the front door and follow him to the room. So, do you have enough glasses?"

"Yeah," said Claire. "There's some plastic cups in the bag Sylvia packed, but we need some ice."

"Well, I guess since no one's supposed to leave the room, I get to be the gofer." Scott reached across Claire to pick the ice bucket up off the table. "Back in a minute." Scott nodded his head toward the door hoping Claire would get his message.

"Girls, go ahead and start on the pizza before it gets cold. I'll hold the door for you, Scott." She followed him to the door.

Scott opened the door and waited for Claire to come up behind him. "How are the girls doing?" he whispered.

"I think they're fine. They're discussing motives for murder and who the motives might belong to."

"Oh, yippy. That sounds entertaining."

"It's better than listening to them cry all night," offered Claire.

"That's for sure," said Scott rolling his eyes.

"What do you mean?"

"I just spent the last thirty minutes listening to Abby cry like a baby as she confessed to killing Sue by wishing her to die."

"You're kidding," responded Claire trying not to laugh. "Was she serious or just looking for you?"

It had never occurred to Scott that Abby might have wanted his attention rather than his sympathy. "Good grief, you are joking, I hope."

"Not necessarily. According to what the girls tell me you are about the hottest piece of walking male flesh around."

Scott actually felt himself getting hot with embarrassment as she waited for his reaction. "Girls exaggerate. And Abby had real tears. Well, I think they were real. But you could find out for sure by asking Shy how Abby and Sue got along."

"Okay. Do you have any more information about how Sue died. It would really help to know if they suspect poison like Allison or if it's something contagious. Let's face it, having Allison and Sue sick at the same time could be a coincidence."

"Do you really think so?" Scott asked, hoping she'd say yes.

"No, but I'm hoping. It's better than murder."

"Ya think?" teased Scott.

"Yeah, I think. Now go get some ice. I'm hungry."

"Claire," he felt he owed her some explanation regarding Abby's confession, "I know the girls talk and I've heard the rumors. As far as I'm concerned, my kids are just that: kids. I've never touched one of my students, male or female."

Claire wanted to believe him. She stared into the clear blue eyes and wanted to trust him. "Go get the ice before the girls send out a search party for you."

When Scott returned with a full bucket, Claire was still holding the door for him. She followed him into the room and found all three girls watching them. "What?" asked Claire. "What?"

"Hey, Mom, do you want us to leave the room for a while?" asked Shy.

Now it was Claire's turn to blush. She threw her daughter the Mother's special "I want to ring your neck" look before answering with an unrelated question, "How's the pizza?"

"Nice try, Mom," answered Shy giving Claire a quick wink. "Did you go to Alaska for that ice, Mr. Krammer."

"No, your mom was telling me about your most embarrassing childhood moments," said Scott. He walked across the room and

Dead Tones

placed the ice bucket on the counter. The thought of an ice cold drink and a good piece of pizza made him salivate.

Shy had a flashback to the time she had her head stuck in her potty chair, "Ahhh, I don't think so." Her mom was sworn to secrecy on that one. Shy glanced at her mother as she filled a blue plastic cup with ice.

Claire smiled innocently back assuring her daughter that the childhood secret was still safe. "Actually, we were wondering if Sue had any enemies. Seems that Abby confessed to killing her."

"My God, like you're kidding. Right?" gasped Andrea.

"Well she did confess to wishing Sue dead," admitted Scott as he sat down in the chair near the window.

"Wishing? You've got to be joking," laughed Shy.

"Abby's always been melodramatic," added Sarah.

"She was certainly dramatic tonight. I could barely get out of her grip," said Scott glancing at Claire who had taken part of the bed claimed by Shy. He didn't realize how incriminating his words were until they were flying through the air. He'd have done anything to reel them back. He could hear Claire saying *I told you so.* "Was she mad at Sue?" he continued.

"Oh yeah. She was flipped out for the last two days," admitted Andrea.

"That's right," added Sarah, "we are so used to her tantrums that we kind of ignore them, but she was using several colorful terms to describe Sue."

"Thursday, she stood at the top of the stairs and yelled, 'Sue Walsch is a whore.' I wasn't so surprised. Abby claimed Sue had stolen Bobby. She was spittin' fire," said Andrea.

"Do you think she'd want revenge?"

"Oh, she wanted revenge all right," continued Andrea. "She was waiting for Sue after sectionals Friday morning. I heard her say 'I wish you were dead'."

"How'd Sue react?" asked Scott.

"The same way we all do when Abby throws a tantrum. We just kept walking. Abby's a little nuts, but we all assumed she was harmless," said Andrea.

"Wishing somebody dead is harmless. Wishes don't kill," replied Claire.

"Yeah, but what if the wishes turn into action?" asked Shy.

"I don't think so," responded Scott. "She kept saying she'd wished Sue to die. And wish was the key word in her confession." Scott thought about Abby's claim that she wished for death like the Indian's do, but he didn't ask Sarah about it. The idea of anyone wishing someone dead just seemed too far fetched.

"So back to Megan," continued Shy, "is she on our list or not?"

"I don't know any reason to suspect her," offered Andrea. "She never stood out as an antagonist."

"Mr. Krammer, can't you call the hospital about Sue? We don't know if we're trying to find someone who had a grudge against just Allison or both of them," said Sarah.

"Mom, you need to talk with Mrs. Hayes. I'd really like to know if Ali is pregnant."

"Wo. Wait a minute," snapped Scott. "Who in the hell...ooops, sorry girls, who in the world told you she was pregnant?"

The girls were silent. Claire was left to answer the question as all eyes turned toward her. Claire couldn't meet his eyes, and the silence was awkward. The girls had no idea who had passed the rumor to Claire.

"Claire?", he questioned, "who was it?"

Dead Tones

"The same person who told me you were the father," she blurted out not wanting to make the information sound like an accusation.

"Jesus Christ!" Scott jumped out of his chair. This time he didn't worry about controlling his words. His frustration exploded through the room as he paced at the foot of the two double beds and then toward the door. "I can't believe it. My God, why would somebody say such a thing. We never...I never. She had a serious boyfriend."

"I'm sorry, Scott. To your defense, we all had the same reaction to this rumor."

Scott trusted the girls to defend him, but he had his doubts about Claire. "Am I on your *list* yet? If you believe the rumor, you have to put me on the list." His gaze was fixed on the woman who could destroy his life with this accusation. Now he had a vague idea of how she'd felt two years ago. He waited for her to respond.

Shy was terrified. This was the very confrontation she'd been afraid of. If her mother had any desire for revenge, she'd get it now. *Where are your darn spirits now, Sarah? We could use a little help here.* Shy threw a pleading look to Sarah.

Claire had to exonerate him. She remembered her own reaction and that of the girls'. The shock they had shared was minimal compared to Scott's. Without some kind of concrete facts to prove guilt, Claire was going to defend the man standing in front of her. "I've heard enough rumors about you today to write a book, but I've also heard testimonials for sainthood. So finish your pizza. I'm leaning more toward sainthood than crucifixion."

"Thanks, but I've lost my appetite."

Shy glanced back at Sarah and mouthed *thanks*.

"For what?" asked Sarah looking directly at Shy. She didn't realize Claire and Scott immediately stopped talking to look at her. Sarah had no idea what Shy was hinting at, but she had to say something. "Maybe whoever started the rumor did it with the intention of throwing doubt on Mr. Krammer."

"You mean like a cover-up?" asked Andrea.

"I don't know. But nothing like this has ever happened before," admitted Sarah. She was sure eventually the doubt would be thrown in her direction just like her grandmother predicted. "My grandmother said to look for who is the loudest and the one who is hiding would be close by. I guess passing rumors could be in the same category."

Claire took Sarah's speculation one more step. "I think I agree with you. It's possible the rumors are a smoke screen. You know, to keep us from looking in the right direction. It wouldn't be the first time the innocent were slaughtered with scare tactics and gossip."

"You mean like the witch hunts and McCarthyism?" asked Shy.

"Yeah, I guess so," answered Claire.

"Wait a minute," injected Scott, "I don't think rumors and gossip can kill."

"Then you spend too much time in the music room and not enough in the classroom, Mr. Krammer. History is full of people lying to protect themselves. You know like in the days of Hitler and..." Shy faltered in her speech.

"The Spanish Inquisition," yelled Andrea as if she was playing Trivial Pursuit.

"The American Government," said Sarah softly.

"What are you talking about?" asked Shy.

"The American Government lied to my people, and thousands of my ancestors died as a result of the 1830 Removal Act passed by Congress and signed by President Jackson. My people, most of whom already lived according to the white man's law, were stripped of their property and belongings and then forced to march thousands of miles with nothing but the clothes on their backs for shelter."

"That's not exactly the same thing," said Shy.

Dead Tones

"Not exactly, but people still lied for their own gain. It's good enough for me."

Now Abby's comment about Indians *wishing* death on others had new meaning. Scott caught Claire's questioning glance at the girl. If his name was on a suspect list then Sarah's was too. He gulped down the rest of his coke and picked up the remaining piece of pizza. "I get the point and my being burned at the stake is not on tomorrow's agenda."

"So what are we going to do?" asked Andrea.

"For now, there's nothing we can do but listen and stop anybody else from perpetuating the lies," instructed Claire.

"I agree," added Scott, "and try to get some sleep. I'm ready to do the same." Scott, doubting he'd be able to close his eyes, headed for the door. Again, he looked at Claire until she met his eyes and acknowledged his request for her to follow him.

"We have to stop meeting like this," she whispered softly in the small space between the closet and bathroom.

"Why? You afraid of the rumors?" asked Scott trying to ease the tension.

The humor in his words was not portrayed in his voice, and Claire couldn't miss the uncertainty in his eyes. She tried to help by making light of the situation. "These three are on our side, remember?"

"I hope so," said Scott as he opened the door.

Claire stepped out behind him holding the door open with her foot. "Did you catch the comment from Sarah?"

"Yeah, makes you wonder, doesn't it?"

"That's all I'm doing right now," said Claire.

"Thanks, Claire, for sticking up for me in front of the girls. I really appreciate it," said Scott. He never took his eyes off hers. He wanted to see her flinch, to look away in an attempt to hide her doubt, but she didn't back down.

"Scott, I don't really know anything about you; however, if public opinion means anything at all, I have to go with the majority. Shy is rarely wrong in her assessment of a person's character, and Trish knows you better than most of the people here. I will believe them before drowning in this sea of gossip."

"Thanks for being honest even if you are still wondering about me," said Scott. He reached out and touched her hand hesitantly waiting again for her to pull away.

Claire returned the tenderness with her other hand and a smile that warmed his heart. "I'm wondering how to clean this mess up not about your virtue."

"If that rumor catches on, you'll be one of the few on my side. Most of these parents will want to fry my carcass before we get back to Tulsa. Why do you believe me?" he asked.

"Does it matter?"

"To me it does," answered Scott. He pulled her closer allowing the door to close behind her. Her fragrance filled his senses.

Claire had to bend her head back to look into his eyes. "Well," she hesitated for a minute, "it's elementary, my Dear Watson."

Scott finally gave her an earnest smile. "What's so elementary, Sherlock?"

"First, if...and I do mean if...if Allison is pregnant and if you are the father, why would you hurt Sue?"

"Okay, if...and I stress the if...if Sue found out maybe I was trying to silence her."

"Sorry, I don't buy it. Remember, I saw how worried you were about her and Andrea."

"Maybe, I'm a good actor."

"You're not that good," she answered. "You're too honest."

Dead Tones

"How do you know?"

The intensity in his question couldn't be missed. This was important to him, and Claire didn't want to take his feelings lightly. "It's in your eyes, Scott. Just like you looked into my eyes waiting for my reaction to your questions, I can tell by watching you."

Her words, triggering his memory, were like a kick in the gut. The reality of his past was rearing its ugly head. Scott shook his head and let her hand go. "You better get some sleep. I'll talk to you in the morning." Before Claire could say anything, he knocked on the door, so one of the girls would let her in. "Good night."

"Yeah, good night," said Claire when the door opened. His quick exit surprised her. But there was really nothing else to say.

Scott watched her until the door closed. He felt sick inside, no, wicked was more accurate. He'd finally found a woman worth fighting for, one under the age of fifty who didn't want babies, and his past would certainly push her away. He enjoyed children but had sworn years ago never to father a child. The family gene pool was tainted; hence, he turned to teaching to fulfill his longing for a family. Scott unconsciously wiped his hands on the leg of his pants in an attempt to wipe the guilt away. He hadn't done it in years.

Claire had forgiven him for his blundering actions two years ago, and she trusted him. A slap in the face was what he offered in return. Scott hadn't misled her or the students intentionally. He'd worked hard to create a wholesome new life, but living a new life couldn't erase the old. As soon as he'd gained some control, the past jumped up and bit him on the butt. When Claire suggested someone might create a rumor to intentionally destroy him, he knew who it was. There was only one person in Scott's life with that much power and that much hate. His past was knocking at his door.

Scott waited for the elevator door to open, but he actually wanted to jump out the tenth floor window. However, he owed the people who'd trusted him with their children more than suicide. He'd try to pick up the pieces for them, offer a full confession, and take the punishment. The worst punishment he could imagine would be watching Claire's face when she heard the truth. Dying would be much less painful than the humiliation. He wiped his hands against his thighs again just as the door opened.

Claire's attention jumped quickly from Scott's abrupt exit to the strange exhibit she found on the bed closest to the door. Several pieces of green cloth were reverently laid out. Claire couldn't identify the content which had been carefully placed in the middle of each square; however her nose told her cedar was definitely part of the concoction.

"Girls, what are you doing?"

"Sarah's making us a charm to keep the evil away. We're making one for you and Mr. Krammer, too." The excitement in Shy's voice reminded Claire of when she was a little girl coming home from school with some great news to share.

"May I ask why you think you need to charm away the evil?"

"It's just in case. You know," said Andrea. "Better safe than sorry."

Claire couldn't see any harm in their taking childish precaution; however, she did wonder about Sarah's role in what had been happening. Humoring them would get her more information than criticism. "So enlighten me, girls. What's in this magical charm anyway?"

Sarah was very serious in her explanation. "I have mixed three powerful components to protect us. Green cedar, cedar charred by lightning, and tobacco blessed by my grandmother will be tied up in this green cloth. It will protect us from any ghosts that might come in the night."

Dead Tones

"Ghosts?" yipped Andrea, "you never said anything about ghosts before."

"What do you think the spirits are?" asked Sarah. "Spirits, ghosts, evil, this will protect you from all of them," said Sarah as she tied the first of five pouches closed. "Carry it in your pocket or around your neck; it doesn't matter. Just don't forget it somewhere. And please, don't tell Krissy. This is all the stuff I have, and she'll be hurt if she finds out I didn't make one for her."

"Considering the reaction most of the kids have to your magic, I agree," added Shy.

"Why?" Claire asked.

"Oh, it's nothing unusual," said Sarah tying another pouch together. "Most of the kids don't understand Indian medicine."

"When some idiot starts calling my friend a witch, I take it very seriously," snapped Shy.

"They're afraid of what they don't understand. Nothing strange about that," responded Claire.

"Instead of nursing their fear why don't they ask questions?" asked Shy.

"That takes too much effort," sneered Andrea, "it's easier to be afraid."

"Did you ever notice how fear begets fear?" asked Shy.

"Oh yeah. It travels as fast as gossip," explained Claire. "Just like an Oklahoma grass fire."

"Huh?" The girls looked at her for an explanation, but Claire didn't notice. Her mind had drifted back to Scott. Wondering again about his strange departure, she pulled back the covers and crawled into bed.

"Here, Mom," said Shy handing her the small green pouch, "tie this around your neck."

Claire nearly refused the offer then reconsidered. *Ghosts? I don't like ghosts. Well, better safe than sorry.* Claire reached for the protective charm and tied it around her neck. "So, Sarah, tell me about your medicine. My knowledge ends with what's in the movies ShyAnne brings home on those cold January nights. More specifically, please tell me what we could be up against. Like the ghosts."

"I don't know what we're up against. This is a pretty general charm, you know, kinda like somebody taking an aspirin for anything and everything. Grandmother has taught me about the power of tobacco smoke and how to bless the smoke. The blessing is a long process, so she helped me. She's worried about me, about all of us."

Claire sat up, so she could pay better attention to what Sarah had to say. "What about the evil? You keep talking about the evil."

"For us the evil is simply part of the magic. Good and bad are part of a circle. Grandmother and I are the healers; we are one part of the sphere. The night walkers and raven mockers are another part of the same circle of magic."

"You are counter parts of each other?" asked Claire with profound interest.

"Yeah," answered Sarah.

"So you know the power of the other side, of the raven mocker?" asked Claire with intense interest.

"I know how strong it can be, but I can't fight it yet. Only my grandmother can. She is strong enough to turn a spell around."

"Explain that, please. How can you turn around what you can't see?" asked Shy.

"The most common spells are sickness and fever. The kind that doesn't seem to have a cause."

"Like Allison's?" asked Shy.

"Yeah. The raven mocker's the worst. He can actually change into different shapes."

Dead Tones

"Wo," sighed Andrea, "you mean some really fine guy could be a raven mocker?"

Sarah laughed, "No, silly. He usually changes into an animal."

"Oh, man. I'm relieved. Wouldn't that be a waste? Could you imagine some buff guy changing into a scary medicine man just as you were about to kiss him. Ewwwww," said Andrea twisting her lips and closing her eyes to exaggerate her opinion.

"I think you're safe on that," offered Sarah. "His most common choice of animal is the wolf..."

"Yeah, and the hawk," said Shy proudly. When Claire looked at her daughter for an explanation, Shy continued, "I saw it on Walker one night when you were working late." Shy could tell by the look on her mother's face that she didn't quite understand. "You know, Walker, Texas Ranger. Saturday night. Television. He's part Indian. One of the shows was about a raven mocker. I know that now cause the guy kept changing shapes." Shy directed her comments back to Sarah. "It was scary then, but I have to tell you, it's more frightening now that I know it could be true."

Claire wasn't sure how much she was ready to believe. "Just how powerful is a raven mocker?"

"He's strong enough to cause death. He will eat the organs of his victims to add years of life to himself."

"Ewwwww," moaned Andrea. "That's so gross." All three of them listened eagerly to Sarah's explanation.

"Do you know who these guys are?" asked Claire hoping for a positive answer.

"Well, yeah. My grandmother does. But you never know what shape he's using or what spell has been sent or to whom."

"So how do you fight the guy?" asked Claire.

"Well, each spell has a force propelled by its originator, and it has to go somewhere. A strong healer can't stop the spell, but he can turn it around."

"Ya mean like 'return to sender'?" asked Andrea.

"Kinda like that. It can go to another person or back to the sender."

"What about an animal? Why doesn't your grandmother just send the spell to a rat or a spider?"

"No way. Animals have their own mystical qualities. A spell has to be toward a person."

"Is it possible somebody in the band besides you is learning the magic?"

"No, Grandmother would know if there was another. There aren't many of us around."

"Is that all you can do? You have to wait for the raven mocker to send his spell, so you can try to stop it. Doesn't that put you at a disadvantage?"

"If that was the extent of our power, it would. We can cast our own spells like we did last night." Sarah knew immediately that she'd said too much. Claire's next question would be about that spell. Sarah looked at Shy hoping she'd jump in with an explanation. Sarah certainly didn't want to be caught trying to explain the spell she put on Claire.

"Yeah, Mom. Sarah and her grandmother put a spell on Ali, one to protect her."

"Protection's a little late, isn't it?" asked Claire.

"Protection isn't really the right word. It's more like a counter to the evil that's already in her body. In order to be really successful, we have to know what kind of spell has been sent to her."

"What? How many kinds are there?" inquired Andrea.

Dead Tones

"A spell can be mental, physical or spiritual. Mental is the most common; but because Allison's so sick and we don't know the source of the spell, Grandmother's trying to protect her with a physical spell that will counter the illness."

"I hope it works," added Claire.

Shy was relieved when Claire didn't push for more information. "I was wondering if the evil isn't from a fellow Cherokee, will this charm have any power?"

"Like I told you, it's a generic brand of medicine. We use it for everything."

"I think it's time for me to write a story about Cherokee medicine. Do you think your grandmother would talk to me?"

"I doubt it. She's pretty old fashioned. I guess it would depend on why she thought you wanted the information."

"Let's work on her." said Claire with a warm smile. "Good night, girls."

"Night, Mom."

Claire laid awake for a long time thinking about the last twenty-four hours. She'd certainly been living outside her daughter's circle. And Scott Krammer, good Lord, she'd certainly changed her mind about him. Last night, she didn't want to be in the same universe with the guy, and tonight she was holding his hand and promising to help clear his name. Wow. Things could certainly change quickly.

The list of suspects played over in her mind, and she admitted no one sounded like a good candidate for the murderer. There was Abby, her confession less than convincing; Kate and Megan didn't seem to have any possible motive; Scott was as much a victim as the girls, Sarah just wasn't the type to kill; and that was it. *Wait a minute. What about Jennifer? She certainly would've thrown daggers at me this morning if she could've gotten away with it.* Claire finally fell asleep wondering if someone really wanted to destroy Scott with an incriminating rumor. If a person could stir up enough raucous about him, including pregnancy and murder, the stories would certainly taint his reputation. This certainly wouldn't be the first time a teacher was hung by circumstantial evidence and insinuation rather than proof. *Poor Scott.*

CHAPTER EIGHT

Morning couldn't come fast enough for Scott. He'd spent the first dark hours praying for sleep and then waited impatiently for light. When he wasn't pining over the lost career and friendship, specifically Claire, he was cursing his family. He'd resigned himself years ago to the fact his father would eventually find him, but everyday he hoped he'd have more time. After twelve years, he dwelled less on the past and more on the possibility of a future. Maybe that's why this was so devastating. He'd let his guard down.

In the darkness, Scott let the years of obsessive dominance play over in his mind. The third of four children, Scott's early years were pleasurable enough. His father was busy creating his empire and abusing the older children. The old man tolerated only absolute compliance with his wishes. Anything else was grounds for severe punishment. With fear and dominance applied early enough, the children would never be strong enough to challenge him. That was the goal. The youngest brother, two years behind Scott, was a carbon copy of his father. He applied the same tactics on the school grounds that the father used at home and in the office. Scott was trapped between two who would not or could not fight against the old man and one who was every bit as evil. Only his mother offered him hope.

He remembered his mother's long blond hair floating in the summer breeze as she clipped roses from the garden. That was the mental picture he'd saved of his childhood. She had been his lifeline to decency; but when she died, there was no longer a reason to stay. In fact, the morning Scott found his mother laying in a pool of blood with her wrists slit, he left. Ran. Scott's mind played the long hours back for him, like reruns of an old movie. The running, as fast and as

Dead Tones

far as he could before grief and exhaustion made him collapse on the road. Then the tears raked his body until there was nothing left: no grief, no hate, no love. Scott walked away from his home and never returned.

Scott eventually ended up in Chicago where he managed to find a job and anonymity. Fortunately, he was tall even at sixteen and was able to pass for nineteen or twenty. His high school diploma was earned via night school, and college hadn't been so difficult. Scott worked his way through, studying late into the night or early in the morning. He kept a low profile all those years, no clubs, few friends, and no communications with any one from Charleston. Scott knew his father well enough to know he'd be searching for him. The man would want revenge. After all, Scott had committed the ultimate crime against the family: he'd managed to escape.

Scott had never considered his father might kill someone in order to destroy his son: but now that Sue was dead and Allison in a coma, Scott wasn't surprised. His father had often bragged at the dinner table about how some rival had conveniently disappeared. Scott never had the impression that it was a matter of convenience, but more a matter of his father's helping hand.

How could I have been so careless with these kids. I should have known he'd rather destroy me than kill me. What a fool I've been. Scott hated himself for the destruction he'd brought to the very thing he loved most in the world. *So if it's dear old dad, then how is he killing my kids?*

Scott forgot about the rumors. He was more concerned now about making sure no one else died before he got them all back to Tulsa. His goal now had to be their safety which would not be easy. Sunday's events were already in motion. After breakfast, the kids would be taken to the Dallas Zoo and then to Medieval Times for lunch and a show. The tickets had been paid for weeks ago, and the staff felt it would be good for the kids to spend the day together rather than going straight back to Tulsa. After all, only Scott, Claire, Trish and a few of the kids thought there was any connection between Allison and Sue. The doctor's final statement last night had been that Sue had most likely died from respiratory complications due to a viral infection. It would be several days before all the tox screens would be done. The family had requested Sue be sent back to Tulsa for an autopsy, so the ER doctor's educated guess was all they were going to get.

Scott threw back the covers and reached for his pants. Staying in this room wasn't going to provide him with any answers. Walking the hallways might be more advantageous. He needed to make sure no strangers were lurking about. Once he had the kids home safe and sound, he would resign and return to Charleston. There he might be able to call his father off the hunt. As far as answering for the two girls, he'd just have to wait and see. In the eyes of the law, his father should pay, but that would never happen. Scott would rather spend his life in prison than return to his father's grasp, but then that wouldn't satisfy the old man. He might continue killing just for revenge, just to prove Scott could never run far enough to truly be safe. Scott, absorbed in his own thoughts, left his room without noticing the person quickly moving around the corner.

In the lobby, Scott hunted for a telephone. He was surprised to see Claire standing at the first pay phone he came to. She gave him a 'good morning' wave and continued her conversation. What could he possibly say to her? Would she even believe the truth? She'd certainly have renewed grounds for hating him. Oh well, that was going to happen no matter what he said. Now he needed help with the kids.

Claire hung up the phone and turned to find Scott ordering a pot of really strong coffee and two cups from a bellman who'd come

Dead Tones

through the hallway. "I promise I'll make it worth your while if you bring it back steaming hot and absolutely river bottom black."

"Sure thing, sir," said the man. "Where will I find you?"

"We'll be sitting over there." Scott pointed to a secluded spot in the empty lobby.

Claire hadn't planned on being caught in the lobby and especially not by him. She was extremely embarrassed to be seen in literally nothing more than a T-shirt and jeans. Not wanting to wake the girls, she'd quickly brushed her hair and grabbed a key. She wanted to make a fast, very fast exit, but his ordering coffee for two made her doubtful as to whether or not she could get away. Maybe the coffee was for someone else. *That's it. I hope. Why would he order for two and why is he down here? He didn't know I was going to be here.* About the time Claire was sure she could make a quick get away, Scott turned from the bell man.

"Good morning. Did you get any rest?" he asked.

"Not much. I just came down to call the hospital. I think I'll go back and shower."

Scott hadn't noticed her bare feet or the fact that she obviously wasn't wearing a bra until she started for the elevator. "Can you wait? I ordered coffee for us. It might be all you get today."

She hesitated and then caught a glimpse of his bare toes wiggling beneath the hem of his trousers. "Oh, what the hell. How can I pass up the first offer of coffee?"

"What'd Sylvia have to say?"

"Well, she had good news and bad. The test results are still negative. The viral and bacterial cultures are negative. That still doesn't mean Allison couldn't have some kind of infection, but it isn't likely. All the early tox screens are negative too. If Allison took something intentionally, then it's something out of the ordinary. Blood has been sent to the Center for Disease Control in Atlanta and the state lab."

"Is that the bad news or the good news. I really can't tell," added Scott.

"I guess it depends on your point of view. Allison is still in a coma, but she's been stable since late last night. She's still breathing on her own and that's good." Claire thought for a minute about Sarah's spell and reached up to caress the charm still around her neck.

"What's that?" asked Scott.

"Sarah made all of us a protective Cherokee charm last night after you left. She made one for you too, but I didn't think you'd be down here so early."

Scott was surprised at Claire's superstitious nature. "I didn't think you'd be a believer in Indian magic."

"Neither did I, but then I've had lots of surprises the last two days."

"I don't think Sarah's charm can protect me from the evil." Before Claire could challenge him about his last statement, he moved on. "Did you find out if Allison's pregnant?"

"I asked, and Sylvia was certainly surprised at the question. No, Allison isn't pregnant and that's not just Sylvia's opinion. A pregnancy test was one of the first things the doctor did. She also told me about the boyfriend and why the girls have never met or seen him."

"Yes," Scott waited for her to continue.

"Well, I kind of promised Sylvia I wouldn't tell."

Scott almost dropped the issue, but then he had the most bizarre idea. What if Allison's boyfriend was somehow connected to his father? "I need to know."

"Why?" Claire wasn't going to betray a trust without a hell of a good reason, so she waited for Scott to explain.

Dead Tones

The conversation was interrupted by the bellman carrying a large tray which he placed on the table next to Scott. "Sorry it took me so long. I had to brew this stuff up special. None of the chefs in there know how to make 'river bottom black', but I knew what you was talkin' 'bout. You must be from somewhere along the Carolina coast, son."

"Yeah," said Scott looking at the man with the question resting on his lips.

"Ya don't sound like ya grew up round here. I can tell the locals. And not many folks use 'river bottom black' as a reference. But we used it where I come from. Small place near Moncks Corner, right where Lake Moultrie begins it's river run to the Atlantic."

Scott knew exactly where the old guy was talking about, but he was more familiar with the river's entrance into the Atlantic than where it left Lake Moultrie. Scott handed the man a twenty, told him to keep the change, and began pouring Claire a cup of steaming black coffee.

"Thank's a lot, mister. I could a wrestled ya up some bagels or som'thin' for this much money."

"Thanks, but it's not necessary. Go have a beer after work and count your blessings."

"I always do that."

"What?"

"Count my blessings. I don't drink anymore," said the man as he walked away.

Scott handed Claire a cup and poured himself one. He'd stalled long enough. She wasn't going to say another word until he'd explained, and it'd be easier now with no one around. Scott took a drink of the deep black liquid. "Wow, the old fart can really brew a cup of coffee. This stuff could kill a weaker man."

R. Z. Crompton

Claire enjoyed the aroma for a moment and then tipped the cup to her lips. She didn't say anything.

Scott began, "I think I know who would want to start a rumor with the intent of destroying me. There's only one person I'm terrified of and that's my father."

"Your father? Why?"

Without spilling all of the dirty family history, Scott tried to tell her only enough to make his story plausible. "I don't know how he's doing it, but I certainly know he's capable of such a thing. That's why I was wondering about Allison's boyfriend. He might be working for my father."

"I don't think so," answered Claire. No wonder he didn't talk about his past. What an incredulous story. She could verify most of it once she got back to her computer. In fact, if he really hadn't been in touch with his family in seventeen years or so, she could probably find out more than he knew himself.

"What makes you so sure the guy is for real? I thought nobody knew anything about him," said Scott as he refilled their cups.

"Trust me. There's a very good reason."

"Please, Claire, be a little more specific."

"Ali has known this man for many years and so has Sylvia. Sylvia isn't exactly crazy about the idea, but she understands the need for secrecy."

Scott was getting impatient with her beating around the bush. "Claire, give me a break. I swear I won't tell anybody; so, please, just tell me who this secret joker is."

The admonishment was offensive, but it gave Claire an honest look at how desperate he felt. "Do you really think your father would want to track you down after so many years?"

"Yes, Claire. I broke his rule of absolute obedience. There's no mercy."

Dead Tones

"Why did you go into teaching? Why did you stay so long?"

"Believe me, I know how stupid I've been. I should've joined the French Foreign Legion or a drilling rig in Saudi Arabia. Now my students are the victims of my past. All I can do is try and find out who's doing this and then leave town. My career is over, but I don't want to just leave. I owe these people too much."

Claire respected his commitment to clean up this incredible mess, but she still wondered how much of what he was telling her was the truth and how much was his imagination. The further she went with the conversation the more she doubted the whole story. This man, who was near sainthood yesterday, is definitely tarnished material today. "Where will you go?"

"I have to go back," said Scott looking into her eyes. She was skeptical and he didn't blame her. "I have to face him and the family."

A little melodramatic, Scott. You must've taken lessons from Abby last night. "So why do you need to know the identity of Allison's boyfriend?"

"Somebody's gotten close enough to poison Allison and Sue. I haven't seen any strangers in the band room. He's the only one I can't account for."

"I don't think so," snapped Claire. "Allison's boyfriend is the Youth Minister at her church. They've kept the relationship a secret because he could lose his job if the members find out he's been having an affair with one of the students."

"He should. A minister? How can Sylvia condone Allison's actions?" Scott sounded more like a hurt father than a teacher.

"Actually, I wondered the same thing. But the guy is only a few years older than Allison and they've known each other for years. They were neighbors, grew up just down the street from each other. It's really not so strange that they could be in love. As soon as Allison graduates, they are going to get married. He has already applied for a transfer. They'd like to start their married life away from this church."

"Man, I don't blame them for that. The guy's respect will be down the tubes if he stays here."

"I thought you of all people would be more understanding."

"Why? I never played with one of my students," said Scott in self-defense.

"Yeah, I know. You always left town to play. But your wisdom hasn't kept you from being a victim." She was beginning to lose her patience with this man. "If Allison was poisoned because of you, her boyfriend had nothing to do with it."

"Okay, okay," answered Scott feeling ashamed of himself and his family. "I still think there has to be someone who's helping my father."

"So your father moves to the top of the list. We aren't any better off than we were last night," said Claire flatly. She was confused about him and her feelings for him. His story certainly answered several of the questions she'd had about him, but his tale of woe wasn't exactly what she'd expected. "I've got to get cleaned up." She finished the last of her coffee and left Scott sitting alone.

Scott followed her out of the lobby until he was close enough to grab her by the arm. Claire spun around to face him. "Claire, don't underestimate the power or determination of my family."

"Or yours?" she said staring at the vise-like grip he had on her arm."

"That's not fair," said Scott softly and removing his hand.

"The truth isn't always fair, now is it?" Her words stung as much as if she'd slapped him.

As she walked away, Scott found himself wondering if maybe there was more of his father in him than he'd ever been willing to admit. But then he was going to have to be as devious as his father if he was going to get out of this mess without ending up in jail. Scott

Dead Tones

watched the elevator doors close. Claire never looked back. *Well that friendship was short and sweet. Thanks, Dad, you never cease fuckin' up my life.*

Kate came around the corner of the hallway slamming into Scott from behind, "Oh, Mr. Krammer, what are you doing here?"

"Falling off a horse," said Scott imagining a white knight covered in mud. *You're pretty full of yourself, Krammer, to even think you could ever be someone's...a woman's hero. Shit I've been teaching too long. My perspective is warped.*

Scott never heard Kate's first reaction to his ridiculous horse comment, so she grabbed his arm and asked, "Mr. Krammer, you okay?"

"Oh, Kate. What are you doing up so early?"

"I had to call my dad right at six. He wanted to know how we did yesterday."

"And what did he have to say when you told him about Sue?"

"Just exactly what you'd expect. 'I'm sorry' and all that crap. It was hard to explain the emotions we shared and why we went ahead and marched finals."

"Has your dad ever gone on a trip with us?"

"Nope."

"Then I suppose it is hard to make him understand how we feel. At least, he likes you to call with the results. There's lots of parents who just don't care. You're pretty lucky."

"Yeah, I guess so. When's breakfast? I'm starvin'."

"It'll still be another hour or so. You could go back to bed."

"Na, I'll just hang around here." Kate watched Scott until the elevator doors closed. She'd watched him argue with Mrs. Mayfield and wondered if the stupid woman had screwed up again.

*****

Claire fumed all the way to her room. She was as angry at herself for feeling sorry for the idiot as she was at him for being in such a mess. Scott should've faced his father years ago. No wonder he never had a serious relationship let alone got married. He never knew when he'd have to pick up and run. Now he was running again. Rather than stay and fight for the life he'd created here, he was going home to do the job he should've put to rest years ago. How bad can one man be? The door slammed behind her before she even realized she'd unlocked it.

Shy jumped instantly to a sitting position, "What? Ahh, what's wrong? Who's there?"

"Sorry, dear...I...ah..." Claire wasn't sure what to say. Repeating the last few words of her conversation with Scott wouldn't help. In fact, she doubted if they'd believe her. Scott Krammer was still their hero and unless he told them about his past himself, they'd never accept it as truth. "I went down to call the hospital."

Andrea and Sarah instantly joined Shy in a sitting position and waited for the report. "Mom, you could'a called from here. We all want to know how Ali is."

"I wanted you to sleep as long as possible," said Claire.

"So you slam the door when you came back?" asked Shy cocking her head and waiting for a response. She knew her mother well, and slamming doors reminded her of the days when her mom and dad argued.

Claire decided to ignore her observant daughter's last question and to proceed with the report about Allison's condition.

Shy was the first to analyze the information, "So, this is good? Right? Ali's not pregnant, the boyfriend is identified, and she's stable. That means Mr. Krammer's off the hook and the doctors will have time to find out what's wrong with her."

Dead Tones

"Slow down a little. Sylvia told me it could be weeks before the doctors can identify the exact poison," said Claire.

"Weeks? You gotta be kidding!" shrieked Andrea.

"Nope. It's a long process. The doctor will test for the most obvious toxins and work their way from there. The more exotic the poison the longer the identification process," added Claire.

"Wow," sighed ShyAnne, "but at least we can take Mr. Krammer off the list. Right?"

When Claire didn't offer a quick nod of agreement, Shy asked again more forcefully, "right, Mom?"

Shy, why do you have to keep pushing this issue? "We know he's not her boyfriend." Claire didn't want to lead them on, but she had to say something. There was a good chance all the kids would find out more about *St. Krammer* than they wanted to know. Maybe there was a good side to the lesson: this man they continued to idolize was just a man. However, he's not guilty of his father's sins. *Remember this, you idiot,* Claire admonished herself. *Scott Krammer still hasn't done anything wrong except have a rotten father, and again the old cliche is proven true: you can choose your friends but not your relatives.*

"So the rumors we heard are stupid?" Again Shy was waiting for her mother to exonerate Mr. Krammer.

"Yes, but Sylvia asked us not to say anything about Allison's boyfriend."

"You're not serious? How are we gonna save Mr. Krammer if we can't give the identification of the real boyfriend," snapped Sarah.

"Girls, you don't have to say anything about a boyfriend cause she's not pregnant. It doesn't matter. Just defend Mr. Krammer. You don't need a name."

"Mom, you, of all people, know it adds credence to the story if you have all the facts. We'd have to do a lot less talking if we could use the guy's name."

"You can't. For now you're gonna have to sing a song of defense without a name," said Claire.

"Why?" Shy's question was short and direct.

"Because using a name could destroy another person's life. Allison has a legitimate reason for wanting anonymity. Girls, there's a lot more to this story than you realize. Just remember how strongly you feel about Mr. Krammer. Focus on what a good friend and teacher he's been. I have a funny feeling he's gonna need all the friends he can muster. I'm going to shower quick and go find breakfast." Claire walked into the bathroom closing the door behind her.

"Shy, what was that all about?" asked Sarah.

"How should I know?"

"She's your mother," responded Andrea.

"My guess is that she's found out something she's not willing to share."

"No shit, Sherlock. We know that much. So go in there and find out what it is." Sarah nodded her head toward the door.

"Me!"

"Yeah, you. We certainly can't follow her into the bathroom. You could fake it. Tell her you gotta pee. Then don't leave 'til she spills the beans," suggested Andrea.

Shy reluctantly got out of bed and headed for the closed door. "I'll go, but no promises. If she's not ready to talk then she's just not gonna talk, and I could be sitting there all day."

"Gee, that's too bad. I hear the Dallas Zoo is great," declared Sarah.

"You're a lot of help and a bucket of laughs," snipped Shy as she knocked on the door.

****

Dead Tones

The monotonous tone of the heart monitor was the only sound emanating from Allison's room. A soft yellow light kept the darkness from becoming as overwhelming as the silence between the man and woman sitting beside the bed.

An overly endowed nurse in her reflective white uniform tiptoed quietly into the room. "Mrs. Hayes, I'm sorry to bother you, but some lady called. She claims she really needs to speak with you. I tried to dissuade her, but she was absolutely insistent about speaking with you."

"It's okay. I told her to call." Sylvia kissed the limp hand she'd been cradling tenderly and laid it at Allison's side. "I'll be right back, honey." The wood and vinyl hospital chair scraped against the white linoleum floor when Sylvia stood up to follow the over starched uniform to the telephone.

The phone call lasted several minutes giving Philip some privacy with his daughter. He'd been waiting for hours to speak to her, but Sylvia hadn't left the room. Philip moved into the seat Sylvia had vacated to be closer to his daughter's inert body. He wanted to hold her hand and whisper the fatherly things he should've said years ago. "Allison, Ali, honey, I'm so sorry. Please forgive me for...for everything...for just never being what you needed in a father. I can change. Please give me a chance. Please, please, please..." he cried quietly into the soft, slender fingers.

The wasted years of isolation haunted him. He loved Sylvia and Allison the only way he knew how. The same as he'd seen his father do all those years ago. He'd never resented Sylvia for getting pregnant. After all, she hadn't done it alone. He was as much to blame as she was. He'd been angry at himself for giving in to his passion in the back seat of his car. If he'd had any forethought, he'd have at least rented a motel room in order to give that first and very costly event some respect. For some reason, he'd never been able to get the feeling of disgrace out of his mind. He'd disgraced Sylvia and himself by turning their innocent love into a cheap romp in the back seat of that damn car, which he sold as soon as he'd gotten a full time job. All these years Sylvia had assumed he resented her when he was more ashamed of himself than anything else. If he'd been more careful, more level headed, not so damn stupid or horny, the two of them would have had a very different life. Philip had always planned on marrying Sylvia, but he would have waited until after college when he was established in his father's business. Too established for his father to kick him out. When he and Sylvia moved so quickly from back seat passion into the confines of married life, his father had not only thrown him out of the very profitable family business, he banished both of them from the family as well. Philip had kicked himself many times over for not considering the consequences of their premature passion.

Neither of them had come from particularly loving families, and he knew Sylvia didn't really miss her father, but he suspected being cut off from her mother and brother was hard on her. The lack of family ties created a rather hollow feeling from time to time. Sylvia's mother had died years ago, and her father hadn't even called to tell her. Philip remembered the private sobs he'd heard in the bathroom as Sylvia grieved the loss. Her miserable, old son of a bitch of a father still lived in that god awful shack out in one of the coves on Lake Keystone. No, Philip was sure that no matter how bad their life seemed to be, Sylvia knew it was better than her mother's had been.

As for his own family, Philip hadn't crossed the family threshold since the night he'd told his parents Sylvia was pregnant and they were getting married. Philip hated his father for being so pompous and his mother for being too weak to stand up to him. He also hated the man for being such a rotten role model. At eighteen, Philip had become a husband and father in the only fashion he knew, just like his father. He became withdrawn, judgmental, and overbearing. He'd grown up around a dinner table just like the one he sat at now, only now he was the asshole at the head of the table. Until last night when Sylvia had handed him a platter

Dead Tones

of reality, he hadn't realized he'd become a carbon copy of his own father.

Philip had spent the last twelve hours evaluating his sad existence. He had lived the first eighteen years of his life being the center of attention for nearly every activity he participated in. His father expected him to be the best in everything he touched; and, fortunately, Philip had the ability to shine in everything from school work and sports to community service.

The next eighteen years had been spent as a failure. He'd lived in world of self inflicted shame. Sylvia thought he'd been in a prison with walls she'd constructed, but the walls had actually been put in place by his own sense of disgrace. By emulating his father in parenting and living behind his own walls of isolation, he'd alienated the only two people he loved. It wasn't what he wanted and he certainly didn't want Allison's life to end with her not knowing how much he loved her.

Allison's illness, if that's what it was, had cruelly given him the opportunity to examine his life and change, if he had the strength. The next eighteen years didn't have to be a repeat of the past. He may not have the chance to love Allison the way he wanted, but he did have time to love Sylvia, that is if she gave him the time. *I owe her her freedom if she wants it. Syl is only thirty-seven. She has time to start over if she wants to.* "Oh, Allison, come back to me, baby. Come back to me."

Sylvia, standing just outside the door, heard the last part of Philip's gut wrenching plea. She agonized for him and with him. To interrupt him now would only embarrass him and stifle the emotional cleansing. It was too early to hope he'd really change; and if Allison didn't make it, there was no reason to. Sylvia knew she'd never stay with him if Allison didn't go home with them. In fact, she wouldn't go back to the house at all. She waited.

Philip cleared his throat and wiped the tears from his eyes in anticipation of Sylvia's return. The soft amber light would camouflage his red, swollen eyes when she sat down beside him. She was going to have to take the seat at the foot of the bed. He wasn't going to give up the time he had to hold the soft fingers. Eighteen years of holding needed to be done tonight.

Sylvia slipped quietly back into the room. She'd been disappointed at the lack of information Claire had for her. Actually, Claire had more questions than facts, and her insinuations of a murder were chilling. Sylvia stood by the bed for a moment waiting for Philip to return to his seat, but he didn't move. She grew irritated at his possessive claim to Allison's hand. Finally, she sat in the chair next to him.

"So how'd they do?"

"What?" Sylvia was startled by the interruption into her thoughts.

"That was someone from the band?"

"Yes, I'd asked Claire Mayfield to call if she found out anything that might help us," answered Sylvia.

"And?"

"Susan Walsch is dead," said Sylvia. She pronounced the words slowly and deliberately as if she didn't believe what they'd meant when Claire had first told her, as if she needed to hear them again to understand the significance.

"Who's that?"

"Allison's her nemesis. Sue has been trying to take first chair away from Ali for three years, but Ali held on to the coveted position in spite of Sue's desire. Allison told me about Sue's constant challenge to beat her some day, but time was running out. Allison's graduation this spring would put an end to the rivalry."

"I bet Ali'll be relieved to be finished with it," responded Philip.

"Not really. Allison admired Sue's talent and tenacity. Sue was a nuisance, but she made Allison a better player. Ali will be devastated when she find's out Sue is dead."

"What happened?"

"Claire said the doctors aren't sure. They won't know 'til the body is sent back here for an autopsy. But her symptoms were a lot like Ali's.

Dead Tones

The poor girl thought she had the flu. She played the solo Allison was supposed to play and then died on the way to the hospital. Oh, Phil," Sylvia sighed, "that could've been Ali. I guess we are better off here."

"Yeah, at least we still have hope. Did she say anything else?"

"Claire asked several questions about Allison. They're trying to find a connection between the two girls."

"Who are 'they'?" asked Philip turning away from the bed to look directly at Sylvia.

"Claire Mayfield, who took my spot as a sponsor, and Scott Krammer, one of the teachers."

"What are they trying to find?"

"Something, anything that will explain what's happened to our girl," said Sylvia softly. She was surprised at her use of *our*. This was the closest she'd felt to Philip in years. There hadn't been an equal give and take conversation between them for as long as she could remember. After years of orders and criticism, she'd forgotten that once upon a time they had shared vibrant conversation.

"I think you're right. Allison might have been sick, but with two girls down, I guess we'd better accept the fact that someone's intentionally doing this. What about the police? Why don't we call them?"

"Cause there's nothing to go on, but our gut feeling. Even the doctors can't tie the two girls together yet. They don't even know if Sue was murdered."

"You're right. We have to make sure one of us is here all the time. What about the young man who came by last night? He's not just her minister, is he?"

Sylvia wasn't sure how to answer. She's never given Philip much credit for being observant. "What makes you say that?"

"He was too upset, and you were too quick to get me out of the room. I wasn't aware of the need for privacy during prayer. How serious are they and how old is the guy."

"Well, he's her fiance, and he's twenty-five."

"Should I be happy for Allison, or should I just want to kill him?"

"Some of both I guess. He's taking my baby away from me, but he's a wonderful young man."

"How long have they been seeing each other?"

"Two years, more or less. Davis grew up a few blocks away from us, so they've known each other for a long time."

"Davis? Davis Mahoney, the tall, clumsy kid who mowed the lawn for me?"

"The very one. And they both give you all the credit for bringing them together."

"Oh, thanks. You're saying it's my fault they met?"

"Well, I didn't hire him. You did that all by yourself. In Davis's defense, though, he's a great guy and he does love her. Ya know, they're smarter than we were."

"That's not hard," admitted Philip. "A minister's life, huh?" He stopped thinking about what would be in store for them. "They'll never have much."

"It's not the *things* that make the marriage," said Sylvia looking heavy-heartedly at Allison's inert form.

Philip knew she was insinuating that he tried to buy her family life rather than give her and Allison the time they'd wanted and needed. *So I'm a jerk. I can't change the last eighteen years, but I can change the future.* "You're right, and we'll be there to help them. Has he told his folks yet or his boss? I don't suppose it's kosher for a minister to marry one of his students."

Sylvia was surprised at his gesture of kinship. "I think Davis agrees with you. As far as I know he hasn't told anyone but me. He's applied for a transfer though."

"A transfer? To where?"

Dead Tones

"Does it matter? Davis didn't think the church would be real supportive of his obviously clandestine rendezvous over the last two years," offered Sylvia.

"No, I suppose not," sighed Philip. "Ya know, if his family or the church, for that matter, throws him out because of Allison it will be just like what our families did to us. Is she pregnant?"

"Would it make a difference?" she waited skeptically for his response.

Philip thought silently about the question and how he'd felt when his father and mother had been so shocked at his announcement. "It would've mattered yesterday when I was pretending to be my father because he was the only image I had on which to base fatherhood. Stupid, huh?" Philip didn't wait for an answer. "Today, nothing matters but having my daughter back. I don't care if she's pregnant and marrying a little green man with two antennae sticking out of his head. I'd be happy just to walk her down the aisle."

Sylvia smiled in agreement, "Yeah, me too. I think Allison was afraid you'd hate her for falling in love with an older man."

"Older man? Shit, he's still a kid to me." Philip heard the subtle *humph* come from the woman sitting next to him. "Okay, so he's taller than I am and his voice is ten octaves lower than it was when he was mowing the lawn. I can't help it, he's still a kid to me."

"I'm glad you can think of him that way. I don't think the church is going to be that understanding."

"I thought that was the church's job. If they can't forgive their own, how can they forgive anyone else?"

"I don't know, Phil. And I'm not sure what the kids are planning to do."

"Sylvia, I don't want them to leave town."

"Then tell them when you have the chance."

******

R. Z. Crompton

Sean, glad to get out of the room, pushed the down button for the elevator as Jason came up behind him. It had been a long night with Mike pissing and moaning for hours about how irrational females were before falling asleep.

"What crawled up his butt and died?" Jason asked as the two of them stepped onto the elevator. "He was a son of a bitch all night."

"He and Krissy had a fight last night," said Sean.

"Is that all? He's been a shithead to us cause of a girl?" asked Jason.

"Yeah, well in case you haven't noticed, his life has pretty much revolved around that girl for two years.

"He leaves for school in a few months, so they were bound to break up anyway. What's the big deal?"

"Why? High school couples have been known to make it."

"Yeah, they're fools. College is a time to live it up. Who'd want to be shackled to a girl already?"

"Life doesn't end when you get a steady girlfriend."

"A steady girl and a wife are two different animals. One's a freebie and the other's a blood sucker."

"You're the kinda jerk who gives the rest of us a bad name. One date with you and a girl thinks we're all a bunch of sex crazed idiots."

"You and Mike have spent too much time hangin' around those four females. You're both pussy whipped. Do you really think Monica's gonna keep you around after graduation? You'd better plug into reality. She's outta here along with the other three. College is as much a play ground for them as it is for us. It's like the ultimate pizza supreme: a little bit of everything."

"You're full of shit, Jason," spit Sean just as the elevator doors opened. He couldn't wait to get out.

"You don't get it do ya? How can you pick a mate for life when ya aren't even a man yet? You don't know what you're gonna do, where

Dead Tones

you're gonna live. You don't even know what kind a guy you're gonna end up being, how can you know what kind of woman you want?"

Sean didn't say a word. He hated to admit that Jason had some logic to his chauvinistic mentality. Sean remembered how much Alex, his older brother, and later his cousins had changed between high school and college. Sean had spent months feeling cut off from the big brother who'd been the fun loving, party animal. When job hunting started, the teenage boy became a serious young man; and Sean didn't appreciate his brother's metamorphic transformation mainly because he hadn't understood why he felt alienated from the one person he admired the most. Suddenly Alex was closer to their father. They talked about jobs, new cities, insurance plans and a variety of other topics which were boring to Sean. Their relationship was never the same. Alex had turned into a clone of their father right before Sean's eyes. As far as Sean was concerned, his big brother was gone forever.

Oh well, graduation was still months away and he wanted to enjoy his senior year with his friends. There'd be plenty of time to worry about the future after May 12th. And Mike should do the same thing. Sean and Jason entered the dining room without conversation to find several sponsors already enjoying the hot coffee and fresh orange juice.

"Good morning, boys," said Jessica, Monica's mother.

"Good morning, Mrs. Wynthrop. When will Monica be down?" asked Sean. He felt anxious now to set things straight with her. He was sure her mother knew they'd argued the night before. Mrs. Wynthrop never missed a conversation, and what she didn't know for sure, she made up using body language and innuendo.

"It'll be a while. When I left the room, she was just rolling over. Krissy was still in another cosmic realm. They were up pretty late."

"Yeah, I bet they had a lot to talk about," said Sean.

"As a matter of fact, you and Mike seemed to occupy most of their conversation," replied Jessica with an all knowing smile on her face.

R. Z. Crompton

"I guess I'm not surprised." Sean didn't want to discuss his and Monica's disagreement with her mother of all people. Mrs. Wynthrop was a sweetheart of a mom, but privacy was not one of her assets. He knew she'd say almost anything to get a rise out of him and then discuss the whole thing with anyone at her table. Changing the subject to something non threatening was the best thing he could do to save him and Monica from becoming table talk. "So why are we still going to the zoo?"

"Cause all the arrangements have been made," offered Jessica.

"I think we should be going home," suggested Sean.

"Me too," added Jason. "How can we have fun after what happened to Sue?"

"Dale thinks it'll be good for all of us to spend some time winding down. We talked about it for a long time last night. You can do more healing together than separately at home."

"Mr. B.'s a band director not a shrink," said Jason.

"He's more of a shrink than you give him credit for. He has to be to enjoy working with two hundred teenagers year after year. Besides, most of the parents agree with him," stated Jessica.

The conversation was interrupted when the kitchen doors were bumped open and hot dishes of scrambled eggs, hash browns and French toast were wheeled out to be placed on the buffet table. Waiters followed with trays of fresh fruit and muffins. Breakfast was on, and the boys wanted to be the first in line.

Girls began to trickle into the dining room. Some were freshly showered with hair and make-up perfectly done. Others were slightly less inhibited and came to eat in their pajamas. The showering routine was one freshmen caught on to quickly, and it lasted through their senior year. You either showered first and ate late or came down in PJ's and cleaned up in the second wave. Those who didn't adjust to one side or the other had a long wait 'til lunch.

Dead Tones

Krissy and Monica were normally members of the dressed and primped group coming down just as the waiters were beginning to clean up the tables. This morning, however, Krissy wasn't ready to see Mike; and she assumed he'd be looking for her to come in with the stragglers. Dressed in blue and red flannel pants and a stretched-out, over worn T-shirt with a faded Mt. Rushmore on the front, Krissy headed for the breakfast line. The sausage, which was usually long gone by the time she and Monica came down, tantalized her taste buds. Krissy hadn't realized what she'd been missing the last few years.

Monica, dressed similarly to her partner, was still trying to get her contacts to focus. She was more concerned about the sleep she was giving up than the food laid out in front of her, but she picked up a plate anyway placing a single muffin in the middle of it. She was still too sleepy to be embarrassed about her appearance, but her mother wasn't.

Sean had smiled when their eyes met. He didn't care how she was dressed: pajamas or potato sack. He just wanted to set things straight before her mother or some friend blew everything out of proportion. The last thing he wanted was for her to perpetuate the fight between them just to give Krissy moral support. Krissy and Mike had to deal with their own problems.

Sean had been the lead snare drummer the last two years, and he enjoyed the responsibility and the attention. If his beat was off even half a second, the synchronized pulse of the drumline and, therefore, the entire band was lost. For every hour the band practiced, the drumline added another. Rhythms and cadences thumped continuously through Sean's mind. He even brushed his teeth to the rhythmic tap of his foot. He'd been this way for as long as he could remember with anything and everything becoming a drumstick or a drum. Sean didn't want to make a living with his drumsticks, but he'd always have the urge to play. The short term goal was to play for the Aggie marching band at Texas A&M, the best marching band in the world. Then he could satisfy his habit by playing on the weekends for the church or in a little combo somewhere, it really didn't matter. Beating the drums was a stress release, like shopping was for Monica. There was no desire to teach or play for a living. Sean was going to return to Tulsa and take over the family business. He was proud of the strong family tie and the architect firm started by his grandfather. His father was excited about Sean adding a third generation to the firm as soon as he graduated.

Sean wanted Monica to go with him to A&M, but she was hesitant because the school was so incredibly large. Even though ShyAnne was planning to attend, Monica was still dragging her feet about leaving home. Jessica didn't want her baby girl to grow up. Sean was afraid Monica would never be out from under her mother's influence. He wondered if he loved her enough to be married to both of them because Jessie would certainly have her nose in their business. But Jess liked him, and for the most part she was okay.

Sean remembered back to the Saturday morning over a year ago when they all took the SAT test together. The anxiety was high and even though they'd taken several practice runs, there was no way to de-stress the event that would dictate their future. They knew the lowest score needed for their school of choice, the score needed to be in scholarship range and the score they were hoping for. Monica's score had been the lowest of the six. She'd met entrance requirements for A&M but not the scholarship range; and even though Sean knew money was not a problem for her family, without a scholarship, he doubted she'd leave the state.

Krissy was the only one who didn't share her score with the others. It was odd, she didn't seem upset about a low score, but then she didn't brag about a high one either. In fact, Krissy never said much about her grades at all. She studied with the rest of them. Generally she was doing the explaining when there was confusion about a problem; however, she was always the last to offer help. If any of the others could add insight, she kept her mouth shut. On the other hand, Sean never remembered

Dead Tones

Krissy asking for help. Monica wouldn't have made it through advanced chemistry without Krissy's help. Sean got the feeling Krissy was a lot more intelligent than Mike realized, and that was most of their problem. He caught himself wondering about Krissy's class rank as his eyes followed the two girls to the table furthest away.

Krissy and Monica chose a table off in the corner away from the crowd. Their desire to be inconspicuous was short lived because Sarah and ShyAnne spotted them right away. Monica saw Shy tilt her head in their direction and the others followed her. It wouldn't have been so bad if they hadn't all taken the time to clean up. Now that Monica was fully awake, she was embarrassed. Most of the kids left their modesty at home when they went on a band trip. Hours of sleeping on a bus made them victims of bed-head, bad breath and smeared eye make-up, but this was different. She'd had the choice but let Krissy whine her into coming down for breakfast early. Monica had seen her mother's look of disapproval, and she was certain the mother's lecture would be given in due time. The last person she'd expect to see was at the table next to the buffet line. There was no way she could have escaped his line of vision. This would definitely go down in her book as one of her most embarrassing moments. She'd returned his smile as a natural reflex. She couldn't help it. He smiled as much with his eyes as he did his lips. Once she was cleaned up, she would find him again and, preferably, without the jerk Jason hanging around.

Claire and her entourage, made up for the day, came into the large dining room to find several tables beautifully set with white tablecloths, silver and crystal. It was a pleasant alternative to eating subways on the street curb. Large brocade curtains had been drawn to reveal bright sunshine and clear blue skies. Claire was sure the beauty of the day belied the true temperature. Most of the tables were occupied now by a half dozen people or more. A hearty laugh filtered in here and there to break up the fairly subdued atmosphere.

R. Z. Crompton

After being caught in only jeans and a T-shirt and barely a brush through her hair, Claire wasn't about to leave her room again until she was properly attired. She was wearing the second outfit she'd bought the day before at Caché. The chocolate brown stirrup pants with matching black and brown turtle neck had an elegant angora and mink trimmed jacket waiting upstairs. Her soft brown curls had a new freshly washed bounce to them, and the crows feet easily detected this morning were more difficult to spot now that the earthtone eyeshadows and eyeliner accented the color and depth of her hazel eyes.

Jeans were the accepted dress code for the kids. Straight-legged or bell-bottom, high-waisted or hip-hugger in every imaginable shade of blue could be seen in the room. Shy, Sarah and Andrea were no exception in their dress blues; however, there was an added element to their attire. A carefully wrapped, Cherokee good luck charm was in each girl's pocket. Claire wore hers around her neck. When she was dressing, she'd tried to convince herself that the charm was silly; but in the end, she admitted she'd also been spooked by all of Sarah's talk about evil spirits. Deciding there was no harm in wearing the charm, she'd carefully tied it around her neck and tucked it under the collar of her sweater.

Shy and Sarah had quickly filled their plates with French toast and headed for Krissy's table. The fact that they'd gorged on pizza just a few hours ago didn't seem to daunt their morning appetite. Claire was amazed as she watched them spread on the butter, add a layer of strawberries, and then drown the pile in maple syrup. Claire was satisfied with a couple pieces of fruit and a croissant to soak up the caffeine from the strong coffee Scott had given her earlier. Her thoughts were still focused on the conversation she'd had with him in the lobby. She found herself second guessing her original idea that he was paranoid about his father with absolutely no proof. She'd nearly accused him of being as melodramatic as Abby had been. Now Claire chastised herself for being so narrow minded. Something terrible must have happened to Scott as a child for

Dead Tones

him to up and leave his family and to still be so afraid of his father. Just because she'd never known anyone who could be so evil certainly didn't mean it didn't happen. All she had to do was watch the nightly news or read a Time magazine to find out that some monster had tried to possess or control another person to the point of destruction. The reasons were varied, but the pain was always the same.

Claire knew she had the resources to help Scott find out the current status of his family. By midnight she could be plugged into her computer gleaning through the pages of the Charleston paper. Her question now was whether or not to invite Scott to join her in the search. She'd think about it.

Andrea had not gotten much rest and it showed on her face. The girls' conversation had played on her imagination all night. When she wasn't dreaming about someone trying to kill her, she was hearing strange noises in the hallway. When they'd left the room, she walked so close to Claire that Claire wasn't sure if it was her hand in her pocket or Andrea's. Claire felt sorry for the girl and was half tempted to put her on an airplane back to Tulsa, so she wouldn't have to worry about being next on someone's death list. Claire watched what Andrea put on her plate. It was going to be her job to make sure Andrea got home safely. Claire admitted putting Andrea on a plane would give her as much peace of mind as it did Andrea. On the other hand, no one in Tulsa, with the exception of Sylvia, was aware of any danger. In the end, Claire figured Andrea was safer staying with her.

As the two of them followed Shy to join Krissy and Monica, Claire planned some protective strategy. "Andrea, please don't take anything from anyone today. No candy, gum, even a glass of water. Okay?"

"Absolutely, Claire."

"I'll get you anything you need."

"Are you going to take the first bite too?"

Claire wasn't amused at her humor. "If you don't take anything I don't give you, I won't have to take the first bite."

"What about this stuff?" Andrea, wondering if she'd ever be hungry again, looked down at her plate.

"I think this is okay. Nobody in the kitchen knows us."

"Oh, yeah," sighed Andrea as she set her plate down on the table and pulled out a chair.

Shy and Sarah were already sitting beside Monica and Krissy, but there was an uneasy silence among the four. Shy and Sarah weren't used to keeping secrets from their two friends, but they couldn't discuss the conversation they'd had last night. Asking Monica about her unusual state of attire didn't seem like such a good idea at the moment either. So Claire assumed the lack of conversation had something to do with finding a safe topic. Anything would be better than this awkward calm.

"Good morning, ladies," offered Claire.

"Hey, Mrs. Mayfield," responded Krissy sounding almost jovial after her tearful exit last night. Monica barely looked up from her plate to acknowledge the arrival of her friends.

Leave it to Andrea to break the ice. "Krissy, have you talked to Mike yet? Did you guys make-up?"

"No, I haven't talked to him," said Krissy sounding rather matter of factly about the thought.

"So you gonna make-up?" persisted Andrea.

"I don't know. I guess it depends on the conditions."

"What conditions?" questioned Shy.

"I was really upset last night, but then I started really thinking about our future. I want to have fun this year, but Mike's getting so possessive. I just want to be friends again like we were, but I'm afraid he won't understand. I don't want to break up and be enemies; on the other hand, I don't want to lead him on," explained Krissy.

"Why would you be leading him on?" asked Shy.

Dead Tones

"Because our futures are totally different. He's going to teach school, and I'm going to Wall Street."

"Are you suggesting that teaching and finance don't go together, or are you just trying to politely say that a spouse who teaches isn't good enough for you?" asked Sarah.

"I don't care if the man I love collects garbage. Mike wants to come back here; I don't.

"So why can't he teach in New York?"

"He could, Shy, if he wanted to, but there's more to it than that. He doesn't respect me now. What makes you think he'll take me seriously in four years?"

"He doesn't respect you now because you've ahh...never been like totally honest about your grades or your goals," said Shy mocking Krissy's ditzy blond routine.

"She's right, Krissy," said Sarah. "How'd you ever get caught up in that stupid blond routine anyway?"

"When I was younger, that's how I was treated, so I believed it. After spending lots of time with my grandfather, I learned I wasn't so stupid. With a little effort, my grades started going up, but I already had the dumb blond reputation. As my grades improved, I realized that guys didn't like it when I did a lot better than they did. So instead of letting my grades go down, I just let the ditzy blond girl co-exist with the smart one. No one with blond hair and boobs is supposed to have a brain," sighed Krissy. "Do you have any idea how many times Mike came up to me and said 'hey, honey, you're nippin' out. It's like I didn't even have a face."

The other girls snickered. "Krissy, they're all like that. I'm amazed they can even walk down the hallway without falling over." laughed Shy.

"That's for sure. I think they walk down the hallway with little antennae protruding out of their heads as they search anything and everything with a lumpy chest. Then some jerk announces to the entire school body 'gee Angela's nippin' out'," said Sarah. "as if we're supposed to have some control over what our nipples decide to do at any given moment."

This time the laughs were louder and Claire tried to control herself, but she was truly amused at this uninhibited teenage banter. She found herself agreeing in principle with their point of view.

"It's a testosterone thing. The greater the level of testosterone, the lower the brain power," offered Sarah.

"I wonder," said Shy looking around to see who might be listening, "if we walked up to Jason and said your sausage is sticking up, what he'd do?"

"Sausage? He wishes he could be so lucky. Weenie is more like it," snapped Sarah. This time the giggles exploded into raw, gut laughter and Claire was not immune. She hadn't shared in such a medley of girl talk in years. Even Monica, as quiet as she'd been, couldn't ignore the hilarious comment. The table became the center of attention as everyone in the room stopped their own conversations to look at the roaring women. Tears filled their eyes and threatened to ruin all the finely placed eyeliner, but the belly laughs felt good after the tension of last night. Less than twelve hours ago, the majority of this group was in tears of mourning. Time and friends could heal most wounds. Then she found herself wondering about the pain Scott must have suffered for it to have lasted so long. He had friends now, but he still had all the pain. He'd tried to tell her; however, she didn't want to hear. Maybe she hadn't wanted the white knight to fall off the unstable horse.

When the laughter subsided, Shy became serious again, "Why don't you try telling Mike the truth?"

"He doesn't want the truth. He wants a good looking girl to hang on his every word. Someone who thinks he's the center of the universe."

Dead Tones

"Yeah, so what's different about that. I thought that was a pretty common trait among guys," offered Sarah.

"I'm not the bad person here." There was silence. "Look, I don't want to hurt Mike. I want him to be the friend he always was. We've had lots of fun together, but there is no future for us past high school. I didn't understand that before, but the sooner we accept it the better off we'll be."

"Krissy," said Andrea, "just how good are your grades?"

"Above average."

"Krissy, you're hedging again. Tell her," demanded Shy, shoving a syrup drenched strawberry into her mouth.

"Okay, okay. Don't get your panties in a wad. They're good. My grades are really good."

"Could you be a little more specific? Like, what was your SAT score or what's your class rank?" asked Andrea.

Krissy hesitated for a moment. She hadn't told anybody her exact score, only hinted. But if she was ever going to learn to sing her own song, she might as well start now. "My score was a fourteen-twenty and my class rank is six."

A gasp of disbelief came from Andrea and Sarah. Claire was simply better at controlling her response. Shy was the first to speak. "A fourteen-twenty? My God, you're a genius."

"Holy cow, six out of a thousand. I had no idea you were so smart," gasped Andrea. "That's wonderful."

"No, shit," said Sarah. "Now I understand why you didn't want to tell Mike. He thinks he's pretty hot stuff when it comes to brains. This will really take the wind out of his sail."

"This will knock out his entire lung capacity," said Shy.

"Well, if you want him to understand you, then you'd better be honest with him," offered Sarah.

R. Z. Crompton

"Ya know, Krissy, rather than just breaking up with him if you let him find out gradually about your grades and where you're going to college, he might break up with you. Then you have the opportunity to be brave and accept the reality of incompatibility without looking like the bad guy."

"You mean make it look like it's his fault?" asked Krissy as she put her rumpled napkin back on the table.

"You have the option of controlling how Mike and others will view the situation. It's all in the wording," said Shy.

Claire found the conversation enlightening. She hadn't realized how well she'd taught Shy the game of *frame or be framed,* but not only had she learned it well, she was passing the rules on to her friends. Claire wondered how much of last night was Shy's word game or Sarah's spirits. She played the events over in her mind as she reached up to stroke the charm tied around her neck. The sequence of events was more than just a word game.

"Ya know, that's a really good idea. Thanks. I do have to give Mike some credit though. After coming down this morning, I realize part of what Mike said last night was true. Life does go on. Just look around. We're all up eating breakfast as if nothing out of the ordinary happened. Oh, sure, the conversation is a little quieter than usual, but we're off to the zoo just liked we'd planned," finished Krissy, as she put the last piece of sausage into her mouth.

"Krissy, don't you feel bad about what happened?" asked Shy.

"Of course I do," defended Krissy. "But I was still hungry when I woke up this morning. Last night I was really upset about Sue's death, but this morning my body is concerned with its own survival. Life does go on. Now, what he said about Sarah's voodoo is a different matter." Krissy looked directly at Sarah, "I believe in you and your magic, especially after what you did with Mrs. Mayfield and all." Krissy could tell by the look of dismay on the faces across from her that she'd spoken

Dead Tones

out of turn about the spell Sarah had used on Claire. "Ooops, was that still a secret?"

"Krissy, you and your big mouth. Have you ever kept your mouth shut?" snapped Sarah.

Finally, Monica joined the conversation in an angry tone, "Really, Krissy, you're getting to be as bad as my mother. I find it absolutely astonishing that you've managed to keep so many secrets from Mike." She finished the last drop of orange juice and pushed away from the table. "I'm going up to get dressed." There was no invitation for Krissy to join her. They all watched her pick up her purse and turn her back on them. No sooner had she exited the dining room doors, than Sean was seen following after her.

"Well, I guess Sean's going to try and make up. Should I tell him she's not really in the right mood for apologies?" asked Krissy.

"Actually, I think you should keep your mouth shut," snapped Shy. She knew by the look on her mother's face that she'd be doing lots of explaining when they got back to the room.

Claire was not so surprised. It helped her understand how she'd managed to get caught up in something she'd have never agreed to forty-eight hours ago. As many times as she'd played over conversation with Shy and Rennae, Claire could never figure out where she'd lost the game. In fact, she hadn't even figured out how Rennae managed to show up at just the most opportune time. And then there was the infamous Scott Krammer, what about his convenient seat right next to hers? Claire found herself stroking the charm, yet not knowing when she'd actually put her fingers around the small pouch. Shy noticed her mother's superstitious gesture.

"Krissy, you'd better hurry up," suggested Shy. She wanted to talk to Sarah and her mother without Krissy's big ears relaying information to her big mouth. The only secrets Krissy could keep were the ones about herself. "We're supposed to load the buses in forty-five minutes."

R. Z. Crompton

"Really, oh shit. Ooops, sorry, Mrs. Mayfield. I gotta hurry." Krissy pushed her chair back and quickly made her exit.

"Shy, we still have over an hour before the buses leave. Why'd you lie to her?" asked Sarah.

"Really? Gee, I guess I miscalculated the time," said Shy smiling sweetly. "Oh well, by the time Krissy figures it out, she'll already be upstairs."

"So, why?" asked Andrea.

"Because I thought I owed my mother an explanation, and I didn't want Krissy to hear anything we had to say."

"Good idea on both counts," said Claire. She looked at Sarah, but her next question was directed at her daughter. "So tell me about this spell I'm under."

"I didn't actually ask Sarah to use any magic. She just told me not to worry about convincing you to come along," shrugged Shy trying to look innocent.

"It was my idea, Claire...ah...Mrs. Mayfield." Sarah figured the formal address might win her some points, but it was too late for sucking up. "We needed you to come with us. I just asked the spirits to help you get over the anger. It's been a long time."

"And Krammer? Why was he part of your package?"

Sarah didn't drop her eye contact with Claire when she answered, "He wasn't part of my package; he was part of your anger."

Claire couldn't deny the allegation. "Good magic, Sarah. I guess it worked," said Claire, again finding her fingers wrapped around the charm. This time the gesture had more respect. "I'd really like to talk to your grandmother when we get back."

"I'll see what I can do, Mrs. Mayfield," offered Sarah.

"Oh, come on, Sarah. You put a spell on me, but you still can't call me by my first name?" Claire smiled at Sarah and then at Shy. The anger was gone. It felt good.

Dead Tones

Andrea cleared her throat in order to get Sarah's attention. "Can I ask you a question?"

"You can ask. I might not answer," responded Sarah.

"You used to go to church," stated Andrea.

"Used to? I still do," said Sarah.

"Well, doesn't the Christian religion conflict with your Indian magic?"

"Not really. There's lots of similarities."

"Yeah?" Andrea's voice was full of doubt.

Shy had wondered the same thing and found herself waiting for Sarah's explanation. "So give us some examples."

"Supposedly, God made people keepers of earth. We knew we were keepers of the earth long before Christianity came to this continent. We didn't need you to tell us there was a Higher Power in the universe. We use the word spirit when you use angel. In the circle of life, there is good and evil. I pray; you pray. Sometimes I pray to God and sometimes to the spirits. In fact, when I put the spell on Allison, I asked God to help me convince the spirits to use their power to protect Allison. Now, I don't really care if it's my *spirits* or your *angels* standing over Allison, as long as she's protected from the evil trying to hurt her. Want more?"

"I'm impressed," said Claire. "I had no idea there were so many parallels."

"I'm sorry," interrupted Andrea, "but casting spells is a little too satanical for me. I think you're trying to force similarities to ease your inner conflict."

Everyone stared at Andrea. Shy knew she was extremely religious, but Andrea had taken the charm just like she and her mother. As far as Shy was concerned, she didn't care where the power came from right now, she didn't want to be a victim. "If you believe the spells are so terrible, then why did you take the charm Sarah made for you?"

Before Andrea had time to defend herself, Sarah came to her rescue, "You call good Christian magic miracles, right? I'm sure we could argue the fine points of our selected faith for hours, but it won't change a thing. I have learned childlike faith is much more profound than looking for absolutes. If we understood religion in absolutes then we wouldn't need God, would we?"

Shy suddenly understood why Sarah had seemed so distant these past few months. Her youth was being replaced with wisdom. Shy was surprised Sarah even wanted to spend time with her immature counterparts. She was sure that they all provided Sarah with immediate and humorous case studies every time they were together. Shy found herself wondering whether or not Sarah had any mutual fun with them or if the group was merely a periodic assignment from her grandmother.

"Can I keep the charm?" asked Andrea.

"Of course," answered Sarah. She knew that was as close to an agreement as she was going to get.

Claire's attention was drawn to the doors as Scott came into the room. His absence had been obvious. By now all of the staff and sponsors had made an appearance. Only the stragglers were still coming in hoping to find some tidbits left for breakfast. Claire tried to put herself in his place. The man was certainly carrying around a heavy dose of guilt and probably fear as well. He believed himself to be the cause of at least one death and possibly more. *What a rotten way to start the day.* She watched him fill a glass with juice and then pick up a lone muffin left on one of the platters. She assumed he'd join the table where Dale and several of the other sponsors were finishing up, but he didn't.

Scott had seen Claire and the girls long before he'd entered the room. After a quick clean-up, he'd spent most of his time wandering around the hallways and watching the lobby. If any strangers were hanging around, he wanted to know about it. Unfortunately or fortunately, depending on the point of view, he didn't see any suspicious characters and

Dead Tones

felt silly for acting like some super spy. He'd watched nearly everyone, including Claire, enter the dining room. Strangely, he felt more of a bond with Claire than any other adult on the trip. In spite of their feisty discussion, he needed her help.

"Good morning, Scott," said Claire when he was close enough.

"Good morning, everyone. How's my best soloist this morning?" asked Scott looking down at Andrea.

"Honestly, Mr. Krammer, I've been a whole lot better. Claire is a great bodyguard and all, but I'm tired of this game."

"Me too, Andrea. How 'bout the rest of you?"

Shy and Sarah nodded in agreement, "Yeah, we're doin' okay."

"Sarah, Claire told me you have something for me," said Scott in more of a question than a statement.

Shy and Sarah both shot the questioning look at Claire. They didn't think she'd even seen Scott since last night. How did he know about the charms? Obviously, they were wrong.

Scott pulled out a chair and sat down. He wasn't going to wait to be invited because he was afraid Claire wouldn't offer. At least, she hadn't told the girls about their conversation, or they wouldn't have been so surprised that he knew about the charm Sarah had made for him. He'd also expect more of the cold shoulder treatment from them. Scott glanced at Claire and offered a smile of thanks. He'd make it official on the bus.

"I have yours," said Claire. "I'll give it to you on the bus. The last thing we need is for somebody to see us passing Indian charms around the table."

"Sounds like a good idea," said Scott.

Shy's curiosity was eating away at her. She'd waited in the bathroom the entire time Claire was in the shower and nothing. Claire talked about the weather, the competition, Krissy going to Princeton, and a host of other things. But every time Shy asked about who she'd seen downstairs or who she'd talked to, Claire just talked on about something totally irrelevant. Now, she was sure it'd been Mr. Krammer. She might not be able to bait her mother, but he was a different story, she hoped.

"Mr. Krammer, did Mom tell ya Ali's not pregnant? Good news. huh?"

"Sure is," answered Scott looking at Claire. She gave a slight jerk of her head, and he instantly knew to cover himself. "But this is the first I've heard about it. Am I still considered the boyfriend?"

"No," answered Shy disappointedly. She was sure he was the one her mother'd met. He was the only one who could get her angry enough to slam doors. "You've been cleared of that too."

"You sound disappointed, Shy. I'd expect that reaction from Jessica, not you," teased Scott. If Claire hadn't told them about his father, then she had a good reason. He needed to talk to her alone before Shy or Sarah caught him in another slip. "So, who's the boyfriend?"

"We don't know. Mom won't tell us. Did she tell you?" asked Shy.

"What makes you think we've had time to talk?" Scott shoved the last bite of his muffin into his mouth and stood up. "I've got to check on some of the others. Andrea..."

"Yeah, I know. Stay by Claire. What about on the bus? Do I have to sit between the two of you?"

Scott was surprised at his reaction to the question. The natural thing for him to do would be to change seats so Claire could keep an eye on Andrea. However, he found himself feeling strangely territorial about that seat next to Claire. For the short ride to the hotel last night he'd moved to the seat next to Charlie. He wasn't about to spend the entire trip back to Tulsa next to Charlie, and he couldn't hand such a fate to Andrea either. There had to be a way for him to keep the seat he wanted and to protect Andrea at the same time. "I'm not sure, but I'll figure something out. Have you seen Abby this morning?"

"No," answered Shy. She wasn't here when we came in."

Dead Tones

"Scott, are you worried about her? Do you think she would do anything stupid?" asked Claire.

"I'm worried because I'm not sure what she might do. After last night, your guess is as good as mine. She was still pretty upset when I escorted her to her room."

"Who was in the room with her?"

"Jennifer opened the door. I think Kate was in the room too, but I don't know if she was staying or just visiting for a while. I don't think they'll let her feel sorry for herself all night. Both of them are pretty level headed. But I'll feel better when I find her. Meet me at the bus in thirty minutes." His instruction was given to Claire, but all of them were included.

"C'mon, girls. Let's get our stuff down here. We're gonna have to hurry in order to make it in thirty minutes.

CHAPTER NINE

Strolling onto the verdant grounds of the Dallas Zoo sparked the imagination of most visitors, and the Renegade Regiment was no exception. In fact, the kids were glad for the diversion. Small groups wandered off in the direction of their favorite animal while most of the kids headed for the chattering chimpanzees. The sense of something exciting going on was like a magnet for the students. The wild din of the monkeys reminded the parents of the outrageous noise often being emitted from the band room, so they followed along out of curiosity. After the oppressive heat and humidity of the summer, the chill in the air was an invitation for action, and many of the animals were enjoying the chance to frolic in the sunshine. The animated antics of the chimps entertained everyone except Abby. More interested in having some time to herself than she was the animals, she wandered off alone.

Abby finally found solace with the beautiful pink flamingos. Dozens of the exotic birds stood in the shallow pond surrounded by large tropical trees overgrown with deep green vines. There was a sense of peacefulness around the birds, no outrageous chatter and erratic movement like the chimps had displayed. Abby found a bench and eased herself down. *I'm sorry, Sue. I always over react. I never really wanted you to die. Really.* Abby shook her head in disbelief. *I'm going to have to learn how to control this power I have. Oh well, it won't matter. I'll die in prison. If they don't catch me this time, they will the next time I lose control.*

Abby was delusional with this self-declared power. Deeply absorbed in admiration for her new power to cause destruction, she didn't see or hear the girl approach. When the girl spoke, Abby nearly fell off the bench.

"Oops," said the girl, "you okay? Didn't mean to scare ya."

Gathering her wits finally, Abby looked up to find a skinny young girl with light brown hair pulled back into a pony tail. "You scared the daylights out of me. Hasn't your mother ever told you not to do that?"

Dead Tones

The girl pondered the question and then answered, "Nope, I don't think she ever did. Why you so upset?"

"How do you know I'm upset?"

"Cause you're sitting there the same way I do when I'm sad. Only I prefer the cats. I love cats, the fast ones like the cheetah. I never sit by these dumb birds."

"They aren't dumb," said Abby defending her choice. "I see beautiful, graceful creatures enjoying a glorious day."

"Really?" said the girl sarcastically. "I see pink puffs of cotton candy on a skinny stick."

Abby studied the birds carefully, and then shook her head in agreement. "Hmmm, I guess they do kinda look like cotton candy, but I like the stuff. In fact, a big puff of the sticky candy might make me feel better. You from around here?"

"Yeah, I live here. Well, not here at the zoo. In Arlington. I just come to the zoo a lot. So, what's wrong?"

"Why are you so nosy? Do you have a name?"

"Jessica, I prefer Jessie."

"I like Jessie. I know somebody named Jessica. She's...well, she's not a Jessie."

"Why?" asked the girl.

"Jessie sounds more friendly. Know what I mean?"

Jessie shrugged her shoulders in agreement. "Is your problem with this Jessica person?"

"No," laughed Abby. "And you're still being nosy."

"I guess it's my nature. My Aunt always tells me my nose gets me into trouble. So?"

"So. Nothing. You wouldn't understand," sighed Abby letting her shoulders droop in defeat.

R. Z. Crompton

"It doesn't matter if I understand or not. Sometimes talking, ya know, just getting it off your chest, makes you feel better. I don't need to understand as long as you feel better. It works for me when I'm upset."

"It does?" asked Abby. "How old are you?"

"Thirteen. Does it matter?"

"No," answered Abby having the distinct feeling that there was more to this girl than a normal thirteen year old had to offer. She had nothing to lose talking to this girl. After all, Jessie wasn't going to get back on the bus with them. What did it matter if Jessie thought she was crazy. "A friend of mine died last night."

"That's too bad. I know how you feel. Like a huge log is laying on your chest - it hurts to even breathe."

"Exactly," sighed Abby looking curiously at the small girl next to her.

Jessie wasn't quick to offer an explanation, but the question hung between the two girls just waiting to be answered. "First, I had to learn to live without my dad, then my mom. Now I live with my aunt. She's pretty cool."

"Wow, you really had the rotten stuff heaped on ya."

"Yeah, but I got through it. You'll get better."

"I doubt it. I'll be in prison."

That got Jessie's attention. "Wow...prison? Wow!" This was a new experience for her. The kids at school would really be impressed. "Would ya write to me. I'll answer, I promise."

"Yeah, sure. I won't have anything else to do."

"What'd ya do?" whispered Jessie assuming she was about to become part of some dark secret.

"The girl who died last night, I killed her."

"Wow! I thought she was a friend?"

"Kind of, but not exactly."

Dead Tones

"I'd say she was more in the 'not exactly' category. Man, she musta done something really rotten to get you so pissed off. You don't seem like the regular type of heartless killer we see in the movies."

"Thanks, I think."

"How'd ya do it?"

There was a long pause, and then Abby decided to answer. "I ahhh...I wished her dead."

"Ooops." Jessie cocked an eye at the girl next to her. "Are you for real or just a fruit cake?"

"You tell me. I was really, extremely mad at her. I wanted her to die and the next day she was dead."

"I may be only thirteen, but I know you can't wish somebody dead cause otherwise I'd a been thrown behind bars years ago. Everybody wishes that on somebody at least once. But it doesn't happen."

"I hope you're right. I guess it is rather bizarre."

More nuts than bizarre, Jessie thought to herself.

"Abby. Abby, I've been looking everywhere for you," scolded a familiar voice from behind the two girls.

Abby turned around and smiled at Kate, "Oh, hi, Kate. I've met a new friend."

Kate gave a quick nod of dismissal to the girl next to Abby and focused her attention on Abby, "We've been worried about you. C'mon," ordered Kate as she turned to walk away without another word.

Abby looked back at Jessie, "Well, I guess I'd better go with her. I'd hate to get left behind. Thanks. I really do feel better. Take care."

"Yeah, you too, Abby," said Jessie. *One's a fruitcake, a real fruitcake, and the other's a bitch. If that's puberty, you can keep it.*

Abby hustled to catch Kate. "Hey," said Abby gasping for a breath, "I need to use the bathroom."

"Yeah, me too. There's one around here somewhere. I passed it while I was looking for you. Jennifer and I have been searching everywhere for you. I thought Mr. Krammer was going to have a fit when he realized you'd wandered off alone."

"Sorry, I didn't mean to cause so much worry. I just needed some time to think. Now, I really gotta go."

"There, it's right there." Kate pointed to a building marked with a lady on a sign hanging from the roof about twenty yards off to their left.

Abby nearly ran to the small white entrance set in among the trees. She charged into the restroom nearly knocking Shy over. "Ahh..." Abby yelled swerving around to miss the head on collision. "Little desperate, Ab?" asked Shy jumping out of the way.

"Absolutely," she answered breathlessly slamming the small metal door behind her.

"I guess she was in a hurry," said Shy looking at Krissy standing in front of the sink adding the last touches to her hair.

"Looked that way. Did you see Mike trying to stare me down. I know what he's thinking...," stated Krissy. Before she could finish her thoughts, Kate sauntered into the large bright room where tile and florescent lights dominated the decorative theme.

"Hey Kate, I see you found Abby," said Krissy.

"Yeah, I looked everywhere for her. She sounds better than she did this morning, all that doom and gloom shit. I hate pessimism." She stepped into one of the tiny metal stalls and closed the door behind her.

Before Krissy could finish what she'd started, Abby's voice filtered through the stalls, "yeah, I'm much better now. Much, much better." A few seconds later the door opened and Abby, with a smile on her face, stepped out. She walked straight to the mirrors and reached for her purse. "Man, I look terrible. Where's Sarah?" She looked first at Krissy and then Shy.

"We left her with the King of Beasts," answered Shy. "She was visiting with some little kid on an intellectual level we couldn't relate to about the visual power of the mind.

Dead Tones

"Yeah, they were getting pretty intense," added Krissy.

"Neat, I think I'll go over and have a look before we have to leave. I like the big cats. I was getting kinda tired of those silly pink birds just standing there."

"You can walk over with us if ya want," said Krissy.

Kate joined Abby at the sink. She turned on the water before looking in the glass at the girl standing next to her. "Gee, Abs, you sure you're okay? You still look a little pale."

"Yeah, I'm fine. I just didn't put any make-up on this morning."

"Want to use some of my blush? I've got it in my purse," asked Kate. Anticipating Abby's affirmative answer, she reached into her purse.

"Thanks. I'd love to. How 'bout your chap stick? Do you mind? My lips are so sore after playing in the cold yesterday."

"Not at all. Mine are pretty sore too. Here you can have this one. I've got another."

"Gee, thanks." Abby handed the blush back to Krissy and then pulled the small cap off the lip balm. "Ummm, pink lemonade, my favorite."

"Man, mine are really bad too," said Krissy, eyeing the small tube. "Do you mind if I use some of that?" She looked at the small tube in Abby's hand as it was moved around her pink chapped lips, soothing the pain.

"Of course not. It wasn't mine to begin with," replied Abby taking one last caressing pass around her mouth. As she reached around Kate to offer the tube to Krissy's out stretched hand, Kate backed up into Abby. The small tube fell from Abby's fingers and landed on the floor and then rolled under the sink.

"I'm sorry, you guys. I didn't realize Abby was stepping behind me," offered Kate.

The other three girls just stared at the motionless tube of chap stick lying on the floor. Krissy almost snapped at Kate but managed to hold her tongue. Kate was infamous for shenanigans just like this one, and Krissy wasn't going to give Kate the satisfaction of making her angry. She rather play the little game out. "Oh, that's okay. I'll just clean it off. How dirty can it get?" Krissy took the two steps necessary and reached down to pick the chap stick up off the floor. With her fingernail, she scraped the top of the contents into the garbage and then wound the bottom of the tube to expose the untouched portion of lip balm. She put the tube to her lips slowly and purposely moved in an almost exotic sway to exaggerate the application and then handed the tube back to Abby.

Abby completely missed the confrontation. She'd heard some of the girls complain about Kate after a football game or marching practice. But Kate never pulled any of that crap with her, so Abby wasn't going to pass judgement on one of the few loyal friends she had. As far as she was concerned, the other girls were exaggerating.

"Abby you coming with us?" asked Shy.

"Yeah. Kate, you want to come along? We're going over to see the lions. I really want to see the lions before we have to leave." Her comment was more of a plea than a statement.

"No," said Kate watching Krissy's eyes. "I've got to find Jennifer. She'll be wondering where I am. And she's still looking for you."

"Oh, yeah, sorry 'bout that. See ya back at the bus," said Abby.

"Fine with me as long as you're okay."

"Yup. Feel great. See ya back at the bus." Abby quickly turned to follow Shy and Krissy out the door.

Krissy was already hissing her anger. "Do you believe her? What a bitch."

"Shh, here comes Abby," snapped Shy. "Finish telling me about Mike."

That was enough to get Krissy moving in another direction. "Do you believe him? He's waiting for ME to apologize. Staring at me. You know that 'holier than thou' look, that chauvinistic look of superiority."

Dead Tones

"Who ya talking about?" asked Abby when she caught up to them.

"Mike," snapped Krissy.

"You guys gonna break up?"

"I don't know what's gonna happen. Frankly, I don't really care."

"If you break up, do ya mind if I go after him?"

Krissy almost choked trying to hold in her laughter. "No, Abby, not at all. You might be good for him."

Shy shot Krissy a jab in the ribs then reconsidered. Actually giving Mike a taste of 'Miss Fatal Attraction' herself might be good for him.

"I wonder how Monica and Sean are getting along?" asked Krissy.

"Did they even get off the bus? The last thing I heard from them was profound 'I'm so sorry' and 'this was my fault'," said Shy.

"I know. They were holding hands like they'd never touched each other before, but I did see them get off the bus. Ya know, those two are perfect for each other. Not like me and Mike. I mean, we have a great time together, but those two are...are" Krissy hesitated, searching for the right word.

"You mean like a hand and glove, a perfect fit," offered Shy.

"Exactly, they're the closest thing to soul mates I've ever seen," said Krissy.

"I agree. They're really into the way each other thinks. I'm sure they didn't see a single animal today," reflected Shy as the three of them approached the big cats.

****

Sarah watched the massive body saunter toward her The large cat, with its long disheveled mane bouncing with every step, was absolutely fantastic. "So you can actually see him attacking you?" asked Sarah looking down at the small boy next to her. His sandy colored hair was long on the top and pulled back into a pony tail while the sides of his head were nearly shaved clean. The crotch of his pants hung to his knees, and Sarah wondered how he kept them from falling down around his ankles. Sarah not only thought he looked out of place at the zoo, but he also didn't look like the mental type. However, his power of imagination was incredible.

"Yeah, I can see 'im. Can't you?"

"I just can't do it the same way you can."

"Okay, now look at that cat," said Josh. "He's big and he's mean. He'd eat ya if he could. Now close your eyes." He looked at Sarah until she did as he instructed then continued. "You're walkin' through the jungle. Lost."

Sarah interrupted, "How'd I get there?"

"Who cares? Now you comin' with me or not?"

"Sorry, I'm coming," whispered Sarah and closed her eyes again.

"See yourself," instructed the boy. "You're dripping with sweat. The heat is pushing down on you. The humidity is so heavy you can smell it, feel it wrap around you. Only a few rays of sun filter through the green jungle canopy. There's barely enough light for you to see where you're going. A bead of sweat runs down your neck and between your ahh...down your ahh back." Josh nearly lost his concentration. He'd forgotten she was a girl. "A bird screeches overhead startling you. When you look up, you miss the jog in the path and stumble into a giant spider web. You panic, rubbing the sticky web on your pant leg. You want to run, to get out of the heat, out of the darkness. The light. There's light coming through the trees. An opening in the oppressive jungle You run...run for the light. You burst from the darkness right into the jaws of death.

"A lion sits at his watering hole enjoying the last of his small meal. It was merely an appetizer, and now the main course has just jumped into view. You stop instantly realizing your error, but it's too late. Your

Dead Tones

intrusion into the lion's realm has captured his attention. The lion slowly gets up as he sizes up his query. At first, his movement is slow and calculating waiting to see what you'll do.

"The lion charges, rushing toward you."

Sarah flinched at his words. She felt the sweat dripping off her neck in spite of the cool temperature. Then in a brief moment of consciousness, she wondered if Josh's eyes were closed too, or was he watching her?

"You can see the large pink tongue lulling out of the massive mouth, and you know he's marked you as an easy target. His large sharp teeth are still dripping with the blood of his last prey. You glance past the lion and see the carcass by the watering hole. Bones are sticking up through the skin and hair. Blood is everywhere. You see the blank staring eyes swarming with flies. Everything seems suspended in time and space. Your eyes focus back on the dull yellow eyes baring down on you. His great mane of coarse tan hair is blown back from the grotesque face. A slow realization dawns...this will be the last thing your eyes will behold. As the lion leaps on you, a blood curdling scream rises above the jungle canopy. Your scream."

Again Sarah feels herself flinch. She almost opens her eyes assuming the scream is the end of his story, but Josh continues.

"A great pain shoots through you as you feel the lion's teeth sink into your midsection and pull out your intestine. You can feel this king of beasts feeding on you as you suck in your last breath."

"Oh yuck! Yuck, yuck, yuck," snapped Sarah.

"Pretty good, huh?" asked Josh waiting for her words of approval.

"You're right up there with Stephen King.

"Thanks," answered Josh proudly. He didn't see the other girls approaching.

"Hey, Sarah, what's so yucky?" yelled Shy.

"This kid's imagination. I don't know if he's brilliant or sick."

"I'm good, huh?"

"Yeah, kid. Ya had me going. When you got done, I had to pick up my entrails," said Sarah with a big smile on her face

"I didn't drop any entrails."

"Guts," explained Sarah.

"Entrails means guts? Good word. I'll remember that one," said Josh.

"You two having fun with the animals?" asked Shy.

"Josh brings the animals up close and...ah...real personal like. Real personal if you get my drift," smiled Sarah.

"Look at how magnificent they are," said Abby scanning the pride of lions relaxing in the sun.

"I don't think 'magnificent' is the word I'll ever use again to describe this animal," replied Sarah. "Vicious, powerful, omnipotent, but not magnificent."

"Why?" asked Krissy.

"Cause that one just ate me," replied Sarah looking at the gold monster laying among the females.

A deep male voice interrupted the girls. "Hey, girls, it's time to head back to the front gate. Shy, have you seen your mother or Andrea?" asked Scott. He hadn't seen the two of them since the buses had unloaded, and now he was beginning to worry.

The majority of the past two hours had been spent looking for strangers rather than at the animals. Although Scott believed anyone who'd kill a teenage girl just to get even with him was an animal and deserved to be in a cage. Scott knew finding out the band's itinerary would have been easy for a novice to figure out; so for a regular type bad guy, following the band all day would have been a walk in the park or the zoo for that matter. The schedule for the weekend had been printed in several small papers around the Tulsa area; and if the school was called, no one would think twice about giving out the information.   Scott was

Dead Tones

relieved to see Abby's return to reality. That was one worry off his chest. "Abby, what brought you back to earth?"

"I had a reality check with a nice girl named Jessie. She lives around here somewhere. She found me feeling sorry for myself at the flamingo pool."

"I don't have to worry about you? Right?"

"Right, Mr. Krammer. I'm fine," answered Abby. "Thanks for being so worried though."

"It's my job. Now start working your way back to the buses. It's going to take you at least thirty minutes to get back."

"Good idea," said Abby. "Aren't we going to eat lunch? I'm starving."

"If you'd eaten breakfast with the rest of us, you wouldn't be so hungry now," scolded Scott.

"Oh, I know, Mr. Krammer," oozed Abby. "I just wasn't in the right frame of mind."

"No kidding." Scott wasn't in the mood for her fluttering eyelashes or sing songy voice. In fact, he was becoming rather paranoid about girls and what used to be harmless flirtation. "Shy," he waited for her to stop talking to Sarah. "Do you know where your mother is?"

"Nope, haven't seen her. We wanted to see the lions, but Andrea was more interested in the gorillas. Mom agreed to go along with her. It took us quite a while to get over here, and the gorillas are the other direction. Why? Are you worried about them?"

"Maybe. I'll head toward the other side of the park; you guys make sure you get back on time."

"You wouldn't leave us, would ya, Mr. Jazz?" teased Sarah.

Scott and the girls knew he wouldn't leave them behind; however, from time to time kids were misplaced and a lot of time wasted tracking them down. He could just imagine Abby sitting alone watching some exotic animal while the entire band searched the grounds for her. It certainly wouldn't be the first time one of them had drifted into la-la land. "You know better. Please hurry the others along or we'll be late for lunch. You don't want to be late do you?"

"No way," said Abby. Food was always the magic motivator. Hungry kids never missed the bus.

CHAPTER TEN

The black and yellow buses, loaded for the last time, moved north onto Interstate 35 for Tulsa. Scott, exhausted from chasing kids and phantoms all day, gratefully slouched into the seat next to Claire. This was the first time he could remember being happy to have all his sardines neatly packed back into their can. Andrea was safely tucked into the seat Charlie had occupied on the trip down. Charlie had been convinced it was in his best interest to take one of the empty seats on Dale's bus. Scott, grateful when Krissy had also asked to be moved, didn't have to answer why he wasn't willing to sit with Charlie and just give Andrea his seat next to Claire. Krissy didn't want to sit with Mike on the way home, so Scott used both of the girls as an excuse for Charlie to change buses. Of course, having the girls standing beside him expressing their deep gratitude helped make Charlie feel like a gentleman and graciously agreed to move. It was about the only positive thing Scott had managed to accomplish all day.

The afternoon at Medieval Times seemed to last forever. Hundreds of people had crowded into the show area for the jousting tournament, and then the lights were turned down. Scott wouldn't have been able to recognize one of his students from Count Dracula, but he still felt responsible for maintaining some kind of watch. So rather than taking a seat in order to enjoy the seven course meal, Scott had paced behind one row and then another looking for anyone who didn't belong with his group; unfortunately, everyone looked alike in the dark. He had to admit the kids had a wonderful time hooting and hollering for their knight whenever the actor on horseback entered the arena. For most of the students, the tragedy of Sue's death had come and gone yesterday. Oh, there would still be the tears and sorrow when they got back to school; but for today, life was to be enjoyed. Only Claire and her girls shared Scott's belief that someone, besides Abby, had killed Sue.

Dead Tones

The four knights in the tournament were color coded with the corners of the arena, so the fans would know whom to cheer for. Most of the Renegade Regiment had been designated to the green and blue knights while the other guests were cheering for the riders decorated in red or white. The room vibrated with pounding hooves and jeering fans. For Scott, the worst part of the afternoon was when one of the girls would exit alone for the restroom. Scott couldn't follow them into the bathroom, but he was sorely tempted when Abby went in alone. He was afraid her cheery attitude at the zoo was merely a front to put him at ease.

The cheering in the arena was a constant distraction as Scott paced the hallways and aisles. Several times he caught himself watching a knight take a dive rather than who was walking past him. As the various courses were served, knights were defeated one by one until only the blue knight was left sitting atop his horse. The show and the meal were timed to have a simultaneous end, and Scott encouraged everyone to hustle back to the buses.

"Everyone safely tucked in?" asked Claire. She didn't want to talk about his family or Sue. Scott needed to get his mind off his father. He was so intent on blaming his father for Sue's death that he'd been stalking anyone and everyone all day. She doubted if there was even a chance at objectivity.

"I hope so," said Scott, leaning back into his seat and closing his eyes for just a second. He soaked in the soft fresh scent of the woman next to him. "Do you have any snacks left in that magic bag of yours? I'm starving."

"You're as bad as a little kid. We just had lunch," scolded Claire.

"I didn't eat," answered Scott as he tried to twist his long legs into the tiny space.

R. Z. Crompton

"Why not? The food was pretty good if you didn't mind eating with your fingers."

"I don't mind the fingers, and it smelled appetizing, but I was busy watching."

"Watching what? The show? It was entertaining, but the rest of us managed to eat. Were you getting ideas for next year's marching show? Ya know, jousting isn't my cup of tea, but the kids had a great time. Maybe you can do Camelot or something along that line." Claire hoped to get him talking about the future even though she doubted his future would be in Tulsa.

"No, I wasn't looking for show ideas," said Scott with a touch of irritation in his voice. He wasn't in the mood for light conversation let alone humor. "I was searching for anyone who didn't belong."

"Scott, the place was packed. How would you know if any one person was stalking us?"

"I knew it was a long shot," admitted Scott, "but I had to watch. I had to. There was no way I could just sit back and have lunch with a clear conscience. Every time a waiter reached over my shoulder, I would've jumped out of my skin. Now that we're all settled in, I can eat."

"I wish I had something substantial to offer, but I'm down to a couple of cranberry-apple slim fasts and some ritz crackers. Everything else falls into the category of junk food. I do have a bottle of water that hasn't been opened yet."

"Claire, I'm a single man. Junk food's my hobby," said Scott thinking back on all the frozen pizzas he'd had over the years. Cardboard with tomato paste and a little cheese had been his main course for more years than he cared to remember. "I'll take whatever you've got minus the slim fast."

"It's good for you," smiled Claire.

Dead Tones

"Ahh....thanks, but I don't do girly drinks. I'm only thirty-three, Claire. I'll drink that stuff when I'm too old to worry about my manhood."

"Manhood? Girly drink? Why, Mr. Krammer, I do believe that's a sexist remark," teased Claire. She was glad to have him distracted from his search. At least with everyone confined to the bus, he could rest.

"I'm sure it is, so sue me. I'm not into girly drinks." He almost sounded embarrassed. "The water and crackers will do fine for now."

"Hey, Mr. Jazz, can we put on a movie?" The shout came from an anonymous male voice somewhere in the back of the bus.

"I don't care," yelled Scott over his head.

"Mr. Krammer," Jennifer's red curly hair bounced as she came up to the side of his chair. The soft orange cropped sweater accented her beautiful hair. Kneeling down in the aisle, Jennifer placed her hands on Scott's arm and leaned into his body before asking, "are you okay? You jumped around today like the energizer bunny. Is something wrong?"

Scott was surprised at her observation. He hadn't realized he'd been making a spectacle of himself, or that someone had been watching him. For the first time in his career it dawned on him that one of his students might be watching or even stalking him. Jennifer's face was only a few inches from his. He could feel her warm breath on his face, almost taste the mint still on her tongue when she talked. Blush and lip gloss were fresh and the perfume was obvious. Her green eyes stared into him. "I'm fine. Thanks for asking." He didn't want to be curt, but he certainly didn't want to encourage her. She was his student, not a friend in the true sense of the word. He needed to make sure she realized the restrictions society placed on him. She had over stepped the bounds, and he would be blamed for any misconduct.

"Okay," replied Jennifer in a whispery voice. "But if there's anything you need, anything at all, just let me know." Then she stood up and strolled away.

Scott didn't say a word after Jennifer left his side. He couldn't bring himself to even look at Claire. Jennifer's obvious display of affection was not only awkward for Scott; he almost felt it was dangerous. Claire had been right, and what was really embarrassing was that Scott probably still would not have noticed the girl's attraction to him if Claire hadn't mentioned it earlier. How many times had he missed this in the past? Scott was still trying to understand what had just happened when Woody made his first appearance on the television monitors. Toy Story was a great movie, but Scott doubted if it was enough to distract Claire from Jennifer's ridiculous performance.

Claire hadn't missed a single word, but she wasn't about to start this conversation no matter how badly she wanted to distract Scott from being obsessed with his father. If the man next to her wanted to talk then he was going to have to say the first words. There was more to this little tryst than just a school girl's concern for her teacher. Jennifer was marking her territory, her claim on Scott. Jennifer wanted Claire to know this man was spoken for. Claire reached down into her bag for the water and cracker. She decided to offer the remnants of the chocolate chip cookies also.

"Scott...Scott." Claire stated more loudly the second time.

He jerked his mind out of the blank stare and turned toward her, "Yeah?"

"You wanted something to eat?" asked Claire offering what she'd pulled out of the bag. "In fact, you can go through the leftovers yourself."

Scott had completely forgotten about his hunger. He couldn't get the smell of the sweet perfume out of his nostrils. It seemed to be

Dead Tones

everywhere. The offensive smell caused his stomach to flip flop. "Claire, is it my imagination, or is her perfume everywhere?"

Claire sniffed the air but didn't detect anything specific. "I don't think so. Why?"

"I can't seem to get away from the odor."

"Here," she offered the crackers. "Eat something. It might help to clear your senses."

"Thanks," said Scott as he took the water and crackers from her. Scott ate all the crackers, but still couldn't clear his nose or mind of the smell. He was beginning to think the smell was psychosomatic, and he was going nuts.

When the last of the water and crackers were gone, Claire knew by the frown on his face that the smell was still with him. He needed a distraction, anything to take his mind off Jennifer's invasion of his space. Against her own better judgement, Claire jumped back to his obsession. "So did you see anyone unusual today?"

"Yeah, I thought all those guys taking nose dives off their horses were a little strange. You couldn't pay me enough to fall off a running horse into a pile of horse shit."

Claire laughed. Scott's sense of humor served him like a shield. "I wasn't talking about the knights."

"I know and no. I feel like an idiot chasing shadows all day."

"Can you tell me any more about your family? Do you have any idea what they've been up to for the last what? Fifteen years or so?"

Scott sighed. He didn't know where to start or how much to tell her, but if she was willing to be his friend and ally in this fiasco then he'd tell her the truth. There was nothing worse than being caught in a lie by the very person trying to help you. Besides, he'd given this friend enough disappointment for a lifetime. He was lucky she was still talking to him. "I've been gone for over seventeen years, and I never even called. At first, I was so afraid my father would have everyone bugged or willing to tell him I'd called that I didn't want to take the risk. Later I just didn't care to know. The only two people I loved were dead. My mother helped me make it through my sister's death, but there was no one left to offer solace when she died. When I saw her in that pool of blood, all I could hear was her voice ringing out 'run, Scotty, run', so I ran and ran and ran. I ran until her 'Scotty' died with her and a man walked away."

Claire felt sorry for the boy crying on the side of the road. She'd never known that kind of loneliness or pain. Life with her asshole husband had been a pain in the neck, but she'd never feared for her safety or Shy's, probably because he knew she'd beat the shit out of him if he ever laid a hand on either of them.

"You didn't tell me this morning about your sister, only your two bothers. What happened to her?"

Scott hadn't thought it necessary to throw out all the family trash, but there was no reason not to tell her now that she'd asked. "Tessa was beautiful like our mother. She had wonderfully shiny blond hair that didn't hang, it floated down her back. I was too young to appreciate her other womanly attributes, but I loved staring at her hair. Now I understand how truly beautiful she was," said Scott turning away from Claire to watch the last of Texas disappear through the window. He had dreams about his mother and sister from time to time, but they always seemed to mesh into one person. Scott wasn't sure when he was seeing his mother as a young woman or his sister. They looked so much alike it was difficult for him to separate the memories. This was the first time he'd tried to think about just Tessa. "Tessa was fifteen when she died. I was almost twelve, I guess. So much went on in the house that I had no knowledge of, I can't be sure of anything. I have a few vague memories of me and Tessa on the swings in the garden. Tyler was several years older than Tessa and already sucked up by the old man by the time I was old enough to have any idea of

Dead Tones

what was going on. Mother tried to stop him from abusing us, but then he turned on her. He was determined to control everything and everyone. We did things his way or no way at all. I remember Tessa crying..." he stopped thinking about the details of the mental picture. "She was in her room. The door was slightly ajar and I could see her on her bed," said Scott slowly. Then he looked at Claire as if a light had just come on, like he'd been in a trance and not realized what he was saying. "I can't tell you what happened. Are you sure you can't smell anything?" Scott was interrupted by the awful odor again.

Claire was surprised at the abrupt end to the story and the change of topics. She wasn't sure if he couldn't tell or just wouldn't tell her the details. It didn't matter. Some family history was better dead and buried with the victims. She caught a vague whiff of something lingering in the air when he turned back to her. This time, however, he'd pulled his outside arm across in front of him.

"Claire, this isn't the place for me to be reliving my past. I know, or at least have a good idea what happened to Tessa, but back then I was too naive to put it all together. Now that I think back about the details, well, it's like a slap in the face. If I'd put it all together then, I'd have found a way to kill him myself. Maybe my mother would still be alive."

"I don't need to know all the details, Scott. You're entitled to your privacy." Now Claire caught herself sniffing at the air between them. "I was just wondering if Tessa's death might have any bearing on what's happening now."

"I don't think so. She wasn't poisoned. I'll tell you later. This isn't the type of conversation I'd want anyone to overhear. Know what I mean? Damn, I can't get rid of the smell." Scott turned around to see if Jennifer had managed to get a seat behind him.

As he turned away from her, Claire had a full dose of the heavy sweet scent. "Scott, Scott."

"What?" he asked turning around to face her.
"The perfume, it's on you," explained Claire.
"What?"
"Didn't Jennifer touch you?"
"Yeah, here on my arm. Why?"
"I think she put the perfume on you, on your arm."

Scott lifted his arm to his nose and inhaled. He nearly gagged in response. "Yuck, yuck, yuck, as the girls would say." Scott maneuvered his way out of the navy sweatshirt without standing up. As he wadded the shirt into a ball, Claire suggested he not throw the foul thing where Jennifer might see it. She reached into the shoulder bag at her feet and pulled out an empty ziplock bag.

"Good idea, thanks. Do you believe the nerve of that girl? I've never been so..so" he hesitated for the right word.

"Sexually harassed might be the phrase you're looking for," suggested Claire. "Feel like you were violated?"

"Yes. Yes, I do."

"You realize the message she was sending was for me don't you?"

"Frankly, I don't care what the message was, it stinks, literally and figuratively. And I find it quite unsettling. I've never been marked before. Shit, I feel like a fire hydrant some dog has just pissed on," said Scott as he squeezed the bag's zipper together.

Interesting comparison mused Claire. "I don't think I'd let her touch me again if I were you."

"When we get back to class, I'll have a little talk with this territorial predator. I'm not going to be anyone's prey."

"Including your father's?" Claire's question slipped out before she had a chance to realize what it would implicate. Was he a hypocrite?

Dead Tones

Scott took the time to consider the pointed question. He'd been running so long from his father that it was second nature. He'd never considered fighting. Scott looked into Claire's eyes, and he knew the answer she was hoping to hear. "I want to fight him, but all I remember is fear. It's one thing for me not to allow a seventeen year old girl to take advantage of me. It's another for me to stand up to the only terror I've ever know. But you're right. It's time to stand and fight."

"Good. Tonight after we get back to Tulsa, we can get on the Internet and pull up any old newspaper articles about your family. It's a place for us to start."

"Can you do that?"

"Yeah. All we have to do is dig up a few numbers in the Charleston area and call 'em up. Pretty easy stuff if you know where to go. You interested? Do you even know if your father is still alive?"

"No. I just assumed he was too mean to die," said Scott. Before he could thank Claire for her help, Jennifer was back at his side. He could smell her coming. A survival reflex caused him to pull his arm as far out of her reach as he could.

"Mr. Krammer, Abby's really sick."

"How sick is really sick, Jennifer?" There was no doubt in his mind that she might try to lure him away from his seat.

"I'm worried about her. She's a pasty white with beads of sweat running down her face."

"She's probably just motion sick," said Claire.

This time Jennifer looked directly at Claire, "I don't think so. She's never gotten car sick before."

The mere fact that Jennifer talked directly to Claire in a civil tone was enough to make Claire believe her. "I'll go back and check on her," offered Claire.

R. Z. Crompton

"No, I'll go," said Scott. "I need to stretch my legs anyway." Reaching up to the top of the gray seat in front of him with his left hand and pushing up on the arm rest with his right, Scott maneuvered his way out of the small space he referred to as a seat.

Claire watched the muscles in his upper thigh and buttocks flex and contract as he struggled to stand up. No wonder he never sat with anyone. The man needed every bit of the space available to be comfortable, and he'd given up that comfort, according to Trish, just to sit with her. She smiled at the view his backside offered in the form fitting blue jeans. *Nice, very nice. You don't spend all of your time eating junk food. There's some working out done to keep those muscles so firm. Humm, jogging or weights?* Claire glanced at his upper body. *I'll guess weights. Gee, I didn't realize denim could be so revealing, Mr. Krammer. No wonder the girls are crazy about you. You'd certainly be surprised if you knew what I was thinking right now.* Claire made a mental note to suggest he wear something besides blue jeans when Jennifer was around, but she'd wait until he was in a better mood.

Scott turned back to see the lingering smile on her face. Without knowing why she was smiling, he returned the gesture and followed Jennifer. Years of experience had taught Scott to balance himself by moving his hands securely from one seat back to another as he made his way down the aisle just in case the bus should lurch, flinging him into some unsuspecting student's lap. *Been there, done that and he didn't like it at all.*

Each set of seats was filled with life, girls or boys, or girls and boys. It was amazing how many kids could get into two seats when Scott could barely get himself into the same amount of space. Comfort had to be the key. There was absolutely no way five kids could be comfortable squeezed into two seats. Eyes glanced from the TV monitors to Scott and back to the movie again. After all these years, Scott still marveled at the power of Disney to entertain even the hard core, the kids who wouldn't be caught dead watching Disney at home because it was too sappy. But on the bus, when everybody was captive to the wise judgement of a few conservative sponsors, the kids could simply enjoy the humorous animated antics without feeling childish.

"Hey, Mr. Jazz, ya want a coke. I got an extra one here," said Jason as Scott approached.

"Thanks, Jason, maybe later. I've got to check on Abby."

"Would you ask if anybody's got some chips? I need something to munch on while I watch the movie. It's a habit, ya know?"

"Yeah, I know. There's nothing like a good movie and a bag of junk," said Scott.

"You got it. So will ya ask around?"

"Just yell, Jason, like you always do," suggested Scott, "it's easier."

"Hey! Anybody got some chips?" The deep voice boomed through the back of the bus.

Scott watched the bags and boxes of various crackers, cookies and candy instantly appear. He was sure the only time these kids weren't eating was when they had a horn in their mouth. At least he knew where to get some decent junk food when he was done checking on Abby.

The heavy, labored breathing could be heard from several seats away. Scott's imagination saw a couple of kids having a very passionate moment; but when Jennifer slowed down as they approached the seat, Scot knew his first impression was wrong. Two more steps and he could see Abby straining to get oxygen. He wasn't a doctor, but this was more serious than simple motion sickness. Abby needed help, and she needed it right now.

"Jennifer, go tell Judi to radio Barnett. Tell her we've got to pull off at the next exit. Ask Claire to get back here with her water. Hurry," ordered Scott.

Jennifer ran back toward the front of the bus yelling for Claire.

"Hey, be quiet. We can't hear the movie," snipped Sean.

"Oh shut up, Abby's sick," yelled Jennifer. "Claire, Mr. Krammer needs you to take some water back to him."

Claire was instantly out of her seat and going down the aisle. She could see Scott pointing at different students, but she couldn't hear what he was saying. Then several of the kids started moving. One handed up a blanket and then a pillow. Several others crowded into the back freeing up some of the space in the aisle, so Scott could move around. By the time Claire reached him, he was trying to help Abby out of her seat and to the floor where she could lie down.

Scott had to pull her up and out of the seat like a dead weight. "Can you stand for a minute, Abby?"

She shook her head up and down, but it was Kate, reaching over Abby's seat from behind, who helped keep her upright while Scott shifted his position in order to help her to the floor.

"Okay, Abby, try to take a couple of steps. Easy, easy. That'a girl," said Scott. He guided her out from between the seats and lowered her to the floor with her head facing the front of the bus, so Claire would have easier access to her head and upper body.

Abby sighed and closed her eyes as she was lowered onto the blanket.

"Abby, when did you start feeling sick?" asked Scott.

She opened her eyes and sucked in a raspy gasp for air. "After...after we got on the...on the bus."

Jennifer leaned over Claire's shoulder now and added. "She told me she was congested while we were at Medieval Times, but she looked and sounded okay. What are we going to do?" Jennifer had

Dead Tones

made a complete transformation from a hormone driven bitch in heat to a true and worried friend.

Claire poured some water onto the few kleenex he'd had in her bag and began to wipe Abby's forehead and face. Scott looked at her and the message he sent was clear. Somehow one more girl had become a victim. Claire thought he looked nearly as sick as poor Abby.

"Jennifer, did Judi tell you how long it would be before we get to an exit?"

"No, I don't think she had a chance to ask. Do you want me to find out?"

"Yeah, ask Hal. He should know. He drives this route frequently. Have Judi find out if anyone has a cell phone. Tell her to have Barnett call for an ambulance. Go!" he instructed. "She needs a doctor like an hour ago," said Scott looking desperately at Claire.

Claire continued to wipe Abby's face and then her neck. It was more of a comforting mother like gesture than anything else. There was virtually nothing they could do for the girl until the bus pulled off the interstate. Claire never realized how desolate southern Oklahoma was. She tried to mentally calculate how far it was to Oklahoma City. She remembered seeing the sign *Leaving Texas*, and several exits after that, but wasn't sure how many miles they'd covered. She guessed they were at least an hour away from a major hospital. Abby wasn't going to live that long.

Scott shook Abby when she tried to dose off. "C'mon, Abby, stay with us. Do you have any allergies?"

Abby shook her head and whispered, "No, I don't think so. Mr. Krammer, am I dying?"

"Don't think about dying," ordered the man hovering over her, "think about fighting to live."

Abby tried to move her head up and down, but her energy was waning fast. Eyelids fluttered shut.

"No, Abby, stay here," said Claire trying to give her a few drops of water. "We've got to keep her awake, Scott."

"I know," sighed Scott wondering how he'd missed the stranger who'd poisoned Abby. He knew this was his fault. It had to be. The only time Abby was alone was when she'd gone into the bathroom. Had somebody been waiting for her? But that's crazy, how would the killer know Abby would go into the bathroom alone? On the other hand, Scott speculated, maybe the killer was waiting for any girl; it didn't matter who. Abby was just unlucky enough to be the one who made the deadly encounter. However, at least now he was pretty sure he was looking for a woman. After all, if a man had been in the washroom, Abby would have said something.

"Abby? Abby," Scott talked louder and shook her, "Abby?"

Abby opened her eyes, but didn't answer.

"Was anyone in the bathroom with you?" asked Scott. Abby stared up at him but didn't answer. Scott didn't know if she was thinking or if she had even understood the question. He asked again, this time more slowly. "Abby, at Medieval Times, you went to the bathroom alone." She shook her head up and down. "Was anybody in the bathroom when you went in?" This time she made a negative motion.

By now the movie had been turned off and everyone on the bus knew Abby was fighting to stay alive. Faces, etched with fear, appeared around the sides and over the tops of the chairs. Shy and Sarah were in the seats two rows in front of where Abby and Jennifer had been. Kate and Megan were seated behind Abby. Now they watched Claire and Scott intently.

Dead Tones

ShyAnne turned away from the scene on the floor and motioned for Sarah to do the same. They sank back into their seats before Shy asked, "what do you think?"

"I honestly don't think she's got a chance in hell. We're too far from help. The poison has too much time to do its work," whispered Sarah.

"How did someone poison her and why? Abby didn't play the clarinet."

"Doesn't...she's still alive."

"Okay...she doesn't play the clarinet. We were expecting Andrea to be the next target not Abby."

"It proves we've got the wrong motive," sighed Sarah.

Shy shook her head wondering, "but what can Allison, Sue and Abby have in common? I didn't think they ever spent much time together."

"The motive may not be so obvious to us," said Sarah pensively. "Where's your charm?"

"Here, around my neck," answered Shy, rubbing the small green pouch tied around her neck. "Do you think it might help Abby?"

"I don't think so. She's too sick. I don't have enough power. Does Andrea still have hers? She believes it will help."

"She's afraid. I think she'll do anything to protect herself even if it doesn't make sense to her. I know I would."

"I wish my grandmother was here."

"Me too," agreed Shy. Both of them stood up as Jennifer came back down the aisle.

Jennifer returned with Judi at her heels. "Dale has called for an ambulance. We aren't waiting for an exit. The closest EMSA has already been dispatched. As soon as we see the lights the lead bus will let us know. All five buses will pull over to the side of the highway. Dale doesn't want to waste any time sitting at a rest area. Mary,

David's mom and our nurse on bus three, said to keep her awake. Slap her face if you have to. Make her stand up."

"But she's sick," insisted Jennifer. "She should be lying down."

Scott understood the orders given by Mary and why. Mary wasn't thinking sick. After Sue's strange death, Mary's mind had jumped to the same conclusion as Scott and Claire: poison. "We've got to keep her awake," said Scott. "C'mon, Abby. I'm going to lift you up. Focus. Abby. Abby!" Scott grabbed her chin between his thumb and fingers shaking her eyes open.

"Huh?" sighed Abby trying to focus her eyes.

"Mr. Krammer, what's going on?" asked Jennifer. "In the movies, they only keep a sick person awake when an overdose is involved. Is that what you think? You think Abby tried to kill herself?"

"No," said Scott. He felt like Jennifer had slapped him. He couldn't tell her the truth without causing a panic among all the kids. Abby was on her feet now, but she wasn't really lucid. Looking at Claire for advice, he waited. The silence was broke by a moan from Abby.

"Mr. Krammer?" questioned Jason from several seats away. "We have a right to know what's happening."

"Yeah, first Sue and now Abby," added Mike. "Are we missing something here?"

"Don't forget Allison," said Kate. "She was the first one to get sick."

At this point, he might as well explain his suspicions. He was out of options. "We don't know if there's a connection or not, but..." he stalled. Scott had trouble keeping Abby upright and concentrating on the conversation.

Dead Tones

"But what?" snapped Jennifer, "I can tell you Abby didn't have the guts to kill herself, and Sue didn't have a reason. So that means somebody did it for them. Right? "

"I think it's somebody who's with us on this trip," added Kate. She looked around at the faces.

Scott stared at her. What was he going to say now? He still felt it was his fault, but he hadn't poisoned anyone and had no comfortable explanations to offer about his family. Again he hoped Claire would step in.

Claire read the plea for help on his face. "Take it easy. There's absolutely no proof of any connection between Allison, Sue and Abby."

"I'd say there's a hellava connection," growled Jennifer. "Allison's in the hospital, Sue's dead, and Abby here is about to join her."

"Huh?" whispered Abby trying to turn her head toward the sound of her name.

Claire continued, "Scott, I mean Mr. Krammer and I share your concern. We were suspicious about Allison's sudden and unexplained illness. Then Sue's death, but we still don't know why Sue died. How can we call the police or accuse anyone if we don't have any facts?"

Jennifer looked around the bus. She was calculating. Judging each face. Claire knew what she was doing as she watched Jennifer's eyes move from one face to another. The girl was wondering the same thing Claire had asked herself. Who wanted to kill the girls? Jennifer had one advantage though: she knew the kids better than Claire did. And, Claire realized, Jennifer was more devious than Shy or Sarah. She didn't know if this was an advantage or not, but Jennifer could see angles the rest of them didn't.

Jennifer's eyes stopped on Sarah. "You," she snarled, "you and your damn magic."

There it was. Jennifer didn't have to say anything else to get the fire going. This was exactly what her grandmother had predicted, and she knew this was just the beginning.

Mumbled tones rose from the others as everyone turned to see Sarah's face flush red. Claire didn't like the way the conversation was going. Jennifer was looking for somebody to blame and Sarah was going to be her chosen target. Claire had to remind herself that this was the same girl who'd wiped perfume on Scott's sleeve. She was a conniving bitch, or maybe a better adjective was witch. Claire was distracted when Jason added his two cents worth.

"Yeah, I agree with Jennifer. I saw the charm you've got around your neck. You're practicing your spells on us, aren't you?"

Sarah tried to defend herself but couldn't quite formulate the words. She'd tried to harden herself for the predicted onslaught, and yet she still found herself on the verge of tears. At this moment there wasn't much she could say. "I didn't do anything wrong. Somebody..."

"Save it for the cops," snapped Kate.

"Wait a minute," screamed Shy, "you can't do this. Sarah's our friend. We've known her for years."

"Give it a rest, Shy. We've all known each other for years, so that argument doesn't stand a chance. One of us is killing, and I think it's her. She's the only one learning and practicing a pagan religion," said Jennifer.

Sarah thought about her grandmother's words and instantly knew Jennifer was the *one yelling the loudest.* Now she had to find out who was the *one standing close.* It was Sarah's turn to look over the crowd of faces.

Scott couldn't stand by and watch Sarah take the blame for this. He considered his father a more likely suspect than Sarah. Abby, her head hanging to her chest, was so still Scott forgot he was still holding her.

Dead Tones

"Abby!" screamed Jennifer. "Abby, wake up."

Claire reached for Abby's face, but froze when she pulled up the chin and looked into the lifeless eyes. Abby was dead.

Screams erupted as the others saw what was only inches from Claire. Scott wasn't sure what had happened until Claire said, "you can put her down now."

"No! No!" yelled Scott dropping Abby's body to the floor, and instantly maneuvering himself into a position to do CPR.

Claire bent down beside him and calmly reached to close the staring eyes. She didn't believe Abby could be revived, but they had to try. They had to try. After several minutes of mouth to mouth and CPR, Claire touched Scott's arm. He wouldn't stop.

CHAPTER ELEVEN

An EMSA unit, dispatched from Norman, Oklahoma, intercepted the five buses between exits eighty-six and ninety-one on Interstate 35. As soon as the lights of the ambulance were seen, the bus convoy began to slow down and work its way to the side of the road. Scott was still trying to revive Abby when Hal maneuvered his bus over to the shoulder. A man and a woman, waiting anxiously for bus four to make a complete stop, rushed onto the bus as soon as the doors opened. Stunned students had already been instructed to stay in their seats and out of the way. Scott didn't move away from Abby's inert body until the woman bent down beside her.

The couple worked quickly and efficiently for several minutes before declaring Abby's fate. There was nothing they could do for her. The man radioed the hospital for instruction. Since Abby's death was unexplained and certainly unusual, the paramedics were instructed to notify the Highway Patrol.

Scott, on the verge of tears, slumped into a seat beside Abby's body. He had nothing to say this time when Jennifer vehemently blamed Sarah for Abby's death. Jennifer was certainly distraught, but Claire wasn't' sure how much was real grief and how much was fear. She'd spent all day with Abby, and Claire was sure Jennifer realized she could have just as easily been the victim rather than Abby.

A couple of Highway Patrol cars were already on the scene with the officers directing the traffic to slow down and move into the left lane. This allowed the paramedics the freedom to move from the ambulance to the bus without having to worry about being struck by a

Dead Tones

non-observant motorist. Once the officers were informed of the situation on bus four, they called for back-up.

The first task for the Highway Patrol was to completely detour the traffic around the convoy of buses and ambulance. With a half dozen patrol cars, ambulance and five buses, the string of flashing lights seemed more like a carnival than what was quickly becoming a crime scene. The kids were instructed to get off the buses, so the officers could conduct a complete search of all five buses. While some patrolmen searched, others questioned the kids in some type of orderly fashion that no one but the officers could understand. All of the students were questioned about their contact with Abby over the last twenty-four hours. Eventually, a series of events from Allison's sudden illness to Sue's death and finally to Abby were laid out for judgement.

As long as there had been a flicker of hope, most of the girls had held the tears in check; but when Abby was officially declared dead, optimism was replaced with tears for Abby and fear for themselves. The fear factor was a new emotion for most of them and it allowed for a sense of panic to take root. Several students, hoping their parents would drive out and rescue them, used Mary's cell phone to make their desperate plea as soon as they got off the bus. Unfortunately, Tulsa was too far away for the parents to be of any help. So in spite of the desire to recover their respective children, the parents were discouraged from making the trip. The buses would mostly likely be on the road long before any of them could drive the one hundred and fifty miles. Dale emphatically argued that he wouldn't leave a few dozen students standing on the highway waiting for Mom or Dad to drive up, and he certainly couldn't detain the entire group once the Highway Patrol was finished with their work.

Pacing angrily on the highway side of the buses, Claire was so selfishly absorbed in her own thoughts that she didn't notice the kids' anxiety. Several students, not bothered by the idea of snakes or spiders, chose to wait impatiently in small groups on the grass. Those who weren't crying speculated and pointed blame. Jennifer told at least one person from each of the other buses that Sarah was the guilty party. After all, hadn't Abby and Sue both been on the same bus with her. Gradually, the majority of the students moved from the concrete where Claire was waiting to the grass. Rumors and tales of killing spirits gripped everybody's imagination. This was a nightmare, and Jennifer was writing part two.

"I always knew she'd do something evil," said Jason. "I could see the danger in those coal black eyes."

"I agree, have you ever walked into a class room and seen her staring. She watches people," added Megan.

"She's not watching; she's making bad magic and we're her guinea pigs," declared Jennifer.

Claire wished they'd just waited until they'd gotten back to Tulsa to call the police, but then she knew the paramedics were required to notify the nearest law enforcement agency whenever they encountered an unexplained death. The questions and search took forever. Several of the girls had succumbed to their bathroom needs and had no choice but to use the john on one of the buses. At first they were denied access even though the search in the first two buses was complete, but at Dale's insistence, the officer's reluctantly allowed access to only the first bus. The boys who had to answer the call of nature opted to relieve themselves in the great outdoors.

"Look, there goes Jason," said Monica. "He just meanders away from the rest of us, gazes out into the darkness for a few minutes and then nonchalantly returns to the group. Does he really think we don't know he's taking a leak?"

Sean stood with his arm wrapped around her protectively. "He doesn't care if you know or not. The man's gotta go, so he's gonna go. Would you rather have him pee on your foot?"

Dead Tones

"Of course not," she snapped, "but if we have to use that stuffy, stinky toilet on the bus then you guys should too."

"You should be glad we can go outside. Imagine how stinky the little cubby-hole would be if all of us had to use it. Besides, we're notorious for peeing on the seat."

"Animals, you're all animals," said Monica, the top of her head coming just above the tip of his chin, cuddled closer into Sean's shoulder. "I'm scared."

"Me too," added Sean. "It's hard to imagine one of us is a killer. I feel really bad now about Allison. I just figured she was sick."

"We all did." Monica stopped talking when the officer came up beside her.

"Excuse me, miss. Do you know where Sarah Morning Star is?"

"I think she's with ShyAnne Mayfield," answered Monica. "They went over to bus one to use the bathroom."

"Thanks. Have either of you ever heard Miss Morning Star talk about spells and magic?"

"No, I haven't," said Sean.

"Me either. And I think you've got the wrong idea about Sarah," offered Monica in Sarah's defense. "Sarah is learning Cherokee medicine from her grandmother. There's nothing sinister about it."

"Not unless she's practicing on her fellow students," replied the officer.

Monica took a breath preparing to continue her defense, but Sean gripped her tighter around the shoulders in an understood gesture to keep quiet. She stayed silent. The officer moved away.

"Don't say anything," whispered Sean. "If he asks again, just say the same thing."

"But it's the truth. Sarah doesn't talk about what her grandmother teaches her."

"I know, but when you get all defensive, it makes her sound guilty. And don't forget, she really did use a spell on Allison and Mrs. Mayfield," said Sean.

"Oh, yeah. I forgot."

"It was to protect them, but you know the cops. If she used one type of spell, then they'll assume she could use the other," explained Sean.

"You're right. We'd better find Krissy. She'll spill her guts if they ask her," said Monica. "Have you seen her?"

"No, but Mike's over there with Jason, so Krissy's probably on the other side of the interstate. It's too bad they can't come to some kind of understanding, but Krissy's being too stubborn," said Sean.

"I don't think she's being so stubborn. She's just never stood up to him before."

"So why now? Why on this trip, when things are so rotten already, does she have to take a stand?" asked Sean.

"Trust me. She has her reasons."

"As long as they don't drag us into the fight, I don't care if they ever make up." Sean leaned down and kissed her on the forehead. "C'mon, lets go find Krissy before the cops do."

****

The officer walked up behind Sarah, "Miss Morning Star?"

"Yes?" said Sarah as she turned around. She wasn't surprised to see the uniform. Not many people addressed her formally.

"I'm Officer Belford. I need to ask you a couple of questions."

"Okay," answered Sarah as if she had a choice.

"Do you know what this is?" The officer held a round black stone in the palm of his hand.

Dead Tones

She knew instantly what it was, but she'd learned months ago from her grandmother to mask her inner feelings and thoughts. "A black rock," she answered flatly.

The officer smiled at the simple answer, "Yes, but does it have any other significance?"

"Is it supposed to?"

"Look, Miss Morning Star, I don't want to play word games with you. I know you all want to get back to Tulsa, but no one is leaving until we get some answers. Now, I understand you're learning about Cherokee medicine from your grandmother. I also know that along with the good goes the bad."

"Sarah, you don't have to answer anything," suggested Shy.

"Girls, this is a simple question," responded the officer in an exasperated tone. "I'm not pointing blame or suspicion. I'm just gleaning information pertinent to this investigation, so we can all go home."

Sarah sighed before answering, "Yes, I know what it is. It looks like the type of black stone somebody would use to make bad medicine."

"You mean it might be used to evoke bad magic?" asked the officer.

"Yes, but the black stone by itself has no real power," explained Sarah. "Where did you find it?"

"In the dead girl's pocket," answered Belford. "And I was told the other girl," he looked at his notes before continuing, "Sue Walsch was her name, she had one in her clarinet case."

"Was it wrapped in anything?"

"No. Should it have been?" Before Sarah could answer he held up his hand. "No, don't answer that, at least not right now. And for your own sake don't tell anyone else either. That little tidbit of information might keep you out of jail." He looked at Shy.

"My lips are sealed," she offered.

"If a friend asks, pretend you don't know what he's talking about. Make sure you tell your lawyer if you get to that point."

Before Sarah could ask what he was talking about, Belford walked away. "Wow, that was weird," she said softly.

"Sure was. What did he mean about the black stone?" asked Shy.

"Who? I don't know what you're talking about," said Sarah with a grin on her face.

"Don't start with me, Sarah. I'll tell him you put a spell on my mother," threatened Shy.

"Oh, all right. I suppose you're safe. Remember last night?" she whispered.

"Of course I do."

"Well, think about the process we went through. The black stone, all by itself, doesn't have much power."

"I get it..."

"Shh. We don't want anybody else to get it. Do you think this means Andrea's no longer in danger?"

"In my opinion, we're all in danger until the killer is caught," answered Shy.

"I'd sure like to know who told him about the black stone in Sue's clarinet case."

"Yeah, better still, I want to have a look in Allison's locker," added Shy.

"Good idea. Me too. Let's go find your mom. Maybe she knows who's doing all the finger pointing."

"You have to ask? I'll lay you twenty to one it's Jennifer. C'mon. I'm freezing." Shy wrapped her arms around herself in an attempt to get warm. The temperature was dropping quickly in direct

Dead Tones

response to the increasing north wind. "Maybe the cops'll let us get our blankets off the bus."

"I doubt it. They won't let us back on until they're finished searching, and they naturally saved our bus for last."

****

Anticipating the evening chill, Claire had managed to grab her jacket as they filed off the bus only to be stopped before stepping into the dark night. Everyone had to empty their pockets and purses, but the simple action of reaching for her coat had brought her the extra thrill of a body search.

The officer stopped her just as she stepped to the entrance of the bus. "Sorry, ma'am, but if you're gonna take anything off the bus with you, I'll have to search you."

Claire didn't want to freeze; however, having this man touch her seemed like a worse fate than the cold. The officer was taller than Claire, but not nearly as tall as Scott. His broad shoulders filled the uniform to the brink of popping off the buttons. She wondered if he was really so muscular or if he'd chosen a shirt one size to small just to enhance his ego. He had a strong square chin and short, nearly buzzed hair. Claire couldn't quite make out the color of the short bristles. He had the ominous look of a man used to having his way, of a man more likely to enforce his kind of law than a man who upheld the law. The cocky smirk on his face, kind of a half smile, made Claire regret she'd even picked up her jacket. "Then I'll leave the coat here," said Claire.

"Sorry, ma'am. At this point I have to insist. Would you please step out of the bus and up along the side," slurred the officer in his syrupy southern slang.

Claire tried to keep her professional face on; however, she could feel the blush growing in her cheeks when the officer ran his hands slowly over her butt and then up between her legs. In the darkness he could linger as long as he wanted because no one could see what he was doing. Everyone, except Scott and two other officers had exited the bus, to meander through the darkness. Scott was being questioned by the two officers still on board while she was left at the mercy of this ultra-conservative, Neo-Nazi jerk with his expensive sunglasses hanging at the V of his stiffly starched shirt. No matter how insistently Claire told herself he was only doing his job, she couldn't shake the feeling he was gaining more pleasure than he would've from searching a man. This man was not conducting a search. He was having his own private caress. When his intruding fingers tightened on her inner thigh, Claire's embarrassment turned to anger, and she jumped away.

"I guess you're clean, Ma'am." Their eyes met in the dim light escaping from the doorway, and his audacious smile lingered until Claire turned away. The officer quickly returned to the bus.

Claire seethed with anger as she played and replayed the man's assault. He didn't deserve to wear the uniform.

"Mom, we're freezing," declared Shy. "Can we get our coats or a blanket?"

Shy and Sarah were visibly shaking, and Claire knew most of the others had to be cold also or would be soon. However, she wasn't looking forward to confronting Mr. Neo-Nazi again. In the hour or so since her first encounter, Claire hadn't seen the man step off the bus. She couldn't believe it took so long to search a bunch of seats.

Scott finally walked around the front of the bus to find Claire and the girls shivering in the cold night air. "They still have more looking around to do before the paramedics can take Abby's body off the bus. Let's see if we can get something to warm you guys up," suggested Scott.

Dead Tones

"Sounds good to me, Mr. Krammer," said Shy, "mom's already got her coat. Good thinkin', Mom." Shy and Sarah headed toward the door.

"Scott, don't let them go back on the bus," snapped Claire.

"Why, Mom?" asked Shy. "We're freezing. The cops'll let us grab a couple blankets."

"Trust me on this, girls. I don't want you going back on the bus."

"I'll go with them, Claire. We only want a few blankets. They've finished searching most of the seats." Scott was baffled by her strange reaction.

"You come with me, Scott. We'll grab as much as we can," said Claire.

Scott took the two steps necessary to stand between Claire and the girls. He knew her well enough to trust her judgement, but he wanted to find out why she was afraid for the girls to go back on the bus. "What's wrong with you?" Scott whispered.

"I don't want them to be in there with that asshole." Claire looked up to find the offensive man staring down at her. Scott followed her gaze, but before he could ask why, Claire headed for the door. On the first step, Mr. Asshole was waiting for her.

"Can I help you, ma'am?" he slurred.

"The kids are freezing out here. We need some of the blankets and coats."

"Why, sure. I don't mind if you come on board, but only you. Wouldn't want you plantin' evidence or takin' somethin' off we haven't found yet. Know what I mean?" The officer stepped off the bus allowing Claire to move in front of him.

One look at the predatory cop and Scott knew exactly why Claire didn't want the girls at his mercy. Scott tried to follow Claire, but the man cut him off. Scott instinctively wanted to throw his fist into the guy's jaw, but assaulting an officer wouldn't do him much good when added to the story he'd already told them.

"You have to wait here. I can only keep an eye on one of you at a time," ordered the officer.

Claire couldn't move fast enough up the steps. The man, taking two steps at a time, moved in behind her. Claire felt his breath on her neck and his hand brush around her waist. She turned to face him while he was still one step below her. The advantage made them eye to eye. Claire mustered all her bravado and delivered her best threat. "If you touch me again, you'll be wearing your balls around your neck." She never broke eye contact with him, but she did slightly lift her knee. "Do I make myself perfectly clear?"

The officer jerked away inherently knowing to protect the *jewels* before answering, "Why...yes, ma'am. Sparkling clear."

"Fine," she hissed. "Now if you want to grab a couple of those blankets for us, we'd really appreciate your thoughtfulness." Claire moved into the stirring wheel, allowing the man plenty of space to move past her, then she descended the steps to find Scott waiting with a curious gleam in his eye.

"What was that all about?" he asked.

"We had a misunderstanding, but I think it's all cleared up," explained Claire, realizing Scott had heard what she'd said to the man.

"You okay?"

"I am now; but if he'd called my bluff, I'd be in big trouble," said Claire with a great sigh of relief.

"I was so busy with his partner earlier that I didn't realize you two already had a close encounter, but I knew the problem as soon as you referred to him as Mr. Asshole. The guy reminded me of Jennifer."

"Me too. Only I had to stand still for the body search," she cringed.

Dead Tones

"Are you serious?" asked Scott looking down at her. "Sorry, Claire. I'm bigger than he is, you want me to punch him in the nose?"

"Nope," said Claire, "if there's any punching to be done, I get the honors and it won't be his nose I aim for."

"I certainly hope we never have that kind of misunderstanding," smiled Scott.

"Me, too, but if in doubt, you might want to have a jock strap handy. Did you tell them about your father?"

"Seemed like as good time as any. If I'm going to stay and fight, I might as well get started now. I know it's going to be late when we get back, but is your offer to check the Internet still open?"

"Absolutely," answered Claire. She heard the officer's foot steps near the entrance of the bus and turned away from Scott.

Scott stepped in closer to her and put his arm tightly around her shoulder. Rather than stepping up to the bus, he held her beside him making the officer step completely to the ground. Standing a good four inches taller than the man in uniform, Scott reached out with his free arm to take the blankets from the officer's hands. "Thanks. How much longer do you think we'll have to be out here?"

"Another thirty minutes or so, sir. We've decided to send an escort back to Tulsa with you and have the semi searched there. No use tearing everything apart out here in the dark."

"Makes sense to me. This has been really hard on the kids. We need to get them home as soon as we can."

The man seemed so much shorter when he was standing toe to toe with Scott. Claire realized he used the steps on the bus to his advantage. *The scum. If I hadn't moved up the steps in front of you so we were the same height, you would've taken advantage of me and your badge again. So how do you like looking up?* Claire wanted to ask him, but decided not to push her luck. He was still the one with the gun, and she imagined he could make life pretty tough for Scott if he wanted to. Again the thought of his hands creeping up her inner thigh made her shudder, and she nudged closer to Scott. It's odd how one man can be so repulsive and another is not. Claire found herself reminiscing about her feelings for Steve and then for Scott. *It's amazing how time and events can change one's outlook.* Claire found herself wondering if her feelings for this little scum bag standing in front of them would ever change. The only thing Claire knew for sure was that things always change.

Instinctively, Scott tightened his grip. The sense of territory crossed his mind and he knew Claire would be insulted by this idea. So he wouldn't tell her he enjoyed the warmth of her body next to his, or the way her fragrance teased his senses. As long as she needed him to act has a shield, he'd stay as close as he could.

"Mr. Krammer, thanks for the blankets," said Shy, running up to grab a blue and white striped blanket from his grip. His possessive grip on her mother's shoulder did not go unnoticed. "I see Mom's not so cold anymore. Way to go, Mom."

"It's not what you think," explained Claire.

"It's not?" asked Scott looking down into her soft hazel eyes.

"No, and you know it isn't." Claire felt her heart skip a beat and a warmth fill her cheeks, but she didn't move away from her source of heat. The warmth she felt was more than just physical and she knew exactly where the fire was burning. It'd been a long time. Too long.

"I think this is exactly what it looks like. Face it, mom, he's pretty cute," said Shy smiling at her mother.

Shy, Sarah, and Krissy were not the only ones to watch the exchange between Claire and Scott. In the darkness, it was difficult to know if anyone was within hearing distance, but the light coming from the bus was enough for several people to watch Scott Krammer, without any obvious reason, put a strong, warm arm around Claire.

Dead Tones

Trish was especially glad to see the exchange between the two of them, but seething rage festered in the heart of another not so far away.

"Shy," said in that special motherly way expressed Claire's feelings to her daughter. Shy knew the tone of voice very well and decided she would have a happier homecoming if she dropped the issue of her mother and Mr. Krammer.

"Here, these are heavy," said Scott, handing the other blankets to Shy. "Offer the rest of these to whoever is shivering the most."

Shy passed the arm load to Krissy and turned back to Scott. "Mr. Krammer, do the police really think it's murder?"

"Probably. At least they think all this is highly suspicious. Unfortunately, without an exact cause of death, they can't draw any conclusions about the three girls."

"Holy cow! Murder," said Shy not wanting to believe him. "I never really thought this was possible. Know what I mean? Up 'til now, it was more like a game."

"I know," answered Claire.

"Is Sarah a suspect?"

"We all are," Scott answered.

"You know what I mean. Some of us are higher on the list than others. Where's Sarah on the list?" demanded Shy.

Sarah stood listening intently, but she knew the answer. "I'm at the top, right?"

"You're right up there with me, kid. I think we're the first two names on this so-called list," answered Scott trying to sound matter of fact.

Sarah wasn't as surprised as Shy about this admission. "They still have you on the list? Mom, I thought we had all this cleared up," said Shy.

Before Claire could make excuses, Scott started his explanation. They'd find out on Monday anyway, and he really didn't want these girls, especially these girls, to hear the story mixed with the rumors and innuendoes, which would surely be added to the facts. By Monday afternoon, Dale would be informing him of the school board's decision to suspend him until this mess was cleared up. After all, it wouldn't look good for a murder suspect to be teaching school. Parents would have a field day with him. By the time Scott had finished telling most of his story to Shy and Sarah, the buses were being loaded again. However, Jennifer had to make one last stand.

"What's going on over there?" asked Scott pointing to the crowd hanging back from the buses.

"No idea, but I guess we'd better find out if we ever want to get home" said Claire.

The two of them didn't have to walk far to understand the trouble. Jennifer's voice rang out louder than necessary. "I refuse to get back on that bus with a killer, and I don't understand how the rest of you can walk around here just waiting for her to put another spell on one of you."

Murmurs rumbled through the crowd.

Scott pushed his way to the center to find a wild eyed Jennifer standing as if to challenge anyone who disagreed with her. "Jennifer!" Scott snapped at her. "Stop it. You're creating a panic that won't serve any of us."

"If we get back on that bus, someone else will be dead before we get home."

"Excuse me," came the slow southern drawl which Claire recognized immediately as belonging to none other than Mr. Asshole. He puffed up his chest and pushed through the crowd. "Just one minute young lady. All of you listen to me. Now we've not had a lynchin' in this here state for as long as I can remember, and you're not gonna have one while I'm on duty. Is that clear?" bellowed the man. "And just in case you don't know, it is still illegal to lynch a

Dead Tones

person just cause ya don't happen to like his or her religion. There will be an officer on each bus, and I personally guarantee no one else will die. Now get your carcasses, and I'm speaking heavy on the 'asses' part, on a bus, so we can get out of here. Now MOVE!" The order was not questioned.

Jennifer was effectively silenced and everyone lined up to get on a bus. Scott looked down at Claire. "Okay, so Mr. Asshole redeemed himself slightly. Are you going to thank him personally?"

"I think I'll just get my carCASS on the bus."

"Me too." Claire was surprised to find out only ninety minutes had elapsed by the time they were on the road again. The ride home was long and silent. No one ate or drank anything for the next three hours. Those who could sleep did, the others gazed out the window at the shadows of the night and wondered.

R. Z. Crompton

CHAPTER TWELVE

The feeling of being home hit Claire when she turned off S. Yale Avenue into Southern Pointe. The front porch light was on as well as a small light in Claire's office. She punched the button on the garage door opener and waited. Claire reached over and touched Shy on the leg, "Honey, we're home."

"Good, I can't wait to get into my own bed. Do you suppose Aunt Nae brought Hairy back. I really want a big hug from my dog."

"I'm sure he'll be waiting for us. She knows I don't like having the house empty when I get home."

"Gee, Mom, I thought you didn't mind being alone."

"I like having Hairy to greet me as much as you do. And don't start with me about Mr. Krammer."

"So it's Mr. again. Well, at least you're not calling him just Krammer or worse."

"Honey, I'm really beat. Was there a point to your last comment or did I just not get it?" asked Claire as she opened the car door.

"Thanks for going. Considering all that happened, I felt much better having you along. Man were there a bunch of cops waiting for us back at the school or what?"

"I didn't think they were ever going to let us leave. I bet Mr. Barnett'll be there all night. How many times can they ask the same question?" asked Claire.

"I wish Sarah and I could've looked through Ali's locker."

"Why?" asked Claire.

Dead Tones

"The police told Sarah they found a black stone in Abby's pocket and that one was in Sue's clarinet case. We wanted to see if there was one in Ali's locker. Maybe Mrs. Hayes found one in Ali's purse or backpack. Would you ask Mrs. Hayes the next time you talk to her?" asked Shy.

"Is it important?"

"The officer who talked to us out on the highway seemed to think it could be," explained Shy, reaching for her pillow and blanket and then letting a jaw stretching yawn escape. "I'm going to bed. Sure glad B. isn't having practice in the morning. I'd never make it."

"I want to get my bag out of the trunk first, then I'm right behind you. Let Hairy out, would ya? And turn on the garage light. It's dark out here."

Shy could hear the big yellow dog yipping at the door. She turned her key in the lock and opened the door. "Hey, boy." Shy rubbed the floppy ears and reached for the light. "Go see Mom."

"Here boy," said Claire. The dog was instantly at her side rubbing up against her leg. "I love you too, Hairy." Claire set her bag on the ground, closed the trunk and reached down to caress the dog. "Were you good for Nae?"

Claire wasn't sure if she really heard a noise, but Hairy's ears perked up and a slow rumble in his belly turned into a deep growl. "What do you hear, boy?" asked Claire. She looked across the moon lit cul-de-sac and nothing moved. The headlights from up the street grew brighter until the car pulled around the circle in front of the house and stopped. "Maybe it was the car we heard, Hairy," said Claire not sounding so sure of herself.

Hairy was not satisfied either, his white canine teeth still exposed and ready for any unsuspecting prowler. He didn't move from Claire's side.

R. Z. Crompton

The car was a dark color Claire couldn't identify without sunlight, but the man inside had to be Scott. She just wasn't expecting him to drive up in a Corvette. Claire knew the car's outline as well as she knew that of a Jaguar. The only two cars she hungered for and would never be able to afford.

Hairy's growl intensified as he watched the strange man approach. The hair on his back stood straight up and the dog let out a fierce warning which stopped Scott in his tracks.

"Hairy, sit," commanded Claire. She stroked his head and the dog backed down, but he didn't take his eyes off the man standing at the edge of the driveway. "Good, boy. Okay, Scott, he won't hurt you," said Claire with a smile on her face.

"Where in the hell did you get the man eater?"

"He does his job well, don't you agree?"

"Are you sure I'm safe?" asked Scott taking very slow steps.

"Yeah, just walk up to him and hold out your hand, so he can get your scent."

"You're joking right? This is the first dog I ever believed could actually eat a human being."

"Only men, he's trained to know the difference," Claire tease.

"And that's supposed to make me feel better?"

"Scott, this is Mr. Hairy Monster. Hairy this is Scott." At the sound of his name, the dog looked affectionately up at Claire and then back at Scott. The growls subsided and the nose began a general inspection for approval. "He usually isn't quite so aggressive, but something spooked both of us just before you drove up. Sorry he scared you. By the way, don't ever try to get into the house without me or Shy around. If you do, I have no doubt he'll find you very tasty."

Dead Tones

"I'm absolutely sure I'll have no reason to try," Scott said while he reluctantly let Hairy finish his inspection. "What if he doesn't approve?"

"He ate the last guy Shy brought home," explained Claire. She picked up her bag and headed for the door. "C'mon, Hairy, let's go in. It's cold out here. Man, this cold snap sure took care of the flowers." Hairy took one last look around the front of the house and fell in behind Claire and Scott.

"Now I know why Shy doesn't date much."

"She trusts Hairy's judgement as much as I do. Just the good guys get in. By the way, nice car."

"Thanks, it's the only advantage to not having a family, but it's not a substitute," said Scott with a touch of melancholy in his voice. Then to change the subject he continued, "When will I know if I pass Hairy's test?"

"When he doesn't eat you. I'm surprised you got here so fast." Claire's free hand automatically reached up to press the button which closed the garage door behind them. However, the person crouching behind the holly bush next door still didn't move.

"The police let me go after I told them the whole story again, about my own disgusting childhood and everything I knew about the girls. Dale sat in on the questioning which saved me some time. He knew most of my background, but not the part about why I ran away. I don't know if I'm glad or disappointed that he told me to take tomorrow off. I thought I'd have a couple of days before he suspended me."

"What'd he say?" asked Claire.

"To find a lawyer."

"That's not exactly a suspension," offered Claire. Scott shrugged his shoulders in response. She moved through the utility room and into the kitchen. Shy had left all the lights in her path on as she'd

R. Z. Crompton

made her way upstairs, so Claire gave a brief tour as they walked through the house. "We'll work in my office. That way. It's the room with the computer." She pointed down the hallway. "I'm going to change quick and start a pot of coffee. Make yourself at home."

Scott watched her move out of sight and then went into the large spacious room she'd pointed to. Flicking on the ceiling light, he did a quick glance around the room and went to turn on the computer. He wasn't sure where or how to start the type of search Claire had offered, but he did know he'd sit here all night if he had to. Any information she could find might help him keep his job.

Scott's attention drifted to the books sitting around the room and eventually to the bookcases behind him. Claire had quite a collection of reading material. Scott picked up one of the cheap paperbacks shoved into one side of the case. *An Angry Lover* was etched in silver across the front of the book. The binding was creased in several places indicating where she'd over stressed the binding. Scott focused on some of the other crinkled titles lined up in the case. *So, Mrs. Mayfield likes reading trashy novels. This information might come in handy.* Most of the books, he assumed, were resource material. Titles like *Surviving in the Wilderness* and *Cooking with Mother Nature* showed a completely different side of the woman.

"So, I see you've found my weakness," said Claire walking up behind him. She'd changed into a purple satin jogging suit.

"You've got quite a variety of books."

"I enjoy a diversity of topics," explained Claire. "I guess that's why I like writing. A lot of these spark an idea for a story. And when I have to write about a particular restaurant, it's a lot easier if I understand the type of cooking."

"I thought most people kept their cookbooks in the kitchen." Scott's statement was more of a question.

Dead Tones

"Only people who like to cook. I enjoy the finer points of culinary art, and I like savoring the chef's masterpiece; however, that doesn't mean I like to cook. Shy and I are experts at conjuring up quick meals. In fact, Albertson's Deli chicken is the best fastfood we've been able to find. A few pieces of chicken, a fresh loaf of french bread along with a quick salad and we've got a nutritious meal for just a few bucks."

"I'm a sucker for their pesto pizza," added Scott.

"Yeah, but the chicken is cheaper, and Hairy likes chicken more than pizza."

"Oh, of course, I forgot Hairy would certainly have a vote in the dinner menu," said Scott looking down at the dog keeping watch at the large window. "Does he always sit like that, staring out the window?"

"Only when he's sure something is going on out there." As the two of them watched, Hairy's head twitched from side to side. His ears were alert listening for the slightest sound.

"Why don't you just let him out?"

"He's supposed to guard the house not the neighborhood," answered Claire.

"What about these?" Scott pointed to the rows of overused paperbacks.

"Simple entertainment, like your car I suppose."

"How 'bout the rescue and survival books? You don't strike me as the outdoor type," said Scott.

"You mean you can't imagine my dangling by a rope off a cliff in the Red Rocks of Nevada or hiking, with only a small pack, through the Holy Cross Wilderness in the Rocky Mountains?"

"Only in your imagination do I see you doing something so...so exciting."

"Good choice of adjectives. My daughter thinks I'm nuts. Honestly, though, you're right. So far my desires have not come to fruition."

"What do you mean?"

"I've been fascinated by the rescue stories coming out of the mountains for years. Shy and I go out to Beaver Creek and Vail skiing whenever we get the chance. After my divorce, I had time and energy to give to my personal interests, and the mountains were at the top of my list. The Search and Rescue teams are made up of mostly volunteers who spend years just training to go on a mission. There's no pay for these unselfish people and very little recognition. Their pay is the personal satisfaction and thrill derived from doing a job that needs to be done."

"You know these people?" asked Scott.

"I've interviewed and written about several of the groups. Who do you suppose needs rescuing more, men or women?"

Scott was sure this was a trick question, but he had no idea which way to go. "I don't know, women because they don't have the stamina?"

"That's the logical answer, but not the right one. Men are notorious for doing stupid macho things, like skiing through an avalanche area. A rescue team more often than not is called in by the smarter female partner to find her counter-part who has gone off into the wilderness to prove his manliness only to be found dead under a couple feet of snow."

"Is that why you like researching the rescue teams? It gives you more ammunition to use against us?"

"No. I like the mountains, and I need something to suck up my interests and energy after Shy leaves for college."

"Aren't you staying here?" asked Scott with a strange sense of loss building in his belly.

Dead Tones

"I don't think so. There's no way I can come into this house knowing she'll not be coming home for dinner," said Claire. The lump in her throat threatened to break her. Thinking of Shy's leaving was Claire's nightmare. She could live her life with no one else as long as Shy was coming home. When Shy harassed her about needing somebody else in her life, Claire couldn't admit that Shy was the only one she needed or wanted. Claire was determined to focus on ShyAnne for as long as possible. She didn't want any other person taking time away from her daughter. There'd be plenty of opportunities later for new people and places.

"So you're going to hang from cliffs as a distraction from your loneliness?" Scott didn't wait for an answer. "Wouldn't it be safer just to move to campus with her. Lots of people go back to college when their kids do. You could still write your stories, but you don't have to risk your life."

"I can't follow my daughter off to school. That's sick. I'd be proving her right. She already thinks I'm a lonely old woman. Nope, I've already made plans to sell the house and move to Colorado. Don't you tell her this. As far as she knows, I'm staying here. Her leaving is as natural as...as"

"Ripping your heart out with a butter knife?" added Scott.

"Ummm, yeah, that's pretty close," answered Claire. She didn't want to go any further with this topic. "I haven't told a living soul about my plans. I trust you can keep a secret."

"Let's see, I've hidden my identity and background for over twelve years. I think I've proven my ability to keep my mouth shut," promised Scott. *So Claire Mayfield isn't as tough as she wants everyone to believe.* He had one more question to ask, but Hairy interrupted.

The dog suddenly turned into a fierce monster leaping at the window. His hind legs thrust him forward as his front paws reached for something outside. Scott was aghast. He'd only seen this type of fury in the movies.

Claire rushed to the window and pushed Hairy over so she could have a better look. Scott was instantly beside her. Their eyes combed through the darkness. Hairy let the two of them have his window because he needed an appropriate amount of space to express his protective nature. Hairy moved to the next window and than ran to the front door. It was important for any possible intruder to understand that Hairy had the entire perimeter of this property guarded.

"There, see the shadow!" Scott pointed at something on the other side of the cul-de-sac.

Claire's eyes followed his finger, but she couldn't make out anything in the darkness. "I don't see anything."

"I did. I know I saw someone in black or his shadow over there between those two houses."

"All the yards over there are completely fenced, and we all have good sized dogs. If anyone is lurking about, the other dogs will start barking."

As if on cue, the chorus of canine howls brought the lights on in two of the yards just across from them. The figure jumped to life scurrying up the street taking refuge behind bushes from one house to another. Scott and Claire watched the illusive waltz until the body was out of sight.

"You want to call the cops?" he asked.

"You've got to be kidding. I've spent too much time being questioned tonight. Besides, by the time a car gets here, the guy will be long gone," said Claire.

"I suppose you're right. With Hairy here to jump through the window if the guy comes back, I doubt if you have to worry."

Dead Tones

Claire didn't give the Peeping Tom another thought. "Shall we get to work?" She walked to the desk, pulled back her chair and punched in some commands. "Pull up a chair. The coffee will be done in a few minutes."

Scott quickly did as he was told while Claire pushed more buttons.

"You ever ride the Internet, surf the web and all that stuff?" asked Claire.

"Yeah, but for music, not old newspapers."

"What do you do besides teach jazz band and write solos?"

"My computer and I don't just write solos. I compose all the parts of the marching music and visuals," explained Scott trying not to boast.

"I'm impressed, all the music?"

"All the music. During the summer and my free nights, my computer and I create shows for a half dozen or so other bands, just depends on how many requests I get and how intricate the show will be," explained Scott.

Claire had stopped punching buttons and watched his lips move. "Really? You can do all that?"

Scott fidgeted in his seat. He wasn't used to bragging. Only Dale knew about his summer job. "It's easy. A director gives me a theme to work with, then I go for a long run. The music and a picture work around in my head until I see a show developing on a field. I can hear the music, see the colorguard, even the number of marchers on the field. Then I go back to my computer, work up the score and drills, and send a finished product via the Internet a few weeks later. If the director wants to make any changes, it's fairly easy."

"Wow, I'm impressed. I'm also not the only one who spends a lot of time with a computer," said Claire.

"True, however, my extracurricular activities don't have me hanging off a cliff somewhere," offered Scott giving her a big toothy grin. Their eyes locked.

Claire hadn't been this close to him, this vulnerable. She couldn't move, couldn't breathe. Hairy's cold nose on her hand broke the spell. "Oh, Hairy, did you get the bad guy?" Breaking eye contact with Scott, she stroked the golden neck resting on her arm.

"I can see why you put such great faith in old Hairy here. He's the only chaperon ShyAnne needs."

"I'll get the coffee. Can you think of the name of the paper in Charleston? If you can, type it in." Claire stood up and walked away.

Unfortunately, Hairy didn't move a muscle. His big brown eyes scrutinized every inch of Scott's body. He cocked his head from one side to the other and finally swaggered over to test the new guy.

"Are we going to be friends?" Scott asked the dog. "Is this your way of making the first move? Well, I accept." Scott reached his hand out and rubbed the dog's broad yellow chest. "Tell you what, I'll rub your chest, scratch your ears, and even feed you from the table if you'll just leave me alone with her once in a while. Deal?"

Claire was back before Scott had a chance to put anything in the computer; and as if living up to his end of the bargain, Hairy walked out of the room. "Glad to see you're not going to be his next meal."

"Me too. And I don't remember the names of any papers. Sorry."

"It's okay. Are you from Charleston proper or a smaller area?"

"Our family home was out of town, but my father's business was in Charleston. He was a big shot, so anything about him or the family will make the big paper. However, you need to look for a Kraminski, not Krammer."

Claire looked away from the key board, but didn't say anything.

Dead Tones

"I felt it wise to change my name. Harder to track me down that way."

"I understand. So is your first name really Scott?" she asked.

"Yes and no. It is now because I had everything legally changed, but I was Andrew, Andrew Kraminski before my mother died."

"And your father's first name?"

"Randolf. He's a lawyer, and if you don't owe him money then he's probably put you in jail at one time or another. He dabbles in the ponies. Trades diamonds with a broker out of Denmark, and plays with a number of other things I can't remember. All I know is that he has created a small empire and he's in charge. He's good and once a client owes him, he owes forever."

"Sounds like a terrible man."

"He's a feeder, like a shark."

"Let's find out what he's been up to." Claire clicked away. The information was tapped in and up came a series of dates and pages from the local papers in the Charleston area. Claire turned on her printer, so Scott could read the family happenings for the last fifteen years. There was plenty to read.

****

The first article dropped out of the printer into Scott's hand. "This one's about my sister." Scott dropped it on the desk. He'd seen it the morning after her body was found. Claire picked up the page after she'd instructed the computer to print the next story. She perused the page quickly. The body of Tessa Kraminski was found on the banks of the Intercostal Waterway near the south end of the Isle of Palms. Claire didn't have to read the entire article to understand what had happened. The sixteen year old had been brutally beaten to death and her body thrown out into the swampy area between the ocean and the mainland. "Did they ever catch who did this?"

"My father did it," said Scott flatly. "Remember when I told you I saw her on her bed crying? My father was standing over her with a belt in his hand. I could hear her stifled screams for hours. I never saw her again. I'm sure my father dumped her in the swamp hoping a gator would drag her off."

"I'm sorry, Scott. What's that one about?"

"Oh, this is a good one. My father got the Man of the Year Award. What a crock. Here's one about my mother's death. Get this, after I ran away, my father actually hinted to the police that I might have killed her. I should have expected something like this."

Claire looked through the stories as Scott handed them to her. There were several about legal cases Randolf had won, and then about his quest for a senate seat. "That's just what you needed was your father in the Senate."

"Hey, hey. Look at this. Here's a new twist. When my father tried to organize a manhunt for me, my older brother stood up to him. I guess the my brother inherited enough of the old man's backbone and my mother's conscience to stand up to him after all. How 'bout this bit of news?" Scott leaned back in his seat and handed the paper to Claire.

"Jordan Kraminski, Jr., your brother?" Claire looked up and saw Scott give an affirmative nod. "Your brother testified against your father for tax invasion. What happened?"

"I don't know. Where's the next article?"

"Oh, yeah. Just a second." Claire pushed the button and out came another story.

"Look! Look!" Scott was out of his seat. "Yes, yes, you old jerk. Mom wanted to destroy you; and by taking her own life, she

Dead Tones

managed to start the process. Thank you, Jordan. May you rest in peace, Mom."

"What?"

"Jordan Kraminski, Sr. was found guilty and had to sell off most of his business assets and the estate to stay out of jail. The stress caused a massive stroke, and he was put in a nursing home."

"Did Jordan call off the hunt for you?"

"Yeah, says here that he completely exonerated me by telling the police how bad my father was. He's sure Mom took her own life. Good Lord," Scott paused again and dropped the paper to his side.

"Is 'Good Lord' bad or good here?" asked Claire.

"I'm the sole beneficiary to my mother's will. I didn't even know she had money of her own. This is incredible. I mean it may be only a few dollars and after all this time, Jordan or Zack might have laid claim to it. It doesn't matter. It just feels good to know my mother wanted to take care of me."

"Who's Zack?"

"My younger brother. I haven't seen his name at all."

"Here," said Claire looking at her computer screen again. "Here's Zackery Kraminsky, what a yucky name. Just a minute."

Scott was standing at the printer waiting. His breath caught in his throat. "He's dead. Jordan must have sent him to school in Switzerland as soon as Zack was old enough, cause it says here that Zack had been there for several years. He died while mountain climbing in the Alps. See I told you messing around in the mountains is dangerous."

"You don't seem too broken up about your brother's death."

"Are you kidding? Zack was a carbon copy of my father. Worse in fact. No, God did the world a favor when he took Zackery. Is there anything else?"

R. Z. Crompton

"That's about it. A few short items. I'll have them printed out." Claire picked up the stories she hadn't read while Scott waited at the printer for the new ones.

****

The November morning sun was up long before Claire, Scott or even ShyAnne fluttered an eye. Hairy had eventually given up on Claire and cuddled in next to Shy's exhausted body around four in the morning. He always knew when she was too tired to push him off the bed. However, by mid-morning, he was desperate for Shy to get up.

"Hairy, go get Mom," mumbled Shy as she pushed the cold wet nose away from her face. The dog didn't go far. He'd already tried to wake Claire and didn't even get a push in the nose.

At the high pitched whine, Shy rubbed her eyes and threw off the covers. "Okay, boy, I'm coming."

Hairy ran for the door and then back to give her a push on the leg. "Yeah, yeah, I'm coming." Shy stumbled down the steps, past the office and toward the front door. When she pulled open the door, Hairy squeezed past and made a dash for the lawn.

"Wow," whispered Shy, "wow." She was dumbfounded. A black Corvette was parked in front of the house for everyone to see, and most of them knew none of her friends would drive a car like that. Shy knew the car. She saw it everyday in the school parking lot. "Wow," was all she could say. Hairy sat at her feet now waiting to get back into the house, but Shy stepped back closing the door before Hairy could run inside. A quick yelp brought Shy out of her trance and the door opened.

In spite of her desire to go find her mother, Shy decided it would be more tasteful and mature to get dressed and out of the house as quickly and quietly as possible. She tiptoed back down the hallway

Dead Tones

and past the office doorway. On this passing she saw them. Scott was sprawled out on the sofa, legs hanging freely over one end. A stack of papers rose and fell with his chest and a hand rested on the floor. Claire had relaxed in the recliner and was laid back comfortably, with several pieces of paper scattered on her lap and the chair. One arm rested on her thigh and the other was draped over the arm of the chair.

"Well, what do we have here?" questioned Shy in a voice certainly meant to jerk them out of the deep sleep. "I thought I'd raised you better than this young lady. Letting a virtual stranger spend the night? What will the neighbors think?"

"Good morning to you too, dear," said Claire rubbing her eyes.

"Mom, I hope you don't think this qualifies as a date," said Shy, nodding her head toward the long stretching body across the room. "By the looks of you, I don't exactly think this was a romantic interlude."

"Give it a rest, Shy. We were looking for information about Andrew Kraminski."

"Who in the world is Andrew Kra...Kra..."

"It's me," answered Scott still yawning. "That was my name before I had it changed. I guess we fell asleep."

"I'd say that's a pretty accurate conclusion. I wish I had a camera now. The kids would love to see this."

"You don't need to say anything," suggested Claire as she picked up the papers off her lap.

"Did you get anything good?" asked Shy.

"What do you think, Scott, should we tell her?"

"If we don't tell her, she'll tell the whole school she found us sleeping together."

"Then we could hang her at dawn," teased Claire.

"Would one of you talk, please?" begged Shy.

"I found enough information about my family to know my father couldn't possibly have done this."

"That's great, Mr. Krammer. But how do you know?"

Scott gave Shy a brief summary of what he'd gleaned from the articles. "I should've done this years ago. Certainly would've made my life easier."

"Would you have stayed here, Mr. Krammer, or gone back to Charleston?"

"I would've stayed here. This is my home now, has been for a long time. Unfortunately, I'm not sure I'll be able to stay after all this mess is cleaned up; it may never be cleaned up as far as the parents are concerned. I know there's been rumors going around about me for years. This might be all that's needed to get rid of me."

"You can make a living anywhere, Scott. With your music connections, all you need is a computer," suggested Claire.

"You mean like in Colorado?"

"Maybe," she answered.

"What are you guys up too?"

"Nothing. Are you going to school today?"

"Yeah, if I hurry, I can get there before third hour starts. You going to tell the police what you found?"

"Of course, they'll find out anyway with a little checking. It's not like we really had to dig deep to find this stuff," answered Claire.

"Ya know, Claire, if I tell the police right away, then Sarah's going to be the top suspect. If I wait and let them dig up the information on their own, we might have more time to find out who is doing this."

"I see, but the longer you let this fester, the harder it's going to be to get the school to reinstate you," said Claire.

"Remember, Dale didn't actually say I was suspended. There hasn't been time for that. He just told me to get a lawyer. But

Dead Tones

Sarah's another story. With Sarah as the only suspect, the police might not have any choice but to arrest her. The arrest would stay on her record forever. If we don't find out who's doing this, Jennifer is going to keep up this witch hunt until the cops won't be able to ignore her."

"Jennifer?" said Shy. "The other night Sarah said to watch for who is yelling the loudest and the killer would be close at hand."

"Yeah, I remember something like that. So?" asked Claire.

"I think we need to find out more about Jennifer's friends, and I need to find out if Mrs. Hayes ever found a black stone in Allison's stuff."

"I'll find out about the black stone. You get ready for school."

"Thanks, Mom. And make sure you ask her if it was wrapped in anything. I've got to get going. If Sarah goes to school, those kids will eat her alive. If she doesn't, then I need to see who's saying what."

"Will you be straight home?" asked Claire.

"No, I think I'll go over to Mama C's Pizzeria. It's the big after school hang out, and I want to eavesdrop. Jennifer always goes over there. Do you want me to bring you and Mr. Krammer some pizza?"

"No, I forgot I've got to go over to Bourbon Street Cafe for dinner. If I don't get their story done, it won't be ready for the Sunday paper."

"Bourbon Street Cafe, the one on 15th street?" asked Scott.

"As far as I know the other restaurant isn't open yet; so yes, the one on 15th."

Scott sounded like a little boy. "There's going to be another one."

"Yes, that's why I'm going down to see Kevin," answered Claire.

"I love that place. The music is fun."

"You make the music sound like a participatory sport."

R. Z. Crompton

"I guess it is. Once a month, the Sunday afternoon jazz session is open to anyone who wants to join in. I love it. I try to get the kids to come with me sometimes; but Sunday afternoon at the Cafe is the best, and it's my time to get lost in jazz."

"Mom, you gonna see Blake or Kevin, or one of the other managers?" asked Shy.

"Both Kevin and Blake, I think. Dave and Paul, the other two managers, aren't available today. Why?"

"I was just wondering if Blake was going to be there."

"Why?"

"Cause he's so incredibly hot. That's why. Are you happy you made me admit it in front of Mr. Krammer? By the way, since you spent the night with my mother, can I call you Scott?"

"No, you may not call him Scott, but you can come with us," Claire said, not realizing she'd just invited Scott to go along.

"Us? Who's going with you?" asked Shy.

"I guess I thought you," said Claire looking at Scott, "might be willing to go with me considering your love for the place. Sorry there's no live music tonight."

"Yeah, I've got good reason to celebrate. Shy why don't you join us when you're done at Mama C's. Come have dessert with us," suggested Scott.

"You don't mind if I intrude? I mean, I'd really like to see Blake again," said Shy.

"What's so great about Blake? I've known him since the restaurant opened, and he's just a guy."

"He's a dead ringer for a young version of Robert Redford. The guy is drop dead gorgeous," oozed Shy.

"There's more to being a man than just good looks," suggested Scott.

Dead Tones

""He's unbelievably nice, but he's too old for me. All I get to do is look," said Shy.

"And you, what do you think of this extremely buff man?" asked Scott looking at Claire.

"I like Kevin. He's tall, dark and handsome. That's good enough for me. However, he's too young for me, so alas, I'm caught in the same spot as Shy. I only get to look."

"Is that the only reason you go down there?" snipped Scott.

Claire and Shy looked at each other and back to Scott. Shy was amazed. Scott Krammer was jealous.

"We go for the fantastic food. The great service is an added benefit; and the scenery, well that should be listed as one of the Eight Wonders of the World."

"Okay, okay. I know all those guys, and they're good but not that good. You're making fun of me." Scott knew he sounded ridiculous, but he couldn't stop himself.

Claire and Shy smiled and laughed, but it was Shy who dropped the issue of age at their feet, "Mr. Krammer, you're in the same category as those guys: too old for me and too young for Mom and too good looking not to notice. So why'd you get so jealous? Hey, I gotta get going. See ya tonight, about eight, okay?"

"Yes, dear. We'll be watching for you."

Scott knew exactly why he was jealous and so did Claire. Neither said a word about the comment until Shy left the room. "I'm sorry, Claire. I had no right to act that way. I'm not used to listening to girls talk about men."

"Scott, you're kidding aren't you? Your students talk that way all the time, and you want me to believe you never hear it."

"I don't care when the girls at school talk about that way. You two are different. I've got to go. Can I pick you up tonight?" Afraid she might say no, he didn't wait for an answer. "Six-thirty? I think I'll call my brother this afternoon."

Claire still had a silly grin on her face as she shook her head in agreement. She knew she should've been mad at him, but she just couldn't find any anger. He was cute when he was jealous, and this was the first date Claire had had in a long time. Maybe her matchmaker sister would be happy now.

****

Mama C's Pizzeria, conveniently tucked behind Woodland Hills Mall on Memorial Avenue, was the favorite hang out for Renegade Regiment. After a Friday night home game, the place vibrated with school pride, although the noise level was definitely higher after a win. This Monday afternoon, the place was alive. Everybody and their Aunt Martha had a theory about Sue and Abby. Jennifer and Kate, along with the other clarinet players sat at the long table below the television screen, but the sound had been muted.

"Do you believe the nerve. I almost fell over when she walked into second hour," said Kate.

"If she knew what was good for her, she'd be out looking for a lawyer," offered Jennifer.

"I bet she thinks her magic will save her. Did you see how fast everybody went through their lockers this morning after the police found that black stone in Sue's extra Clarinet case," snickered Megan.

"No kidding. If the cops had found the stupid thing while they were searching the semi last night, the whole effect would've been lost," Jennifer admitted.

"Yeah, you certainly took a good look through your stuff, Jen," stated Kate as she took another bite of the vegetarian special. "Umm, this is so good. I can't understand why I'm so hungry."

Dead Tones

"You didn't find a rock in your locker. Believe me, that'll affect your appetite," said Jennifer.

"You didn't find one of those stupid rocks either."

"Well, I expected to, and I know how I felt while I was looking through all my stuff. My breathing increased, I was sweating. It was terrible. I almost passed out."

"You had an anxiety attack, that's all. Now go get something to eat before the guys get here. You know they'll take every last piece on the buffet," said Kate.

"How can you be so calm about this? One of us could be next," replied Megan. "I felt the same anxiety as Jen when I was going through my stuff. When my fingers wrapped around the jaw breaker I'd bought yesterday, I almost peed my pants."

"There's the guys. C'mon, Megan, let's get something to eat. Even if we aren't hungry, the pizza's pretty good. Hey, was there any of the cinnamon apple up there, Kate?"

"Yeah, but you'd better hurry. Look," Kate pointed at the two girls coming in the door. "I can't believe her nerve. It's Sarah and Shy."

Jennifer and Megan stared at the two girls walking through the door. Jennifer had been furious when the officer stopped her last night, but this afternoon there were no cops around. "C'mon, Meg. My appetite's growing as we speak."

Shy and Sarah knew they were walking into the fire. The rumors had been growing all day. Each class Sarah had walked into brought long, leering stares. By lunch time, Shy knew if they were going to find out what was happening, then they had to be in the middle of the action, and this was definitely the place to be. The kids always flocked to the television and moved the smaller tables together. Shy and Sarah settled for a spot as close to the television as they could get without pulling up a seat right next to Jennifer. No use trying to hide. Their plan had been to start the kids talking and then watch the flames take off. Sarah's theory put Jennifer at the center of the turmoil. Sarah scrutinized every person at the table with Jennifer and calculated the odds as to who was capable of murder. One of them was setting her up to take the blame for Sue and Abby.

"Well, you were right, Shy. Everybody's staring. If they weren't talking about me before, they are now," Sarah said watching the faces.

"Let's grab some pizza. I'm starving," suggested Shy.

"Shy, you don't have to do this for me. I heard some of the kids calling you 'Indian lover' in Chem. Doing this for me will alienate you from everybody else."

"Thanks, but don't worry about me. When all this is over, I can tell each one of them to kiss my ass. We'll look like the only two with a brain. Now hurry up before those eating machines get the really good pieces."

"Wait a minute, if you're so smart then why don't you let the guys clean the platters? There will be steaming hot replacements any minute."

"Good idea. See, that's why I hang with you."

"Yeah, well, you might really get hung with me if we don't find out who's doing this. Were there any bread sticks up there?"

"No, but they'll probably come out with the next pizzas. I want some of the cheese pizza without tomato sauce. This is the only place in town where I can have pizza my way."

"You amaze me! How can you have a pizza without sauce? It's the sauce that makes a pizza."

"No it's not. It's a pizza pie, silly. You can put anything on a pizza crust and have a pizza pie. I like my pies made without tomato sauce. You like the bread sticks topped with chocolate and powdered sugar, so don't tell me how weird my taste buds are."

Dead Tones

"I like anything covered with chocolate. And I've seen you put away more than your fair share of chocolate breadsticks after a game."

"Yeah, well they have a particular appeal after the hype of a game. Nothing like some sugar and caffeine all in the same bite."

"Ya know, I'd love to look through all those purses at Jennifer's table. Somebody over there has at least one more black stone tucked deep down inside."

"How do you know that?" asked Shy, trying not to gawk at the others. When she looked back at Sarah, Shy felt foolish for even asking the question. "Cause your Grandmother told you?"

"I can feel it myself, Shy. There's still more to come."

"Can't you get the police to search everybody's purses and lockers?"

"No, they need a little more to go on than my feelings. I don't know if they believe I'm innocent because of the black stone not being wrapped in cloth or because they don't believe in the magic at all. In which case, I'm not guilty because I don't have any magic powers," said Sarah.

"I don't care what the police believe as long as they don't lock you up before we find out who's really guilty. How's your mother taking this?" asked Shy.

"Not well, not well at all. She blames my grandmother for all this trouble."

"Why? Your Mom's full blood Cherokee. I thought she'd be more understanding."

"You've got to be kidding. She's full blooded by birth but not by heart. As far as my mother is concerned, the Cherokee left their heritage in the history books. When we started living with the whiteman, she believes we walked away from our old ways. She doesn't understand how important it is for us to keep the religion and the magic alive. There are lots of elders in Tahlequah who remember their parents telling them about the Trail of Tears and how they survived. They were only children then, but they still remember and they told their children. Now those children are the elders, and they tell us what it was like. They are a direct link to our heritage. We don't have to read about our history; we can live it through the stories. She wants me to stay home until this goes away. I tried to tell her that it's not going to disappear, and that I have to fight. If I even mention my grandmother in front of her, she gets nuts."

"What about your father?"

"Now that's different. Grandmother is my father's mother. I wouldn't be learning the magic if it wasn't for my father's support. I hate fighting with my mother, but sometimes our soul dictates a louder call to order than our parents."

"Does your father think you need a lawyer?"

"Oh, yeah. My mother does have some influence over him. We are going to meet with a man tomorrow morning. Dad doesn't want me to wait until I'm arrested to seek advice. Ya know, my mother insists that if I wasn't learning the magic, I wouldn't have been accused. And I can't argue with her on that one," said Sarah almost defeated.

"So let's get to work. I've got to meet Mom and Mr. Krammer at eight."

"Your mom and Krammer have a date?"

"I'll never doubt the power of your spirits again. Krammer was at the house all night. I found them asleep in mom's office this morning."

"I can think of a more comfortable place to start an affair," said Sarah.

"Yeah, right. They were searching the Internet for stuff about Krammer's family," Shy explained.

Dead Tones

"And?" questioned Sarah while she watched Kate, on the other side of the room, dig through her black leather backpack.

"And they found everything he needed to clear his father. Are you listening to me?"

"I'm listening and watching. I know most kids can't do more than one thing at a time; however, I can watch and listen simultaneously. So why is the father suddenly cleared from wrong doing?"

"It seems the old man got what he deserved. He's been confined to a bed for more than ten years. He can't talk, or move, but he's mentally alert."

"Wow, that'd stink. It's like...like being zipped into a sleeping bag; and when you wake up, the zipper's broke and nobody can get you out. Okay, so where does that leave us?" asked Sarah.

"Nowhere, absolutely nowhere. We know it's not you, so it must be one of them," said Shy nodding her head toward the long table below the television screen.

"Why one of them? There's over a hundred band kids who aren't even here," Sarah added.

"Because one of them is hiding behind Jennifer. And I think it's a clarinet player," Shy said looking over the animated figures around the table.

"Why a clarinet?"

"Because only a clarinet player has easy access to another clarinet player's case and locker. It's a logical excuse to say 'I'm looking for a reed' or 'I need so and so's music' or 'she has my hair twisty'. See what I mean? Now if a drummer, or any guy for that matter started going through Sue's locker, I'd think it was rather strange," explained Shy.

"Makes sense. I'm impressed with your logic. Now how 'bout this. I think the connection among the three victims is Mr. Krammer."

"Really? Why?"

"Think about it. Allison was spending lots of time with Krammer learning the solo, then Sue quickly becomes the center of his interest."

"Yeah, but Abby doesn't fit. She didn't play the clarinet."

"No, but she did have a big chunk of Krammer's attention the night Sue died," explained Sarah. "Remember? He told us how she'd cried and cried in his arms. He even had to escort her upstairs. Then at the zoo he kept asking about her."

"True. Everybody knew he was worried about her. Do you really suppose that's enough of a link?" asked Shy.

Sarah shrugged her shoulders. "I don't know, but it's all I've been able to come up with. I was actually hoping Mr. Krammer's father would turn out to be the guilty party, but that would've been too easy."

"Look, here comes the fresh pizza, and all this thinking makes me hungry." Shy pushed back her seat and made her way to the buffet.

Jennifer, who'd been watching for Shy and Sarah to get in line, intercepted them before they reached the buffet. "You can't eat here. You might poison the food," accused Jennifer. She was standing with her hands on her hips and her feet shoulder-width apart. The girl had squared off and was waiting to complete the challenge she'd started the night before. Her witch hunt mentality had been overcharged all day, and this was the moment she'd been waiting for; but this time there was no Highway Patrolman to step in with the civil rights shit. The room grew silent with Jennifer's first comment.

"Back off, Jennifer. We have as much right to be here as the rest of you," defended Shy. She stepped slightly in front of Sarah in an attempt to make Jennifer understand that if she wanted a fight, she was picking it with Shy.

Dead Tones

"I don't think so. We're," she stopped and pointed back to the table where she'd been sitting before continuing, "the majority here, and we say you can't share our food."

As if an instant replay of the night before had started on the television screen, Jennifer heard a husky voice interfering with her desired confrontation.

"Wait just a minute here." The kids, who didn't know the voice, knew the face when the man entered the room. The owner didn't tolerate any teenage shenanigans in his place; and over the years, he'd seen it all. The most important lesson he'd learned was to step in early while there was still time to defuse the tension. "Young lady," Mike was looking directly at Jennifer, "you have no right to come into my establishment and determine who is served and who isn't. Do I make myself clear?"

"But you don't know what she's capable of," stammered Jennifer. Her red cheeks were filled with rage.

"And according to Mr. Barnett, neither do you."

"Mr. B.?" questioned Jennifer.

"That's right. He called me this afternoon to fill me in on the hostility level. Seems you are making allegations which have no foundation. And you can't do it here."

Jennifer didn't say a word. She'd been shot down again, so the only thing she could do now to maintain a little dignity was leave. She marched back to the table, picked up her purse, and left. The other kids at her table watched in silence.

Mike turned to Shy and Sarah, who were still standing by the buffet. "Sorry, girls. I hope you'll stay."

"Is the pizza as good as it always is?"

"Of course," answered Mike with a warm smile.

"Then we stay," said Sarah, picking up a plate.

Krissy came through the door only seconds after Jennifer's bitter exit. She quickly made her way to ShyAnne and whispered, "Wow, who got Jennifer's panties in a wad. She was stringin' out a line of curses that would embarrass even a drummer."

"Hey, Krissy. Jennifer's always got her panties in a wad. Where have you been?" asked Shy.

"I decided to have a talk with Mike. I really didn't want us to start hating each other; on the other hand, I can't go back to being his little blond bimbo anymore," said Krissy

"So how much did you tell him?" Sarah doubted if Krissy had come clean about her grades and where she was going to college. "If we have to cover for you, you'd better tell us what's still a secret."

"I explained how I got caught up in the 'clueless' routine, and that it was just an act. At first he didn't believe me. Men! Even after I told him my class rank and my SAT score, he didn't believe me. We had to actually open the chemistry book, so he could quiz me before he accepted the fact that I'm smarter than he is."

"Did you tell him about Princeton?" asked Sarah.

"Good heavens, no. He can only handle so much at a time. I thought I'd let him digest the grades first," answered Krissy.

"So are you two still going out together?"

"It's on hold for now. I suggested we just let things mellow out for a few days until all this mess with Sue and Abby is cleared up. We don't have a deadline we have to meet or anything. Now what's been going on? Where's Monica and Sean?"

"They didn't want to get caught between you and Mike, so they went down to the Central Library to study," answered Shy.

"Good idea. I don't want them to think they have to take sides in this. There's no reason to. Sarah, if you need help with any homework or studying, just let me know," offered Krissy.

Dead Tones

"Thanks. I'm okay for now; and I think this will be cleared up in a few days, one way or another."

"Sarah, I was just thinking how lucky you've been," said Shy.

"Lucky? I'm missing something."

"Each time Jennifer has challenged you, someone has stepped in on your behalf, first the officer and then Mike. Neither of them gave her the chance to argue," explained Shy.

"Grandmother put a spell on me. She asked the spirits to protect me. Her magic is stronger than mine. I just hope she's strong enough."

****

Bourbon Street Cafe was the newest and hottest restaurant in Tulsa. Cajun food was the rage and Bourbon Street made the best. Walking through the front door was an instant trip to New Orleans. The music was an entertaining mix of jazz and Creole. And the food? Well, the food was an erotic experience. Claire loved everything from the cajun popcorn and fried alligator to the more elegant Oysters Rockefeller. All of the chef's secret recipes were good, but Claire's constant favorite was Mardi Gras Snapper. Nothing she'd ever had compared to the delicate shrimp and crab madeira sauce which smothered the white snapper.

Scott and Claire sat in a booth, one on each side of the table. Claire ordered the traditional New Orleans Hurricane to sip on while she discussed the new restaurant with Kevin, who had slipped into the booth beside Claire. Scott had the more potent Sazerac Cocktail. Claire told him it was the New Orleans version of a Manhattan, one would curl your hair as fast as the other.

"So Kevin, when will the new restaurant be open?" asked Claire.

R. Z. Crompton

"The 81st and Lewis location should open the doors in a few more weeks. You know how hard it is to give an exact date. Until the decorating is done and the tables set, anything can happen to push the opening day back. Scott, you willing to play for us?"

"Can't wait. You give me a day, and I'll be there. You're using the same theme, aren't you?"

"Absolutely, Claire would shoot me if I changed the menu. The place is bigger though, and we've added a fireplace and fountain."

"More important is whether or not you've fixed the parking." said Claire.

Kevin laughed. He knew parking at the 15th Street location had been a challenge. "Yeah, Claire, parking won't be quite so exciting. But ya know, lots of our clientele like a short walk after eating such a fantastic dinner. They claim it's good for their new-found cajun soul. Any other questions?"

"I'll call you if I need anything. You want to preview a copy before I send it in?"

"Nope, I'll read it in the paper. I've got to get back to work. Hey you guys come back on Sunday. The Tulsa Jazz Society is playing. Bring some of those kids you keep telling me about, Scott."

"Sure thing," answered Scott.

Shy was disappointed to not find Scott and Claire sitting beside each other when she arrived, but then that was probably too much to ask for. They were just finishing up their main course when she walked in.

"How was school today?" Claire asked.

"Interesting, very interesting," answered Shy as she slid into the seat beside her mother.

"I take it you don't mean intellectually interesting," said Scott.

"That's for sure. I couldn't think about anything except Sarah. By the way, how's Allison?"

Dead Tones

"She's the same. Sylvia said she looks like she's just sleeping comfortably, like she should wake up any minute. And yes, she found a round, black stone in Ali's purse, but it wasn't wrapped in anything. Sylvia threw it away cause she thought it was just a rock. Is this good?"

"It just means Sarah's right so far. She expects at least one more to show before we can find the killer. Mr. Krammer, when will you be back at school? We could really use you to help keep a lid on the rumors. You don't have any idea how bad things are. I swear, Jennifer was ready to have a knock down, drag out fight right in the middle of Mama C's this afternoon. She's obsessed."

"I know. Dale called me this afternoon. He said it was pretty bad; and now that I'm off the hook, he wants me back tomorrow.

"Did you guys hear or see anything that'll help?" asked Claire.

"No, not yet. But Sarah thinks the link is you, Mr. Krammer."

"Me. How does she figure that?" he asked incredulously.

"You spent so much time with Allison, then Sue and finally Abby when she broke down Saturday night."

"Okay," said Claire, "but what about Andrea? He spent lots of time with her."

"I don't know. Maybe there was never time to kill her. She was always with one of you. You might have saved her life," replied Shy. "Her folks are keeping her home until this is over. She can have outside contact via the phone and television. That's it."

"Frankly, I agree with her folks. If what you say is true, then she's the next target. Since Jennifer's making such a fuss, why don't you think it's her?" asked Claire.

"Because Sarah's grandmother said the killer is hiding behind whoever is making the loudest noise. Jennifer definitely fills the bill on loud. Besides, if she was guilty, I don't think she'd be making such a fuss. It just draws more attention to her. No, Sarah and I think somebody is encouraging her to be the instigator, and I can't wait to prove that Jennifer's wrong. She deserves a full dish of crow."

"Hello, ShyAnne." Blake was standing just behind Shy's left shoulder.

Shy had to turn completely around to soak in the full pleasure of Blake's presence, and then she wondered how he knew who she was. "Hi, Blake."

"What can I get for you?" His smile almost made her melt.

"I came to have dessert with Mom and Mr. Krammer. I'll wait for them. How 'bout a coke while they finish dinner?"

"Coke, coming up."

Shy watched him walk away and then turned a questioning eye to her mother. "How did he know my name?"

"We told him you were coming," answered Claire.

"Is that all?"

"That's all," said Claire innocently. "We were talking to Kevin and asked Blake to keep an eye out for you. You certainly look nice. I know you didn't dress like that for school."

"I stopped home first to freshen up," replied Shy. The velour top was a deep red with black swirls creating a subtle animal print. The skin tight turtle neck certainly accented her assets. The shirt dropped just to the top of her black jeans. Shy's long curls were placed meticulously to one side of her head and then left to cascade down her back. The desired effect was to look completely natural, not placed and sprayed with cement. The teenager had aged ten years since her mother had last seen her. Fortunately, tomorrow she would be back in the T-shirt and ponytail.

"By the way, I had to take my marching horn over to Tulsa Band. A couple of the keys are bent. Paul said it would be done tomorrow afternoon. Can you stop over and pick it up for me, or do you just want me to charge it?"

Dead Tones

"I'm afraid I might forget. You're right there by the shop, so just charge it," said Claire.

"Mr. Krammer, did you find out anymore about your family?"

"I certainly did. I actually talked to my brother for the first time in nearly eighteen years. I had no idea it had been that long until he reminded me. I left when I was sixteen, six years in Chicago and twelve years teaching; well, time does move right along."

"And?" asked Shy waiting to find out if Scott was still feuding with his family.

"And he wants me to come home as soon as possible."

Shy's face nearly fell into her lap. She couldn't believe he'd go back after all this time. "Are you going?" she asked, not wanting to hear the answer.

"Of course, I'll probably go out for Christmas. Unless, I get a better invitation," Scott said as he looked at Claire.

Shy didn't miss the exchange, but she certainly must have missed a good part of their earlier conversation. "What are you talking about? Are you moving back to South Carolina or not?"

"Moving back? Good Heavens no! Why on earth would I do that?" Scott finished the last bite of his Chicken Bon Tempes and pushed his plate back.

"Well, that's what I want to know?" asked Shy.

"I'm going back to see my brother and his family and to settle some legal matters which have been pending since my mother died, but I'd never move back. There's too much sadness there."

"Okay, now what about this other offer you hinted at."

"I'm waiting for your mother to invite me to go skiing with you."

"I didn't know we were going skiing for Christmas," said Shy.

"I didn't either," answered Claire. "But it sounds like a good idea."

Blake came back to the table again without Shy seeing his approach. "So, have you guys decided on dessert?"

All three blurted out, "Beignets!" The delicate pastry covered with powdered sugar was a New Orleans tradition; but with the Bourbon Street Cafe's added rum sauce, the dessert was heavenly.

"With rum sauce?" asked Blake.

"Of course," said Claire while Shy and Scott just shook their heads in agreement.

CHAPTER THIRTEEN

The evening at Bourbon Street was easy and pleasant. Shy enjoyed watching the warm exchange between her mother and Mr. Krammer; and as much as she wanted to stay while they had an after dinner cappuccino, she was tired and as always, there was homework to be done.

When Shy unlocked the utility room door, she immediately wondered why Hairy wasn't waiting for her. He was always at the door. "Hairy, Hairy." The dog didn't come. Shy looked through the kitchen and the office, then headed upstairs to her room. "Hairy." Shy was getting more worried with every step. When she flipped on the light in her room, Hairy was curled up on her bed. "There you are." She walked into the room.

The remnants of Hairy's evening fun were scattered on the floor. "No wonder you're hiding, you bad dog." When Shy had hurried home to change before going downtown, she threw her jeans on the bed. Shy surmised that Hairy had nosed his way through her pockets until he found the old saxophone reeds she'd taken out of her case before leaving the damaged horn with Paul. "I hope you didn't swallow any of those things. It'll make for a really uncomfortable day tomorrow," she said as she reached over to pet the dog. He'd barely made a move. "I'm not that mad, Hairy." Hairy still didn't move, and this had Shy worried. "I'll go down and get you some water."

Hairy whined when she turned to leave. "It's okay, boy. I'll be right back." Shy hurried to the kitchen for the water. Hairy wasn't acting like himself at all. Mom would be home soon; she'd know what to do. Shy grabbed a bowl, filled it with water and ran back up the stairs. "Here you go, boy." Hairy lifted his head to drink and then closed his eyes. "You sleep for a while. I'll sit here and do some homework." ShyAnne opened her backpack and reached inside for her Chemistry book, but that's not what she pulled out.

The round black stone lay ominously in the palm of her hand. "Oh, My God! My God!" Shy instantly dropped the stone on the bed as if it might burn a hole through her skin. Then she did the only thing she could think of; she called her mother.

Claire was surprised to get a call at Bourbon Street. Her first thought was that Shy had had an accident on the way home. "This is Claire Mayfield."

"Mom, Mom, come home!" Shy's voice was filled with panic.

"Calm down, dear. Are you okay?"

"No, I'm not okay. I found the next stone. It was in my backpack."

"We'll be there in fifteen minutes. Lock the doors. Hairy will let you know if anybody's about," Claire ordered as she motioned for Scott to hurry.

"He can't, Mom. He's sick. I found him on the bed, but he won't get up."

"Lock the doors, then call the vet. We'll run him over as soon as Scott and I get there. I have a bad feeling about this."

****

Claire and Scott found Shy sitting on her bed with Hairy on her lap. "Mom...Mom, I'm really scared. He won't get up." Big tears streamed down her face.

"I know. I am too. Let's get Hairy to the clinic." Claire walked over to the bed and bent down to the dog. "Hi, my friend." Big brown eyes looked helplessly up at her. "I know you don't feel good," said Claire fighting her own tears when Hairy moaned.

"The vet's waiting for us," said Shy.

"Let me carry him," offered Scott. Scott easily picked Hairy up and headed for the door. Claire and Shy followed at his heels. "Scott, let's take my car. There's more room in the back seat."

The quick ride to the veterinary clinic brought only moans from poor Hairy. Claire held the dog's head in her lap and stroked the soft spot right between his eyes. "Hang on, Hairy." The vet's office was only about a mile from the house. The tires squealed, as Scott turned the corner onto Yale Avenue and then made the quick left and finally turned into the clinic's parking lot.

Shy was out of the car before it came to a complete stop. She ran to the office and knocked on the door. By the time the doctor's face appeared, Scott was waiting to carry Hairy in.

"Claire, what's wrong with him?"

"I don't really know," she answered, but the possibilities ran frantically through her mind.

"When I got home, he was laying on the bed. He hasn't moved," explained Shy.

Claire's mind, quickly calculating Hairy's daily routine, came up with only one logical answer. "I think he's been poisoned."

Shy and Scott looked stunned.

"Any idea how?" asked the Doctor. "Could he have gotten into something outside, in the garage, household cleaners. Anything might help me."

"Three of Shy's classmates have been poisoned in the last three days. Two of them are dead."

"And how does Hairy figure into this?"

"Yeah, Mom. What are you getting at?"

Dead Tones

"A black stone was found with all three girls, and tonight Shy found one in her backpack. I think whatever poisoned Hairy was meant for Shy."

"Really, Mom? You think Hairy got what was meant for me?"

"Considering the events of the last couple of days, the black stone you found, added to the fact that Hairy rarely has the opportunity to get into anything which could hurt him, yes. I think it's very likely."

"Oh, my God. My God. It's my fault. Hairy, I'm sorry I left my jeans on the bed." Shy looked at her mother and then explained to the doctor. "When I got home, I knew Hairy had gone through my pockets cause the junk was laying on the floor."

"What was in your pockets?" asked Claire.

"The garbage from my horn case. I always try to clean it out before I leave it with Paul. There were a couple of old reeds and some old notes from Sarah, old candy wrappers, and...and" she thought for a minute, "oh yeah, and some gum."

"That's it," said the veterinarian. "Dogs love gum. Something about the chewing action that intrigues them."

"The poison must have been put on the stick of gum, then it was re-wrapped and slipped into your case," Scott added.

Now the doctor seemed more urgent in his motions. First he drew some blood and set the vials in a holder. The next step was to start intravenous fluids. "Did you see any signs of vomit?"

Shy answered, "No."

"Should I assume this is intentional?"

"You mean like in murder? Yes. It's cold blooded and carefully thought out. The police, as far as we know, have only one suspect. But we know she didn't do it," explained Scott.

"Do the doctors know what killed the girls?"

"No idea," answered Claire.

"How long since the first girl?"

"She went to the hospital on Friday. She's still in a coma, but breathing on her own. The other two, one on Saturday and another Sunday, are both dead.

"So either the killer learned to up the dosage to make sure the job got done, or the severity of the reaction is directly related to the amount ingested, and the killer is willing to take his chances. What were their symptoms?"

"All three thought they had a flu bug, so nobody suspected a problem until it was too late. The other problem is that the first one got sick here in Tulsa, the next in Dallas, and the last one on the way home; so none of the doctors saw all three victims in order to make comparisons. In each case, it was like starting from the beginning. Allison had a fever, congestion, and maybe some vomiting. Sue and Abby had the fever and congestion, but I think Abby's reaction was more violent because she died the quickest," explained Claire.

"Hum, either the killer is very smart or very lucky," said the doctor.

"I don't think smarts or luck has anything to do with it," Shy said angrily. "I think it was just a matter of fate. If we hadn't left town, only Allison would be sick. I think Sue and Abby were after thoughts on the part of the killer."

"Why?" asked Claire?

"Cause if we hadn't been going out of town, Mr. Krammer wouldn't have needed another soloist right away," explained Shy.

"I think you might be right. Doctor, do you think you can save him?" Claire asked.

"I don't know. I'll be with him all night. You guys go home and get some rest."

"I'd rather stay with my dog," said Shy. "It's my fault he's so sick. The least I can do is give him some loving."

Dead Tones

"He won't know if you're here or not, ShyAnne. So go home and get some rest. I'll call you if he...when he wakes up. Claire, I'm going to assume the doctors have run all the logical tox screens that can be done locally and come up negative. I'm going to rush Hairy's blood samples to the State Diagnostic Lab along with a stomach sample. There's a good chance that he hasn't digested all of the poison. In the meantime, I'm going to treat him with Lasix, just in case there's any pulmonary edema, and with steroids. I'll tell the veterinary toxicologist to start testing for the more exotic possibilities rather than the most logical. The doctors haven't had much luck with logic, so we'll be more aggressive."

"My guess is that the poison has no taste or smell," added Claire.

"How do you know that, Mom? Hairy doesn't care how anything tastes. He eats it anyway."

"I know it doesn't matter to Hairy, but I think one of the girls would've noticed a strange taste or smell on a piece of gum."

"Oh, yeah," said Shy.

"When you get home, would you look for any pieces of gum he didn't swallow, so I can have it tested as well."

"Thanks, for everything. I really appreciate you coming in like this."

"It's my job, Claire, and you can show your appreciation when you get my bill. Now go and let me get to work."

Reluctantly, Claire and Shy followed Scott out of the clinic. They got into the car for the short ride home. Shy broke the silence, "We all had Sarah's charm, but poor Hairy, he didn't have anything to protect him. That poison was meant for me. When I find out who did this, I'll kill him myself."

Claire felt exactly the same way, but said nothing until they got back to the house. "Shy, I'd like you to stay home with me tomorrow."

"Mom, you know I can't do that. I have to go to school; for Sarah and Hairy, I have to be there. Jennifer is ready to have Sarah burned at the stake."

Scott pulled into the driveway and turned off the car before interfering with their discussion. "Shy, I agree with your mother."

"Fine, you can agree with her all you want, but that doesn't mean I'm staying home. I can't." Shy didn't wait for her mother's argument. She got out of the car and headed for the back door before either of them could stop her.

"I understand how she feels," said Scott. "On the other hand, there's not a chance in hell that I'd let her out of this house."

"I guess I'd rather have her alive and hating me than dead and wishing she'd listened to her mother. Do we have an alternative?" asked Claire. "I'd better go see if Hairy left anything for the doctor to have analyzed."

"Do you think the doctors at the hospital might like a sample, too?"

"First, let's see if there's enough for the vet. Hairy doesn't usually leave much behind," said Claire as she walked up the stairs with Scott right behind her.

"Ya know, there's an issue here we haven't had time to address yet."

"What's that?" asked Claire without stopping to turn around.

"Assuming Shy and Sarah are right about the girls' connection being me, then how does Shy fit into the scenario?"

"Good question, I don't know."

"I do," yelled Shy from her room.

Scott and Claire entered Shy's room to find her sitting on the bed. In her hands were the broken reeds, a few pieces of saliva-soaked paper and a couple wads of gum. "This is all that's left. Will it help?" asked Shy in a defeated tone.

Dead Tones

"It might. Here, give me the gum. I'll throw the rest away. Now explain your theory about Scott," requested Claire.

"It's easy, Mom. Look where he's at. Last night, tonight."

"She's absolutely right," sighed Scott. "Remember the Peeping Tom last night?"

"The what?" asked Shy. "I don't remember any Peeping Tom."

"It was after you came in the house. Hairy and I were still outside. I thought I heard something, but then Scott drove up. After we came in the house, Hairy went and did his 'there's a stranger out there' routine. Scott and I saw a figure moving along the bushes up the other side of the cul-de-sac. When all the other dogs started barking, the guy took off. I didn't think anything of it, until now. If I'd let Hairy out, maybe we'd know who was behind all this."

"If I hadn't come over, Shy wouldn't be the new target."

"Yeah, Mom. It's not fair. I'm the target, but he's hangin' out with you. No fair."

Shy's meager attempt at humor didn't seem to lighten the spirits. All three of them felt guilty for one event or another. *If only, if only,* was the beginning of each silent thought.

"So what are we going to do about that?" asked Shy as she pointed at the black stone on the end of her bed.

"I think we should do the same thing we did with Andrea," suggested Scott. "She's still alive."

"Yeah, and under lock and key. No thanks. The killer moved on to a new target, and Andrea is still scared to death. I can't do that," said Shy.

"I'm open to intelligent suggestions," offered Claire.

"I go to school tomorrow and put absolutely nothing in my mouth, not a piece of candy or gum, no water, or even the end of my pencil. At least, that way I can see who's surprised that I'm still around."

"I don't like it," said Scott. "We're only guessing that the poison was on a stick of gum. It could be anything."

"Mr. Krammer, if I stay home and you go back to school, the killer might find another target. On the other hand, if I know not to put anything in my mouth, we have a chance of drawing her out."

"Why did you use 'her' this time? We've never attached a gender to the killer," asked Claire.

"If Mr. Krammer is the connection, then I think it's a girl who's obsessed with him."

Scott and Claire looked at each other and instantly remembered the perfume Jennifer had put on the sleeve of his sweatshirt. "Jennifer," they said in a tone of agreement.

"No, it's not Jennifer," said Shy emphatically. "She's too obvious."

"What if it's not an obsession, but a grudge?" asked Claire.

"I like that idea, Mom."

"I don't," said Scott. "Come to think of it, I don't like obsession either."

"Who has a grudge against you?" asked Claire.

"I don't know," said Scott shifting his weight from one leg to the other.

"What if Jennifer is hiding behind Jennifer?" said Claire.

"Huh? You lost me on that one, Mom," said Shy.

"Did you know Jennifer wiped her perfume all over Scott's sleeve last night just after we got on the bus?" Shy shook her head no and Claire continued, "I don't think we can overlook the fact that Jennifer is obsessed with Scott. I think she's a more likely suspect than Sarah is," suggested Claire.

"She is as obsessed with getting Sarah convicted as she is with Mr. Krammer. The girl just doesn't have all her electrical circuits moving in the same direction," said Shy.

Dead Tones

"If that's your way of saying she's a little nuts, then you're right. I wish I knew what the police were thinking," Scott added as he flipped his car keys around his fingers.

"I've got to run this gum over to the clinic, you and Shy stay here and think," said Claire.

"No way. You aren't going out alone. You and Shy get some rest. I'll drop this stuff off on my way home. Let's make sure everything is locked up before I leave," offered Scott.

"Ya know, Mom, this house doesn't feel the same without Hairy here."

"I know. You want to sleep downstairs with me?"

"Not a chance. If the killer gets in, your room is the first place he'll...she'll go. I'm safer upstairs."

"Thanks, that makes me feel better," said Claire.

Before Claire got out of the room, Shy asked the last question, "Do I go to school or not?"

"Will you promise to keep your mouth shut?"

"Absolutely, dying is not on my agenda."

"Good night, dear. Try not to worry about Hairy. He's a tough, old guy."

"Good night, Mom."

R. Z. Crompton

CHAPTER FOURTEEN

Claire had a miserable night. She'd tossed and turned until the sun came up. Every time she moved a leg, she was reminded of Hairy's absence, then she prayed. She heard Shy in the morning and decided to join her for breakfast. Claire was in the kitchen before Shy, so she called the vet. Hairy hadn't changed, which was good according to the doctor.

"Morning, Mom. Did you get any sleep?"

"Nope. This makes four nights in a row that I've been deprived. You're young, you can get by on no sleep. I'm old, it shows when I don't sleep. Just look at these eyes." Claire looked straight at Shy so she could get a good view of her mother's eyes.

"Gee, Mom, you're eighty if you're a day," replied Shy as she poured herself a glass of grape juice. "I don't think it's the lack of sleep as much as it is drinking that stuff you call coffee."

"Thanks, your sympathy is overwhelming."

"I don't see how you and Mr. Krammer can drink that stuff. And speaking of Mr. Krammer, you two are certainly getting along well."

"Oh, the coffee remark was slick. If you wanted to know about us, you didn't have to beat around the bush. Just ask."

"So tell me about you and Mr. Krammer."

"Nope, there's nothing to tell," said Claire trying to hide a smile.

"Mommmm, tell me what's going on. Am I gonna have a new daddy?" Shy asked in a high pitched, little girl voice.

"No, we just get along nicely. We have more in common than I realized, and I like having him around. I'll tell you more after all this mess is cleared up. Is your good horn at the school already?" Claire poured herself another cup of coffee and put a bagel in the toaster.

"No, I've got it upstairs. Ya know, if I hadn't taken my marching horn into Paul yesterday, Hairy wouldn't have gotten sick."

"Stop, Shy. I know how you feel. If I hadn't invited Scott over to look up his father's background, you wouldn't be a target. And if you think we feel guilty, think about how Scott feels. He has to deal with the fact that he might still be the cause of this whole mess. What he doesn't realize is that he's a victim too."

"You're right. I've got to hurry. And I know what you're going to say. 'Be careful'."

"And don't forget the 'I love you' part," Claire said walking over to give her daughter a big hug.

"What are you going to do today?"

"I'm going to get on the Internet and find out everything I can about exotic poison."

"You go, girl," said Shy with extra emphasis on girl. "I'm impressed, Mom. Do you think you can help the doc save Hairy?"

"I'm gonna try," said Claire. "I spent the whole night thinkin' about my dog. I can't just sit and wait. I've got to run to the bank later this morning. Do you need anything?"

"My dog. Just my dog."

****

Claire had spent several hours in front of her computer. The information turned over and over in her mind, but there was nothing that would help Hairy. She was hoping somebody surfing the Internet would find her questions on one of the bulletin boards and E-mail her an answer. In the meantime, she decided to make her run to

Albertsons, the local supermarket which conveniently housed one of the Bank of Oklahoma's branch offices.

The cold spell was definitely over as the temperature was already in the high sixties. The sun was bright in the mid morning sky. Too bad Claire's mood didn't match the beauty of the day. She pulled into the Albertson's parking lot at the intersection of 81st and Yale. She appreciated being able to do her banking, get groceries and pick up a quick meal at the deli all in one place. Now, if they could just add a dry cleaners, she could run all of her regular errands with just one stop.

Claire took the deposit out of her purse and waited in line. Her mind was still going over the last list of poisons and the symptoms she'd downloaded. She didn't see Derrick open the bank's office door.

"Claire, hey Claire."

"Oh, good morning. I didn't see you," said Claire.

"Well, that much is obvious. What's going on at Southside?"

"Oh, Derrick, it's a real mess."

"Can you come in for a minute?" Derrick held the door open for her, then he followed her, letting the glass door close behind him. "The story was all over the paper this morning. The early morning news showed dozens of reporters talking to kids as they arrived at the school."

"You're kidding. I had no idea."

"Did you have your head buried in the sand this morning?"

"No, I was searching for information about poison. I bet the killer's latest victim didn't make the headlines."

"Why? Who was the victim?" asked Derrick.

"Hairy, my dog."

"Oh, Claire. I'm so sorry. Is he...did he..."

"He's at the vet's office, but I have to find out what kind of poison it was."

Dead Tones

"Now I understand why you're searching. By the way, I met your sister last Saturday."

"My sister? Rennae? She was here?"

"I knew she had to be related to you. Good Lord, you two look exactly alike. You've talked about her before, but you never told me how much you resemble each other."

Claire was instantly on guard. She'd forgotten all about the last conversation with her sister. Rennae was just sneaky enough to go looking for Derrick. "What did she say?"

"Well, we had a very interesting talk."

"Oh, I bet you did," said Claire. Her sarcasm should be directed at Rennae, but Derrick was the only one available.

Derrick smiled. He'd had a great time visiting with Rennae. Claire was a good friend and he played the game for her, but now he wanted to see how she would react. "I'd completely forgotten that we were having lunch together this week. Which day? Tuesday or Wednesday?"

Claire squirmed slightly. "I'm going to kill her," she whispered softly, but Derrick still heard her. "I'm sorry she put you on the spot. I didn't mean to set you up. Frankly, I didn't think she'd come all the way over here just to go to the bank."

"I have a funny feeling she didn't come to do any banking," added Derrick. "She suggested that we might not be eating lunch at a restaurant. In fact, she was under the impression that food might not even be on the menu."

"I'm going to kill her," said Claire only this time she didn't try to hide her irritation. "Okay, you caught me. Rennae and ShyAnne have been harassing me about staying home too much. Friday night I might have made a few hints that we, you and I...umm...enjoy a special kind of lunch from time to time. I'm sorry." Claire could feel the flaming red in her cheeks.

"I'm the one who's sorry. I'm sorry that you were only hinting; however, if you ever need me to stick up for you, just call."

"You aren't mad at me?"

"Of course not. You flatter me. I figured if you were hinting at an affair, you must need the cover. When she started hemming and hawing about our special lunches, I knew something was going on; so I played along. That was the most fun I'd had in months. She seemed so surprised when I confirmed everything."

"I bet she was. Thanks, Derrick."

"Tell me about the band trip. When Rennae told me you had actually agreed to go, I was shocked. How did you and the director get along?"

"Actually, we got along very well."

"Oh, don't tell me you don't need my services anymore."

Claire blushed again. "We're friends."

"You and I are friends. From the flush of your cheeks, I'd say you either are, or you would like to be more than friends with this band director. What about the girls who died? Do you have any juicy details that weren't in the paper?" asked Derrick, pulling his chair into his desk, so he could lean in closer to Claire.

"I know Shy was the next intended victim, but somehow Hairy got a hold of the poison."

"How did you ever let her go back to school today?"

"She's determined to find out who's doing this."

"I thought everything pointed to the Indian girl."

"Everything points to Sarah being set up, not to who did the real crime."

"Let's see, two girls played the clarinet and one the flute and Shy the saxophone."

"Yes, do you see a tie we missed?" asked Claire intently.

"Nope, all I see are instruments," Derrick shrugged.

Dead Tones

"The reeds?" The thought rolled over in Claire's mind. "Hairy got into Shy's pockets and chewed up her reeds. That's the connection." Claire jumped out of her seat and reached for Derrick. She kissed him quickly on the cheek before saying, "I've got to go." Claire nearly ran for her car. Dale had called off marching band rehearsals until the deaths of Sue and Abby were resolved but...she calculated the time. In a few minutes, Shy would be sitting down to start jazz band.

Claire had to cover four miles in less than ten minutes. *Please, God, be with me. Don't let her put that horn in her mouth.* Claire pushed harder on the accelerator. She was at the intersection of Sheridan and 81st, eight minutes; two more miles down and four minutes 'til the bell; Claire turned north at Mingo. She had only a mile to go and two minutes before class would begin. The yellow light turned red, but Claire wasn't slowing down. She pulled around the circle in front of the school, shoved the car into park and threw open the door. Claire noticed several people hanging around the front of the building. She assumed they were reporters hoping to get a quick word with a student or teacher. *Vultures waiting to pick away at the afternoon roadkill. They should close the school.*

The bandroom door was slightly ajar and Claire could hear the notes ringing through the air. All the heads turned toward her when she came rushing running into the room.

"Mom, what are you doing here?" asked Shy. Scott was as surprised as Shy, but he didn't say anything.

Claire didn't know what to expect when she barged into the room, and now she felt rather silly. In the calmest voice she could manage, Claire said, "Shy, I need to talk to you."

Shy moved around her music stand and walked to the back of the bandroom where Claire stood waiting for her. "Mom, what's wrong?"

"Did you put that horn in your mouth?"

"Not yet, I was just soaking down a new reed." Shy held up the small wet piece of wood.

Claire felt her heart skip a beat, "Shy, I figured out how Sue, Allison, and Hairy were poisoned."

"You did? How?"

Without saying a word, Claire simply looked at the thin piece of wood held in Shy's fingers.

Shy followed her mother's gaze and stopped at the tips of her own fingers. "The reeds?" she asked and then anticipating her mother's next question, Shy answered, "I just unsealed a new box this morning. I bought it yesterday when I was at Tulsa Band."

"Thank God. I was terrified. Now get your stuff."

"Why? I can't leave."

"Yes, this time you're going with me," ordered Claire.

"Mom, we agreed," pleaded Shy.

Claire didn't raise her voice, but her tone carried all the meaning she needed to make herself completely understood. "ShyAnne, this is no longer negotiable. I saw you put this tiny piece of wood in your mouth a million times on my way over here. I know you promised not to put anything in your mouth, but neither one of us thought of this. I am not going to spend the rest of the day wondering what else we didn't anticipate. I'm not going to spend another minute wondering if you'll still be alive tonight. Been there, done that and won't do it again. You are all I have, all that I live for; and I will not gamble with your life. Now get your stuff, we're out of here."

The body language between mother and daughter left nothing to Scott's imagination. Something had happened to change Claire's mind about letting Shy remain at school, and he wanted to know what it was. The students, having been on edge all morning, also watched this mother daughter exchange with great interest. Scott had hoped

Dead Tones

playing a little jazz would distract them from the growing sense of panic. He was wrong.

"Claire, what happened?"

With her back to the band, Claire hadn't seen him approaching. In fact, she hadn't even noticed that the other students had stopped playing. If any of them heard what she'd said to Shy about the reeds, there would be instant bedlam. "Scott, I think the poison was put on the reeds."

"No." He tried to whisper his astonishment, but found it nearly impossible. "No." Scott shook his head running all the facts through his mind over and over. "I can't believe...I don't want to believe someone, one of us, could be so diabolical as to poison an instrument, but...I think you're right. Remember when I told you Allison thought someone had gone through her locker? Now I believe her."

"What's really sad is that Sue might have been an accident," said Claire.

"Mom, are you serious?"

"When I was with Sue Saturday morning, she told me she was out of reeds, so she got one out of Allison's locker," explained Claire.

"Are you serious? I had no idea Sue was in Allison's locker."

"Poor Sue," was Shy's response. "But what about the black stone the police found in her case?"

"It was found after we got back. The killer had plenty of time to plant it. In all the confusion Sunday night when we got back, it would have been easy to open Sue's locker and slip the stone into her extra case," added Scott.

"I'd be more inclined to think she was an intended target if we'd found the stone in the case that was on the semi, the one she had in Texas," said Claire.

"I agree," replied Scott.

"How's Sarah today?"

"She's not here this morning. Her father made an appointment with a lawyer. It's probably a good thing cause the reporters would have devoured her. They asked everybody about 'the Indian girl'. It was terrible. I almost punched one guy in the nose when he asked if I was afraid to go to school with a witch."

"If the police don't come up with an answer real quick, the Superintendent is going to have to close the school," said Scott.

"But none of the deaths happened on school grounds," Shy responded leaning up against the brick wall.

"Doesn't matter. The trip was a school sanctioned activity. We might as well have been sitting right here in the parking lot," explained Scott. "It's going to get worse. We'll be lucky if we get to take a trip across the river to Jenks next season. Shit, we'll be lucky if we have any students," said Scott realizing the long lasting effect this would have on the entire community.

"One thing at a time, Scott. First we have to find a killer. Then we deal with the future."

"Yeah, you're right. Shy, you go home with your mother. This rehearsal is over. I've got to tell Dale about the reeds, and I think we need to call the police. I want all the lockers and cases searched again. And I think all the reeds should be labeled and sent to a lab. The cops can to that. Don't say anything. I don't want to tip the killer off. Are the reporters still hanging around out there?"

"Oh, yeah. And the way I rushed in here, I'm sure they're expecting something. If I walk out of here dragging my daughter behind me, then I'm just one more parent in a panic, pulling my kid out of school."

"What do you want me to do, Mom?"

Claire didn't answer right away. *Options. I need an option.* "I know I'm not leaving you here. I absolutely refuse to play games with your life."

Dead Tones

"I know, Mom. How 'bout if I leave my stuff with Mr. Krammer. I'll lean on your shoulder and limp. You can say you're taking me to the doctor cause I slipped on a step or something and broke my ankle. But what about my car?"

"Where are you parked?"

"Around on the other side of the building. I was late getting here, so I'm way out in the boondocks. Can we pull around and get it?"

"Sounds good to me," said Claire. "Better than anything I could come up with. Put your horn away and let's get out of here." Shy, feeling almost relieved to be leaving the school, did as she was told.

"What are you going to do?" asked Claire.

"Stick around here for a while. Dale's meeting with the superintendent and then we'll decide what to do about the lockers. I don't want him to get back here and find cops rummaging through the place again. I don't think an hour or so will make much difference. This was the last class I was going to hold today; so once we get everything put up, the room will remain empty."

"I've been searching the Internet for information about unusual poisons. Wow, what an array of options for a killer: snake venom, spiders, roots, herbs, chemicals. I was amazed. Would you like to come over when you're finished here?"

The invitation brought the first smile of the day to Scott's face. Maybe his going home alone night after night was about over. "I'd love to. Thanks."

"Mr. Krammer, I put my stuff in your office. Please keep an I on it. I don't want to find anymore black rocks in my backpack."

"I don't blame you. One is more than enough," said Scott.

"You ready to start the act?" asked Claire.

Shy bent her left leg and leaned into her mother's shoulder. "Yup. Let's go. I think I need to be comfortably eased onto the sofa in front of the T.V. and eating ice cream. That's what you used to give me when I got hurt."

"C'mon. Scott will bring your books home so you can do your homework."

"Ohhh, Mom. I'm hurt, remember?" She put more of her weight on Claire and winced at the pretended pain.

"Look, I've created a monster. Let's go," said Claire taking Shy's full weight and helping her hop out the door.

Several reporters swarmed as they headed for the car. The fake ankle injury meant they had a slow pace all the way. The media people hit them with a barrage of stupid questions. Claire needed to stay calm and give simple direct answers. "My daughter fell. I'm taking her to the doctor." She repeated the answer several times before they reached the car.

"Man, am I glad that's over. Let's stop and see Hairy on the way home," said Shy.

"You can stop for a minute, but I'm waiting for a bunch of information to come in, so I need to get home," answered Claire.

****

Claire put all the pages about poison that she'd down loaded out on her desk. She looked from one page to the next, trying to categorize the symptoms. There were so many to consider, and the symptoms often overlapped. No wonder detecting the exact poison was extremely difficult. Claire fidgeted in her seat and found herself wondering more about what Scott was doing than about the pages on her desk.

Shy came through the door to see her mother tapping the end of her pencil on the corner of the desk. "Did you find anything?"

Dead Tones

"No, the symptoms that lead to death are often so much alike. Ya know, there are only so many ways to die, but there's dozens of options here. Since I have absolutely no medical training, most of this has no meaning to me. How 'bout you? Did you get a hold of Sarah?"

"Yeah, I strongly suggested she stay at home."

"Will she take the advice?" asked Claire.

"I think so; it was the same advice her attorney gave her. From the sounds of it, her mother is ready to tie her to her bed if she tries to leave the house."

"Smart woman," said Claire. "Did she say what the lawyer thought about the state's case against her?"

"He said it wasn't very strong. Everything so far was just circumstantial. He told them not to worry, but you know how mothers are," offered Shy.

"Yeah, I know exactly how we are. We worry. It's in the job description."

"I appreciate your worrying about me, but Sarah's spell would've protected me. It did last night," stated Shy as she looked over her mother's shoulder.

"I know, but I also know if you tempt fate too often, you will lose. You can have all the faith in the world, but a wise man doesn't gamble with the gift of life."

"Hey, Mom, that fish looks just like the one Kate and her dad had in our biology class last year."

"Really?" Claire looked more closely at the picture and then at the description. "You said Kate helped her dad do research, and the fish looked like this."

"Yeah, pretty much. They had several different samples. Some looked almost like flowers. Why?"

"Does Kate have any kind of history with Scott?"

"Gee, I don't think so. She plays the clarinet, so she's not in jazz, and she's never had a solo," Shy explained, shrugging her shoulders. "Gee, if they had a history, I don't know about it."

"Isn't Kate a good friend of Jennifer's?"

"Yeah, yeah," said Shy slowly catching on to Claire's thinking. "You mean like in 'look for the one yelling the loudest and the one who is hiding will be close by'?"

"Exactly. She plays the clarinet, she's a good friend of Jennifer's, and she has access to exotic poison."

"But why? What's the motive?" asked Shy.

"I don't know, but I'll go back to the school to talk to Scott. You take this information to the vet and then stay there." Claire handed Shy a piece of paper. "I don't want you running around until we know for sure Kate's the guilty party." Claire reached for the phone, "Hello, I need to speak with Sylvia Hayes." There was a short pause. "Yes, it is an emergency. Thank you," said Claire in a disgusted tone. She hated having to justify her request to speak with Sylvia.

"Hello," said the hesitant voice on the other end of the line.

"Sylvia."

"Claire? What's the emergency?" asked Sylvia.

"Allison, how is she?"

"The same. Why?"

"Did she have any vomiting before you took her to the hospital?"

"Yes, it was terrible."

"Have the doctor test her blood for tetrodotoxin. It's a puffer fish poison. Did you write it down? I hope it helps. There's no antidote, but the doctor can treat the symptoms better if he knows what it is. It's a long story. Okay, I gotta get going." Claire was moving away from her desk before she hung up the phone. At least this trip wasn't a race to save a life. Shy was safe.

Dead Tones

****

Scott took another drink of the cold coffee and turned back to his computer. A band director in Utah had asked him to work on a show, and this was as good a time as any. He couldn't leave until Dale got back, so he might as well get some work done. Scott reached up and wiped the sweat from his forehead. The janitors must have adjusted the thermostats after the cold spell. It was so warm.

"Hello, Mr. Krammer. How are you today?"

"Kate, what are you doing here?"

"Oh, I thought I'd come in and check on you."

"I'm fine, Kate. Don't you have a class or something?" Scott felt uncomfortable having one of the girls just drop in. After what he'd experienced with Jennifer, he didn't want to find himself in a compromising situation.

"No, I only have a couple of classes in the morning. I'm finished for the day. Are you sure you're feeling okay?"

"Yes, Kate, I'm fine." Scott's agitation with the girl was growing. He wanted her out of his office. *Damn, it's getting hot in here.* "I really have to get this work finished, Kate. If there's nothing you need, I really have to concentrate."

"Go ahead. I don't mind. I'll just sit here real quiet like." Kate sat down in Dale's chair and stared at him.

"Kate, what's going on? You're acting very strange." Scott tried to catch his breath, but his chest was so heavy. He struggled to inhale.

"That's better, Mr. Krammer, I think you're starting to get the message."

Scott strained to inhale. The reality of her question about his health was beginning to sink in. A flash of Abby struggling to inhale raced through his mind. "Kate, you...you killed Sue and Abby?"

"Sure did, but Sue was an accident. How was I supposed to know the dummy would go digging through Allison's locker."

Scott drew in as much oxygen as he could. "Why did you kill your friends? Why?"

"I'm impressed, Mr. Krammer, that you would still be so concerned with the dead. I would've expected you to be more interested in keeping yourself alive. Let's see, you want to know why I killed Allison, or at least tried to kill Allison. I guess she didn't suck enough of the toxin out of her reed to do the job. Sue certainly got a heavy dose."

Scott was visibly struggling to suck in oxygen. "Aaaaahhhh." He tried to reach for the telephone.

"No. No," said Kate. She walked over to the desk and pulled the cord out of the wall. "Ya know, I tried everything to get your attention, but you always had a favorite, which meant I had a rival. I graduate in a few months. I was running out of time, but you...you became more illusive than ever. You gave your attentions freely to Abby, even held her in your arms. I had to kill her to teach you a lesson."

"Buuut...buu...how? All the...the...instru...ments were...ah...locked on the...the semi." Scott grabbed the edge of his desk to help hold himself in his chair.

Kate reached down inside her purse and pulled out a small clear vial. See this? It is the poison I used on you and Abby. I put Abby's on the chapstick I gave her while we were at the zoo. Man, Krissy almost got some of that one. Oh well," Kate shrugged her shoulders, "she's always been a pain in the ass to me. I wouldn't have missed her. So how was the coffee today? A little toxic, maybe?"

Scott looked at his coffee mug, the one he'd used for the last two years. The one the clarinet players bought him at Disneyland. He couldn't believe he was hearing this. He couldn't believe he was dying

Dead Tones

at the hands of one of his students. After all the wasted years worrying about his father tracking him down, and it's a student he should've been afraid of. What an ironic pain in the ass. She knew just how long to wait before coming in to gloat.

Kate rambled on, "And then there's ShyAnne Mayfield. I don't know what you see in her."

Scott shook his head as if to make her understand that she was wrong about Shy.

"Oh, no. Don't try to deny it. I saw you over there. You were outside with Mrs. Mayfield. Ya know, I have to give the woman some credit though cause most parents would never understand a daughter wanting to date her teacher."

The strength Scott had left was used to stay conscious and to inhale.

"And then I just got tired of trying to please you. You were never going to pay attention to me. I was punishing all the girls and then I realized you were the problem. You have been a very bad boy and now I have to punish you. See, I even remembered to bring you a little black stone." Kate stood up and walked over to Scott's desk. She pried his fingers off the side of the desk and turned it palm up. The black Stone was placed in the palm of his hand and his fingers folded one by one around it. "That's a good boy. Now this will be easier if you just go to sleep. Too bad you can't talk anymore, I wanted to hear you say how sorry you are for being so fickle with my heart. Oh, well, too late now. And poor Sarah, she's a sweet girl but I needed someone to blame. And if they don't believe she did it then I have Jennifer set up as the next best choice. After all, everybody knows how you've spurned her. I've got to get going."

Kate was standing by the entrance when the outside door creaked open. She hadn't planned on a visitor just yet. "Shit!" Kate moved back through the office and into the small storage room.

R. Z. Crompton

"Mr. Krammer, are you here?" Jennifer came into the office just in time to see him slip out of his chair onto the floor. "Mr. Krammer! Ohmygod, ohmygod! What do I do?" She knelt down beside the body to see if he was still breathing. "Mr. Krammer?" She shook him and the motion caused the small black stone to roll out of his hand. "The witch! She did this. I know it was her! I'll kill her myself." Jennifer jumped to her feet and ran through the band room, up the tiered sections of the floor and out the door nearly throwing Claire to the ground.

Claire regained her balance as she watched the red hair disappear into the sea of parked cars. *Well, excuse you, Jennifer.* Claire pulled open the band door and stepped inside the empty room.

"Scott, you still here? Scott?" Claire walked quickly down the tiered floor to the office area. "Scott, I found something," yelled Claire again. Claire's breath caught in her throat when she found Scott sprawled on the floor beside his desk. She rushed to his side. His breathing was shallow, but he was alive. "Scott, I'm here. I'll get help." Claire reached for the phone, but couldn't get a dial tone. There was a phone in the bandroom. She'd seen some of the kids use it on Saturday. "Scott, I'm going to call for help. Jennifer's the one. She almost ran me over. I should've known from her first wicked comments on the bus."

Scott tried to mouth his words, but she didn't understand.

Claire was only gone for a second, but it was enough time for Kate to take a quick look around the corner. Scott could see her still hiding in the small storage area. He could see the smile of satisfaction on her face. His eyes closed.

The 911 call was quick, but Claire found herself irritated at the request for an exact address. "Give me a break lady. How many Southside High Schools do we have in Tulsa? A man is dying and you want an exact address. It's the place where all the reporters are

Dead Tones

hanging out. He's in the band room. There's an outside entrance." Claire slammed down the receiver and ran back to Scott.

****

The paramedics, fighting the throng of reporters, loaded Scott into the ambulance. Claire got in beside him. She watched as an intravenous needle was inserted and taped securely to his arm. The paramedics worked efficiently to save his life, but Claire was terrified that it wasn't going to be enough. *If only I'd hurried faster, if only I'd understood her obsession sooner rather than wasting all my time looking for poison.* Claire felt like a fool. She'd given Sylvia false hope and Shy too. She'd show up at the vet's office with a bunch of papers that wouldn't mean a thing. *Damn you, Jennifer. Damn you.*

"Lady, do you have any idea what's wrong with him?"

"No, I mean, I know he's been poisoned, but I don't know how or with what."

"Is this like the girls?"

"Yeah, but Allison, the first girl, is still alive. She's at St. Thomas Hospital. The two other girls died. I'd thought it might be some kind of tropical fish, but now I just don't know. I saw the wrong girl leaving the band room"

"Why the tropical fish?"

"Because one of the girls had easy access to exotic fish, I thought she might be using it to poison her classmates."

"Bizarre, but a good idea. Nobody around here would suspect tropical fish. There aren't too many saltwater fish floatin' down the Arkansas River these days," said the paramedic as he looked at Scott's pupils again. "You say the first girl's still alive?"

"Yes, why?"

"I better radio that in. Might make a difference in how they want to treat him when we get there."

Claire called Shy from the waiting room. Hairy was barely hanging on, and Shy didn't want to leave. The doctor put together a type of treatment for him based on the information Claire had found on the Internet. "Shy, tell him I was wrong. I saw Jennifer running from the bandroom just before I found Scott."

"But, Mom, that doesn't necessarily mean it was Jennifer. Remember how long it took for the poison to work. Mr. Krammer must have ingested the poison earlier this morning."

"True, but if it wasn't Jennifer, then why'd she run instead of calling for help," wondered Claire.

"Who knows what goes through her mind. What would you do if the man you were obsessed with was dying?" asked Shy.

"I'd call for help," said Claire.

"Not you, Mom. Pretend you're Jennifer."

Claire thought for a minute and then said, "Revenge."

"Sarah. I'll be there to get you in ten minutes."

"I'm going to call Sarah. What's her number?" Claire scribbled the digits on a scrap of paper. There was no answer at Sarah's home. *Maybe they're in Tahlequah for the day.* Claire left the emergency room to wait outside for Shy.

Within minutes, Shy was pulling through the parking lot and up to the emergency room door. Claire hurried to the car. "There was no answer at Sarah's home?"

"What do you want to do?" asked Shy as she maneuvered her car out of the parking lot.

"Let's drive by Sarah's place; she might be outside."

"Did you call the police?" asked Shy.

"Yes, I told them I saw Jennifer running from the bandroom. I'm sure they'll go to her house first," explained Claire.

Dead Tones

"Did you tell them about the tropical fish thing?"

"Yes, but I think the officer thought I was crazy. When he said 'Why, Ma'am, there's no tropical fish here in Tulsa,' I kind a got the feeling he had some doubts about my mental condition."

"I sure wish you'd break down and get a cell phone," said Shy.

"I won't need one after you leave for college. You'll never want to call your old mother."

"Of course, I want you at my beck and call, especially when I need you to send money," said Shy.

"That's not exactly going to convince me, but I sure wish I had one today. Can't you drive faster?"

Several minutes passed before Shy pulled off 51st into Sarah's subdivision. "Look, there's Jennifer's car. Should we go back and call the police?"

"I don't know." Claire was frustrated. If they left, Jennifer might hurt Sarah before they got back. If they stayed, she might hurt all of them. "You call the police, I'll see what's going on, and tomorrow we get a cell phone for each of us." Claire opened the door and got out. "Hurry!"

"I will. Be careful!" Shy caught a glimpse of her mother hurrying up to the front door as she pulled away.

Claire knocked at the door, but there was no answer. There had to be people around. There were two cars in the driveway and Jennifer's at the curb. Claire stepped off the front porch and headed around to the back of the house. The closer she came to the fence the louder the voices became.

"Jennifer, I didn't hurt anybody."

"You're lying. I found the black stone in Mr. Krammer's hand," sobbed Jennifer. "I know you did it. It had to be you!"

Sarah's voice was very calm, "Jennifer, I didn't put any spells on Mr. Krammer. I've been home all day."

R. Z. Crompton

"Yeah, practicing your black magic," screamed Jennifer.

Claire knew Jennifer was frantic in her accusations, too frantic to think straight. She looked over the fence and could see Sarah and her parents standing by a large pile of leaves. Jennifer was standing out of Claire's line of vision. Claire hesitated opening the gate only because she didn't want to trigger some crazy action by Jennifer. She didn't know if the girl had a weapon of some kind. As long as Jennifer was just yelling, Claire didn't think she could cause any real harm.

"I don't practice black magic, Jennifer. And you cannot hurt me or my family while we are here. If you believe I have powers, then you must believe that I can protect myself in my own home. Leave here before I tell the spirits to destroy you. You are on my sacred ground, and I can certainly protect myself and my family," threatened Sarah.

Claire appreciated Sarah's bravado. There was silence and she could imagine Jennifer looking around, waiting to see the spirits. If Sarah had any tricks handy this would be the ideal time.

"I want you to die, Sarah Morning Star. And God help me, I'll be the one to end your miserable witchcraft!"

"We all die. But today is not my day. Can you say the same?"

Again there was silence. Sarah was winning the battle of words. Claire heard the door slam and seconds later the front door flew open and Jennifer ran for her car. She let a string of curses fly that Claire had only heard in the movies.

"Sarah, are you guys okay?" asked Claire as she hurried into the backyard.

"Mrs. Mayfield, how long were you there?" asked Sarah. Her mother was giving her a long hug.

"Long enough to know that you outsmarted her. Good job."

"Thank you."

"I'm proud of her," said Mrs. Morning Star. "I guess she's learning something from her grandmother besides the magic."

Dead Tones

"Shy went to call the police. Did Jennifer have a weapon?"

"Oh, yeah. She had some kind of hand gun. I don't know what it was, but I'm sure it could have done the job. Is Mr. Krammer really dead?"

"Not yet, but he's really bad. I saw Jennifer running away from the bandroom. Shy and I wanted to warn you, but there was no answer when we called. Now I know why," said Claire.

"I'd like to go to the hospital and see Mr. Krammer," responded Sarah.

"I think you should stay right here. Jennifer isn't likely to bother you as long as you stay home. There's nothing you can do for Mr. Krammer," answered Claire.

"Yes, there is."

Claire had no response. She knew what Sarah was hinting at, and Claire couldn't argue with her. Sarah was the only one who seemed to have any insight into this whole affair. "Sarah, do you still think Jennifer's innocent?"

"Yes, if she had killed Sue and Abby, I don't think she would've been over here flopping a gun around."

"You're right about that. What does your grandmother say?"

Sarah's mother was astonished at the recognition Claire gave to the magic. She tried, in fact, wanted to ignore the old ways. "We don't talk about Indian medicine here."

"I'm sorry, Mrs. Morning Star, but Sarah's medicine has been very helpful to us."

"Really? You believe?" asked Sarah's mother.

"I had my doubts in the beginning, but not anymore. Everything she said has been true; every spell she used has worked. So I was wondering if she had any new feelings or ideas."

"No, Mrs. Mayfield, I'm sorry. I haven't talked to my grandmother today."

ShyAnne and the police came through the back gate wondering what had happened to Jennifer. "Are you guys okay? That was Jennifer, wasn't it?"

Sarah explained how she and her parents were out raking the autumn leaves when Jennifer showed up waving a gun around and threatening Sarah and her parents. "I knew she couldn't hurt me here, but I was still worried for my parents," explained Sarah.

"Do you know where she went? We'd really like to talk to her," said one of the officers. "She was seen running from a crime scene, and threatening people with a gun isn't exactly legal."

"Sorry, she didn't say and we weren't asking," answered Sarah.

"Is there anything else we can do for you?" asked the officer.

"I don't think so. We're fine," said Mr. Morning Star. "I think we'll stay inside with the doors locked tonight. I don't want another unexpected visit from that crazy broad." The remark lightened the mood and brought a smile to everyone's face.

"Let's go Shy. I want to check on Scott."

"Call me, Shy, if you have any news," Sarah requested wishing she was going to the hospital with them, but she knew she couldn't leave her parents.

"I will. Take care," said Shy as she and Claire walked back through the gate. "So what now, Mom?"

****

Sylvia and Philip, leaving Allison's bedside for only the necessities, had kept their diligent vigil since their daughter had been admitted on Friday. This was the fourth day with no change. Davis came as often as he could, and Philip always vacated the chair closest to Allison, so the boy could hold her hand.

"Mr. Hayes..."

Dead Tones

"Please, Davis, call me Phil. We've been sitting here for better than three days, and we're going to be related soon. Please call me 'Phil.'"

Davis appreciated the way Philip and Sylvia had taken him in. This was no time to be arguing. "Phil, I've been thinking about your job offer, and well, I understand how you feel about not wanting Allison to leave town. If I have any trouble with the church accepting our marriage, and if Allison agrees, we'll take that offer."

"Thanks, Davis. Sylvia and I appreciate it. Have you told your folks yet?"

Davis didn't answer, only shook his head in an affirmative nod.

"Didn't go so well, huh?"

"No, Sir. Not very well at all. My father said I was throwing away everything I'd worked for over a girl."

"I heard the same speech from my father, so I know exactly how you feel. Don't worry, son, Sylvia and I will stand by you. Won't we Sil?" Philip reached out and touched her hand. The walls of isolation were gone. The man she had been waiting for was finally here.

"Yes, Phil, we'll be here for them."

"I've got lots to make up for," said Philip looking down at the fluttering eyes lashes.

"...make up for...what, Daddy," whispered Allison so softly that Philip barely heard her voice.

"Ali! Ali!" He reached for her hand and cried, then he thanked the Lord for his second chance.

"Daddy, Davis, Mamma."

"Yes, baby," said Sylvia. "We're all here. Waiting for you to get back." Sylvia bent down and kissed her baby on the forehead.

"Daddy, you aren't mad at me?"

"Of course not, baby. Why would I be mad at you?"

"Because of Davis." Allison tried to reach up and touch Davis' hand but didn't quite have the strength. Davis finished the gesture and gratefully stroked the slender fingers.

"No, honey. I approve of your choice."

"What happened to me?" asked Allison.

Sylvia didn't know if she should tell her everything or not. Maybe just a little bit for now. "You were really sick on Friday, and I brought you here."

"C'mon, Mom. That much I already know. What was wrong with me?"

Philip answered, "We aren't exactly sure who did this, but we know someone poisoned you."

"Poisoned Me! Holy shit...Oops, sorry, Dad. I didn't think anybody hated me that much," said Allison. "Am I going to be okay?"

"The doctor said if you wake up, you should be fine," explained Sylvia.

"Daddy, it was so strange, so strange. I was floating in a very bright place and there were angels floating all around. But sometimes the angels sounded a lot like Indians doing a chant. Strange very, strange. But I heard you, Daddy. And I love you too." Tears rolled down her cheeks.

Philip leaned over the bed and whispered, "can you ever forgive me?"

"I never held anything against you, Daddy."

"Honey, I love you," and her Daddy cried with her.

****

Claire wondered for a moment about going back to the hospital, but decided to check one more place before giving up. "Shy, do you know where Kate lives?"

Dead Tones

"Yeah, why?" asked Shy.

"Let's go and see if Jennifer's car is parked out front?"

Shy headed south on Mingo. Kate lived east of the high school in Broken Arrow. The subdivision was new and several houses were under construction. Shy meandered around a couple of trucks before turning onto the right street. "Okay, there's the house, the red brick with the dark blue door, and there's Jennifer's car. What now?"

"Let's go knock on the door. Nothing like a little direct confrontation to draw out the truth," suggested Claire.

"We can't do that." Shy was dumbfounded.

"Why not? What's she going to do? Shoot us?" asked Claire jumping out of the car.

"Wait a minute," whispered Shy as she ran after her mother, "what about not gambling with my life?"

"Fine. Wait in the car if you don't want to play," offered Claire.

"This is for the police. I think we should call them," demanded Shy.

"Can't, don't have a cell phone," said Claire continuing her walk to the front door. "Look, Jennifer doesn't even know we were at Sarah's house, and Kate doesn't know we suspect her either. So just play along."

"Mother, what are you going to say? I've never seen this crazy side of you!"

"Maybe it's Sarah's spirits," offered Claire.

"What do I do?"

"Just follow my lead. I've got an idea." Claire walked up the three porch steps and knocked on the door. Before Shy could utter another objection, the front door was pulled open.

"Mrs. Mayfield, Shy, what are you doing here?" asked Kate.

"We were wondering if we could talk to you for a minute. I've been doing some research, but I need some help. Shy told me you know about tropical fish. Is that right?"

"Yes," answered Kate with a touch of skepticism in her voice.

"Do you mind if we come in?" Claire didn't wait for her to finish the objection that was just beginning to form on her lips. She pushed past the girl at the door and came face to face with Jennifer. "Well, Jennifer, I'm surprised to see you here. How are you doing, dear? You were so upset when you ran out of the bandroom." Claire's voice oozed with empathy.

"Mrs. Mayfield, I didn't do it. I swear, I didn't do anything to Mr. Krammer," sobbed Jennifer.

"I know you didn't," said Claire as she walked up and put her arms around Jennifer's shoulders. "Let's go in and sit down. I think we can all help Mr. Krammer." Claire led the weeping girl into the small, elegant living room with Kate and Shy just a few steps behind them. A staircase wound up the long outer wall of the living room to the loft upstairs. The vaulted ceiling made the room look much larger than it really was.

"Jennifer, you're sure Sarah did this, right?" Claire caught Shy's wondering look and gave her the nod to play along. "Well, we have our doubts about her too. That's why we stopped over."

"Really?" asked Jennifer trying to get the tears under control. "Do you finally believe me?"

"Oh, yeah," added Shy reluctantly as she sat down on the light blue recliner.

"Well, we think Sarah might be guilty, but we really don't believe she's using Cherokee medicine. We talked to her mother this afternoon, and Sarah doesn't have any powers."

"You mean there's no magic?" asked Kate. "Please sit down."

Dead Tones

"Nope, no magic at all," said Claire as she and Jennifer sat down on the sofa. "We think she's using some kind of poison, something that's very hard to trace. Shy told me you're a wonderful scientist, Kate."

"I dabble," answered Kate.

"Oh, I think you are far more talented than you give yourself credit for." Claire glanced around the room at the family pictures on the walls and piano. Obviously, Kate had no siblings. Every picture portrayed only three people. The cute little girl had matured into a gorgeous woman.

"I've done some research, but it's really hard to find specific information about poison. And I found it incredibly hard to understand." Claire paused for effect and then continued, "Can you tell me if it's possible to extract poison from an animal?"

"Well, I suppose it is. I've seen people milk a rattlesnake for its venom. Did you have a specific animal in mind?"

"I don't know. Shy told me your research is with tropical fish. Anybody could buy a tropical fish, right?"

"Yes, so?" Kate was still hedging.

"The doctors have not been able to identify any type of poison yet. So that means the toxin has to be very unusual and nobody would suspect tropical fish poison in Tulsa. We need your help to prove that it's possible to buy a poisonous fish, extract the toxin and then use it to kill."

"Gee, Mrs. Mayfield, that's a pretty wild scenario," said Jennifer with great interest. "I'd never think of anything so complicated."

"Your dad sells the kind of fish I'm talking about doesn't he?" asked Claire.

"Well, yes," answered Kate.

"So anybody could buy one?" continued Claire.

"I suppose."

"I assume there are other dealers in town?"

"I believe so," was the slow, careful answer.

"Is it possible to extract the poison?"

Jennifer jumped into the conversation before Kate could formulate a careful answer. "Oh, yeah. I've watched Kate do it lots of times, downstairs in her father's lab."

"Jennifer," snapped Kate.

"What? You know all that stuff. You even showed me how to do it. How to cut down at just the right place to extract the poison," continued Jennifer.

"Shut up, Jennifer!"

"Why? I saw you put the stuff in that little glass bottle. I saw...I saw..." Jennifer paused for a moment, thinking back to what it was that she'd really seen, "I saw a bag of black stones beside the notebook.....you.. you said they were for...for somebody special. Kate?"

"Shut up, Jennifer."

"No, Kate. The little black stones were from Sarah right? Sarah did this. I know Sarah did this! It has to be Sarah! Right, Mrs. Mayfield? RIGHT??"

Claire didn't say a word.

"Please, Mrs. Mayfield! Help her! If it's Sarah then why won't you help, Kate?"

"Jennifer, SHUT UP!" yelled Kate.

Jennifer didn't want to believe what her mind was suggesting. Reality was knocking on the door, but she wasn't going to let it in. Her best friend had killed the only man she'd ever loved. Jennifer stared at the girl stepping slowly for the door. "It was YOU! You killed Abby, but why? Why...How could you do that?! And the others? Allison and Sue! And..and then Mr. Krammer! Oh my GOD! I've been blaming Sarah all along and it was you!" screamed Jennifer. She

Dead Tones

was standing now, facing Kate. "You stupid, conniving Bitch! I hate you!!! You'll pay for this, I swear you will!!" screamed Jennifer.

Kate started to turn and run, her fear increasing with every second! But Jennifer was furious and her fury made her the more dangerous of the two. Claire and Shy heard Kate being tackled in the foyer. Jennifer was going to have her revenge, and Kate would lose most of her hair in the process. They could hear Kate's pain filled screams along with Jennifer's continued cries of hate and revenge.

"I think we should call the police now," suggested Claire.

"Wow, Mom. I'm impressed, you played the two of them against each other perfectly. How'd you know?

"Just a good guess, I figured somebody was encouraging Jennifer; and with the poison information we got this afternoon about the tropical fish, Kate was the logical choice. They had to be together. After Jennifer's traumatic afternoon, I was sure she'd look for morale support. Kate played Jennifer for a lovesick fool. I've no doubt that if things hadn't gone her way with Sarah, she would've found a way to blame Jennifer."

"From the sounds of it, Jennifer's got the winning hand now."

"Thank me later. If this wasn't so tragic, I'd be laughing at the two of them. There's nothing so sad as two women fighting over a man who would never belong to either. Go call 911, dear. I'll check on our girls."

CHAPTER FIFTEEN

Another Sunday afternoon at the Bourbon Street Cafe and the music had the whole place swingin'. Claire and Scott, along with Shy and her friends, squeezed around the front corner table. They finished off the afternoon treat of Beignets and rum sauce, then sat back to enjoy the entertainment.

"Hey, Scott, how come you're not playing this afternoon?" asked Kevin.

"Not for a few more weeks. I'm just lucky to be here," answered Scott.

"So, I heard. It's a good thing you know somebody who's smart enough to save your sorry skin, or you'd be six feet under this week," added Kevin with a smile.

"I know. I thank her everyday." Scott had his arm around Claire's shoulder and pulled her closer. "I, honestly, would have never expected Kate. Until she showed up in my office, I had no idea it was her."

"Are you still dying for a cup of coffee in the morning?" asked Shy.

"Hah, hah, you think you're funny, don't you?" The entire group laughed at Scott's answer. "And just for your information, I have given up coffee for the time being. Even the thought of it turns my stomach." Again the laughter erupted.

"How 'bout me? I almost got a belly full of the poison she gave to Abby. I threw out every tube of lip balm I had," said Krissy. "How did Kate know about using the black stone to point finger at Sarah?"

"She probably did some basic research. It wouldn't be hard to find the information, but she didn't go far enough. Sarah told us that

Dead Tones

in order for the black stone to have any real power, it had to be wrapped in purple cloth. She knew enough to scare the other kids, but not enough to be credible to anyone who really knew anything about Cherokee magic," explained Claire.

"Ya know, I still don't understand why Allison's symptoms were different for Sue's and Abby's," said Monica.

"That's easy. After Mom and I found all that stuff about poison, we realized Kate was using more than just one type of toxin to confuse the doctors," explained Shy.

"And the rest of us," said Scott.

"How does it feel to have the girls fighting over you, Mr. Krammer?" asked Sean.

"Really rotten. I've done some serious thinking about the past few years, and I can't imagine what set Kate off. I don't remember a single event that would have triggered her," said Scott.

"Yeah, well that's not saying much. You didn't know Jennifer had a crush on you until I told you; and come to find out everybody, except you, new she was crazy about you. Kate knew Jennifer was just a little off balance, or she wouldn't have been so obsessed with you. She got Jennifer all worked up about Sarah's magic and then set everything into motion. If Jennifer couldn't sell the idea of Sarah's guilt, then Kate figured she could pin it all on Jennifer." explained Claire.

"Wow, what are good friends for?" Krissy asked in a tone seething with sarcasm. "What's going to happen to Kate and Jennifer now?"

"Well, I guess it's no surprise," said Scott, "Kate's going away for a long, long time; and if she ever gets out of jail, I don't want to be easy to find. I heard that Jennifer's going to a boarding school at semester time."

"Gosh, we're gonna miss her. Kinda like a tooth ache." announced Shy. "Do you think we'll be having band next semester?"

"Of course, but I bet the instruments are kept much cleaner. You should've seen all the reeds Dale found in the garbage Wednesday morning. He said there was enough wood to make an addition to his garage."

"Yeah," added Shy. "Most of the kids bought one of those tiny cedar boxes that lock for their reeds and mouth piece, me included. I bought mine this afternoon."

"Are you serious?" asked Claire. "Don't you think you're getting a little carried away?"

"Would you want to stick a horn in your mouth after all this? Lots of the brass players are getting the boxes too just cause they thinks it's cool to have the locked cedar box. Come to think of it, the box is rather chic," said Shy.

"Chic? You even think about 'chic' at this age?" asked Scott.

"Of course, I do," said Shy, looking around to see if Blake was around.

"How's Hairy?" asked Kevin.

"He's better," said Claire. "Ya know, he's kind of a hero in all this. If he hadn't gotten a hold of Shy's saxophone reeds, I don't know if we'd have figured out what was going on in time to save Scott. As soon as Shy told the doctor about the poison, he knew what to do."

"So I owe my life to a man eating dog?" asked Scott.

"You owe some to Hairy and some to me," said Claire with a smile.

"It's just great having all of you here," said Kevin. "I've got to get back to work. Hey, and thanks for the great article, Claire."

"My pleasure."

"Mr. Krammer..." said Sean.

"It's Scott now. I'm not a teacher anymore, just your friend."

Dead Tones

"That's gonna be hard to get used to. I mean, like you've always been there," said Krissy.

"Everything changes. You're all going to be leaving in a few months anyway. I'll still be in town, at least until the fall. Where's Mike?"

"I'm not sure. We've kind of gone separate ways. He's hanging around with Jason these days."

"Oh, that'll be a really mature experience," muttered Sean, but Monica jabbed him in the ribs before he could explain to the others about his feelings regarding Jason's outlook on college life.

"How about Sarah? Why didn't she join us for our celebration?" asked Monica.

"She's with her parents in Tahlequah. There was some kind of ceremony this weekend," explained Shy.

"I didn't think her mother did the Indian heritage stuff," said Claire.

"I think they are working on a compromise," replied Shy.

"Good idea," said Krissy. "I like compromises."

"Scott, aren't you mad about getting fired?" asked Shy.

"Not at all. Dale had to do something, If he didn't find a scapegoat, then the board would have fired him."

"But why couldn't he have picked somebody else?" asked Krissy.

"I was the logical choice, and I told him so. After all, I think a lot of the kids and their parents thought I was somehow responsible for all of this. If I hadn't volunteered to resign, there's a good chance Dale would've been forced to get rid of me in another year or so anyway. Actually, I'm ready for a change, a clean start. Who knows where I might end up. Maybe in Colorado," he said squeezing Claire's shoulder again.

Claire liked having Scott around. He'd quickly become a good friend, and she needed one now that Shy was going to be leaving.

Everything changes, and change is good. It keeps the spice in living. "Who knows," she added, "You might end up hanging from a cliff somewhere in the mountains."

Dead Tones

The Renegade Regiment actually won second place at the Regional Finals in Denton, Texas in November, 1996. The Band did go to the Winter Guard International Friendship Cup in St. Louis, Missouri where it won first place and became National Champions. All of the events in this novel are fiction; however, I had endless help and inspiration from the Renegade Regiment.

R. Z. Crompton

I want to thank Nichols Junior High School and all the students who participated in the creative writing workshop last May. Jessica Leser's work was the most compatible with the Dallas Zoo scene. I want to give Jessica credit for contributing the imaginary walk through the jungle, page 213. Approximately eighty students wrote for me, and picking the best was very difficult. I decided to print four excellent pieces here for your entertainment.

*****

By Justin Poynter

I open my mouth, but I can't yell. I try to run, but my legs are locked. Standing there, I am terrified. All of a sudden the lion leaps up, but it has the legs of a human. "Manuel, what are you doing here?" I asked.

"This is my summer job, man," he replied.

I feel really stupid at my cowardice; but, in a way, relieved it's only Manuel.

"What are you just standing there for? Come help me with this lion display for the showcase," said Manuel.

We take the display over by the snack counter. After hauling the lion puppet, Manuel and I sit down and talk about the school year over a couple of cokes.

We talk for only a couple of minutes before Manuel says, "My boss gets angry if I take long breaks, so if he asks, just tell him I was telling you about the show."

We finish our cokes, and I run off to find my friends.

Dead Tones

Tiffani Morris

You are so nauseous you can taste the crumb biscuits and sweet succulent molasses, which Imal, the guide with whom you've lost all contact, served for the mid-morning snack, coming up. You feel the burn of hydrochloric acid in your mouth, and all of a sudden out comes your biscuits and molasses right on an ant hill. Out comes giant man-eating ants, so you jump back just in time to get out of the way. Then you realize the lion is right behind you, licking his big chops. You see a giant bead of drool stream from his moth. He starts after you, but much to your surprise, he saunters past and starts gobbling up what was once your snack and the ants as well. When the lion is finished, he strolls to a nice shady place, flops down heavily, and closes his massive, limpid brown eyes.

Natalie Stalmach

The lion's eyes locked onto mine. I wanted to run, to get away. My whole body screamed with danger. I tried to turn, but couldn't. This majestic, deadly creature had a strange hold on me. Its luscious mane and beautiful eyes had me transfixed. I could only stare at it in awe and admiration. As it walked slowly toward me, I noticed its sculpted body, one of nature's many wondrous creations. It came so close to me; I could see its slow, rhythmic breathing pattern. The lion gave me one last look and turned away just as quickly as it had come, as if in some way sensing my purpose and understanding my awe.